THE KING OF FAERIE

ALSO BY A.J. LANCASTER

The Lord of Stariel
The Prince of Secrets
The Court of Mortals

THE
KING
OF
FAERIE

STARIEL: BOOK FOUR

A.J. LANCASTER

Published by Camberion Press, Wellington, New Zealand

Printed by KDP Print.

A CIP record for this book is available from the National Library of New Zealand

ISBN 978-0-473-53925-2 (paperback)
978-0-473-53926-9 (Kindle)

Cover design © Jennifer Zemanek / Seedlings Design Studio

ajlancaster.com

To everyone trying to finish a long-term project.
But mostly to me, for finishing this one.

PART I

A BREWING STORM

AN OMINOUS PLANT

W YN ARRIVED PRECISELY on time, but there was no sign of either train or package as he drew the pony cart to a halt, the sudden cease of hoofbeats leaving a hollow absence in the still morning. Fog clung low to the ground, and the dark train tracks disappeared into blankness on either side of the platform. His instincts prickled at the sheer ominousness.

Weather isn't an omen, not here in the Mortal Realm, he reminded himself. Fog was a perfectly natural phenomenon, the result of damp spring weather and ground-air temperature differentials. Not at all dangerous. But his sense of oncoming doom refused to abate in the face of this excellent logic. Instead, his magic shivered in restless patterns under his skin, as if it knew something he did not, and a faint hint of petrichor hung in the air. He pushed it down, as he had been doing so often lately, smoothing his thumbs over the leather of the reins to steady himself.

The horse snorted, as if it sensed his unease. Or perhaps it merely objected to his proximity. Harder to fool animals than humans; Stariel's horses had always known there was something wrong with his scent, and it tended to put them a little on edge even though they were accustomed to him.

Out of habit, he checked the sky. A pointless action, even if it hadn't been obscured by fog, for the moon had set hours ago. Not that he needed to check its phase in any case; he already knew there were still five days left until the moon reached full.

He shook his head at his own foolishness and climbed down, leaving the pony cart hitched. As he approached Stariel Station, the billowing grey clouds drew eerie shapes around the straight lines of the station.

Small scuffling noises came from the platform, and he leaned on his leysight to identify the person hidden in the shadow of the ticket office. The sudden awareness made him suck in a breath, not because of the man's identity—unsurprisingly, the stationmaster, Mr Billington—but because of the heady combination of leysight with land-sense. He still wasn't used to that, the way the faeland—*his* faeland, now—surrendered information so freely.

This is my home now. As always, an uneven murmur of joy and guilt accompanied the thought, the latter beating a name in the hollow beneath his sternum: Cat, Cat, Cat.

Cat, who was trapped because of him.

He called out to the man as he came onto the platform, not wishing to startle him. "Good morning, Mr Billington."

"Morning, Mr Tempest," the stationmaster responded cheerfully without turning from the door. There was a snick of the lock tumbling, and the stationmaster froze as if his own words had only just caught up with his ears. His shoulders hunched. "I mean, Your Highness."

There was an edge in his tone, halfway between accusation and question. It was the first time the two of them had interacted since Wyn's identity had come to light—reasonable for the man to be cautious of him, even if it stung a little.

What exactly did Wyn want to achieve here? He could play the coolly distant royal, if needed. Would Hetta want that of him? His heart twisted, worry and wonder twining in equal measure. A few weeks ago, before the world had tilted on its axis and shaken every priority into realignment, he would have known the answer to be a firm negative; Hetta wasn't a woman with much concern for rank. Now…would there be some advantage in it for her, if he made sure everyone acknowledged his title? An advantage for their child?

Child. The word slid through his mind like ice-water, and he shied from it, mustering a friendly smile for the stationmaster. *When in doubt, appear harmless.*

"Ah—I see my reputation precedes me." Wyn wrinkled his nose. "But the formal address is unnecessary. It seems foolish to stand on ceremony, given the length of our acquaintance. And given that you once yelled at me for raiding your plum tree." That had been Hetta's idea, not his, years ago, before she'd left Stariel.

The stationmaster's expression softened. It was difficult to mistrust someone you'd seen young and sticky with fruit stains. "You and every other youth in the county. Including her lordship, if I remember correctly." He coloured faintly, and Wyn knew he was wondering about Wyn's relationship with Stariel's lord.

Wyn and Hetta hadn't yet publicly announced an engagement, but they'd *un*officially announced their intentions to Hetta's family, and the Valstars weren't exactly discreet, though he couldn't truly blame them in this instance. All of Prydein knew there was *something* between Hetta and him now.

"They were very superior plums," he said diplomatically.

"Aye, and still are. This year's crop looks set to be the best we've ever had." Mr Billington smiled, but there was still a tension to him, and he examined the space behind Wyn as if expecting wings to sprout. *You'd know if I were in my fae form,* Wyn always felt like telling people. Wings weren't exactly discreet, and neither were horns.

I haven't changed, Wyn wanted to say. *Not fundamentally. I'm still just Mr Tempest, good-natured steward, practically human, and certainly nothing to fear.* But he couldn't pretend things were the same as they'd always been. All Prydein now knew who and what he was. There could be no more pretending. "Don't let me keep you," he said instead, gesturing at the ticket office. "I am merely awaiting the arrival of some seed barley." And the other package, of course, but best not to draw attention to that.

"The train's running late," Mr Billington said, unnecessarily. He grimaced at the fog. "Not surprising, really. It's the slick tracks as much as the visibility. Probably be another ten minutes at least." He let himself into the ticket office. "You're welcome to come in and wait out of the chill, if you'd like...sir," he said cautiously, waiting for Wyn's reaction to the address.

Wyn didn't particularly feel the cold, but he recognised a peace offering when he saw one.

"Thank you." He ducked into the small space even though in truth, he would have preferred to spend the time pacing the length of the platform. A restlessness had hold of him this morning, and his feathers itched under his skin. But continuing to settle the stationmaster's anxieties was a better use of ten minutes than brooding. He rifled through his memories.

"Tell me, how goes your Johnny?" he asked. "He must be nearly finished with his apprenticeship?" Johnny was the stationmaster's nephew, and he and his wife doted on the young man. He'd taken an apprenticeship with a cabinetmaker down in Alverness, or so Wyn had heard.

The stationmaster grinned. "Only six months more, he reckons," he said, and the ten minutes passed quickly as he spoke of his nephew's accomplishments, his career prospects, and the sweetheart he was apparently courting. Warmth kindled in Wyn's heart, the reminder of domestic successes and concerns a pleasant one.

Mr Billington eyed him sidelong. "We've told him he needs to finish his apprenticeship before he asks the lass, though—otherwise how will he afford to keep a wife?"

"Sound advice," Wyn said, deliberately disingenuous. *Can I afford to keep a wife?* The question briefly amused him, having never considered it from that angle before—it was a very mortal construct.

"Of course, we've told him he must have care for the girl's reputation, in the meantime."

Oh dear. Well, on the one hand, he couldn't fault someone for caring about Hetta's good name. On the other, the judgement in the stationmaster's expression rankled, since Wyn would have liked very much to announce an official engagement to all and sundry—but the obstacles preventing him from doing so weren't ones that he could explain in casual conversation.

Firstly, Hetta's queen is expecting me to return to the capital in the role of King of Ten Thousand Spires before she announces our engagement—and that is no longer possible. Secondly, my own High King needs to grant me permission to marry a mortal—and my godparent still hasn't returned with word of how to find him, and they told me not to summon them until full moon if they didn't return earlier.

Fortunately, the long, mournful blare of the train horn saved him from finding a more sensible response.

"Ah, there she is, eleven minutes late," the stationmaster said, glancing at the clock with something like satisfaction at his earlier prediction. They both left the ticket office to watch the train roll in.

The engine drew to a halt with a slow grind of brakes, the weight of the iron warping the leylines in a way that made all Wyn's muscles tense. He forced them to relax. Iron resisted fae magic, but it wasn't painful. Why should it bother him so much this morning? Perhaps it was only that he was already on edge, and the fog made the train's emergence vaguely menacing, its lights creating narrow beams in the white.

The train attendants moved briskly, throwing open the doors

to the luggage carriage and ferrying the mailbag and other items marked for delivery onto the platform. The attendants closed the doors and hopped back aboard, while the stationmaster walked the length of the train and blew his whistle to sound the all-clear. The train began to move again, pulling away into the fogbank.

Wyn was scanning for the package of books he'd come for among the train's leavings when his gaze fell on a small pot plant next to the seed barley. The stationmaster made some remark, but he didn't hear it over the sudden thunder of his pulse. The stunted, leafless stick of thorns was only a few inches high, black as pitch, but it seemed to suck in what little light there was.

No.

No, it couldn't be what it looked like, not here, not *now*, not sitting in the perfect ordinariness of Stariel Station like a viper. He leaned on his leysight and blinked against the glare of the plant's magic. His instincts hadn't been quite as ill-informed as he'd told them. *Maybe stormdancers have more foresight than I thought.*

Gritting his teeth, he resisted the urge to blast the cursed plant with a lightning bolt. A stiff envelope was tied to the black stem, and as he leant down to examine it, a taste of cherries and beeswax bloomed on the back of his tongue. He knew the signature and wished he did not.

Tearing the envelope free, he stared down at the mocking words written in Princess Sunnika's hand: *I am calling in my debt, Prince Hallowyn.*

2

LETTERS AND INVITATIONS

H ETTA TOUCHED THE end of her pen to her mouth and frowned down at the unfinished letter in front of her. Unfinished was being generous, as so far she'd only gotten as far as:

Dear Lord Arran,

We have not been introduced, but you have no doubt heard of my ascension to Lord of Stariel.

An inane beginning, since of course the Chair of the Northern Lords Conclave knew who she was. She looked down towards the lake for inspiration, but the waters were hidden by the billowing fog, making it seem as if the terrace where she sat was adrift in a vast cloud. Pulling her woollen wrap around herself more firmly, she drummed her fingers on the wrought-iron table. A more sensible person might've sat inside on a day like today, but she'd felt too restless to be cooped up by walls.

Now, assuming Lord Arran wasn't so old-fashioned that the mere act of an unmarried, unrelated woman writing to him turned him irrevocably against her, how exactly did one phrase the thing? What she wanted to say was simply: *you'd better jolly well ratify my membership on the Conclave. I don't have the patience for this nonsense, not when I've got bigger fish to fry.*

Or, more humiliatingly, *Please, I really need this. So far I've managed to make a mess of lordship on nearly every front, and I can't afford another. Not when I'm running out of time.*

She placed a hand on her abdomen, still as flat as it had been the last time she checked five minutes ago. Was the gesture an impulse that affected all women in her condition? Or only those paranoid about being discovered?

Giving herself a shake, she began to pen a watered-down version of her sentiments, though the result made her wrinkle her nose. She wasn't a watered-down or apologetic woman, and she didn't want Lord Arran to believe her one. But did it matter what Lord Arran thought of her character, if he supported her on the Conclave? Once her membership was ratified, they couldn't exactly un-ratify it; as far as she knew, membership was lifelong. There'd be plenty of opportunity for tactlessness later, after she'd proved herself to all the naysayers. Out-of-wedlock pregnancy, malicious gossip, and rocky start to lordship notwithstanding.

Still, the resulting insipid letter left her with a sour taste in her mouth. With a sigh, she signed and sealed it before she could change her mind, put it firmly in the 'done' pile, and surveyed the rest of the papers spread before her. *News next*, she decided. At least keeping track of what was going on outside the estate didn't require any pretence from her, even if it was likely to be similarly exasperating.

Some minutes later, a familiar spark burned bright in her awareness. "You know," she said without looking up, "I think we might be losing our infamy. There's no mention of you in today's paper, although one of the letter writers claims 'fae monsters' ate three of his sheep." She raised her head. Wyn was padding over the damp stones, silent as a cat, carrying a stunted pot plant in one hand. *"Are there fae that eat sheep?"*

"I am partial to lamb myself," he said, straight-faced. "But yes, there are any number of lowfae that might eat sheep, though I don't know if they're at fault in this instance. Sheep are entirely capable of getting themselves into trouble without the need for any fae intervention."

Lifting the teapot, she poured him a cup of the green tea he preferred. Steam coiled in the cold air.

"And how is our seed barley that you were so keen to fetch yourself this morning?" They both knew it wasn't barley that had sent him out.

"The books arrived," he answered, slightly sheepish. "I've put them in my office."

"You know I *will* set the books on fire if you treat them as an iron-bound set of rules that I have to abide by," she warned. Wyn had tendencies. He'd mostly been keeping them in check, but she wasn't going to live with nine months of him trying to coddle her, which he *would* do if she gave him the least encouragement.

"I hope I am subtler than that." He placed the stunted pot plant on the table with a kind of grim care, as if it were an explosive and not a rather unassuming botanical specimen.

She frowned at the plant. Stariel's awareness sharpened, information flowing between heartbeats. The land didn't much care for the plant, sniffing around it with deep suspicion. A hint of candles and cherries, the taste magical rather than literal.

"It smells like Princess Sunnika's magic," she observed after processing the signature. "What is it?"

"A dusken rose." Rakken's voice cut through the fog. Wyn's brother emerged out of the whiteness and stalked up the terrace steps in a blaze of fury. "Get out of the way and I'll destroy it."

"Honestly, Rakken, I'm not going to let you electrocute a

houseplant before I even know what it is or why it's here, so you can stop boiling over with storm magic."

Rakken bared his teeth. The gold threads in his dark hair trembled free despite the fact that there was no breeze, and his bronze-and-green wings furled out to their full breadth—which would've been more impressive if his wings weren't clipped as neatly as a hen's. He was using glamour to disguise that fact, but glamour didn't work on her anymore, not since she'd become Stariel's lord and gained the Sight. Why did Rakken bother with the charade, knowing that? Maybe it was simply to needle Wyn.

Rakken's glare shifted to Wyn, who'd half-risen at his entrance. "And you, brother? Will you let this thing live? Have you not betrayed the Spires sufficiently yet? Are you now actively *helping* our enemies?"

Stariel curled around Rakken, responding to her anger. <No, sadly we can't just throw him out,> she told it regretfully. And she understood Rakken's emotional state to some extent. If *her* sister were trapped somewhere, she'd be simmering with frustration too—but it didn't make it acceptable for Rakken to take his temper out on *Wyn*, who wanted Catsmere back just as much as he did. Especially since Rakken had been busily ignoring them for weeks.

"I'm not thrilled this is here either," Wyn said. "But you cannot ignore the message it would send if we destroyed DuskRose's gift."

"And what if that's *exactly* the message I wish to send?" Rakken said silkily, folding his wings with a snap. The anger in him was vast and terrible, and somehow even more alarming when he smoothed it under a veneer of civility.

"If you've quite finished?" she asked, pouring herself more coffee. "Could one of you please explain what, exactly, a dusken rose is?" She clinked the pot softly with her cup. Both brothers winced.

"A dusken rose is a rare magical flower native to Princess Sunnika's court," Wyn said, slowly settling in his seat again, all the time eyeing his brother as if he thought he might need to leap up at any second. "And one closely associated with DuskRose's royal bloodline."

Hetta considered the stunted black stick. It didn't look like it would be flowering any time soon. "I'm assuming this 'gift' has more than just symbolic meaning?" She put down her cup and reached out a finger towards the plant. Both Rakken and Wyn froze, but neither moved to stop her. That, and Stariel's lack of reaction, made her continue.

The texture was smooth and slightly waxy, and it almost hummed against her skin, the sense of foreign magic intensifying. Stariel gave an unimpressed huff.

"I can feel the magic in the stem, but Stariel doesn't seem to think it's dangerous." She was confident of that, even if she and Stariel's communication remained imperfect; like Wyn, the land tended to err on the side of caution.

"DuskRose wants you to plant it," Wyn said, extremely neutral. "To build a Gate between Stariel and the Court of Dusken Roses."

She frowned and hazarded a guess based on what she knew of fae magic. "I'm assuming a Gate is some kind of portal, and that this dusken rose is to give us a resonance point?"

"Yes," Wyn said. "A Gate is a type of permanent portal in a fixed location. They require substantial energies to build as well as an anchor to act as a resonance point, but once they're constructed, they are more stable than portals and require little magic to activate and use. They also bypass wards against translocation."

"And if I use this, er, anchor to build a Gate between Stariel and DuskRose...?"

Rakken bristled. "An insult."

"An insult to ThousandSpire," Wyn clarified. "A Gate between two faelands...is symbolic."

"Princess Sunnika spoke of an alliance," she mused, wrestling with an instinctive rejection of the idea. The princess *had* helped her on more than one occasion. But Hetta kept remembering the cold fear of nearly losing Wyn in Meridon, thanks to a member of DuskRose's court. That hadn't strictly been Princess Sunnika's fault, but on the other hand, it wouldn't have happened if Princess Sunnika hadn't sent her handmaiden Gwendelfear to spy on them in the first place.

It didn't help that Wyn had once been engaged to Princess Sunnika, nor that he still owed her a favour. Hetta wrestled with the urge to set the plant alight, and Stariel perked up its ears.

<No,> she told it firmly. <Allies are a good thing, in theory at least. Let's not burn bridges quite yet.>

"Are Gates permanent once you've made them?" she asked.

"In theory, one can destroy a Gate. But to do so would be an act of war."

"Do not trust the Court of Dusken Roses, Lord Valstar," Rakken warned. "It's no coincidence that they've sent you this while the Spires are under a curse. They wish to take advantage of the power vacuum. They're trying to secure their place as the most powerful court of Faerie." Something dark flickered in his expression.

He truly hates the Court of Dusken Roses, she realised, faintly surprised. She knew DuskRose and ThousandSpire had been at war, but the emotion still seemed uncharacteristic for Rakken, who'd planned—and technically, succeeded in—a coup against his own father with a cold-blooded lack of sentimentality.

"What happens if I don't plant it?" she asked Wyn, who was still looking at the plant as if he could bore his way through it.

"It will insult DuskRose," he said heavily. "Dusken roses aren't given lightly, and Gate anchors even less so. A great deal of magic went into making this."

"I note that you fail to mention *your* debt to DuskRose, brother," Rakken said, snapping his wings irritably. "Is this what they asked of you, that you play their advocate?"

An infinitesimal pause. "Yes," Wyn admitted.

Hetta stared hard at him. "And are you going to?"

There were a lot of things glinting in the deep russet of his eyes, too many and too complicated to name. He sighed and pulled a stiff blood-red rectangle from his pocket. The florid gold ink of the handwriting was familiar; Princess Sunnika had used the same ink in her last note to him as well. Why did the princess have to send him so many notes, anyway?

Rakken's tone was mocking. "Oh, little Hollow, still keeping secrets. Still letting everyone else pay the price of your mistakes."

"The debt is *mine* to pay, and so I intend to tell Sunnika," Wyn told Hetta, ignoring his brother. His words tended to become more precise in direct proportion to how agitated he was. They could have sliced stone now.

Rakken laughed. "She's your lord now, Hallowyn. It's *entirely* within her rights to discharge oath-debts on your behalf. Oh, didn't you know that? Didn't he tell you?" he said innocently as Hetta narrowed her eyes at him. He flashed a dagger-sharp grin. "Are you still both pretending nothing has changed and that this play-acting will become real if you try hard enough?" He waved viciously at Hetta's engagement ring.

"Go away, Rakken," she said quietly.

He dropped his mocking act. "He will never be human, Lord Valstar, for all he hides his feathers from you."

"*Go,*" she repeated, and there were hints of Stariel in her voice.

Rakken shrugged. "I have spellwork to be doing anyway." He gave Wyn a passing glare. "*Someone* has to think of freeing the Spires."

The fog quickly enveloped Rakken, but she could still feel the blaze of his presence through her land-sense as he walked away— heading back towards the Standing Stones. He'd haunted the Stones these past weeks, trying to find a way back into ThousandSpire, but the curse that had locked the Spires into stasis had blocked any and all of his attempts.

"Sometimes I want to strangle your brother."

"Entirely understandable," Wyn said lightly. He nodded at the blood-red card in her hand. "It's an invitation to Kurayanni at the Court of Dusken Roses, one of the more significant seasonal celebrations in their calendar. In one week's time. The dusken rose is to give us a way to get there. Sunnika has asked for your attendance in payment of my debt." His expression was fierce, the gold motes in the russet of his eyes glittering. "It is *my* debt, Hetta."

Hetta considered him. "*Our* debt."

"Are you trying to claim this from me?" His voice was dangerously soft, and he'd gone all icy fae prince despite not actually changing forms.

"Yes, I am," she said, adding quickly, "but *not* because of what Rakken said. This is our debt because we're *in this together.* Of course I'm not going to decide a course of action without you; but similarly, you're not going to settle this without regard to *me.*"

She could see him fighting that, the stiff lines of his body saying just how little he liked the idea. She waited.

Eventually he closed his eyes and gave a short, tight nod.

She put a hand over his. "Thank you."

He breathed out, the line of his shoulders loosening. "I am not sure delivering this unlovely botanical specimen deserves thanks."

"That's not what I was thanking you for."

He gave her fingers a gentle squeeze. "I know."

Giving him a moment, she read the card and then propped it up against the dusken rose's pot. "Is the invitation simply an excuse to pressure us into planting the rose or do they actually want us to attend this Kurayanni event?"

"Both. I imagine Queen Tayarenn would like to take your measure."

Hetta didn't much relish the idea of a fae queen sizing her up, or of planting foreign magic within Stariel's borders. She thought of her letter to the Conclave's chair. Was DuskRose's queen more or less likely to approve of her than Lord Arran? Queen Tayarenn wouldn't care about the things humans found scandalous, but she might still see Hetta as lacking. Presumably DuskRose's queen didn't have difficulty controlling her own faeland.

Hetta reached out to Stariel. <We're getting better at communicating, though, aren't we? And today's experiment will be a chance to prove what we can do together.>

Stariel sent her its standard response when it didn't quite understand but was nevertheless attempting to be generically reassuring: the stone roots of the Indigoes.

Wyn was gazing unseeing into the fog in the direction his brother had taken. "Rakken isn't wrong that the timing of this takes advantage of the Spires' curse." His voice was soft, worried. "I thought Lamorkin would return before now. I thought...I didn't think it would take them this long."

They'd asked Wyn's godparent if they knew how to contact the High King, or if they knew his brother Irokoi's location, since Irokoi had hinted he knew more about the Spires' curse. Lamorkin, who liked being cryptic far more than necessary, had stated they'd return with answers by the full moon, and then disappeared without further comment. That had been weeks ago now.

"Full moon is on Thursday night. Not so very much longer to wait," she said, though it wasn't much comfort. She'd hoped to know more by now too.

Perhaps she ought to make another effort to hunt through Stariel's library for information. For all she knew, there were entire shelves of notes detailing everything from the colour of the High King's eyebrows to his dietary preferences hidden somewhere in the disorder. *We really must get the library contents properly catalogued at some point.*

She sighed, knowing already how long the estate's to-do list was. If only Marius hadn't been so determined to return to Knoxbridge so quickly; he'd always been much better at searching through the mess than she was. Perhaps she should enlist some of her cousins to help? Aunt Maude had arrived with several of her brood yesterday, and cousin Ivy was bookish. Hetta made a mental note to ask. Ivy didn't need to know exactly why she needed the information.

Her gaze fell once more on the blood-red invitation. "What happens if you don't pay Princess Sunnika back the favour as she's asked?"

Wyn didn't meet her eyes, but she could tell his fae nature was still lurking close to the surface by the way the shadows of his features deepened, becoming subtly more angular. "I can live with a broken oath."

She huffed. "Yes, well, perhaps we can at least consider if there might be some alternative before you *immediately* leap to sacrifice yourself?"

He gave a soft laugh, the hard edges of him softening. "Perhaps." The warmth in his eyes woke an answering warmth in her, fond and gooey as caramel. His attention grew sharper, more assessing, but he managed to bite off the query before it could form.

She couldn't help smiling, even though she'd put a limit on the daily number of times he could ask after her welfare for exactly this reason. "I'm fine. And you're up to three already today."

"Technically, I didn't ask; it does not count."

"It does if I can see you thinking it that hard."

He diplomatically took a sip of tea instead of responding, and Hetta decided on the spot that complications of all varieties could wait. She rose—intending to kiss him—but a wave of dizziness rose with her. Pinpricks of sweat broke out behind her knees, of all places, and the world swam in a nauseating way. Grabbing the table for balance, she sagged back into her seat and laid her head on her arms.

"Hetta? What's wrong?" The alarm in Wyn's tone was a sharp contrast to the gentle hands on her shoulders. He'd moved faster than humanly possible.

She lifted her head warily. "Nothing, I think," she said after a pause to check the world had indeed steadied, the dizziness ebbing as soon as it had come.

"That was *not* nothing."

"Nothing inexplicable, I mean. I remember Cousin Cecily had dizzy spells early on, before she had her girls. I think I just stood up too quickly."

Cecily's little girls were six years old now. Hetta had been in Meridon studying illusion by the time they'd been born, but she remembered some of Cecily's pregnancy. This was normal, then. It was fine that her body was doing alarming things without her say-so. She swallowed.

Maybe she should ask Cecily for advice. Or her stepmother. Or, in fact, any of the other innumerable women among her relatives who'd gone through this.

Of course, that would also mean telling them that she was pregnant.

At some point I'll no longer need to tell them because it'll be obvious. How long, exactly? She was fuzzy on the finer points of such things, but at least several months, surely? Another thought swam up guiltily. *It might not stick, though.* Many women didn't widely share their news until the babe had quickened, for that reason. *And if I'm one of them, I don't want to bear my entire family's condemnation for nothing.*

Wyn frowned worriedly down at her. "You should eat something."

"I will, shortly," she agreed.

He still looked worried, but his gaze had unfocused, and she suspected he was running through his own memories of her various relatives' past pregnancies. *I wonder if he paid more attention than I did?*

"You're going to be very tiresome once you've read those books, aren't you?" she reflected.

The corner of his mouth curved up guiltily. "I…yes, probably."

She ought not to encourage that sort of behaviour, but since she hadn't actually gotten the kiss she'd wanted earlier, she tugged him down. The fog created a small bubble of privacy with just the two of them inside.

"Bloody hells, Hetta, do you have to paw at each other in public?" Her cousin Jack strode along the terrace, his face screwed up in disgust.

She sighed and extricated herself. Not just the two of them, then. "Would you prefer we pawed at each other privately?"

Jack's eyes narrowed, but he didn't take the bait. "I'd prefer you kept your appointments. Are we going to try this business at the Heathcote before the estate agent turns up or not? Is that one of Marius's?" He frowned at the table, and she remembered the dusken rose.

"That's a problem I haven't yet decided how to deal with. I'm inclined to procrastinate, at least for today." She threw a questioning glance at Wyn. "Unless it's going to start sprouting the second we leave it alone?"

"I will put it in the greenhouse under wards," he said, and then grew stern. "While you eat breakfast—*before* you experiment."

RIVER EXPERIMENTS

H AVING WOKEN AT an ungodly hour, there were any number of things Marius ought to have used the extra time for: prepping for the tutorials he was taking later today; re-working his thesis proposal for the eleven-thousandth time; catching up on the latest journal articles.

Instead, he was doing none of these things. Instead, he was doing something monumentally ill-advised, standing on the banks of the river in the early dawn light, about to spend precious sleep time on experiments—and not the sort of experiments he could put in his thesis proposal.

Though it's not as if I would've slept much anyway, he thought. *So, really, what am I losing out on?* Sleep had become an elusive creature of late, his nights torn into fragments by strange dreams. They weren't always nightmares, but they were almost always unsettling, full of people he didn't recognise and impulses he didn't understand. Last night he'd been a linguistics student who'd somehow become trapped in the Professor of Modern Languages' office—a location he'd never actually set foot in during his waking life—whilst lists of nouns and verbs sprouted teeth and menaced him. Marius hadn't realised he knew that much about declensions in the first place, or that they were preoccupying his subconscious so. The night before, he'd dreamed of a pretty tavern wench in a pub he didn't recognise and felt a desire for the girl that confused him utterly upon waking. *Maybe I'm going mad.*

This, at least, was a familiar demon. *I can't be mad,* he told his inner pessimist firmly. *Someone would have told me by now.* His father, for one; Lord Henry had never held back on his opinions of his eldest son. A grim reassurance, but reassurance nonetheless.

But Hetta and Wyn were worried about you after Aroset's attack, the pessimist argued back. *They didn't want you to return to university to see out the rest of term—what if it's because they knew something might be wrong with you? What if Aroset permanently injured your brain?*

I'm not so easily broken. He hurled the words back forcefully, because he so badly wanted them to be true. His family loved him, but they saw him as fragile, made him see himself as fragile when he was around them. Returning had been a refusal to be that fragile man they thought him to be.

Also, you didn't want to be in the same house as Rakken for an extended period, the relentless inner voice added.

Marius carefully drew his thoughts back from that dangerous topic. Instead, he checked once again that he was alone. This wasn't a highly frequented section of river even at more civilised hours, and he was shielded from view of the old towpath by a handy willow in any case.

Dawn was breaking gently above the thin whorls of mist, the sun a pale disc amidst the spires of Knoxbridge's buildings in the distance, gentle gold infusing the landscape. Extremely pretty, but it was difficult to appreciate it within the prickle of his own self-consciousness. *No one can see you,* he reassured himself. And it wasn't as if he were doing anything wrong, was it? If someone did come, they probably wouldn't even give him a second glance. Right. These reassurances didn't stop the itch on the back of his neck, as if an invisible audience were watching and judging his every move.

Are you sure it's not guilt rather than self-consciousness? his inner voice added helpfully. *In which case, you can stop worrying; no one from Stariel is here to see what you're up to. You can betray them all in comfortable secrecy.*

I'm not betraying them!

Hetta would understand, wouldn't she? He was just being *sensible* about things. Someone had to be. Gingerly, he pulled the case from his pocket and extracted the modified quizzing glass. He was no artisan, so although he'd eventually managed to glue the rowan-wood in place, the result was a bit rubbish. Still, good enough to test a theory, he hoped.

He held the quizzing glass up to his spectacles and surveyed the river. This would be a lot easier if he didn't have to look through two sets of lenses, but it was necessary unless he found a handy fae within the three feet of the world he could see properly without his spectacles.

Marius didn't have the Sight, not really, though Wyn had theorised that he might be able to learn it, as an offshoot of his resistance to compulsion. But sometimes he did catch the odd ripple in the world, not *seeing* things exactly, but getting a prickling sense that there was something more present than met the eye. He'd gotten the sense of something unseen down here the other day, and moreover this spot seemed like the kind of location that might appeal to lowfae, with the banks left to grow naturally rather than cut into straight canals. All his reading suggested fae had always been more strongly associated with natural spaces. The books suggesting this were admittedly folk tales and children's stories, but Wyn *had* been uncomfortable in the city when they'd been there recently.

Although that might've just been due to the warrant out for his arrest at the time.

Thin tendrils of mist curled lazily over the dark waters, and Marius's heart stuttered as he spotted—no, it was only a pair of swans, feeding amidst the reeds on the opposite banks. He lowered the glass, disappointed.

Step two, then. He pulled out a vial from his breast pocket. It was an awkward juggle to smear some of the mixture it contained on the quizzing glass, and he wrinkled his nose at the oily mark he managed to leave on his gloves in the process. He'd have to think of a more efficient dispensing method, if this worked. At least the green, herbaceous smell was pleasant enough. The yarrow was the strongest, but there were other plants in the mixture as well, combined with small iron filings. He'd decided to start with a rough approximation of the same mixture that had had such an effect on Wyn when thrown by the bank manager's wife last year. If it worked, he'd take out ingredients until he could figure out which individual one was the key, or whether it was the combination.

Perhaps a glassblower could make quizzing glasses with a hollow section that one could then add the liquid into? He mulled over the problem, considering and discarding ideas as he continued to survey the river through the quizzing glass. How were quizzing glasses made? He was so preoccupied with wondering that he'd almost passed over the swans again when he realised the flock had multiplied—and that none of them were swans.

He inhaled sharply. The fae swans didn't have feathers, or rather, their feathers didn't seem to be made of the same stuff as birds' were (What *were* bird feathers made of anyway?) but in any case, these creatures had bodies and wings adorned with pale, lace-like waterweed. Silver flashed as they moved, as if there were blades hidden amidst their weed-feathers, and their beaks were sharply silver too, cutting daggers of dawnlight with their deadly beauty. There were five—no, six of the creatures.

Keeping his eyes on them, he lowered the quizzing glass. The shapes blurred, caught halfway between swans and whatever sort of lowfae they actually were, as what he knew fought with the glamour they were casting. It made his head hurt, so he held up the modified quizzing glass again. The blurriness resolved into the creatures' true waterweed strangeness. Marius followed the fae swans' lazy path as they swam along the riverbank, both fascinated and appalled that he'd successfully found lowfae in Knoxbridge.

It all felt faintly surreal, blurring the boundaries of proper placement. Stariel was for wild magic and strange happenings; Knoxbridge was supposed to be a place of order, knowledge, and things fitting neatly in their assigned places. Even if the fit he'd thought waited for him here wasn't quite as neat as he'd remembered it being. He'd thought he was coming home, but instead it was as if he'd gone to don a beloved coat only to find it had somehow shrunk in the wash.

The fact that Knoxbridge was heartily pretending fae didn't exist wasn't helping. Some days he felt like he was going quietly mad, trying to reconcile a series of things that couldn't be reconciled: Marius-before and Marius-now; fae and mortal; botany and magic. *And now fae swans*, he thought, watching the lowfae's serene movements. Were there fewer of them than there had been before?

Something hit him hard in the leg.

He flinched back with a cry of pain, his other foot landing on slippery grass. *I'm not actually going to fall into the river, am I? Not even I'm that unlucky, surely?* he had time to think as he over-balanced and slid down the slope and, indeed, fell into the river.

"Fuck!" The cold shock of it had him scrambling to his feet. The water came nearly to his waist, his trousers heavy and billowing as he pulled himself up onto the bank, creating a mess of muddy grass about himself in the process. Delightful. At least he hadn't dropped his spectacles, though a patina of muddy river water now fogged over the world. He half-reached for his handkerchief to wipe them clean before realising not only that his gloves were filthy but that said handkerchief would now be soaked.

"Gods bloody damn it!"

An urgent voice at the back of his head reminded him that something had caused him to fall into the river in the first place and perhaps he should be paying more attention to that than clean handkerchiefs right now?

He looked around wildly. One of the fae swans lurked further up on the riverbank, and Marius met its black, fathomless eyes with a bite of fear. He could make out every crisp detail of the creature's strangeness, even without the quizzing glass. Perhaps the cold and shock had made his brain realise it ought to be paying better attention. The lowfae had seemed harmless from a distance; it didn't seem so now.

Mind you, maybe it's just the angle. Even a real swan would be fairly alarming from this vantage point. But its beak looked awfully sharp, and were those claws rather than the webbed feet of a waterbird?

"Er, was there a reason you bit me?" he asked it, for lack of any other option. The fae swan puffed out its strange feathers, and Marius was just thrilled to see that he'd been correct in his earlier observations: there were indeed what looked like sharp blades hidden in the curves of its wings. Excellent. *Cygnus horribilis.*

"I suppose you weren't expecting anyone to be able to see you. Sorry." He wasn't sure what made him carry on with the one-sided conversation, but it was better than trying not to stare at the bladed wings. "No, I've no intention of hunting you or your flock. None whatsoever." He shot a quick glance towards the rest of the creatures. Oh no. Several of the fae swans were considerably smaller than the others. "Or your babies." He held up his hands to show they were empty. "I was just watching, because, er..." *I'm trying to figure out how to negate fae magic* didn't feel like the right thing to say, somehow.

The creature made a low ominous sound and began to blur subtly at the edges. Marius got the sense it was doubling down on its glamour. He pinched the bridge of his nose and went to fish about for the quizzing glass with the other hand. He came up empty and realised with a sinking feeling that he'd lost it in the river.

He started to get up. "I'll just go then, shall I?"

The fae swan—and he really must find a better name for them—spread its wings, blades flashing, when—

"Good morning! I say, shoo, you silly bird, shoo!"

The fae swan made an indignant honking noise at the woman who was carefully making her way down the riverbank towards them. Then it resettled its wings with a hiss, and Marius swore he could hear it thinking scornfully, *you're not worth the trouble*, before it gave him one last glare and flounced back to the river.

Marius looked up at his would-be rescuer, conscious of his general state of disarray and of the fact that she'd just seen him menaced by—to all appearances—a perfectly ordinary swan. A familiar tide of hot embarrassment began to rise. Perhaps he could brush her off and put this whole incident behind him as quickly and anonymously as possible. Her next words put paid to this hope.

"You must be Mr Marius Valstar. I've been looking for you." She beamed.

He pulled himself to his feet, feeling his ears heat. "Yes?" he said cautiously. "I don't believe we've met, ma'am."

She was a youngish woman, a similar age to himself—*ha, young-ish!*—dressed in smart but modest clothing, hair pulled back into a neat bun beneath her hat. There was something orderly about her that made him think of lists and notebooks.

She held out a hand. Marius blinked at it. Women didn't usually offer handshakes. But then, they didn't usually approach muddy strangers on riverbanks at dawn either. Should he ignore her breach of etiquette and take her hand? Deciding it was far more awkward to ignore it, he reached out gingerly and then hastily pulled back before their hands could touch.

"Forgive me," he said, holding up his muddied gloves.

"Oh," she said, withdrawing. "Fair enough. Ms Orpington-Davies." She gave a little wave in lieu of a handshake. The smooth *Ms* startled him. He knew the modern address had found fashion amongst a particular sort of woman, but he didn't often hear it.

Ms Orpington-Davies also wore spectacles, horn-rimmed ones that were thicker than his own. The eyes behind them were dark and intelligent, and he felt uneasily exposed beneath them. *This isn't a chance encounter; she wants something. Information.* And there were really only so many topics people would seek him out for information on. He somehow doubted Ms Orpington-Davies had an interest in botany. A dull throb began at the base of his skull.

"You're a reporter," he said flatly.

"Well, yes," she said. She gave him a charming smile. "But please don't hold it against me! I promise I don't bite." She batted her eyelashes in a manner he knew was supposed to be disarming.

He shook his head and started walking back up the bank to the towpath. She followed.

"What do you want?" he asked.

"To interview you, of course! Although I understand perfectly that you probably wish to change right now. What a peculiarly aggressive swan that was!" Her voice was warm with understanding, and she held out a card. He took it out of sheer reflex. "Perhaps we could set up a time—"

She hadn't seen through the lowfae's glamour then. "Interview me about what, specifically?"

"I was hoping you might be able to tell me more about fairies. Obviously, our readers are highly interested in the topic at the moment."

He stopped and narrowed his eyes at her. "And why are you

asking me?" He knew why, of course, but he wanted to see if she'd say it: *everyone knows your sister is involved with a fairy.*

To his surprise, she dropped some of her artless manner and pinned him with those intelligent eyes.

"There are eyewitness accounts of an altercation between you and a fairy woman with red wings at Celerebank Station in Meridon in March."

'Altercation' was a mild word for Aroset's attempt to kill Wyn with lightning in a crowded part of the capital city. For a moment all Marius could see were golden eyes, gleaming with triumph, fear a live thing in his belly. He pushed the memory away. The throbbing at the base of his skull intensified, sending rootlets up to his crown and around to his temples. Fantastic.

"The public deserves to know if there will be further attacks."

"There won't be," he said heavily. "She won't be coming back any time soon." No one had seen Aroset since the Spires had been locked in stasis, which was compelling evidence that she was trapped there. Marius couldn't imagine Aroset not causing chaos if she was freely wandering the human world.

"What makes you say that?" A trace of excitement crept into Ms Orpington-Davies' tone, and she had half-reached for her breast pocket, an automatic habit, to retrieve her pen and notebook.

Marius frowned down at her. "I haven't said I'll give you an interview." Besides, something about this whole situation didn't quite fit. "What paper did you say you were from?"

"I am the Society Reporter for *Lady Peregrine's Society News.*" She said it with calm dignity, he had to give her that.

Still, he turned on one heel and began to stride along the towpath. It was abominably rude, but he didn't trust himself not to say something even ruder otherwise. It'd been *Lady Peregrine's* that had started the original ugly rumours about Hetta.

Ms Orpington-Davies followed him, though she had to pick

up her skirts and trot to keep up with his long stride. "Please, Mr Valstar! I understand you're probably angry about that article, but that wasn't me—and wouldn't you rather correct the record?"

He couldn't walk the entire way back to town with a pleading woman chasing after him, could he? Maybe she would give up?

She showed absolutely no sign of giving up as they moved in their strange parade—him with his head down, his wet trousers flapping as he walked, trying to ignore her as she trotted tirelessly a pace behind him, peppering him with questions and justifications.

He tried not to care, even though the awkwardness of it all made him want to crumple into a ball—or alternatively, break into a sprint and run away from the entire situation. But no, literally running away from a reporter wasn't a good idea—he could already see the headline: *Lord Valstar's Brother Dodges Questions, How Suspicious!*

"What about these wing worshippers, then? Do you endorse them?"

He lost his rhythm. "Wing what?" he asked, slowing down despite himself.

Ms Orpington-Davies was slightly breathless when she caught up. "Wing worshippers. That's what they're calling themselves."

He curled his muddied fingers. "I don't know what you're referring to." But he guessed nothing good, from that name.

Ms Orpington-Davies pursed her lips. "I suppose you wouldn't have; they're new but quite fervent supporters of fairies." She rolled the word 'fairies' around thoughtfully. "Zealots, by all accounts. They seem to be based in Greymark, but there hasn't been much published in the papers yet."

"Why not?"

She laughed. "You're very free with your questions for someone who refuses to answer any!"

He narrowed his eyes. "You were told to bury the story," he guessed. It wasn't much of a guess, given how angry Queen Matilda had been at one of her advisors—the Earl of Wolver—who owned a good chunk of Meridon's press, including *Lady Peregrine's*. And in fairness, all the papers the earl owned had refrained from printing any more mud about Hetta since. Not that it had stopped others from filling the gap. Marius carefully didn't think about *why* the earl had taken up a personal vendetta against Stariel in the first place, though even skirting the knowledge made his insides writhe with shame.

She heaved a deep sigh. "Yes. Well, not me personally. But yes. But that won't hold forever—not with the upcoming Conclave." She paused hopefully, waiting for him to comment.

He sized her up as they came to the gate between the towpath and the commons. Small brown cattle looked up from their grazing as he put his hand on the latch. Could he simply close the gate in her face? No, that would be too rag-mannered. He stood indecisively and frowned down at her.

"Look, I sympathise with your ambitions of breaking into political journalism, but I still have nothing to say to the press. Your editor doesn't know you're here, does he?" Because this wasn't society reporting, what they'd been speaking of. Ms Orpington-Davies saw this as her chance to prove she could do more than write about what hat everyone was wearing this season or who was engaged to who. His developing headache throbbed, like a bruise being prodded.

Ms Orpington-Davies looked annoyed. "I won't be the last to approach you; others will think of it soon enough, and many of them will be far less open-minded." She sprouted notebook and pen. "But speaking of society reporting, our readers are *very* interested to know more about Prince Hallowyn. Is it true he's engaged to your sister?"

Oh, to the hells with it. He relatched the gate with them both firmly on opposite sides. It would give him a head start. "Good day, Ms Orpington-Davies."

He fled, as fast as dignity would allow. Damn it, she was right, though—there would be more where she came from. He needed to warn Gregory. And Hetta.

By the time he made it to his little brother's accommodations at Maudlin College, *without* the reporter in tow, thankfully, the sun had risen sluggishly above the town. He spent some time knocking before Gregory opened the door to his room with bad grace. There were dark shadows under Greg's eyes, and he absorbed Marius's warning with monosyllabic grunts.

"So just—watch yourself, will you?" Marius finished.

Gregory just rolled his eyes and mumbled that he wasn't an idiot and of course he wasn't going to talk to the press. *Where did my even-tempered little brother go?* Greg had thrown off Marius's efforts to help him adjust to life away from Stariel, determined to be independent. The age difference between them yawned, an uncrossable chasm.

Brotherly concern prompted him to ask, awkwardly, "How are you going, otherwise?"

A shrug. "Fine. You don't need to babysit me."

Not exactly an answer to inspire confidence, but Marius didn't see what else he could do, so he left Greg to enjoy his hangover alone. So far, he was doing a brilliant job of looking after the sibling in closest geographic proximity to him. How was he supposed to do any better with the ones so much further away?

I just hope you know what you're doing, Hetta.

4

REAL ESTATE ISSUES

W YN LEFT THE anchor under wards in the greenhouse and wished he could leave his worry behind with it. Instead, he carried it as a cold weight in his chest as he, Jack, and Hetta made their way to the Heathcote. Another complication, at a time when that was the last thing they could afford. Did DuskRose suspect he was currently attempting to contact the High King via Lamorkin? Did they know Hetta's position in the mortal world was far from unassailable? Oh, they couldn't take Stariel from her, but if the Conclave opposed her, it seemed unlikely the mortal queen would continue to support their union.

Especially since I unintentionally misled her.

By the time the three of them arrived at the old Heathcote cottage, the fog had thinned out, but it was still damp here on the Moors. Hetta held up a sketch map of the local waterways in one hand, and she looked from it to the cottage thoughtfully. The cottage's occupants, Mr and Mrs Healey, stood nearby, watching with cautious interest. The baa of sheep and newborn lambs came at intervals, muffled by the fog and the hills, making it hard to tell where any one sound originated.

Hetta seemed entirely recovered from the earlier episode of dizziness. *And she did eat something before we left,* Wyn consoled himself, sneaking a look at her profile as she frowned at the cottage. That was important, wasn't it? *Eating for two,* that was the phrase people used. If only he'd had more time to read the books; but there would be time later. There was still time.

"And this'll stop it flooding?" Mr Healey was saying doubtfully. A path of churned mud led to the cottage. The Healeys had been fighting a war of slow attrition against the nearby stream, and this year they'd lose it, if something wasn't done. In the warmer parts of the estate, the earliest-blossoming fruit trees, apricots and cherries, had begun to bloom, but the apple tree by the Heathcote cottage was yet to join them. Its branches stood bare and left glistening by the fog.

"In theory I can shift the drainage pattern," Hetta said, lowering the map. Her gaze unfocused.

Stariel's attention gathered around them, and Wyn drew in a sharp breath at the sensation. Jack did likewise, throwing him an inscrutable look for their shared reaction—their shared land-sense. They both belonged to Stariel now.

"Hmmm. Stariel is rather reluctant to shift the drainage." Hetta's grip on the map loosened, and only Wyn's quick move saved it from ending up in the mud. Hetta didn't seem to notice as she turned to the farmer. The pine and new grass in her signature had strengthened, and the unfocused look in her eyes made Wyn uneasy, as if it weren't only Hetta looking out of them. "How do you feel about the cottage moving instead? I think that would make things significantly easier."

Mrs Healey looked extremely alarmed. "Won't that damage the cottage?"

"I'm only moving it a few feet," Hetta assured her absently. "It's just the way the land falls. If it were slightly more *here*, I could tweak the drainage pattern only a little...*there*." There were odd echoes in her voice.

Faeland and faelord, he thought. *His* faeland; *his* faelord, the two signatures becoming indistinguishable: pine, damp earth, spring grass, and a hint of coffee. The leylines began to glow and swell, as if a current somewhere upstream had been diverted. He bent towards the magic, like a flower turning instinctively towards the sun, clamping his teeth together with the effort of keeping his wings from spreading forth.

When the leylines shifted, in Faerie and Mortal both, the earth under the cottage rippled, and the tenants gasped. He heard them only distantly, hypnotised by the re-aligning drainage patterns and plant roots; moving the cottage ten feet was a superficial feat in comparison.

The world re-settled, altered, the great stir of magic dispersing. The cottage stood safe but now located on a natural rise in the field. The old apple tree beside the door had shifted with it, with one notable change. Its previously bare branches were now thick with pink-white blossom, green leaves unfurling even as they watched.

A giddy feeling gripped him, as if he'd just knocked back half a bottle of whiskey. Hetta's cheeks were flushed, her lips pink and parted softly in wonder, and stormwinds, he wanted to shed humanity and kiss her with all the fierceness of the storm.

Until she swayed.

He moved without thought to catch her, scooping her up into his arms. The impulse caught them both by surprise, and Hetta blinked up at him with that echo of ancient faeland still in her expression even as the entirely womanly curves of her pressed against him. He held her tight against his chest and wrestled with an alarming urge to sprout wings and take off with her in his arms. In the sky she'd be safe, his instincts suggested. *No*, he told his instincts firmly. *She wouldn't be. Not with my mediocre flying skills, aside from anything else.*

He knew the moment the woman won out over the faelord, because Hetta gave an impish smile and wriggled.

"Not that this isn't impressively manly, but you can put me down now. I just misjudged a bit, unpicking myself from Stariel, and the magic came free rather suddenly." He was doing a poor job of hiding his thoughts, because she quickly added, "It's not...anything else. I'm fine. And yes, that does count."

"You all right, Hetta?" Jack asked with a frown.

"*Yes*," Hetta said firmly. "Just a momentary dizziness." She smiled brightly at the tenants. Too brightly? But now wasn't the time to ask.

Mr and Mrs Healey watched with interest as Wyn reluctantly replaced Hetta on her feet. Mrs Healey had one hand to her breast, and a deep, heartfelt sigh escaped her as she looked from Wyn to Hetta.

"That's so romantic," Mrs Healey murmured. Her gaze went to Hetta's engagement ring. "May we offer our congratulations?"

"Thank you," Hetta said; Wyn echoed her. Jack's mouth twisted, but he remained silent; he wouldn't argue about the wisdom of Hetta's decision in front of others. "Let's go check that everything shifted properly."

They checked the cottage. The tenants were cautious at first, but eventually they concluded that the cottage had shifted without damage. Wyn got Hetta to sit down, by dint of insinuating to Mrs Healey that it would be appropriate to take tea in the cottage to celebrate its new and improved location.

Jack watched Hetta with slitted eyes but didn't object. Mr Healey was effusive in his thanks, which Hetta accepted uneasily. Wyn knew she wondered sometimes if she was worthy of her position. *You are*, he tried to communicate silently. *A thousand times more worthy than my father was of the Spires; more worthy than your own father was of Stariel. More worthy than me.*

He was getting distracted, watching Hetta too closely. *She said she was fine*, he scolded himself sternly. *You are fretting too much.* But the state of calm equanimity that had never before failed him felt as far away as full moon.

"These are rather beautiful teacups," Hetta remarked, examining hers. "I don't think I've ever seen this pattern before."

Mrs Healey beamed. "My nan left them to me. She got them as a wedding gift when she married my grandfather." She slid a sideways glance at Wyn, who chose not to react. First the stationmaster, now this. Was there something in the water today that was making *everyone* mention weddings?

They were about to take their leave when Mr Healey sized up Wyn and said, "Been seeing strange creatures around...sir." Wyn was growing tired of that pause of uncertainty, though he was glad the man had settled for addressing him as steward rather than prince. Perhaps he ought to send round some sort of notice clarifying the matter?

"What sort of creatures?" Wyn asked.

Mr Healey's shoulders went up, but he looked Wyn straight on. "Fairies, I think."

Perhaps Wyn should include a helpful footnote on fae terminology in that same notice.

"Can you describe them?" Hetta asked.

Some of Mr Healey's tension eased; he hadn't been sure he'd be taken seriously. "Little things," he said, bringing a hand up to demonstrate. "Big ears, gold eyes. And other ones, like small deer but with only the one horn."

"And colourful coats. They were beautiful creatures," his wife added.

"The horned ones are called starcorns," Hetta said, her expression softening. "The ones with the ears—" she looked to Wyn.

"Brownies," he confirmed. "They have a fondness for milk, if you want to bribe them to keep out of the pantry. Sometimes they can be persuaded to do household tasks for the same. The large brooding man with the wings is my brother, but please don't try bribing him with milk." They all laughed. Nervous laughter, admittedly, but it nonetheless cut a fine thread of tension in the small cottage.

"They're not dangerous, these...starcorns and brownies and the like?" the farmer asked.

"No," Hetta said firmly.

Wyn couldn't have mortals thinking fae were safe. "Some fae *are* dangerous," he warned. Hetta frowned at him.

"Some *people* are dangerous, fae or human," she said.

For some reason, Mrs Healey was smiling as she looked between them, but it was her husband who spoke. "That's fair enough," he said.

"ARE YOU *TRYING* TO make life as difficult for yourself as possible?" Hetta asked as they walked back to the pony cart.

He didn't pretend not to understand. "It's safer that they don't think of fae as tame things. Not all fae are like starcorns—not even *most*, not by a long shot."

She frowned but to his surprise didn't continue the argument. Did she look paler than before? Her fingers dug into his arm. He made a wordless sound of inquiry—it didn't count if he didn't actually ask the question aloud, did it?—but she only shook her head.

"I thought the wyldfae usually hid themselves from people?" Jack asked.

"They do," Wyn confirmed. "But there are a great many more wyldfae here now than there have been for the past three centuries. And some wyldfae may be feeling...playful. Or curious, at least, to see mortal reactions now that the Iron Law has been rescinded."

The High King had lifted the Iron Law only last year, around the same time the old Lord Henry had died.

The thought caught at him. When *exactly* had the Iron Law come down? So many things had occurred in the interim that he'd never wondered at the coincidence, that the death of Stariel's old lord should coincide so closely with the return of Faerie. But he was suspicious of coincidence on general principle.

Jack heaved a sigh. "Wonderful," he complained. "Just wonderful."

Hetta swallowed when they reached the cart. "I think," she said faintly, "that you should go to the Dower House without me."

"Hetta, please, don't—" Wyn objected, but she released his arm and *vanished* in a swirl of pine and coffee. He glared at the blank space she'd occupied, stretching his leysight as far as it would go, but it didn't extend as far as the house. Still, Stariel was unruffled, which meant she had to be safe; the land would be in uproar if she wasn't. "Seven stormcrows."

"Bloody unnerving when she does that," Jack agreed. Hetta had learnt how to translocate within the faeland recently, and she'd been using it more and more since. "She all right? She didn't look well, before."

"She *said* she was fine," he said plaintively, which made Jack give a bark of laughter.

But Jack's amusement was short-lived. He turned away from the spot Hetta had so recently vacated to look once again at the blossoming apple tree, his brows drawing together. Wyn knew that expression, and knew moreover that it did not bode well, but all Jack said was, "Well, we better get on then."

Jack remained ominously quiet as they took the pony cart to the Dower House, and Wyn used the reprieve to try to pull himself together, once again pushing down the restless curls of his magic. What was wrong with him today?

The estate agent met them on the steps of the house. The building had seen substantial refurbishment recently; the workmen would complete the last of the repairs this week. The agent wasn't from Stariel, and he gave Wyn a speculative once-over as they made the introductions. At least the man's thorough appraisal held no hint of fear, and he managed to maintain a cautious professionalism as they toured the house.

Jack was less professional, growing progressively more irritable with every room. Wyn knew he—alongside most of Hetta's relatives—wasn't much in favour of the house being rented out to strangers, however much it might help the estate's finances, but it was unlike Jack not to put aside private dislike in the face of public scrutiny.

By the time they reached the second floor, Jack was glowering like a thunderhead. Wyn took advantage of a moment when the agent was distracted by inspecting the bedrooms to pull Jack aside in the hallway.

"Whatever is making you scowl at me so, can you put it aside at least for the next half-hour?" Wyn asked in an undertone. "We aren't exactly presenting a united front, and we need this to go well. For Stariel." The initial bank loan had already been spent—on repairs to the Dower House, and phone lines and elektricity to the House and some of the nearer settlements. The further-flung parts of the estate were still without. The release of further funds depended on them showing the bank that the estate could indeed meet their cash-flow projections.

A muscle in Jack's jaw worked. "Yes, let's think of Stariel," he ground out, just as the estate agent re-emerged.

"Does the upstairs bathroom run hot water?" The man looked between Jack and Wyn, as if he could read the tension there.

Wyn's words appeared to have had some effect; it was clear Jack was trying to put his dark mood aside as he responded. The problem was that Jonathan Langley-Valstar was a poor liar, and his smile held far too much gritted teeth to be plausible.

Wyn applied himself to the task of compensating for Jack and putting the estate agent at ease. Such a thing had become harder, now people knew what he was, but harder was not impossible, and the man's wariness eased as they walked through rooms covered with drop cloths.

They paused in the entry hall, and Wyn asked if the agent had any further questions. The man rocked slightly on his heels, and Wyn anticipated what he was about to say even before he asked delicately, "Ah, this fairy business…?" He shaped the word with a grimace, eyes darting everywhere but to Wyn's face. "Any prospective tenants will want to know if they're likely to encounter any…issues."

What issues did the man mean? Briefly, Wyn considered telling the man that Hetta had already evicted the flock of piskies that had previously inhabited the Dower House's attics. But no; that wouldn't be reassuring.

"What do you mean?" Jack asked, aggressively.

The estate agent coloured. "Just, well, it stands to reason…" He turned to Wyn, an unlikely source of sympathy. "Well, people *will* wonder. There was that attack in Meridon, after all. A creature, at the palace." Again, that sweeping gaze behind him, as if wings might have subtly snuck in at some point in the last hour. "And that woman with the red wings."

My sister, Wyn didn't say. Aroset had tried to kill him and Hetta with lightning in a crowded part of the capital city. They'd survived thanks to Marius, who'd given Aroset a nasty case of psychic back-lash at a crucial moment.

"Neither is a danger to the public any longer," he said instead. It was the single good thing to result from ThousandSpire's curse. A hollowness formed under his sternum. Cat had to still be alive, didn't she?

"And Stariel is safe from fairies regardless," Jack put in. Wyn met his eyes—there was something too complicated there for him to read.

The estate agent looked between the two of them. "Right," he said, in the tone of someone who isn't entirely convinced but doesn't want to keep arguing about it. "Well, thank you for the tour. You'll be hearing from me."

They bid him farewell; he'd come in one of the new kineticars, painted a jaunty blue. Wyn and Jack stood outside the Dower House in silence and watched it disappear. The fog was thinning with reluctance, but the dark peaks of the Indigoes were now visible in the distance. Snow still capped their high slopes, but Wyn didn't let his gaze linger on them. Not that it made much difference; the place where his father had died was carved in him so deeply, he could have pointed towards it with his eyes closed even before he'd become magically connected to this land.

Jack didn't immediately climb onto the cart. Instead his attention went to a nearby ornamental cherry tree, just beginning to bud, and Wyn knew they were both remembering how the apple tree at the Heathcote cottage had burst into full, frothy radiance between one moment and the next.

A furrow formed between Jack's brows, tension in the line of his shoulders, in the way his hands balled into fists. He took a deep breath, coming to some decision, and whirled with a crunch of gravel.

Given Jack's obvious displeasure, Wyn wasn't completely surprised at the punch that came his way. What did surprise him was how *hard* it hit; Jack hadn't pulled the blow at all, and Wyn's head snapped back under the force. Pain shattered out from the impact, and his magic jerked at its leash, urging retaliation. *No,* Wyn told it, alarmed at the impulse.

He'd thought letting Jack land the blow might drain the anger out of him, but instead it seemed to be having the opposite effect.

Wyn dodged the second attempt and danced out of reach, his cheek stinging as blood rushed to the surface.

Jack stood panting, a dangerous light in his eyes. "Hetta's breeding, isn't she?" he accused, the old-fashioned term jarring, but Jack often fell back into old-fashionedness when flustered. And he was flustered now, flushed bright red despite his anger. Or perhaps because of it.

Wyn said nothing.

"Bloody *hells*, Wyn! What in Simulsen's name were you thinking?"

Wyn continued in his silence.

Jack grit his teeth. "Don't tell me you weren't thinking, *Prince Hallowyn Tempestren*, because that's damn well not good enough!"

The use of his true name hit like ice water. How *dare* a mortal use his full true name so freely? He sucked in a breath and stifled the beat of primitive rage, wrestling for a control that worried him far more than Jack's temper.

"I was certainly not thinking of *you*, Jonathan Langley-Valstar," he said tightly, wrenching his feathers back under his skin before they could manifest. "This is not your business."

Jack clenched and unclenched his fists at his sides. "Like hell it isn't. How far along is it?"

Wyn reminded himself that Jack had reason for his temper; there were mortal consequences here that couldn't be simply wished away, no matter how much they irked him or Hetta. "Two months, more or less."

Jack did the calculations and flushed a deeper red. "Meridon," he said in disgust.

"Yes." Wyn couldn't help adding drily, "Your mother is a very bad chaperone."

"You are *not* blaming my mother for your utter disregard for honour!"

"No, I do not blame Lady Sybil," Wyn said. "But also, I don't agree that there is anything inherently dishonourable about sex between willing adult participants."

Jack winced. "She's my cousin, Wyn. Could you not talk about it like that?"

"*You* raised the subject."

Jack regrouped. "I don't give a damn about what's acceptable back in Faerie—here you don't, don't—"

"Canoodle?" Wyn supplied.

"*Canoodle* with women you're not married to—"

"And you never have?" A spark of anger flared again in his chest. Jack didn't answer. "I don't have much patience for hypocrisy, Jonathan Langley-Valstar. What you mean is that unmarried *women* should not, but that men may do as they please, so long as they do not touch '*ladies*'." He drove each word in like a dagger, knowing he was being impolitic. "It has always puzzled me how such a thing is to be achieved, given that your society also does not allow relations between men—so who exactly are they to canoodle *with*, then?"

There was a heavy silence. Had he gone too far? But he couldn't take the words back; he'd meant them, after all. "I won't let you punch me a second time," he warned.

"More's the pity," Jack said bitterly. "When in the hells is the wedding happening, then?"

DIFFICULT QUESTIONS

ETTA SPENT SOME time feeling sorry for herself in the bathroom. *Thank goodness for translocation.* Very likely Wyn would continue to love her even if she threw up on his feet, but she'd still rather not test that.

It was also unlikely to impress the estate agent.

She sighed and began to pick out the detail of the lavender-patterned wall tiles, tracing the cracks where the grouting needed repair—like so many things on the wider estate. It would take years to pull Stariel back to prosperity, years in which the unending list of needs and wants had to be carefully prioritised. Lavender wall tiles ranked somewhere far, far below elektricity, farming supplies, and insulation for the cottages.

Distantly, she could feel other people moving about the house, the general sense of them vaguely soothing so long as she was careful to keep from focusing too hard on any one individual. She willed her stomach to stop roiling. Was it going to be like this for the duration? She thought again of her female relatives who'd know more about the business. Her stepmother would be kind. And maybe Phoebe would even keep it secret from the rest of the family, if Hetta asked—though she'd also fuss. A lot. Fussing, however, Hetta could deal with. It was more...telling Phoebe would also somehow make it more *real*.

She snorted. *As if it isn't real enough already!* She sent a bolt of irritation at Stariel on general principles. Had the land had a hand in this somehow? Of course, precautions could fail on their own, but they never had before, and the timing was too coincidental for her liking. If she hadn't been pregnant, could they still have broken Wyn away from ThousandSpire and claimed him for themselves using that line of connection?

Stariel curled around her with faint smugness.

<Don't you dare be pleased with yourself about this! Particularly not if you interfered in some way that caused it!>

Stariel perked up its ears, concerned, but it didn't understand, not really. She tried to explain while she traced the cool edges of the tiles. <I know we're bound together, but you mustn't interfere in my personal affairs like that. *Did* you interfere?> She still wasn't sure; it could've been her fault for not taking Wyn's or her magic into account with her precautions.

Something like a question came back, tasting of storms and cardamom.

<Yes, I *do* love Wyn and I *am* happy he's here and not in the Spires. But I had good reasons to send him away when I did. Just because I want something doesn't mean you should give it to me without asking.>

That was the unsettling point, of course. Had this all happened because she wasn't controlling Stariel as a proper lord should? Was it controlling *her*, rather? She thought of this morning's experiment. Ought she to have let the land change her original plans halfway through? How had previous lords dealt with being so tightly connected to such a powerful yet alien sentience?

And how did one deal with lordship *and* morning sickness at the same time?

Stariel's only response was to send its generic-reassurance impression of stony mountain roots again. Hetta blew out a long breath. It didn't matter, ultimately, how this had come about; it wouldn't change the fact that it *had*.

Her stomach having resumed normal proceedings, she got up and brushed her teeth, then changed out of her working clothes and made up her hair and face, summoning a minor illusion to get her lips the exact shade of holly-berry red she wanted. The routine was reassuring not only in its familiarity but also as a much-needed bolster to her vanity. The face staring back at her didn't look at all like a woman grappling with situations not of her choosing, nor like a lord who couldn't keep either her stomach or her land under control. She looked pretty and fashionable and *free*.

Hetta determinedly pinned a ridiculous confection of a hat to her head, hissing at a moment of unexpected static, and set her shoulders back, deciding to let appearance become reality for today at least.

She went in search of her cousin Ivy with a flicker of guilt for the estate agent. But Jack and Wyn would handle him, and possibly even better for her absence, if she were grimly honest.

Normally Marius was the person she went to for anything involving searching Stariel's library, but Marius wasn't here. Aunt Maude was the family genealogist, which might've been the next best thing, except Hetta would much rather deal with her cousin than her aunt, and she knew Ivy shared her mother's interest without being quite as eccentric about it.

Ivy wasn't in any of the obvious locations, and Hetta made her way down the Northern Tower, thinking of where else to search. Stariel curled around her, a casual brush of interest without any intent, like a cat reminding you that it was there, and Hetta debated whether to ask the land for help—it could certainly locate Valstars with ease, once she'd figured out how to describe which *specific* Valstar she wanted, but looking for people within the house was always more complicated and frequently left her with an aching head.

But the drainage experiment had been a success, hadn't it? Even if it hadn't gone entirely to plan. And even if it had felt, for a second, as if Stariel had made the decision on moving the cottage for her, as if she'd been merely a channel for the land's power rather than her own agent. Stariel had only been trying to do what she'd asked of it; they simply needed to work on their communication. Which wouldn't improve if she avoided opportunities to practise.

<Do you know where Ivy is?> she asked Stariel, pausing halfway down the stairwell. She drew up Ivy in her mind's eye. Ivy was only a year younger than Hetta, dark-haired and grey-eyed, leaning on the cane she sometimes used, thanks to a deformity affecting her right leg. Stariel puzzled at the description for a bit before eagerly pulling Hetta up to the west wing.

She became the curtains in her Uncle Percival's gloomy bedroom, a moth scratching at her worn brocade as she reeled from the sudden change in perspective. Her uncle was still asleep, a lump beneath the bedclothes, his snores loud as a saw. It wasn't sight, exactly, this sense of the world, more a disorienting awareness of location. She could feel the water flowing through the pipes of the central heating in the walls as strongly as she 'saw' the room.

Thank goodness Uncle Percival was doing nothing more interesting than sleeping late; she'd so far managed to avoid the worst invasions of her relatives' privacy, though she feared it was only a matter of time.

<This isn't the Valstar I was looking for, though I suppose he does sometimes use a walking stick too,> she allowed. <But Ivy is considerably younger.> She tried to feel her way back to her body, not liking how strongly and quickly she'd been sucked out of it, but instead she bounced locations again, like a ball thrown from one end of the house to the other.

"Can we pleeeease have one now?" little Laurel wheedled the cook, looking longingly at a plate of fresh biscuits. Willow, Ivy's youngest sister, stood next to her, wearing a similarly begging expression. "Just one?"

<*Too* young,> Hetta qualified. Perhaps age wasn't a good method of identification for a thousand-year-old faeland. She attempted to pull her attention away from the kitchen. Perhaps if she pulled back far enough, she could get more of a sense of who was where in the house. All the Valstars gave off a spark to her land-sense, more so than other humans. Almost a little like—

Fae, a flock of them, crowding in the Tower Room. The piskies chittered and dove, and she was part of their giddiness as they danced between rafters, performing for their audience, the slim, golden-haired girl—*Alexandra*, murmured a tiny voice at the back of her mind, but the name washed over her, meaningless—who was sitting on the window ledge with a sketchbook and laughing at their antics.

She streamed up and out the window into the golden sunlight filling the courtyard, dancing on air currents with the flock, weightless as a bird.

Something shunted her out of balance, and the warp and weft of the magic wavered.

"Hetta!"

Meaningless sounds, but the world kept shaking, and suddenly she was no longer part of the wind but back in a lump of flesh, slumped against the wall as something—someone—shook her shoulders.

"Henrietta! Can you hear me? Wake up, girl!"

Worried brown eyes in a wrinkled, kindly face. There was a long, stretched moment without meaning or familiarity, and then awareness and recognition both slammed into place. She was still in the stairwell, and she didn't seem to have fallen so much as slid gracelessly down the wall, her legs sprawled on the steps. Grandmamma was leaning over her, hands shaking Hetta's shoulders.

"I'm fine, Grandmamma." Stariel swirled around her, and she could sense its confusion and concern. <I'm fine,> she repeated mentally, for the land's benefit.

Grandmamma stopped shaking her, though she looked extremely doubtful. "You didn't respond for half a minute, love. What were you doing?"

"I was talking to Stariel, and I got a bit…caught up." This wasn't the first time she'd had trouble after immersing herself in the land, but previously she'd always eventually found her own way back. Would she have, this time? What if Grandmamma hadn't found her? A shiver went down her spine.

<*Why* did I get so caught up?> she asked Stariel. The land didn't know. It brushed up against her like a parent soothing a fretful child, sending stony foundations of reassurance. She was growing tired of that image.

<I'm not a child,> she told it irritably. It didn't disagree, exactly, but that sense of being brushed strengthened.

She got up off the floor, resisting the urge to press a hand to her stomach. "Did my father ever…" She wasn't sure exactly what she was asking, but if anyone would know, it would be Grandmamma. "Or Grandfather? Did they ever get lost?" She didn't remember her grandfather—her father had inherited as a very young man.

Grandmamma shook her head slowly, her expression uncharacteristically serious. "Marius—*my* Marius—used to say there were times it felt like being a trout trying to swim upriver. But mostly the land was quiet, then. And Henry…"

Grandmamma was nearer ninety than eighty, but Hetta had never really thought of her as *old* before. But now her shoulders drooped, and her eyes grew faraway and full of sadness. "The magic unsettled him; it got worse over the years. Sometimes I wonder if that was what started the drinking. But then, Henry never did need much excuse for that."

"No," Hetta echoed softly. She thought of one of the last times she'd seen her father. He'd been drunk and shouting, *No child of mine is going to bloody magic school!* She'd been eighteen and shaking with anger, shouting back. *Disown me then, because I'm going and you can't stop me! I don't need you or this stupid estate anyway!*

She'd left the estate not long after that argument, amidst the bitter shards of too many things said. He hadn't come to the station to see her off.

She put the memory away. "Do you know where Ivy has got to?"

Her grandmother pursed her lips. "She's in the rose garden. But the neighbour's boy has come to see you."

Hetta blinked. "Angus?" Lord Angus Penharrow was no boy, but then, Grandmamma probably viewed anyone under fifty as such.

"That's the one."

Thank goodness I'm looking my best, was Hetta's first, trivial thought, followed immediately by suspicion. Why was Angus here? They weren't exactly enemies anymore, but that didn't make them friends either.

Ivy would have to wait.

SHE FOUND ANGUS IN the sitting room, and he rose with casual confidence as she entered, all easy smiles, curly brown hair and broad shoulders. If only she could hate him; that would make things simpler. But the problem with the countryside was that you couldn't avoid people as easily as in town; you kept meeting them while out riding or at the local fair or at someone's dinner party. *Or when they turn up uninvited at your house.*

"You could have warned me you were coming," she told him. "I actually intended to be out on the estate this morning."

"I'm glad I caught you then," he said, taking in her appearance with a distinct note of appreciation; at least her efforts hadn't been wasted. In one hand he held a pretty cake box to which was tied a folded leaf of paper. "This is from my mother; she's written down the recipe for your cook." One corner of his mouth lifted. "Apparently it's a sought-after one."

Hetta reached out with some confusion to accept the gift. As she did so, her fingers brushed Angus's and a shock zapped between them—a literal one. She sprang back with a hiss of surprise.

"Still a spark between us," Angus remarked with a grin, setting the box down on the side table.

"Mildly irritating static only," she said firmly. She frowned at the cake box. "Angus…not that I don't appreciate it, but—"

"Why is my mother sending you cake?" he finished. She nodded, and some of the teasing drained out of him. He sighed. "She sends her congratulations on your engagement."

"Oh." Of course the wider district would've heard of Hetta's engagement by now, lack of official announcements notwithstanding; it wasn't the sort of news you could keep quiet. Not that they'd actually tried. Hetta reflexively rubbed at her ring, which she'd started wearing openly because dash it all. It was a deceptively simple design in silver, containing a single stone that had once been part of a powerful translocation spell. Stariel's influence had turned the gem into a sparkling gold and blue. "Please thank her for me." *I notice you don't bring your own congratulations*, she thought of adding, but that would be petty.

Something about Angus stiffened, as if he hadn't quite believed the news until she'd confirmed it—or as if he'd hoped for a different answer. *Oh, Angus.* But if he'd felt so strongly about her, he shouldn't have betrayed her. Not that that would've changed things between them, ultimately, but it certainly hadn't *helped*.

"One of the villagers told my sister. I take it you got Her Majesty's permission, then?"

"We did." That wasn't *really* a lie. They'd gotten Queen Matilda's permission. They just hadn't quite met her conditions yet. Details, details.

She waved for Angus to sit.

"I must have missed the engagement notice," he said as he seated himself.

"Oh, there wasn't one," she said airily. "They're not compulsory, you know. In any case, Her Majesty wants to announce it herself at the Meridon Ball."

"And when is the date for the happy event?"

"We haven't decided."

"Not in a rush then, are you?"

"Why should we be?" She had the sudden feeling that Angus *knew*. But that was just paranoia. He couldn't possibly know; she and Wyn had told no one of her pregnancy, and the only person Hetta knew who could read minds was her brother Marius—though he didn't know about his talent—and he was safely distant at Knoxbridge University until the end of the term. "It's my business whether I rush or not."

"Oh, aye," he agreed with a sudden grin. "But I would've thought you'd be eager to tie the knot sooner rather than later—or that he would. But maybe fae are more cold-blooded creatures."

The remark irritated her. Wyn wasn't a *creature*. "I'm certainly not going to share those kinds of details with you, but since you're so anxious for my happiness, rest assured I've no complaints on that front." She lowered her lashes and smiled a slow, deliberately sensuous smile. Pettiness be damned; a childish part of her wanted to provoke him. Besides, the idea that she was an innocent lady with no idea of what passed between men and women was frankly ridiculous.

Although you currently find yourself in the exact situation all those societal rules are designed to prevent, a small voice pointed out. She ignored it.

Angus laughed, full-throated. "I deserved that, didn't I?"

"Yes, you did," she informed him primly. "For being vastly improper. Now, why are you here? Me accepting your apology sheep wasn't encouragement to drop in whenever you feel like it." Angus had given Stariel a small flock of his coveted slateshire sheep in recognition of the wrong he'd done them. It was a very Northern custom. "I suppose it's about the Conclave?"

"I know it'll take more than 'apology sheep' for you to forgive me," Angus said, mouth curving at her turn of phrase. "But yes, the Conclave is one of the things I wanted to discuss. I'm holding a house party before the Conclave, to which I've invited several of our peers, including the Chair. I thought it might be a good chance for you to meet Lord Arran, give you a chance to show some of what you've been up to here."

She sat back in her chair. "Are you *campaigning* on my behalf?" She hadn't even sent her own letter to the Conclave's Chair, and here Angus was having already secured his attendance at a house party! Part of her wanted to refuse to be involved with it out of sheer pique.

He shrugged. "I owe Stariel a debt worth more than a few sheep."

The thought flashed through her unbidden: *Angus Penharrow will deal well with fae.* They too weighed the world in terms of oaths and debts.

Angus continued. "Lord Arran is old-fashioned, but also fair-minded. Or he can be." He canted his head. "So I can send around a dinner invitation without your biting my head off, then?"

I don't need your approval or your help, she wanted to say. Instead, she wrestled her emotions into something that resembled graciousness. This wasn't a time for pettiness, not when this was so important for Stariel. And Angus *did* owe Stariel, even if it rankled to accept his help.

"I'll try not to. Hopefully Lord Arran will favour me more rather than less upon closer acquaintance."

"Well, you've impressed every Northern lord you've met so far."

"All *one* of them." Guilt dragged a nail down her throat. It wasn't that she didn't enjoy flirting—quite the opposite—but it wasn't as fun when she knew Angus might take it seriously. "Don't flirt with me, Angus," she said quietly, fiddling with her ring. "And if—if you think speaking in my favour to the other lords will somehow make me *not* marry Wyn, then I'd rather you didn't."

"Don't insult me, Hetta." He said it lightly, but there was a warning growl in his tone. "I know you've more cause than most to doubt my integrity, but I actually *do* pride myself on my honesty." He grimaced, because they both knew he'd lied to her, and more than once. "I won't pretend to be thrilled at the match—"

"You shock me."

He snorted. "—but it doesn't change my duty to my own people and to the wider North. I meant what I said in Meridon. We cannot afford for the North to be divided against itself. Not given"—He glanced at her ring and finished lamely—"events."

A heavy silence fell. How was she supposed to treat him now? It had all been simple when he'd courted and then betrayed her. How dare he try to make reparations for his actions and make everything complicated again? How dare he help her? And most egregiously, how dare she need it?

"Thank you, then," she said, dredging up a graciousness she was far from feeling.

He jerked his head. At least he was as uncomfortable receiving her thanks as she was giving them.

"Is your fiancé available?" he asked, shaping the word like a slice of lemon.

"No, he's out on the estate."

"I take it the business with his sister is done then? Can I use his name again without drawing fae monsters down upon us all?"

"You can," she confirmed. She nibbled on a biscuit while she thought about how much she wanted to tell Angus. But he'd had to suffer through a monster attack at the theatre thanks to Aroset, so he probably did deserve a bit of the truth. "The succession in ThousandSpire is still unsettled, but I don't think Princess Aroset will be sending any more monsters."

Angus met her gaze, something close to accusation in his eyes. "What about others? There *are* more fae out there, aren't there? How does one evict unwanted fae guests?"

She thought of her tenants and their description of the starcorn and hazarded a guess.

"You've seen wyldfae at Penharrow?" She explained the different ranks of Faerie. "Lowfae are usually wyldfae as well, which means they don't belong to any particular court. Though since Penharrow isn't a court, I don't know how you'd know where they were from or what they were. Most of the lowfae I've seen are fairly harmless, and they keep themselves hidden from humans for the most part. The lesser and greater fae are more like us."

She had a pang of sympathy for Angus. She could kick out unwanted lesser and greater fae with only a thought through her bond with Stariel, but Penharrow wasn't a faeland.

Angus grew thoughtful and she ate another biscuit, suddenly famished.

When he spoke, she suspected it was the question he'd really come here to ask all along: "And how," he said slowly. "Does a mortal estate *become* a faeland?"

6

STORMS

THE QUESTION ROLLED in her like a struck gong all day, and she repeated it to Wyn later that night.

"What do you think the first Valstar offered the High King, to make Stariel into a faeland?"

They lay entangled in Wyn's bed, beneath the rafters. The reason for this choice of location was mainly that her own room shared a wall with her sister Alexandra's. *I should shift rooms,* she thought absently, tracing a line down from the hollow at the base of Wyn's throat. There would be hells to pay if anyone found her here, though the chances of that were slim, given the combination of her illusion and Wyn's glamour. *At least if we actually manage to get married, I won't have to sneak around my own dashed house!*

Wyn hummed thoughtfully, the sound vibrating against her fingertip. "I do not know; it's never specified in the tales. Perhaps he merely impressed the High King with his power. Faelands… I wish I knew more about them. All I know about their creation is that they need a link to a living soul to sustain themselves. The longer they go without a ruler, the more they risk coming unravelled. Maybe that's why Cat…" He trailed off. The slow beat of his pulse under her hand was the only movement in his body.

She wrapped her arms around him. "Ivy said she'd help search the library, but she doesn't think we have any records from that time." The original Lord Fallstar had established Stariel more than a thousand years ago—centuries before the Iron Law came into being. "Perhaps my ancestor gave the High King a good deal on sheep," she mused. Stariel's 'wealth'—if you could call it that, given the state of their finances—lay in natural resources.

Wyn laughed, returning her hug. "If so, Penharrow will be well placed to bribe him."

"*We* will be well-placed to bribe him." She sighed. "In another season or two. If we find tenants for the Dower House. If the bank will extend the rest of the loan."

"True." He paused, his fingers tracing up along her side suggestively, sending little sparks of awareness through her. "Although I confess, I don't wish to speak of finances just at this moment." The russet of his irises was black in the dim light, but the motes of brandy-gold in them glowed slightly. She didn't draw attention to the fact; Wyn was sensitive about showing the fae side of his nature, especially without meaning to. She did, however, wrinkle her nose at his black eye. He healed fast, which in this case meant the black eye had already progressed past the red-and-swollen state to the spectacularly black-bruised state.

She traced the edge of it gently. "I still can't believe Jack *punched* you!"

"He's very loyal to you," he said placatingly.

"And I can't believe you *let* him punch you."

Wyn didn't deny it. "I thought it might make him feel better."

"Did it?" She hadn't seen her cousin since the morning, as Jack had taken himself off to the pub instead of attending dinner. Wyn had cast a minor glamour over the eye, but no doubt the rest of the family would still hear of it eventually.

She felt his sigh through his body, and his hand flattened on her side, sadly abandoning its distracting movements. "Not noticeably, no."

"Did it make *you* feel better?" She shifted against him encouragingly, and his fingers resumed their slow tracing.

His lips curved. "Ah. I'm becoming obvious, aren't I? No, it didn't actually."

She poked him in the ribs. "Regardless, you're not to let any more of my relatives hit you!"

"I feel it's only fair to give Marius the opportunity if he wants it." He took on the mild expression he used when he was being deliberately provoking.

"You know Marius won't do any such thing." Marius had a better rein on his temper than Jack. He would, however, be hurt that Jack had yet again found out something important before he had. It didn't sit well with Hetta either. "I want to tell him I'm pregnant," she said in a rush.

The gold motes in Wyn's eyes gleamed brighter. "You know I'm in favour of doing so."

"The others…I don't want them to know yet. Not until we can set a date. Or until it becomes unavoidably obvious." *Or the reverse.* She didn't say the words aloud, though guilt wormed in their wake.

"The books suggest this may be several months yet. They were unhelpfully vague on the exact amount of time. The dizziness you had this morning is apparently relatively common but will probably not last for the duration." He half opened his mouth and then shut it again.

"I feel fine," she said in answer to his silent question. "Though I appreciate the effort you made not to ask me for the fifty-seventh time today."

"The book I read today did suggest tact was called for when dealing with pregnant mortals. Apparently they can be prone to irrational anxieties," he said, deadpan.

"In which case, are we sure it's *me* that's the pregnant one?"

"There, there," he soothed, patting her head. "Try to rid yourself of irrational anxieties."

Oh, he was so appealing like this, teasing her with his white-blond hair tufted into disarray. So she kissed him.

"Hetta," he groaned, bringing his hands to her hips.

"Irrational, am I?"

He chuckled, the sound shifting into a deeper rumble of pleasure as she nibbled her way along his jaw. She moved down his body in lazy spirals, enjoying the freedom of her position, lust a coil low in her belly. Sitting back on her heels, she let her hands wander lower, and he arched in pleasure at the touch.

What if I asked him to take his fae form? The thought crashed over her like deep, cold water. Would he? Did she even want him to? What if he did only because she'd asked? Rakken's words about Wyn hiding his feathers from her echoed in her ears, and the request half-formed on her lips. But there was something undoubtedly libido-quelling about voicing the question aloud. She knew in her bones that Wyn would do nearly anything he thought would make her happy, but she didn't want him to do this for *her*.

Wyn twisted them so their positions rearranged, and she gasped as her back pressed into the mattress. She'd kissed quite a lot of men; none of them compared. Maybe it was the sheer amount of practice she'd had with Wyn, but she suspected not. He kissed like coming home, and yet there was that edge, as if a storm could somehow be tamed. He kissed in dizzying contrasts, and it drove her wild. *Oh, I love you*, was all she could think, the beat of it aching in time with the rain on the roof, the rhythm of their bodies.

She lost track of things for a while. The rain's intensity increased, and in the distance came the rumble of thunder, followed by small flashes of lightning, throwing the chamber into a series of still-lifes.

When she could think properly again, snuggled under Wyn's arm, unease looped its way around her chest and tightened. Wyn was fae. Could they really keep ignoring that fact? Her and Wyn's *child* would be half-fae. She swallowed. Here with them now, carried within her own body. *A baby.* The word still seemed too big, too serious, too much.

How to broach the subject? The storm outside was reaching its peak, rattling against the house. Wyn obligingly shuffled the duvet up before draping his arm around her once more, his hand splayed out against her stomach. She leaned into the touch. He was gloriously warm, but then, he always burned hotter than she did.

"Wyn, our child will be—"

But before she could say anything more, Stariel blazed into alertness, and charge swarmed over her belly in a burst of elektric blue fire. Wyn's magic flared in the same instant. The lightning forked from her skin to his fingers, up his arm and across his shoulders, and fizzed into a ball of charge in his other hand as he rolled off the bed and strode to the balcony, threw open the doors, and flung it out into the night.

"Ow," she said weakly, in confusion rather than pain—the shock had been mild, like picking up a hairbrush full of static. "What was that?" Wyn had been struggling with his powers ever since they'd increased, but he'd never lost control in her presence. Had he done so now?

His face was ashen. "It wasn't me," he said grimly. His gaze fixed on her middle. "Maelstrom take me, but that wasn't me."

7

MINOR ELEKTRICAL CHARGES

"Are you all right?" he asked Hetta, as the cold night air swirled around him. How powerful had that charge been? It had felt tiny, but his judgement wasn't sound; as a stormdancer he was immune to everything short of an actual lightning strike. What had happened? Where had the magic come from? Or, since the answer to that question was obvious if not palatable...*why* had it come from there? He stared at the smooth skin of Hetta's stomach, ice crystallising in his lungs.

"I'm fine," Hetta said. "It wasn't painful, just surprising. It felt like a bit of static." She sat up and frowned at her stomach. "If it wasn't you, did that come from where I think it came from?"

"What does Stariel say?"

Hetta pursed her lips, and her eyes went distant. "It came from me. Or rather, our child," she confirmed. "Stariel is concerned but doesn't seem to know what it means. Wyn, why is our child giving off *minor elektrical charges*? Is this *normal*?" Her voice went up on the last word.

My child. Seven stormcrows. He balled his hands into fists and clung onto his mortal shape. He would not lose control. He would *not* panic. *Doom*, his instincts said helpfully.

"I don't know, but I don't think so," he said. Maybe he was wrong; stormwinds take him, he *wanted* to be wrong.

He shut the balcony doors before turning his leysight on Hetta. She shone bright as a star, blazing with both her own and Stariel's magic as the heart of this land. He couldn't make out the separate spark at her centre even knowing it was there. "Your power swamps the leylines too strongly for me to read much."

Hetta's lips quirked. "That sentence made a surprisingly amount of sense to me. Is it going to happen again, do you think?"

"I don't know," he said again. He closed the distance between them, pulling her into his arms and burying his face in her neck. "I think we may need to ask for advice. Which I don't much enjoy admitting."

He felt Hetta smile against his shoulder before she asked, "Who are you suggesting?"

He hesitated. "I can think of two people who might be less ignorant than me. Lamorkin knows many things. They might know this."

Hetta didn't point out that his godparent was currently who-knows-where, but her expression said it well enough.

He continued reluctantly. "The other is…Rake. He's older than me—he might remember our mother's pregnancies." It was a strange thought, because the pregnancy Rakken was most likely to remember was when their mother had been carrying *Wyn*. "Or even if he doesn't, his knowledge of magic far surpasses mine." And thank the High King his brother couldn't hear him admitting that; it would make him insufferable.

"Is he likely to tell us anything, though?" Hetta asked.

"He owes you a steep debt for giving him sanctuary here. You could demand this information and much more before it would equal the value of that."

Hetta blinked at him. "That's…not why I gave him one of the spare bedrooms, but useful to know." She frowned down at herself again. "The static happened earlier today as well, though that might've just been coincidence. But I'd like an answer sooner rather than later if there's one to be had."

"I do not want to wait till morning either," he confessed.

She gave a weak smile. "Good thing the fae don't care about unmarried mothers."

He hugged her, wishing he had words to convey all he felt. She was right; Rake wouldn't care about that. He wouldn't be scandalised by her pregnancy, but Wyn had no idea what his reaction might be beyond that, not in the violent mood he'd been in lately. Would Rake help them? If it had been a full fae child—but it wasn't. How much would that matter to his brother? Would he see it as yet another betrayal on Wyn's part? He wished, not for the first time, that Catsmere were here; he felt surer of her reaction than her twin's.

They dressed. Hetta had come to his room after the household had gone to bed but hadn't bothered to change into her nightclothes first. There was a routine to it now, a comforting familiarity that filled Wyn with softness despite his worry. He'd never given much thought to mortal women's undergarments before—other than as a line item on a laundry list back when he'd been filling the role of housekeeper—but the shapes and textures of Hetta's fascinated him: the blush of her skin through the sheer fabric of her chemise, the soft silken sound stockings made as she drew them up her legs. Wyn found the mortal attitude towards nudity tiresome, but he had to admit it added an extra dimension to seeing Hetta like this. It was the intimacy rather than the eroticism of it that made his pulse quicken.

Or rather, not *only* the eroticism. He wasn't a stone.

Mine, his instincts whispered, with a possessiveness he wasn't sure what to make of. It had too much in keeping with those odd moments earlier in the day, when he'd struggled to keep from turning Jack into a smoking crater. Or to keep from launching skywards with Hetta like a cantankerous eagle.

"I didn't realise putting on a sock required such intense concentration," Hetta teased, startling him out of his reverie.

"Perhaps no one has ever taught you proper sock-donning etiquette then," he said primly, finishing the task and pulling on his shoes. "Butlers are known for their understanding of correct attire, after all."

"You're not a butler anymore, Wyn."

"I remain in possession of excellent butlering skills. And I *am* still the steward." What did he hope to achieve by raising the point? They both knew his status at the estate had evolved into something more complicated. Hadn't it? The thought rose, unbidden: *Does Hetta wish that there wasn't a child and that I'd accepted ThousandSpire's throne?* Hetta loved him, he knew, but it didn't change the fact that she hadn't chosen this freely, any of it.

Hetta held his gaze, but in the end only said, "I prefer fiancé." She held out a hand. He took it.

They made their way through the hushed darkness of the house, and Hetta summoned a small magelight to bob above them as they crept downstairs.

"I don't know why I thought being lord would mean less sneaking through my own house in the dead of night," she reflected.

He chuckled. Around them, the house creaked as the storm wore itself out on the stones.

"Did you sneak around the Spires at night, as a child?"

Memories bubbled up. ThousandSpire was a dark court, which meant the night there was a time of deep, still power. He'd been a quiet child, skirting the edges of the court after it descended into sadism and savagery. After his mother had left. But he didn't want to speak of that. He fished about for a softer memory, before everything had gone so horribly wrong, before he'd fled his home court in fear of his own father.

"Irokoi used to take me night-flying before he lost his eye. Before Mother left." And just where *was* his oldest sibling? Irokoi had appeared via astral projection and given Wyn a cryptic message to pass on to Catsmere: *sleep is not death*. Wyn had come to the unhappy conclusion in the weeks since that Koi had *known* what Cat was planning, but he still didn't understand why. Maybe Lamorkin would know when they returned.

"Catsmere told me about your mother. She said King Aeros was worse after she disappeared."

"I don't remember him very well before that." It made him uneasy, speaking of his father, and he checked the urge to draw up his ley-sight. His father was dead; he could not touch them now.

Hetta squeezed his hand. "Where do you think she went?"

It was an old question, an old hurt, its sharpness worn smooth and hard from years of wondering. He didn't want to talk of it, but perhaps it was better to speak the words in the dark now, so that they might be over and done with.

"I like to believe she had a compelling reason to leave, that she still lives, and that something prevents her from returning." A bitter and childish hope, he knew, but the alternatives seemed worse: that she was dead; that she stayed away by choice. "I try not to dwell on it."

He'd helped kill one parent and the other had abandoned him, willingly or not. *What kind of parent will that make me?*

EMBROIDERED DRAGONFLIES

W HEN HETTA KNOCKED on Rakken's door, he answered it wearing an extremely immodest dressing gown. It wasn't so much the fact that it was silk, black, and embroidered with golden dragonflies as that he wasn't wearing anything *underneath*. He was in his fae form, and the garment was constructed to allow for wings, but it meant the only thing preventing the garment from sliding down his body was the knot behind his neck—and it didn't look like a very secure knot. A distracting quantity of muscular brown skin was already on display.

She couldn't help a feminine flutter of admiration, though she hoped none of it came through in her expression. She'd grown resigned to the fact that Rakken oozed sensuality in the same way pigs couldn't help their stench. It was simply a mildly irritating fact of life, or possibly a character defect. *At least I know it's not just me.* Even self-righteous Aunt Sybil had a distressing tendency to melt into silliness in Rakken's presence.

Rakken's eyes gleamed. "Did you knock merely to enjoy the view, Lord Valstar?"

"I have no taste for half-plucked pigeons," she said, because he deserved it. Wyn laughed softly behind her.

Rakken's wings rustled, the sheared primaries not so obvious with them folded behind his back. Had she offended him? Maybe he was sensitive about his damaged wings and that was why he never appeared without them glamoured to perfection.

But Rakken chuckled, a deep, sinful sound. "Ah, yes, you prefer your prey unfeathered. And bruised, apparently." He noted Wyn's eye.

Throwing a fireball at him would be childish, she told herself. Particularly when they wanted his help.

"That's none of your business, Rake," she said.

"I have not given you leave to call me thus, Lord Valstar."

"Well, if you're going to be my brother-in-law, it's ridiculous to keep calling you 'Your Highness'."

Both fae froze. Sometimes she was reminded forcibly that Rakken and Wyn were brothers; they reacted similarly to strong emotions, analysing the situation before they'd let themselves act. Rakken broke out of it first. He leaned one arm against the door-frame and considered the pair of them through half-lidded eyes. The hem of the silk robe lifted a couple of inches. Hetta fixed her gaze firmly on the lintel.

"A bold prediction," he murmured. "Given I cannot imagine the High King is pleased enough with Hallowyn to grant him such a favour, even if you had any notion of how to find him."

"The High King must also know how to free ThousandSpire from its curse," Wyn pointed out. "So you should be glad we're trying to find him."

Only the sudden brightening of Rakken's eyes betrayed his interest; they glowed briefly in a way that was more than metaphorical. *I shall have to ask Wyn about the specifics of why that happens.* Without making him feel sensitive about it—she was fairly certain he didn't know he sometimes did it too when they were alone.

"Ah—and that's the crux of it, isn't it? It's all about your precious mortal—though stormwinds know how you can justify dragging her into this, when you claim to care about her so. Do you fool yourself that the High King will favour this match?" Rakken smiled, and it wasn't one of mirth. "Or can you tell me that your primary motivation truly is Cat and the Spires?"

"I'm trying very hard to resist the urge to singe your eyebrows off, but I will if you keep being so deliberately provoking. What does it matter how Wyn prioritises the various things that *all matter to him a lot*, including saving Catsmere?" They shouldn't have come. How could she reveal vulnerability to someone so crackling with animosity?

"If ThousandSpire matters so much to him, then why does that dusken rose still live?" Rakken shifted. How could the sound of silk on bare skin be so loud? She met his gaze, which actually helped matters, because there was nothing sensual in his expression. His eyes were hard and cold. "Why are you here, Lord Valstar?"

She shook her head. "For nothing. I've changed my mind. Good night, Your Highness."

Before she could turn to leave, Rakken reached out and grasped her wrist, quick as a cat. A spark of elektricity sizzled over her skin with an audible crack. Rakken jerked back, the gold threads in his dark hair glowing for a second before the energy dissipated.

Stariel swirled around her, unsettled just as much by the faint citrus of Rakken's magic as the sudden static. Wyn stepped in front of her, his stance uncharacteristically aggressive, and she tasted the spice of his magic on the back of her tongue. Despite everything, she pressed a hand to her mouth to prevent a burble of laughter escaping. It was just so very posturing.

Some silent message passed between the two brothers, and Rakken's eyes widened. The citrus faded, though the storm lingered.

"High King's *horns.*" Rakken looked between Wyn and Hetta, and a slow smile spread across his face, the softest she'd ever seen there, as if he was too genuinely taken aback to add his usual edge. "You are with child, Lord Valstar." It wasn't a question.

She put her hands over her stomach and was then immediately annoyed at herself for the impulse. How had Rakken known? She hooked her arm into Wyn's in gentle rebuke, but he didn't abandon his position between her and Rakken.

"I am," she said reluctantly. Did she *look* pregnant, somehow, already? It was probably just some magical fae thing, but it made her self-conscious anyway. Two people in one day figuring out her secret didn't bode well. "Congratulations on your future uncle-ship."

Rakken blinked. "Indeed." He blinked again. "A half-human niephling." He turned introspective, playing absently with one of his lapels. It didn't improve the dressing-gown situation; or rather, it improved it in an entirely inappropriate direction.

She fixed her gaze on Wyn's shoulder to resist the nearly overwhelming impulse to look down.

"Does your brother know?" Rakken asked her suddenly.

"I have *two* brothers, you know," she said. She knew which brother he was asking about, but the gods knew Rakken took every opportunity to answer *her* questions with that sort of fae nonsense. Besides, she didn't trust Rakken's interest in Marius—not since the revelation that her brother was telepathic.

But Rakken didn't dignify this with a response, merely raising one cool eyebrow and letting the silence grow.

She sighed and shook her head. "Neither of them knows yet. Don't you dare tell Marius before I do." Not that she was sure how Rakken would achieve that, since Marius was in Knoxbridge and the two weren't in communication, but it seemed worth giving the warning anyway.

"I doubt anyone will need to tell him once he sees you in person. Or is he to remain absent for some time yet?"

She narrowed her eyes at him. Why did he care when Marius

returned? It could be simply because Rakken wanted some warning of his arrival, but she'd never gotten the impression that the telepathy worried Rakken. *Not like it worries me*, she thought guiltily. But it wasn't unreasonable to find it unsettling, was it? One ought to be safe to think whatever one liked in the privacy of one's own mind. Especially from one's older brothers.

I'm sure Marius wouldn't look at people's thoughts on purpose, she told herself sternly. Though as Marius had no idea he was telepathic and no conscious control over the ability, the thought wasn't that reassuring. She hadn't liked keeping it secret, but Rakken had warned that Marius might lose whatever subconscious control he'd gained if he found out about his ability.

"Why do you wish to know?" Wyn asked, and there was a thread of something in his voice that Hetta couldn't quite interpret; a hidden bait he was daring Rakken to rise to.

But Rakken answered with unruffled ease. "I should like warning of telepaths crossing my path." He considered Hetta critically and made a thoughtful sound deep in his throat. "Interesting. The energy fluxes are more unstable than they should be, aren't they?"

"That's why we are here," Wyn said tightly. "Is that...normal?"

Rakken canted his head, the smell of his magic intensifying. Stariel grumbled. <It's all right. I think,> she reassured the land.

"I don't think so, but I need to examine you more closely." He held out a hand commandingly for Hetta's.

"Can we do this somewhere other than the hallway?" Her heart beat rabbit-fast. Rakken didn't think it was normal. What did that *mean*?

Rakken straightened. "Very well, but not here. My wards will interfere. The Green Drawing Room will suffice." He gestured for them to remove themselves from his doorway. Apparently Rakken saw no issue with striding through the house in a state likely to cause a riot.

Wyn sighed. "Stop needling Hetta and put some clothes on first."

Rakken shrugged. "As you wish." He shut the door.

Hetta slipped a hand into Wyn's. "Sorry."

His russet eyes were amused. "For what? You've no need to apologise for Rake." He looked pointedly at the door and raised his voice. "Rake is the one showing poor taste and an even poorer sense of humour, pretending he does not know the conventions as a guest of this house."

Rakken pretended he hadn't heard Wyn when he re-appeared a little later, dressed. He'd adopted Spires fashions for the past few weeks. Possibly only because that comprised the bulk of his wardrobe, but she knew he owned at least some mortal clothing because he'd worn it in Meridon. Was it all a dig at Wyn not accepting his fae side? Or was it simply that Rakken felt alone here, cut off from his homeland and his twin? It was hard to believe Rakken was that sentimental, given that the only emotion that occasionally broke through his dispassionate mask was rage, but she knew from experience that anger could be used to hide a wealth of other emotions.

They went to the Green Drawing Room. This had been her mother's favourite room, and the essential décor hadn't been altered since she'd died—which meant it was now somewhat shabby. An old, gentle grief wedged its way into Hetta's heart. She'd never known her mother. And now Hetta was—well, in a state that made one feel the lack more than usual.

Rakken ignored them and sank down onto the rug with casual grace, crossing his legs and resting his hands palm-up on his knees. His wings draped behind him, but his shorn feathers didn't touch the floor. He made an impatient gesture for Hetta to join him. Wyn stood sentinel by the door, tense as a bowstring.

She sat down facing Rakken and took his hands. Citrus and storms rose, but whatever he was doing wasn't intrusive. Even Stariel didn't do more than eyeball it suspiciously before subsiding.

She waited, trying not to fidget. Around them, the house creaked.

She was starting to recognise the nuances that distinguished Wyn's storm signature from Rakken's. Wyn's was like rain fallen on long-dry earth; Rakken's held more of a drenched greenery smell.

Rakken's eyes snapped open; his brow was furrowed.

"What?" Wyn's voice was all edges.

Rakken spoke with a kind of care she wasn't used to seeing from him, and it made unease shiver down her spine. "There is growing storm magic within you, Lord Valstar; I believe that's what is causing the static."

"Is it dangerous?"

"To you—no, I don't think so. Or at least, not at present. Even mortals aren't so sensitive, and the amount of charge is minute."

"And to the child?" Wyn asked.

She saw the answer in Rakken's eyes. "I am sorry, Lord Valstar. I think, if the energy fluxes aren't stabilised…the child will not reach term." There was an uncharacteristic gentleness in his expression, and Hetta wanted to hit him for it.

"Why?" Her voice came out flat.

Rakken tilted his head. "You are mortal, Lord Valstar. He is not. Perhaps it isn't a stable combination."

"One of my ancestors was fae."

"True. Perhaps that, and your bond to this faeland, is why this was able to begin at all."

"I meant, if one of my ancestors was fae, then half-human, half-fae children are clearly an entirely possible combination. How sure are you that static isn't a perfectly normal side effect in such cases?" She wasn't sure who she was trying to convince.

Rakken spread his hands, the surrender too easy to be satisfying. "True. Perhaps I am wrong. Even so—" He hesitated.

"Say it," Wyn growled.

Rakken drew his wings tight against his back as he rose. "I think this is not a normal level of power, even for a full-blooded storm-dancer child." He looked old suddenly, the lines of his face sharper.

She *felt* the pressure drop, unnaturally swift. Thunder rumbled nearby, the storm that had been fading abruptly renewing in energy. Vortexes formed over the Indigoes, the wind speeds increasing to gale force.

"Wyn," she chided, mentally taking hold of the vortexes and smoothing them out. Wyn had gone outwardly as unreadable as stone, but the fae edge to his features would've been a tell even if she hadn't just had to save her inhabitants from surprise emotional flooding.

"What if we had *sengra*?" Wyn asked suddenly.

"Perhaps. Perhaps a sufficiently strong bond between you would allow your magic to stabilise the child's. But if so, it would need to be done swiftly," Rakken said.

"How long?"

"I'm not an expert, brother. I do not *know*. A week? A month? The power levels are already growing alarmingly."

Hetta didn't appreciate being left out of a conversation that was about *her*, ultimately. "What are *sengra*?"

Rakken answered. "The physical manifestation of a successful marriage bond between fae. In your case, one approved by the High King." To her surprise, he flared out a wing, brushing Wyn's shoulder softly. "I am sorry."

He left, in a rare show of tact.

"Well," Hetta said, getting off the floor. "We shall simply have to find the High King on a slightly more urgent timetable than we thought. Or perhaps Stariel can help stabilise these 'energy fluxes', given enough time to explain the concept." She tried suggesting it to the land and received only confusion in response, but sometimes that only meant she needed to reframe the question. Sometimes.

Wyn still hadn't moved. Rain pelted against the windows, and

a flash of lightning lit up his features, stretched taut and skull-like.
When he spoke, his voice sounded like it came from far away. "I
won't blame you if you don't want to continue with this, Hetta."

She blinked, not following his thoughts. And then she did follow
them, all at once and horribly, and anger rose in her, hot and sharp.
"What exactly are you suggesting?"

He wouldn't meet her eyes. "I know you didn't choose this. I
know it has forced matters between us to fall a certain way. And
now, if this…'unstable combination'…" The air spiked with the
scent of thunder, but he exhaled carefully, keeping it from further
fuelling the storm outside. "I will not blame you if you choose to
let this end."

"'This' being our child," she said. He flinched. "Is that what
you want?"

His eyes snapped to hers, a hint of iron in them. "This is—storms
above—this is one thing that is not about what I want, Hetta."

"Oh, sometimes I just want to shake you!"

A crease formed between his brows, uncertainty creeping into
him as he scanned her expression. "I—I mean, if you want—that
is…" He put a hand on the back of a chair, as if for support, and
trailed off inarticulately.

How dare Wyn be too flustered to string coherent sentenc-
es together? It softened the white-hot edges of her anger, and she
wanted to be angry at him for putting this on her. Because if there
was one thing she knew for certain, it was that Wyn was already
attached to their baby, even if it wasn't quite a baby yet. She strode
angrily to the curio cabinet and began pulling open drawers.

"It's in the bottom right," he said, correctly guessing her intent.

She located the bottle of whiskey her father had secreted—she
was still finding them even so many months after his death—and
clonked it down on top of the cabinet. The amber liquid rebuked
her. Bitterly, she fished out a crystal glass in the shape of a mushroom

from amongst the curios, but when she un-stoppered the bottle, the smell made her stomach turn. She re-stoppered the bottle angrily and thrust it back into hiding.

"Dash it!" She went to the window and threw up the sash. Cold, rain-drenched air poured in, erasing the sharp scent of the whiskey. She closed her eyes and drew several deep breaths. "Dash it all."

When she turned back, Wyn was watching her the way one does snakes and explosives.

"Hetta—" He made as if to move towards her.

"Sit down!" He obeyed, sinking down onto the chesterfield without losing any tension, as if he feared any move might be the wrong one.

She began to pace. "Yes, of course I didn't choose this! Of course I've wished it hadn't happened, or at least, not right now! Of course I've thought how much easier it would be if it just went away! Of course I've thought of ending it! And of course I'm not going to!" Her voice wobbled and she blinked rapidly. "Lamorkin is going to come back and tell us what the High King wants, and we're going to do whatever we need to do, and our baby is going to be *fine*." The fury was receding under an alarming urge to burst into tears. She glared down at him.

He held out an arm, and she sank onto the couch beside him, curling against his side with something between a laugh and a sob.

"Tell me you don't want this child, that you're not already attached to it."

He held her so tightly she could feel his heart racing.

"Tell me!" Why was she being so unreasonable?

A long sigh. "I can't, Hetta."

The wind from the open window sent the curtains furling and unfurling like great wings. Neither of them moved, even though she knew Wyn would be itching to close it.

"You were right, though," she said quietly. It was her turn to avoid his eyes. "I—I'd thought about it. Ending it." He didn't say anything, rubbing small circles on her shoulders, his cheek resting against her hair. It made it somehow easier to speak. "One of my friends, when I worked at the theatre. She—well, you don't need magic to end such things, if you know who to go to. But I…don't want this to end. I didn't realise quite how much until now. Even though it would make everything easier." She swallowed and made herself look up at him, trying to read his expression. "Are you angry?"

A faint crease formed between Wyn's pale brows. "Ah, forgive me, but I don't follow?"

"That I thought about not keeping it?" All her guiltiest thoughts swam to the surface. "That I told you to leave, that I chose Stariel over you. How can you not be angry about that? How can you possibly not *mind*?" To her disgust, she felt tears welling. What was wrong with her?

"Ah." Comprehension replaced bewilderment. He squeezed her more tightly. "Your first duty is and should be to Stariel, love; it would be unfair to hold that against you. Though I admit it's some consolation that Stariel has since attached itself to me so emphatically." She felt him pluck at his land-sense. "As for the other, I meant what I said before; I wouldn't blame you for not wanting this child. Stormwinds know I struggle with things outside my control—I have no high ground from which to judge you for feeling the same."

"Stop being reasonable! I want you to be angry!" She sniffed. "Dash it, why am I being so weepy?"

"You're allowed to be weepy," he soothed.

"Don't treat me like I'm not being irrational!"

"You're not being—"

"I *am* being irrational!" She wiped the tears away, annoyed at herself. "Stop not minding!"

"Ah—all right?" he said cautiously. "What do you want me to

say?" She could tell he was trying not to laugh, and she wanted both to strangle and kiss him.

"Go and close the window—I can feel you fretting," she grumbled.

He did so, slipping back to the couch before she could really mourn the absence of him. "Hetta, my love…" He paused, and his eyes burned. "I'm glad you want this." He kissed her, slow and intense.

The grandfather clock chimed midnight, and they listened to the day turn over, the gongs settling into the fragile intimacy between them. She drew her legs up and settled against him, drawing in the warmth and familiar spice of his scent. Breaking the hush, she asked softly, "Tell me about *sengra?*" She tried out the shape of it.

His answer was equally quiet. "Fae marriage is not quite like the human sort. It's more…official."

Hetta frowned. "Human marriage is very official—especially for me. You *do* remember that little trip we made to Meridon to get Queen Matilda's permission?"

Wyn grinned, a sensuous note flaring in his irises. "Certain highlights do come to mind."

She prodded him. "That's exactly the sort of attitude that got us into this situation."

"Well…that's not exactly an argument against it, given the circumstances. It's not as if you can get *more* pregnant." She prodded him again, and he gave a soft huff of laughter. "Official isn't quite the right term, then. It is more…fae take marriage very seriously. Fae, especially greater fae, hardly ever marry. It isn't tied up with inheritance and children the way it is here. My parents were not married, and there was nothing unusual in that. As far as I know, there are no married monarchs amongst the upper courts, though there are many small courts in Faerie I did not keep track of. I know of a small handful of political alliances between courts cemented by marriages."

"It's about oaths," she guessed. Without really trying, she was aware of the throb of the dusken rose, all the way out in the greenhouse, buried even as it was under wards.

"Yes, and tying oneself deeply—and magically—to another. For royalfae, almost the only reason to do so is for important alliances."

"Your engagement to Princess Sunnika." She'd known that was supposed to end a war between two warring courts, but she hadn't appreciated the full magnitude of the commitment until now.

"Yes."

Gwendelfear had called him 'oathbreaker', she remembered. "Did the High King specify *you* in particular had to marry Princess Sunnika, or was it more of a general 'go and make peace by marrying two important people from each court' instruction?"

"I don't know." He wrapped his arms around her. "I seem to be saying that a lot lately. I wasn't directly involved in the negotiations; Father simply summoned me and told me what was required of me. I caught only a glimpse of the High King." Awe coloured his tone. "He was… They say if he favours you, he will assume the form of a greater fae of your court."

"He looked like a stormdancer then?" But it wasn't the High King that rose in her mind's eye; it was Wyn as she'd still so rarely seen him, blue-hued wings edged with silver, horns dark against his moon-white hair. *Would* their child have wings and horns?

Will they feel they have to hide their feathers too?

Wyn was shaking his head. "I saw him for only a second as he left; I don't know if he was aware of my presence. It was like looking into the heart of a star."

And this was the person they were going to try to negotiate with. She tried to rally her spirits. "A star with a fondness for sheep trading, I hope?"

His laugh trilled out, silvery and delighted, and nearly disguised his despair. She turned her face up to him. "We *will* figure this out," she told him firmly. She refused to consider any other possibility.

9

ANGSTING IN THE NIGHT

FTER HETTA HAD fallen asleep, Wyn prowled the house. If he kept moving, perhaps he could keep from thinking, from feeling. He padded across the cold courtyard and climbed the tower, the dregs of the storm beating against the shield of air magic he formed out of habit.

He leapt atop the parapets, the winds singing to his blood, the urge to change and unfurl his wings nearly unbearable. But he'd been so close to losing control earlier, when he'd strengthened the storm without meaning to. Stormwinds knew how much worse it would've been had he been in his fae form, with consequently more power to draw on. The Heathcote was far from the only vulnerable location on the estate—who might be hurt, if he rained down out-of-season flooding simply because he couldn't control his anguish?

This isn't a normal level of power, even for a full-blooded storm-dancer child.

The hair on his neck stood on end. Hadn't Gwendelfear said something similar, when he'd been chained beneath Meridon, about all of King Aeros's brood being unnatural?

"Oberyn!" he called into the night. The name shivered out, and he felt Stariel's leylines spin in eddies around it. To speak the High King's name, to try to summon him…it was madness. "Oberyn!" He balled his hands into fists. "OBERYN!"

There was no answer. Of course shouting into the darkness was unlikely to fix matters. Yet bitter disappointment filled him as he stood there, staring blindly into the night.

He dropped his air shield and bared his teeth, daring the storm to lash him. But the storm was nearly spent and refused to cooperate with his mood, the rain a light hiss that merely dampened him in slow, unsatisfying degrees. Mortal weather; so rarely narratively sympathetic.

The tower door opened behind him with a protest of hinges, and he made an absent note to see it oiled.

"I wish Cat were here." Wyn flung the words without turning, half-hoping they might make Rakken strike at him.

A soft pad of footsteps.

"We both wish that. I certainly would rather she dealt with your wallowing than I; she always had more patience for it."

"You know for sure she's alive?" He needed to hear the words aloud.

Rakken moved to stand next to him, looking out over the dark countryside. "She's alive. I cannot locate Koi, but I don't think he's still in ThousandSpire. He knew what Cat planned. She *planned* it, Hallowyn. And she didn't tell me."

Wyn wished for his wings, to return Rakken's earlier gesture of reassurance. Wing touches were intimate, for stormdancers, reserved only for family and close friends. "We'll find a way to free her."

Rakken gave himself a shake. "She would feel the same as I, if she were here. A *child*, Hallowyn."

Something splintered in Wyn's chest. Rake *understood*, understood in a way no one else here did, mortal as they were.

"Yes," he said, throat tight.

Rakken held out an unstoppered bottle that Wyn recognised as one containing the potent sloe gin that was Stariel's homebrewed specialty.

"I don't remember giving you permission to raid the cellars."

"And I don't remember asking for it. Mortal alcohol has a certain kick, doesn't it?"

Wyn took it anyway, drinking straight from the bottle. The bitter-sweet taste burned its way down his throat.

The rain eased off, the sudden cease of sound making the darkness larger. Rakken raised an eyebrow at Wyn's dampness; his own shield of air had kept him perfectly dry.

Wyn handed him back the bottle. Rakken laughed, low and bitter, but accepted it. "How long are human pregnancies?"

"Nine months."

"And how long has this one been going on?"

Resignedly, Wyn told him.

Rakken did the same mental calculation as Jack, threw back his head, and laughed. "Oh, Hallowyn, how very *precocious* of you. And how nice to have a token to remember your first time by."

Wyn couldn't help the growl that started in his throat, even though he *knew* Rake was baiting him.

"Your time with the mortals has made you prudish," Rakken observed, eyes gleaming.

"Perhaps you're simply not as amusing as you think."

Rakken didn't dignify this with a response, and silence fell between them. In the distance, an optimistic owl hooted in the soggy leavings of the storm.

Wyn spoke reluctantly, because there was no one else he could ask, and he needed to know. He missed Cat with a sharp, piercing ache. Cat was blunt, but he'd always been closer to her than Rake, and it would've been so much less humiliating to admit this weakness to her. Something about Rakken always made him feel as if he were still a fledgling.

"The Maelstrom changed us, you said. My power is still growing. And my instincts are more…aggressive. Being in my mortal form blunts the effect." Had Rakken experienced anything similar, as he aged, or after the Maelstrom? But Rakken merely raised an eyebrow at him until Wyn grudgingly added, "I'd like your advice."

"Twice in one night, you seek the wisdom of your elders? Wonders never cease."

Lightning flickered irritably in Wyn's veins, and he quickly smothered it.

Rakken took another swig of the gin and grinned. "Very well then, little brother. You do know you're a storm prince, don't you? It's our nature to feel the turn of the world and seasons, to ring with the primal call of blood to blood. You treat what you are as an awkward costume, to don when necessary and tuck away the rest of the time. The only thing that surprises me is that you got away with such behaviour for so long, and that your instincts have only now begun rebelling."

"If you're trying to be reassuring, you're failing."

Rakken slid him a look, the glow of his eyes an eerie green. "How you lived in mortal form for ten years, I do not understand."

"I couldn't have done it if my power hadn't been fractured by my broken oath." A truth he'd come to realise in the time since he'd been made whole.

Rakken turned and hoisted himself up on the parapet so that his ruined wings draped over the edge. Wyn echoed him, though remaining wingless. How often had they sat in a similar way atop the rocky towers of the Spires?

Not that often, admittedly; he and Rake had never been that close. But with Cat, and Irokoi, often enough.

Rakken's mind had clearly taken a similar turn. "If it lives, the child will belong to FallingStar," he mused.

"Yes. If it lives." How he hated that *if* and the fact that he was the cause of it.

To his astonishment, Rakken once again fanned out a wing to brush Wyn's shoulder. If Wyn had been in fae form, their feathers would have slid over each other. Rakken didn't acknowledge the gesture of reassurance, merely folding his wings back along his spine.

"Half-human *and* not bound to the Spires. Oh, you are fortunate you killed Father, Hallowyn. I'm not sure whether his triumph at a child would trump those two facts."

Wyn was silent. Technically, Stariel had killed his father, but he'd known what would happen when he'd translocated him here. It had been an act of desperation, to save him and Hetta both, but it didn't change the outcome. Now his father's bones were buried beneath the earth of this faeland, and Hetta carried a child of King Aeros's bloodline. A stormdancer child.

"Still, it's a relief to know you *are* capable of ruthlessness on occasion. You may need it, to come through this with your feathers intact."

"You sound like Cat." Cat had always called him too soft-hearted.

"Someone needs to represent her in this, since she's not here to speak for herself." But there was less bite to the words than before. Rakken sighed and handed him the gin.

Wyn took it, not reassured. They drank sloe gin as the clouds thinned and revealed a gibbous moon. Five days—four, now, technically—until it was full, until Lamorkin had promised to return. Would his godparent be able to help them?

His thoughts ran in unfocused eddies, spinning around the two halves of his life. He should have better appreciated the decade of grace before the Iron Law was revoked. There had been no Hetta for much of it, after she'd left for Meridon, but also no one had eyed him like something dangerous, and no one had suffered because of him either. His heart clenched. He did not regret his father's death, but he wasn't the only family member Wyn had lost in this.

"How did Torquil die?"

He felt Rakken's stillness. They hadn't spoken of their brother's recent death, not since Rakken had broken the news that Aroset had murdered him. Wyn hadn't seen Torquil in more than a decade, not since he'd first left ThousandSpire. Now he never would.

"I don't know, precisely." Rakken spoke softly. "I had barely registered his return to ThousandSpire when I felt his presence snuff out. If we'd known what he intended, perhaps we would have reached him before Aroset. Perhaps together, we could have bested her." He sighed. "But there has ever been little trust between us all. He must have assumed we would slaughter him too in a bid to gain ThousandSpire's throne."

"And would you, if Cat wasn't against it?"

Rakken didn't answer for a long time, staring out at the lake as the wind ebbed and its surface settled into a great mirror. Abruptly, he laughed, a sharp sound of glass shattering. "Not now, I think. But then… Ah, what has our bloodline come to, little brother, that I don't know the answer myself, that we have such a history of killing each other for madness or power, parents and siblings both? Perhaps I was hasty to blame you for the whole of ThousandSpire's sufferings. Perhaps we brought this ruin upon ourselves."

"You're a very depressing drinking companion."

Rakken chuckled and held out his hand for the gin. They watched the sky clear and stars spread across the sky, their reflections glimmering in the dark water below. A shooting star blazed towards the horizon, its watery twin below nearly as brilliant. *The Court of Falling Stars*, Wyn thought absently.

"Goodnight, brother," Rakken said, some time later. He slid down off the parapets and looked as if he would say more, his wings shifting. But then he folded them back and left without another word.

Wyn sat for a long time alone, until the darkest hours of the night, until the blurred edges of the gin had sharpened back to cold sobriety. He went back into the house, wandering the dark hallways on silent feet, leaning on his fae side for night vision, not quite admitting to himself where he was going until he stood in front of Hetta's door.

He'd only entered Hetta's room a handful of times during his time as house manager while she'd been gone, and not at all since she'd returned home; they usually met now in his own room, since the risk of being caught was lower there.

Hetta's room still had a sense of being frozen in time, holding the relics of the girl she'd been before she left Stariel. In daylight the walls were papered in faded yellow, but night drained the room of colour. A chink in the curtains let through a single beam of moonlight, painting a stripe in the shadows of Hetta's hair. She didn't wake as he crossed to the windows and closed the curtains properly.

He had a small internal argument with himself despite already knowing he would lose it. Hetta needed her sleep; he shouldn't wake her. There weren't that many hours left in the night, and he'd have to be back in his own room anyway before the first of the servants rose. Even as he thought this, he unbuttoned his shirt.

Hetta half-woke as he slipped in beside her, murmuring a sleepy, wordless question as they re-arranged themselves. The bed wasn't designed for two people, but he didn't mind the excuse to hold her close.

"I love you," he told her, kissing her hair.

"Hmmm," she agreed sleepily, burrowing into his shoulder.

His thoughts grew long and slow-moving as taffy as he listened to the sound of her breathing evening out. Hetta's back was to him, his arm draped over the curve of her waist, just beneath the soft weight of her breasts. Without thinking, he spread his fingers over the warm skin of her stomach. The child had storm magic— *his* child. In self-defence, he hadn't dared to let himself speculate. Hadn't let himself *want*. But on the edges of sleep, the ghosts of possible futures slipped through his guard and curled around his heart. His last thought before darkness pulled him under was of a child with Hetta's grey eyes and auburn hair—and his wings.

He dreamt.

He was a small child, dwarfed by the enormous throne that stood empty atop the dais. He pulled himself up the stairs, flapping his wings to help haul himself over the lip of each one in turn. Panting, he reached the top and backed up until his wings hit cold stone. He could do this; Cat had made it look easy. Taking a deep breath, he ran in a wobbling line, leaping from the edge of the dais with wings outstretched.

He fell, tumbling head-over-heels in an uncoordinated ball of feathers. Pain burst bright as he caught himself. He sat sprawled on the marble floor, lip trembling. He wouldn't cry. Cat wouldn't cry if she fell.

A rich chuckle behind him. "Ah, youngest. A valiant attempt."

Frustration boiled through him. "Why can't I fly?" Even Quil could fly!

His father, huge and reassuring, crouching down. Warm golden eyes. "Because you are not big enough yet. Here." A hand in his, helping him to his feet. "You need to practice strengthening your flight muscles. Hold your wings like this." He demonstrated, his feathers rustling as they unfurled, red and silver, wide and sure.

Wyn mimicked the motion, his father's hands guiding his wings.

Familiar feminine laughter, Father's expression softening at the sound. "May I join your flight school, my love?"

Wyn turned towards his mother and—

He woke.

YOUNGER BROTHERS

MARIUS HAD NEVER been inside a police station before, and he would've preferred, on the whole, not to be inside one now. The atmosphere prickled oppressively, even though he was only standing at the front desk and not, say, in the cells, where presumably it was much *more* oppressive. The back of his neck crawled with an oily sensation that made him want to rub at it self-consciously. *It's just a gift of your overactive imagination; atmospheres are not physical things that leave marks.*

"Good morning, sir. I'm here for Mr Gregory Valstar," he told the officer manning the front desk. He even managed to make it sound polite, despite his churning emotions. *Damn* Gregory. Was he all right? He wasn't sure exactly what Greg had done—a brawl and a broken shopkeeper's window had been referenced by the friend of Greg's who'd found him—but if it had landed Greg here, it definitely qualified as stupid. Hadn't he *told* Greg to watch himself?

The officer had the look of someone dividing time into ever-tinier increments to make it pass more quickly. He gave Marius a tired once-over. Marius knew what he saw: a bespectacled toff, either over- or under-dressed for this hour, depending on whether you considered it too early or too late. Marius could practically hear the unimpressed conclusion he reached: *Gods, another useless academic who thinks he's above us all.* Normally, Marius would wilt under the flat judgement in the man's eyes, but he wasn't here for *himself.* The officer could think what he liked, so long as he got Greg out of here.

The officer referred to a large logbook and ran a finger down the column. "No Valstar listed here. Got a Greg Smith."

Honestly, could Greg not come up with something *slightly* more original? "That's him. He's my brother."

"He's in for disturbing the peace."

"If there's a fine, I will pay it," Marius said wearily. "And I apologise for any inconvenience he's caused." Oh, he would *strangle* Greg when he got him out of here. He gave a grimace he hoped the officer might be sympathetic to. "He's young and stupid, and I'll have his ear for this, but he's my little brother."

He got out his wallet with deliberate casualness. Sometimes, he had intuitions with a strength that was hard to ignore, and right now one was telling him the officer would prefer to be rid of both him and the blond lad, sick of bloody drunken students' kick-ups but most of all the damn paperwork that came with them. He deserved bloody compensation for the waste of his time. At least the lad's brother looked stern enough to take paint off. Let *him* deal with the lad.

Gods, letting our imagination run away with us a tad tonight, aren't we? 'Stern enough to take paint off'—what did that even *mean*? Marius winced as a headache germinated behind his temples.

"How much is the fine?" he asked, unsurprised when the officer named an inflated sum.

"And your name?" the officer said when he'd duly noted down 'fine paid, released without charge' next to 'Mr Greg Smith'.

"Marius Valstar."

The officer nodded and summoned his co-worker, who seemed

equally unimpressed with Marius and the entire situation but went and fetched Marius's errant brother without further ado.

Gregory emerged sporting a brilliant shiner and a wary expression. Relief flooded his features when he spotted Marius, followed quickly by guilty defiance. Shiner aside, he seemed unharmed, and a knot of anxiety unwound itself in Marius's stomach. Thank the gods.

He dragged Gregory out of the office, feeling sick, his head beginning to pound a warning that signalled a truly *terrific* migraine was pending. Lovely. They spilled out onto the cobbled streets of Knoxbridge, lit by the glow of elektric streetlights at this time of night.

"Why did you tell him my name?" Gregory demanded, pulling his arm free.

"Because I had to pay a bloody fine to get you out, and I'm not committing perjury!" Though maybe he should have. The truth was he hadn't thought about it at all, but no way in the hells was he letting Greg turn this on *him*. It wasn't Marius's fault they were here, and Greg could show some small sign of gratitude at being rescued! "What in the name of all the little gods happened?"

Greg kicked at a loose cobble, and they watched it clatter away. Somewhere distant, a dog barked, but the town was as quiet as it ever really got. It was past the hour of drunks and too early for tradesmen.

"Nothing. It was just a bit of a disagreement that got out of hand, all right? You didn't need to come." He gave a laugh that was far too jaded for his age. It made the hair on Marius's neck stand on end.

"Like hell I didn't! You know if I hadn't come, it would've been your Dean bailing you out and packing you back to Stariel shortly afterwards! Do you want to be sent down?"

"That's why I didn't give my *real name*, idiot." Greg shot a wary look at Marius to see how he took the insult, and Marius nearly laughed at his expression. He was still so painfully *young*.

"Watch yourself, brat. I've still got half a foot on you," Marius warned him without heat. *Though let's be honest—he's already far more physically able to take care of himself than you are. You've never actually thrown a punch in anger!* For a moment, he felt Aroset's fingers closing around his throat, and a splinter drove itself into his brain, an echo of remembered pain. He hadn't been able to defend himself at all when it mattered. *Though it's not like punches would have done much against a psychotic fae princess with lightning powers, in any case.*

"Not half a foot! Two inches, if that," Greg protested, recalling him to the present. "But I still don't see why you told them who I was. You're the one who told me to be careful of reporters poking about!"

"Yes, I can see ending up in a holding cell is practically the definition of carefulness! What really happened?"

Greg's mouth grew mutinous. "What I said. I was drunk, and I lost my temper. *It's fine.*"

Marius said something then that he didn't want to say. "It's not fine, if you can't keep your temper when you've had a drink."

Greg went white and looked away. "It wasn't—I wasn't…like that."

Marius felt like a cad. It was a thing they didn't talk about. Greg hadn't borne the brunt of Father's rages, but he'd witnessed them target others. *Namely me*, Marius thought with bitter honesty. It hadn't mattered what he did—*everything* about him had irritated Lord Henry on some level. "*What's wrong with you, boy?*" had been the refrain of Marius's childhood. Usually swiftly followed by, "*Stop blubbering!*"

Marius wrenched his mind away from the memory. "Well, what *was* it like?" What could provoke Greg into an uncharacteristic burst of temper that would make him lash out? Oh. *Oh.* The knowledge came with sudden and piercing certainty. "Someone insulted Hetta, didn't they?"

Greg made a low growl of agreement.

Marius sighed. He understood, he really did, but, "If you're going to punch every person who insults our family, I'm going to run out of funds to bail you out rather quickly. Or, at least, I assume you did punch someone?"

Greg looked offended. "Of course! You didn't hear what he said."

"I can imagine easily enough." Marius had overheard more than he wanted, *seen* more written than he wanted. *I shouldn't read the damned gossip rags.* But it was worse, *not* reading them and then not knowing the reason behind the mocking glances sent his way, the suddenly dropped conversations when he entered a room, the titters of the students he tutored.

"You—you *can't* expect me not to do anything when someone says things like that about our sister!"

"Words exist. Fists aren't the *only* way to settle things, nor do I see that they've been particularly effective in this case. Whoever else was involved in your scuffle wasn't in that cell with you." He put a question into it. It didn't matter who it had been, given how widely the gossip was circulating, but he'd still like to know.

Greg stayed silent.

"At least tell me it wasn't a duke's son or something." The Southern aristocracy was more complicated and more numerous than the Northern, where you were either a lord or you weren't, but they were also more closely connected to the Prydinian throne.

"It wasn't a *duke's* son," Greg hedged.

Marius grimaced. "Earls' sons are not much better."

"I hate it when you do that," Greg groused, accustomed to Marius's flashes of intuition.

"Well, if it was an earl's son, and he insulted you to your face, then you gave him *exactly* the reaction he wanted. You *know* the Southerners love to characterise us all as brutes rather than gentlemen!"

"Pretty sure he didn't want me to break his teeth," Greg said with satisfaction and absolutely no sign of repentance.

Marius rubbed at his temples. "*Think*, Greg! Think who exactly will be dragged into this if that boy goes complaining to his father that some violent Northerner roughed him up! You know there's a reporter snooping about already—I'm sure she'd love to make hay of this if she hears of it. And who do you think that will cause trouble for, when the Conclave is about to meet?"

Greg absorbed this as they passed a bookshop, the sign gleaming with dew.

"Hetta," he said heavily.

Marius felt old and jaded, watching his little brother's righteous anger crumple into the hurt realisation that the world wasn't a fair place, that being in the right didn't necessarily *matter*.

"It's not *fair!*" Greg uttered the age-old words on cue, hands curling in and out of fists.

"No," Marius said. "It's not. I hate it too."

"What am I supposed to do, then?"

"*Not* break innocent shopkeepers' windows, for one."

Greg did look guilty at that. "Did you…did you have to pay for that too?"

"Yes." *And what a gold-plated window it was*, he reflected, remembering the sum the officer had named. He ran a hand through his hair. "I don't have a perfect solution for you. But I do know that if they figure out how to rile you, they'll keep doing it." *Eighteen-year-old boys are not the most emotionally mature specimens of mankind.* "Avoid them if you can, or at least try to avoid getting involved in any more fisticuffs. This won't last forever, and I suspect Hetta will make our name more than merely notorious, given enough time. The same boys who insulted her tonight will make little impact on the world, in comparison."

Had he said too much, or not enough? He knew Greg both

looked up to him and frequently discounted his advice—this was the trouble with being so far removed in age and personality. Unbidden, his mind began to speculate on what the bloody earl's son had said about Hetta that had sent Greg into such a rage. An earl's son… Marius had a flash of horror. The Earl of Wolver didn't have a son Greg's age, did he? Although if he did, Gregory punching him did seem suddenly acceptable. *No*, he told himself. *You're supposed to be the mature adult here.*

The gravel path crunched under their feet. "Are you happy she's marrying Wyn?" Greg said eventually. "I mean…she *is* going to, isn't she?"

I'd be happier if I was surer of the answer to that. Hetta had told him of the obstacles that stood in their way. But Greg wasn't asking that. Wyn was practically another brother to him, but Greg had been badly burnt by the fae when the girl he was courting turned out to be the fae spy Gwendelfear. He'd never quite recovered his equilibrium from the experience. Being made a fool in love cut deep. *Which I know better than anyone.*

Marius winced away from the thought of just how foolish he'd been in his own choices. As if attempting to blackmail his family hadn't been sufficient, John had then shacked up with the Earl of Wolver and spun him a pretty tale of tragedy in which Wyn, Marius, and Hetta had wronged him, prompting the earl to avenge his lover.

"Em?" Greg prompted.

"I think," he said carefully, "that I'm glad we have Wyn on our side, given that things with Faerie seem likely to get more rather than less complicated. And he does love Hetta." He didn't doubt that, though he could wish the pair were a little more *careful*.

Greg made a disgusted noise at this saccharine comment. "Well, I wish they'd hurry up and actually *marry*. It doesn't look good, drawing it out. People will say she's—you know, a light-skirt." He blushed.

I'm fairly sure she is a light-skirt, by standard definition, and has been for some time, Marius considered telling him. He was the only one of the family who'd seen Hetta during her six-year absence, when he'd occasionally visited her in Meridon. She'd drawn a sharp wall around her life there, but he could read between lines. He didn't *want* to read between lines, not when they involved his sister, but, still, he wasn't completely naïve.

"Anyone who insults a woman with that sort of judgement isn't worth your time," he said firmly instead. *Hypocrite*, his inner critic whispered. Hadn't he railed at Hetta about the very same thing more than once?

That was different, though. He was her brother; it was his job to worry.

They walked in silence for several minutes. The colleges of Knoxbridge were sprinkled throughout the township, with the one Greg belonged to on the outskirts. Marius deposited his thoughtful and semi-penitent brother at Maudlin College and began the walk back to his own accommodations. His headache was starting to ease—thank Mighty Pyrania and all the little gods. Maybe it was a sign that he was finally recovering from whatever Aroset had done to him. *What if she permanently damaged me?* Fingers clutching at his throat…

He shoved his hands into his pockets and began to walk more briskly. He walked for a long time, until dawn broke through the mist in a wash of grey light and a small trickle of people joined him on the river path, giving him no more than passing nods. There were swans on the river as well, real or lowfae he wasn't sure, and he squinted at them to no effect, trying to tell. Would the herb mixture work without the quizzing glass, he wondered? He ought to try that next, just to rule it out as a variable.

What was he doing? He had a tutorial to teach this morning, and doing that on no sleep was guaranteed to bring on a migraine.

He forced his feet back in the direction of Shakif College, which was a small postgraduate college named after an Ekaran benefactor. It was located on the opposite side of the Botanic Gardens from Greg's college, so the trip would've been a ten-minute one if not for Marius's meanderings.

The porter was just distributing the early morning delivery into the pigeonholes when Marius came in.

"Two for you, Mr Valstar," he said, handing him the envelopes. "Got a sweetheart, have you?"

He meant it kindly, but Marius still flushed. "Thank you, Mr Singh." He took them from him and tromped tiredly up to his room. It looked out over the four-sided courtyard and faced west, which was a blessing today, since it meant with the curtains closed it would still be dark enough to sleep.

He threw the two envelopes on his desk and frowned. One was a thick, cream-coloured piece with a rather official-looking seal and his name and address written in tight, elegant black ink. The other was unlabelled, and he recognised the envelope as the sort you could buy ten-for-a-penny.

He should sleep, but he'd never been very good at denying curiosity, so he picked up the rougher of the two, fished about for a letter-opener, and tore it open.

A pamphlet stared up at him. A horrible urge to laugh rose up in his throat as he unfolded it and found an illustration that, in a poor light, might've been of Wyn, if Wyn had abandoned his usual neat suit and instead taken up some kind of druid's robes instead. In poorly set type, the pamphlet informed him: "WINGED GODS ARE AMONG US!!! Have You feLt THEIr inflUENCE????"

He did laugh, a choking sound. It looked like Ms Orpington-Davies had been right about the wing worshippers. Gods, imagine what Rakken would make of this sort of nonsense. It didn't bear thinking about, though it was at least better than yet another thinly veiled snipe at his family. Wasn't it? Rubbing at his temples, he crumpled the pamphlet up and dropped it into the wastepaper bin, that seeming the best place to file it.

He eyed the second envelope. "Well, you can hardly be worse than your friend," he told it, picking it up.

It was.

11

ILLUSTRIOUS ANCESTORS

THE NEXT MORNING before breakfast, Hetta once again tried asking Stariel if it knew how to fix the cause of the static shocks, and the land once again returned only worried incomprehension, so she got up, got dressed, and made her way to the library. Surely if she kept digging, somewhere in the library's disorder, one or other of her ancestors must've recorded at least one useful fact relating either to her land-sense, fae-human hybrids, or the fae High King? What was the point of storing all this wretched family history, otherwise!

She walked along the length of the main floor—the library was a two-storeyed room that had been a ballroom in a past life—and drew up in surprise: Ivy, not usually an early riser, was already here, snugged at a desk in the far corner, surrounded by stacks of old books. Her dark head was bent over her work as she scribbled furiously.

"Ivy?"

Ivy gave a start and knocked over one of the stacks, which went cascading to the floor in a paper avalanche. Hetta bent to retrieve it with an apology and saw that the pile consisted mostly of hand-written journals.

"Drat," Ivy said, frowning at the pile. "I'd already sorted that one into date order." She yawned, covering her mouth with a hand, and blinked around owlishly. "Gosh—what time is it?"

"Please tell me you haven't been here all night," Hetta said in dismay. Ivy's eyes were blood-shot, suggesting that this was, in fact, the case.

Ivy wrinkled her nose. "Well, I didn't *intend* to be," she said, stifling another yawn. "But I got Daff to help me locate all of these yesterday, and then the cross-referencing got very involved…" She gestured around at the books in a 'you-know-how-it-is' sort of way. Daff was Daffodil, one of Ivy's younger brothers. Aunt Maude had a penchant for botanically themed names.

"Family journals?" Hetta guessed. The open spreads of several of the books showed various styles of handwriting.

"*Lords'* journals," Ivy said proudly. "We found a whole cache of them buried in a shelf otherwise devoted to cataloguing beetles. No wonder no one knew they were there."

"I don't suppose any of them are from—"

But Ivy was already shaking her head. "None are from the first Lord Fallstar, but *these* ones"—she poked a small stack of battered leather journals triumphantly—"are from Great Great Great Great Great Grandfather, Lord Marius Valstar the first. You know," she said impatiently in the face of Hetta's blank look. "The Lord of Stariel during unification."

"Oh, when the Northern Treaty was signed with the Crown." Hetta did know *some* history. That had been a little over three centuries ago, though sometimes the North acted as if it had been only yesterday. "And around when the Iron Law came into being."

"Well, yes, I wondered if they were linked too," Ivy said kindly, picking up one of the journals. "Though I don't think they did happen at the same time; I think your fairy Iron Law happened the year after unification." She huffed down at the journal. "I have to say, though, that Lord Marius's approach to record-keeping leaves much to be desired. This is the entry nearest in time to when I think the Northern Treaty must've been signed: 'A lot of paperwork. Extra houseguests due to leave by the 20th.'" She made a disgusted sound. "The next entry is for the 25th of the same month: 'Bagged two rabbits, one pheasant'. Honestly!"

A strange feeling rose in Hetta's chest, hearing the words of her ancestor who'd occupied the same role she did now, even if they weren't particularly illuminating words. She wanted to reach across the centuries and ask Lord Marius I whether he'd expected to be lord or if—like her—it had been thrust upon him. How he'd reconciled lordship with personal concerns. Whether he'd doubted himself too.

"Does he say anything about Stariel's magic?"

Ivy shook her head. "Only by inference. Things like 'Stariel is quiet tonight'. Once he worried about 'going too deep', but he didn't elaborate on what that meant."

A chill went down Hetta's spine; she knew what he'd meant. Had that been what she'd done on the stairwell before Grandmama had snapped her out of it? If so, how did one avoid going too deep again?

Ivy didn't notice her reaction, continuing to flick through the journal whilst making small grumbling sounds. "He had a sad life, I think. Look at this, his last two entries."

Hetta craned over her shoulder and read: *Ewan is dead.* There were no other details, but the unadorned words carried grief across three centuries. That entry was followed a week later by a second one: *The cursed queen gave her word. It won't bring Ewan back, but mayhap it will keep the others safe for a time.*

There were no more entries after that.

"Who was Ewan?" Hetta asked, wrapping her arms around herself.

"His youngest son—he's on the wall, look." Ivy got up, stiff and groaning as she fished about for her cane.

"You need to go to bed," Hetta said severely. "You shouldn't have stayed up on my account."

"It wasn't exactly on your account; I'm not that noble. I just lost track of the time. Anyway, the wall!" Ivy found her cane and began to make her way back along the length of the library, to one of the staircases leading up to the mezzanine. Hetta followed her.

The wall she referred to was on the upper floor. On it hung an old heirloom tapestry of their family tree, with the line of lords picked out in gold thread.

Ivy craned her neck to look to the very top, where Lord Fallstar was stitched in faded thread. "That's about all we have of our most illustrious ancestor," she said, pointing at it. "I wish I knew more about him."

Hetta realised she already knew something more than Ivy did about the first Lord of Stariel. "Wyn said he married a fae woman."

Ivy's eyes widened. "Why didn't you tell me that sooner! What was her name? Does he know anything else about her?"

"Er…I don't know. I didn't ask any of that." And now she felt somewhat sheepish for not doing so. It also hadn't occurred to her that the information might be of interest to anyone else in the family.

Ivy deflated and then brightened. "Well, I can ask him myself, I suppose. Where is he?"

"Stewarding."

Ivy sighed and turned back to the wall, saying philosophically, "Well, it's waited a thousand years. I suppose it can wait a while longer."

"I haven't looked at this in years," Hetta said, touching the name of her great-grandfather, Sydney Valstar. A small gold star indicated he'd been chosen to rule. "Grandfather Marius never got his star." Lord Marius II's name was present only as one of Lord Sydney's offspring, his own lordship not yet stitched. None of the family after him were present, as the tapestry hadn't been updated in several generations.

"We're looking for Marius the first."

They traced their way upwards. "Here's Ewan. Goodness, However-many-Great-Grandfather Marius was prolific. *Fourteen* children!" Hetta resisted—once again—the urge to put a hand to her abdomen.

"His poor wife," Ivy remarked. "See, there—Ewan was his youngest son." She pointed at a tiny name above Hetta's head. "Died young, looking at the death date—only eighteen. Never married or had children." A sad dead-end in the Valstar family tree.

"*The cursed queen,*" Hetta murmured, turning the words of Lord Marius's last journal entries over thoughtfully. "But there wasn't a queen in Prydein then, was there, in North or South? You think he was referring to a fae queen?"

Ivy's eyes brightened. "Exactly."

Hetta knew the High King would've been the High Queen then and said as much to Ivy. The gender-changing nature of Wyn's liege had been a strange thing to get her head around, though she supposed less strange than the fact that the fae had turned out to be real at all. After all, the idea wasn't wholly without precedent, even here in the human world. It wasn't quite the same thing, but back in Meridon, Hetta had known some amongst the theatre crowd who went by names and attires other than the ones they'd been born to.

An unsettling shape began to form as Hetta tried to fit everything she knew together. The first Lord Fallstar bargaining with the High King in a past so distant there were no real records left of how Stariel began. Lord Marius I, many generations later, making another bargain with the High Queen at a time that coincided a little too neatly with the beginning of the Iron Law. Stariel's magic ebbing over the last three centuries since Faerie and Mortal had separated.

Ivy had turned away from the wall and was eying her speculatively. "You know, if Lord Fallstar married a fae woman, technically that means Wyn will be the *second* fae marrying into this family, assuming you actually are going to make an honest man of him. Who would've thought you'd turn out to be the most traditional of us?"

Hetta laughed, though the thought sat oddly. So much of her life since returning to Stariel had been dictated by tradition—from the Choosing ceremony itself to seeking the queen's permission to marry. Had the original Lord Fallstar faced the same kind of opposition she was dealing with now? Though the fae wouldn't have been a secret back then, centuries before the Iron Law came into being. "Two fae marrying into the family in a thousand years can hardly be considered a *tradition*," she felt bound to point out.

"Two fae that we know of." Ivy shrugged. "We've started traditions on the basis of less." Her tone grew teasing. "Are you sure you don't want to formally adopt this one, betroth your future children to fae royalty, lock them in tower rooms awaiting enchanted rescue and so on? After all, we have all these appropriately picturesque towers—it seems a shame not to use them."

Hetta carefully didn't put a hand to her stomach.

Ivy continued her thought experiment, oblivious. "Though I suppose technically any children you have would *be* fae royalty, on their father's side. Which does raise the question of whether their land-sense would be tied to Stariel or to Wyn's court. Do you know much about how fairy inheritance works? Would the wings be passed down the line as well? There's no record of that in our own histories, which suggests Lord Fallstar's wife either *wasn't* winged, or it's not an inherited trait with mixed bloodlines."

"*Ivy*," Hetta said plaintively, for her cousin had given her an entire raft of new concerns. Images bloomed in her mind's eye: a small boy with bright russet eyes and the long Valstar nose; a girl with flowing, silvery-white hair. The images flickered at the edges, uncertainly forming the outlines of wings and horns.

She pushed them away. The images were only her own imaginings, not realities—even Stariel couldn't give her any details yet. The land was only connected to the child through its effect on her; it was too early for it to know anything more. Early enough that she shouldn't have really known it even existed yet.

Ivy gave a start, a faint flush rising on her cheekbones. "Oh. Sorry. You know I get caught up."

Hetta wavered, considered confessing that the topic wasn't only of academic interest to her, but in the end only said, "Getting back to the matter in hand, did Lord Marius write anything more about what happened with the fae queen?"

Ivy shook her head. "I suppose he was too busy grieving his son."

Frustration burned in her. They ought not to lose so much institutional knowledge each time the lordship changed hands. There ought to be properly organised records made of this stuff, an instruction manual for Stariel's magic passed down.

"He was still the lord; he should've recorded something this important. Even if—Oh." Hetta's fingers stilled on the tapestry, her focus on the death date of Marius I. "He died too, the same year as his son." But the cold-hearted anger still lurked at her ancestor's failure of duty. She certainly wouldn't leave Stariel's next lord so adrift.

"As I said, he seems to have led a rather sad life." Ivy rubbed at her eyes. "I don't suppose our Marius is due back any time soon? Organising family journals would go a lot quicker with another pair of hands. And legs. Even if he *does* prefer a wrongheaded system of categorisation." She stifled another yawn.

"Not until end of term, I don't think." Hetta sighed. She both wanted and didn't want Marius here.

Ivy slid her a sideways look. "What does Marius think about"— she made a vague gesture—"all this?"

"What do you mean?" Hetta asked frostily.

Ivy didn't take the hint; she'd never been good at reading

tone. "You know—you and Wyn. Fairy royalty. Queen Matilda summoning you for whatever that was about. The Dower House."

"What about the Dower House?"

Ivy blinked. "Er, well, it is a bit different, isn't it? Renting it out to strangers?"

Hetta wrestled with the urge to snap at her cousin; it would be unfair to lash out at Ivy for repeating sentiments that hadn't originated with her. She knew Ivy was only passing on what their wider family was discussing behind Hetta's back. Besides, hadn't Ivy just spent the whole night researching on Hetta's behalf?

Ivy added uncertainly, "Though I don't really understand why it matters so much who lives in it. It's on the other side of the lake, after all."

"Exactly!"

They both turned at the sound of the library door opening. Wyn emerged, looking up towards them curiously. A black kitten trotted at his heels. It was half catshee—fairy cat—and one of three born at midwinter. One or other of the kittens was frequently to be found shadowing Wyn's footsteps, which he pretended to find exasperating. "Am I interrupting?"

"Not at all!" Hetta said, holding out an arm in invitation. "Ivy's been digging through old records—we were just checking the family tree."

He climbed the spiral staircase, the kitten attempting to run under his feet as he did so. It went to butt its head against Ivy's cane, and Hetta hastily scooped it into her arms to avoid a mishap. The kitten gave an indignant mew.

Wyn gave her a swift, assessing look, and she knew he wanted to ask if there had been any more shocks but couldn't with Ivy there.

"Good morning," he said to her cousin instead.

Ivy replied, smothering a yawn. The way she looked at Wyn

made Hetta a little uneasy, and Hetta put a deliberate arm around Wyn's waist. She was going to marry him; her family could jolly well get used to the idea that he was one of them now, fae or not.

Wyn blinked at her in surprise but made no objection, despite the fact that they'd agreed to at least attempt a façade of respectability when in front of an audience. Ivy flushed and looked away.

The kitten wriggled, wanting to get to Wyn, and Hetta held back a laugh as Wyn let it climb onto his shoulders with a long-suffering expression. It curled up and went to sleep there as Hetta told him what she and Ivy had found.

Wyn inspected the tapestry. "There are seven generations between Lord Marius I and your father."

"Is that significant?" Ivy asked.

"Perhaps," he said. "Seven is a significant number, in fae magic." He and Hetta exchanged a glance.

"You don't know anything else connecting fairies and Valstars?" Ivy asked.

"I was thinking earlier about the timing of the Iron Law coming down. I don't know for sure, but I wonder…did it end at the moment of your father's death? Was it bound to the Valstars, somehow?" he said, turning to Hetta.

They all mulled over that. What did it mean, if her family or Stariel had somehow been responsible for the Iron Law in the first place? Hetta shivered. "The timing does seem like too much of a coincidence. But the question is why, isn't it? I don't like all these unknowns," she said.

"Nor do I," Wyn said.

Ivy stifled another yawn. "Well, would your brother know?"

Hetta was almost tempted to loose Ivy on Rakken for the amusement value, but Wyn was already shaking his head. "I have asked him already, and no."

Ivy dug about in her pockets and then gave up with a sigh. "Dash it, I left my notebook downstairs. I still think it's probably worth me quizzing you, if you don't mind, since you're the closest we have to an expert on the subject."

"I have no objection—but, forgive me, I do not think it is so urgent it should keep you from your rest."

"Ivy, go to bed," Hetta agreed.

Ivy rubbed at her head. "Oh, all right—but don't you dare make any important secret discoveries without me."

She left.

Wyn carefully dislodged the kitten and put it down—it gave itself a shake before going to investigate the bottom shelves. Putting his arm around Hetta's shoulders, he drew her closer. "Have there been any more shocks?"

She shook her head. "None since last night. This isn't your fault, Wyn, and you fretting over it isn't going to solve anything."

"Are you not worried?"

She sighed against him. "Of course I am, but I'd rather not dwell on it right now. I'd rather dwell on how we're going to fix it." She frowned at the tapestry. "If my family is in some way responsible for the Iron Law, is that going to make the High King more or less positively inclined towards me?"

"I suspect that depends very much on the *why* of it."

"You mean if my ancestor blackmailed the High Queen into the Iron Law, she's probably not going to look on any requests from me kindly."

"He," he corrected absently, tracing down the lines of the Valstar family tree that ended at Hetta's grandfather. "And yes. Though I never thought the High King likely to look upon me with kindness in any case, given I disobeyed his last directive."

Hetta followed the golden line of thread, imagining it updated to include her father, then her, and from that, her children. She swallowed. "Well, blackmail or bribe, if we can find out what my ancestor used, then maybe we can use it again."

THEY MET RAKKEN ON the threshold of the breakfast parlour. He paused briefly, considering the pair of them with an inscrutable expression, though he seemed less hostile towards Wyn than yesterday.

"If you tell my family anything…" Hetta warned, a hand drifting to her abdomen before she caught herself.

Rakken looked genuinely blank—the first time she'd ever seen that expression—but it cleared after a moment. "Oh, your peculiar mortal customs," he said dismissively. "I can hold my tongue, Lord Valstar."

"Well, good then," she said, unreasonably annoyed. It was all very well for Rakken to wave away the threatening scandal as 'peculiar mortal customs', but neither he nor his home faeland had to live with the consequences.

Rakken wasn't done. "*I* have no intention of adding to the unflattering mortal reports of our people," he added, with a pointed glare for Wyn just in case he'd missed the dig. "*I* am not the one whose name is being bandied about across an entire mortal kingdom."

Not less hostile, then.

"If you would mind removing yourself from the doorway while you needle me?" Wyn said mildly.

"Yes, you're between me and the coffee," Hetta added.

Rakken's eyes narrowed, but he did get out of the way.

"So you've been reading our newspapers, then," Hetta said after settling herself. Her stomach wasn't queasy so much as delicate, as if she'd over-indulged the night before, which seemed very unfair.

Rakken poured himself tea. "They will fear us soon enough, if they do not already." He looked at Wyn again. "You cannot allay those fears by hiding away up here, playing at being human."

"Well, how can we allay them then, in your princely opinion?" Hetta asked.

Rakken laughed. "What do you think the machinery of a proper court is for, Lord Valstar? Even your mortal one. Boxing at shadows, propaganda and promises. Deals cut in back rooms. Marriages of state." He emphasised the last, showing teeth.

"Well, I am technically attempting that, brother," Wyn put in.

"Perhaps the second time will be more successful than the first."

It was perhaps fortunate that Jack stomped into the room at this point. Jack was usually the first of her family to breakfast, being the only one naturally given to early rising. Often, he'd already have been out on the estate before breakfast, though it was clear today he hadn't. He bore all the signs of a hangover.

Wyn crouched and pulled a bottle of Lady Philomena's hangover remedy from the lower shelf of the sideboard, offering it to Jack with an extremely innocent expression. Jack glowered at being so easily read but slouched over anyway to snatch the proffered bottle.

"Nice eye," he grunted.

Hetta frowned; she'd thought Wyn had glamoured himself. Perhaps he hadn't bothered yet.

Jack clearly remained in a bad mood, shooting her a disapproving look as he dumped a measure of the remedy into his cup before adding coffee. He opened his mouth to say something, then stopped himself with a dark glance at Rakken.

"Oh, do not refrain on my account, Jonathan Langley-Valstar," Rakken said sweetly.

Jack coloured to the roots of his hair, but fortunately—or perhaps *unfortunately*—they were joined by several other members of her family. There were more Valstars home than usual right now, thanks to the recent spring equinox celebrations. Hetta's stepmother, sisters, and several of her cousins breezed into the breakfast room oblivious to the tension—or possibly merely accustomed to it, Hetta thought with a sigh. It wasn't as if it were the first time she and Jack had been at odds.

No one else noticed Wyn's black eye though—except her sister Alexandra, who sat down next to him with a frown and said something in a low tone. "I heal very fast," she heard him reassuring her. Hmmm. Alexandra had the Sight, but perhaps she wasn't the only one.

Lady Phoebe beamed at Hetta as she seated herself.

"Hetta, dear, I found the most *wonderful* bridal catalogue! It has several very useful suggestions for summer weddings." Phoebe dropped this announcement with a hopeful question at the end of it. When Hetta merely smiled, she added, anxiously, "You will marry before midsummer, won't you? Or we could combine it with the Solstice celebrations, if you liked? That could work very well!"

"We'll think about it," Hetta said diplomatically.

"Anyone would think you were nervous about taking up married life, what with all this indecisiveness over the wedding date," her cousin Cecily said with a knowing smile. She had taken up the seat next to Hetta. She lowered her voice: "And I wouldn't fret over the wedding night, you know."

Hetta choked on her coffee and met Wyn's eyes. He grinned.

Her cousin Caroline, who was sitting on Cecily's other side and who had once stumbled upon Hetta and Wyn embracing in the map room, rolled her eyes and said loudly, "I'm pretty sure Hetta's not worried about that, Cess."

"Worried about what?" Alexandra piped up from the other end of the table.

"Lady Cecily may be concerned about Lord Valstar developing

an ill-timed allergy to feathers," Rakken said, earning a glare from all parties.

"My brother is being ill-mannered. How are your waterway maps progressing?" Wyn said, firmly changing the subject as Alexandra flushed a brilliant red.

"Oh, um, good."

Hetta threw Wyn a look of gratitude as he did his best to keep the conversation from veering into inappropriate or inflammatory territory, not helped by Jack continuing to glare as if he were considering strangling her, Wyn, and Rakken all; nor by the silk-covered darts Rakken kept throwing out to enliven things whenever he grew bored.

If they never freed the Spires, where would Rakken *go*? He was too sharp for Stariel, a pike in a trout pond; this could never be home for him the way it was for Wyn. Would it be petty to inflict him on Queen Matilda? Rakken was right; there *should* be a fae ambassador in the mortal court, and Hetta didn't want to part with Wyn. But sending Rakken to Meridon would only be a good idea if they could persuade Rakken to act in Stariel's interests rather than his own—about as likely as Starwater freezing over at midsummer.

She reached once more for her cup and winced at the static. Taking a steadying sip of coffee, she looked up to meet Wyn's worried gaze. There was a fae edge to his face, and she wondered that no one else had noticed.

She shook her head subtly—it was fine, and there was nothing either of them could do right now about it in any case. Rakken was watching them both, the green of his eyes like a cat's.

The housemaid entered then, one of the kittens at her heels.

"There's a phonecall for you, my lord. From Mr Marius."

Hetta rested her fingertips on the white tablecloth, winding in a long, slow breath. "Thank you, Lottie," she said, rising.

Four days until full moon.

OLDER BROTHERS

HETTA COULDN'T HELP giving herself a small mental self-congratulation as she picked up the receiver in her study; the phoneline direct to the house had only just been installed. The rest of the lineswork for the estate remained a work in progress, but this small bit of modernity was nevertheless a heartening milestone.

"Hetta?" Marius's voice scratched down the phoneline. "Is that you?"

"Indeed it is, brother mine. You sound like you swallowed a bottle of scotch. If so, I hope it was worth it!

A weary chuckle. "Sadly not. You don't sound terribly chipper yourself."

"A side effect of insufficient coffee and watching Wyn try not to strangle his brother over the breakfast table."

Marius made a sympathetic noise.

"How are the headaches?" she asked.

"Fine, fine." He didn't sound fine. He sounded like someone trying to cut short a thread of inquiry before it began.

Hetta pulled on the thread. "That's not very convincing. When does 'fine' ever actually mean 'fine'?"

"Improving, then. But I didn't call to discuss my health."

"What does *improving* mean?" she pressed. She wished Marius hadn't returned to Knoxbridge so quickly after Aroset's attack. What if Aroset had damaged him in some way they'd yet to realise? And what about the telepathy? Guilt knotted in her stomach. If Marius hadn't left so quickly, would she have had time to rethink the decision to keep him in the dark about his own ability? Was Rakken right about the risks? But she couldn't tell Marius about it now, at the impersonal end of a phoneline.

"It means stop pestering me and remember which one of us is the elder, *Mother*." There was a bite in the last word, and she knew Marius was rolling his eyes.

Her stomach fluttered. "Um, actually, that's a rather apt bit of phrasing. I have something to tell you." She twined the phone cord around her wrist and extended her senses. No housefae or staff lurked near her study, and no one had lifted the other receiver in the house, which sat in a small room off the main entranceway. She let out a breath and said in a rush, "You're going to be an uncle."

A sharp crack made her wince away from the receiver. It was followed by a clatter and muffled swearing.

"Did you drop the phone?"

"What did you say?"

"I'm pregnant."

There was a long, fraught silence at the other end of the line. Marius didn't react well to surprises. Was he gathering momentum to rail at her?

"Who else knows?" His voice had taken on a strange clinical detachment.

Really, *that* was his immediate thought?

"You're the first person I've actually told apart from Wyn. I didn't tell Rakken and Jack, but they each guessed it, separately. Apparently my swooning at the wrong moment gave me away."

"Swooning?! That's—have you seen a physician?"

"*Normal* amounts of swooning," she emphasised, despite not knowing if this was entirely true. "And don't you start—Wyn's already taken to asking me if I'm all right approximately four dozen times per day." She wasn't going to mention the shocks, not until they'd at least heard back from Lamorkin.

"Oh." He lapsed back into silence. What kind of scandalised brotherly reaction *was* this? Didn't he care?

"Well?" she prompted when the silence threatened to go on without end. "Aren't you going to rail at me for failing to uphold the family honour and so forth?"

What was she doing? It was nonsensical to be annoyed that he wasn't yelling at her!

"You're pregnant," he said slowly. "Hells." There was another long pause, as if the wheels of his mind were creaking only glacially back into motion. Then—"Please tell me you've got the High King's permission to marry?"

This at least was closer to the reaction she'd expected. "It's a work in progress."

"*Hetta.*" Her name held a history of echoes, of half-fond, half-exasperated older-brother complaint stretching over years, right back to when they were children, before their father had remarried.

"I've recruited Ivy to the cause." She told him about what they'd found. "I don't suppose you've found anything useful down there?"

Marius made a frustrated sound she knew wasn't aimed at her. "All I've been able to get hold of from the time period is a slightly disturbing set of folk tales—waterhorses drowning people, fae women murdering their lovers, that sort of thing—and a criminally boring thesis on the drivers behind the Northern Treaty that absolutely fails to mention fae in any capacity." Marius had been the one to find the Addendum to the Northern Treaty that said Stariel could make its own treaties with fae courts, separate from the rest of Prydein.

"Maybe you should give me the highlights of that," she said, only half-joking. Stariel had its own copy of the treaty, which she'd struggled through recently to refresh her memory. It wasn't a particularly exciting document. She hadn't found a copy of the Addendum. Or was it too buried somewhere in the chaos of Stariel's library?

"No one needs the highlights of that thesis," he said darkly. "How long have you got until…I mean, when…?"

"A while yet. November, we think." She swallowed as well; mentioning a date made it feel somehow more real.

This time the pause held considerable awkwardness.

"Meridon," he said grimly. "We're rubbish chaperones, aren't we?"

"It wasn't actually only you and Aunt Sybil standing between me and my virtue. I'm not virtuous, Marius, and haven't been for years." But she couldn't help the flush rising in her cheeks, despite herself.

"Yes, I know—but you don't have to *remind* me." He sounded so pained that she couldn't help a huff of laughter escaping. He went quiet again, and when he next spoke it didn't surprise her to find that his thoughts, now that he'd gotten past the initial shock, had begun to spin rapidly towards the wider implications. "The Conclave's, what, end of May? It won't be, er, obvious by then, will it?"

"No, but I'm not an idiot. I've no intention of making this news public before then regardless—or at all, before we're married." The injustice of it burned and made her add, "But it's ridiculous that it should matter to them, given I know at least one of them has a child out of wedlock—and very likely more!"

"Don't pretend it's the same."

"Of course. Because I'm a woman." She picked up a pen from her desk and stabbed it into the notebook in front of her with a satisfying wrench.

"Because the child will be *half-fae* and if the Conclave have any wits, that's what they'll care about, not bloody propriety! What will it even look like? Will it have wings?"

"I don't know! I don't know; Wyn doesn't know. Nobody knows! There hasn't been a child like this for three hundred years at least and there's no one I can ask for advice!"

"Oh, Hetta." There was only softness in the word. "I'm sure you'll be a great mother. You've faced down literal monsters, after all; raising one baby can hardly be worse than that. And you have time to get the knot tied, before it becomes, er, too obvious." A dry note entered his tone. "Plenty of firstborns are born improbably early, anyway."

"But what if—" She didn't finish, but he heard it anyway, homing in on that secret fear not with telepathy but with familiarity. It was an old heartache, intimate to the two of them, though Marius had never, ever blamed her for the fact that her birth had heralded his mother's death.

"You'll be fine, Hetta. Modern medicine is much better than it was, back when…well, anyway, it's different now. You'll be fine."

"I know it's silly to be afraid." Equally silly was how reassuring she found his words, given that he knew even less about this process than she did. She blinked suddenly wet eyes, annoyed with herself. Why on earth should that make her cry?

"It doesn't seem silly at all. I'm terrified," he said frankly. "For one thing, the prospect of being an uncle makes me feel depressingly ancient."

She gave a watery chuckle. "Well, never mind all that. Why were you calling me in the first place before I distracted you?"

"Oh, that." Marius's tone went dark. "More wonderful news on the public relations front." He told her about the reporter approaching him. "I warned Gregory, but I wanted to let you know as well, in case they range further afield."

Hetta wrinkled her nose. "Goodness knows what the locals will tell them, if they do." She hoped any reporters would at least hold off until after Angus's house party and the Conclave; being hounded by the press was unlikely to impress the Northern lords. "But how is Greg doing?"

Marius was a bad liar; she could tell by the long pause that he was censoring himself. "Er, well enough, I suppose. He doesn't really talk to me much—gone are the days of my older-brotherly shine, apparently." His aggrieved tone was genuine, she thought, but also camouflage.

"What don't you want to tell me?" She hunted about and retrieved her pen so she could continue stabbing at her notebook.

Marius hedged. "It's not your fault, Hetta."

"What isn't my fault?"

There was a long sigh down the other end of the phone, and she could see Marius run a hand through his hair. "I've been summoned." All Hetta could think of was fae magic, but his next words clarified that he was talking of a summons of a more mundane sort. "The Earl of Wolver wants to talk to me."

"What?"

"Yes," he agreed darkly. "Apparently the queen, in her infinite wisdom, has made him Chief Inquirer into Fae Misconduct."

Hetta had to stop herself from yanking on the phone cord. "She was supposed to punish him for what he did! Not put him in charge of…whatever he's been put in charge of!"

"Quite. But I don't think I can ignore it. He's out of town at the moment, but he wants me to come up to Meridon when he returns. An official interview."

Hetta didn't want her brother anywhere near the Earl of Wolver, not after seeing the way he'd looked at him with such loathing. "Marius—"

"The earl is *my* problem to deal with." His tone had gone brittle, and she knew his shoulders would be up around his ears. "And I wouldn't have told you anything about it except I know you've the Conclave coming up, and I didn't want you blindsided by the news if it spills over into that."

Hetta glared at her office walls in lieu of her brother and the Conclave both.

"It's *not* your fault," Marius repeated. He paused. "You'll tell me, won't you, if there's…anything else I can do?" Her brother was just as much at sea with the concept of pregnancy as she was. "I could try to take some leave and come up to Stariel before end of term." Knoxbridge's term had only just begun, and as a junior staff member with a patchy academic record, Marius's position was precarious; it was a mark of his concern that he'd even mentioned the idea.

"No, I'll be fine," she said firmly. She knew how important Marius's work was to him, how he mourned the years of ladder-climbing he'd lost when their father had decreed he put a halt to his academic studies. She looked out at the wind-ruffled caps of Starwater. "I'd better go, unless you have any more dramatic reveals to make."

His voice hardened. "Can I speak to Wyn?"

"Jack's already given him a black eye, if you were planning to chew his ear off."

"Bloody martyr," Marius groused. "But I still want to chew his ear off. Humour me this once, sister mine."

Hetta rolled her eyes but nonetheless found herself irrationally cheered by this unreasonable behaviour. *Honestly, I could do without these see-sawing emotions.* "Oh, all right then. I'll fetch him."

13

FULL MOON

FOUR INTERMINABLE DAYS later, Wyn held his breath as the full moon inched above the horizon. He and Hetta stood in Carnelian Hall, her hand warm in his. They summoned Lamorkin in the space between the fireplace and the dilapidated armchairs, freeing a little portion of Stariel's lands from the wards against portals for a time. The connection between Wyn and his godparent felt oddly weak, as if it might snap at the merest touch.

"Lamorkin," he called. "Lamorkin. Lamorkin."

He'd tried to summon Lamorkin so many times without answer lately, and the connection when it finally unfurled was so thin that he feared a repetition of those failures.

But this time, his godparent answered.

The relief was so heady he nearly swayed as a portal opened with a snap in the unwarded circle. A glimmer of wintery daylight before the portal closed; Lamorkin had come from somewhere far, far away.

Lamorkin gave themself a shake of adjustment as the portal snapped closed and blinked up at him from the form of a delicate horse-like creature with six legs. Their fur was a soft fawn-brown, growing longer and more luxurious with every breath.

Wyn smiled. "Godparent. I am very glad you came."

"Good evening, Lamorkin," Hetta added politely, her hand tightening on his.

He appreciated the effort Hetta made to hide how much Lamorkin unnerved her. The rest of her family had been less restrained, at the single appearance Lamorkin had made to Hetta's family before leaving on their mission: a family breakfast weeks ago. Lamorkin had gotten on alarmingly well with Hetta's grandmother, and the two of them had spent much of the meal cackling and swapping increasingly awkward stories while the rest of the Valstars watched with expressions ranging from horror to fascination.

Lamorkin made a thoughtful noise low in their throat, a resonant, eerie sound of caves and songbirds, and shook out their long fur, which had taken on a subtle striped pattern in shades of purple.

"Hallowyn, Hallowyn, Hallowyn," they chided, tilting their narrow head to the side. "Hallowyn Tempestren." There was power in the true names of fae, and using one had a range of connotations depending on context. This one wasn't that subtle; Lamorkin was needling him.

Wyn just smiled, still too relieved that they'd come to be so easily baited.

Lamorkin watched his reaction closely. "You do so like to play pretend-mortal, don't you? It irks you to be reminded of your own nature, doesn't it?"

"I know what I am," Wyn said and then cursed himself for taking the bait. He took a long breath. "Godparent, I—"

"How long does a godparent's bond last, Hallowyn?" Their lips stretched in a mouth that was far too wide for their face, growing broader as they smiled. "Naughty, naughty, princeling," they said slyly, looking at Hetta.

Oh. *Oh.* "But I am so *young*," he complained.

By fae standards, that was. He felt faintly indignant. By rights, he should've been able to rely on a godparent for a good century more—in Faerie. Time moved more swiftly in Mortal, and he aged more quickly while he was here. He should have realised what else that might mean.

Lamorkin began to shrink, their extra limbs twining about each other and merging until they stood on only two legs.

"Young and *powerful*," they agreed. "You've come into your full bloodfeathers." Lamorkin sprouted feathery wings, and their features became fae-like and yet…not.

A child blinked up at them.

Hetta's hold on his hand tightened into a death grip. The child had silver wings and dark horns, and Hetta's grey eyes, big and solemn, and something of her in the shape of their nose, the arch of their narrow eyebrows.

"It's a guess, Hetta," he said tightly. "A *guess*. It's not—Lamorkin cannot see the future."

"I can extrapolate, godson," Lamorkin said. They sounded eerily like Hetta's younger sister Laurel, which probably wasn't an accident. Lamorkin held the form, their mocking expression out of place on the youthful face they'd assumed.

"I would rather you did not." He'd admit weakness so that Hetta didn't have to, her grip tight enough to hurt. "Please."

Lamorkin shook their head, rearranging their auburn locks. "Does it scare you, to see what you're brewing? Perhaps it should." But their lips pursed, turning blue and extending outwards into a long beak. The child melted away into a brightly feathered creature, and the tightness of Hetta's grip eased.

"Yes, and *on* that rather ominous note, do you know how to help us?" Hetta's tone was even, but he could feel the rapid beat of her pulse through their joined hands.

Lamorkin quirked a row of feathers at Wyn.

"She speaks for me," he confirmed. Lamorkin was bound to aid him, not Hetta. "You *are* still my godparent, aren't you?"

"For now," Lamorkin agreed. "Not for very much longer. One cannot be both parent and godchild, Hallowyn."

"I'll miss you." He meant the words—he could not speak an untruth—but if there was ever a time for flattery, this was it.

Lamorkin's eyes crinkled, the closest they could come to a smile with their beak.

"So sentimental, princeling." But he knew they were pleased. "Ask your question," they instructed Hetta.

Hetta told Lamorkin about the static and what Rake had said. Lamorkin's eyes grew thoughtful, into lamplike pools that they turned on Wyn.

"The instability isn't surprising, with your sire, Hallowyn, now that I consider the matter. Aeros was already ancient when you were born." They flicked their tail thoughtfully. "What *is* surprising is that this little spark has lasted this long without burning out. Perhaps you will be my godchild a while yet."

"What if we get the High King to marry us?" His voice came out flat. "Rakken said *sengra* might help."

Lamorkin tilted their head and was silent a long, long time. The walls grew closer, and Wyn longed to unfurl his wings and be gone, gone, gone, away and into the sky.

"Yes," they said. They smiled, showing sharp teeth. "Yes, I think it would help."

Relief and anticipation so heady it again threatened his balance. "Did you find him, godparent? Will he grant us permission to marry?"

"He has set you a task."

"Which is…?"

He waited impatiently as Lamorkin grew taller, sprouting antlers and wings as ribbed as a great bat's. Lamorkin settled themselves into their new form, flexing their wings and stretching the moment out. *Hetta is right; the fae are too inclined to melodrama.* It was certainly effective though; he held his breath, chest tight with anticipation.

When they spoke, their voice had deepened, and a shiver ran down Wyn's spine. Was this the High King's voice?

"The task is thus: if the rulers of ThousandSpire and DuskRose approve your union, present yourself to the High King and he will grant you a boon."

Hetta made a sound of disbelief. "Does literally every royal we know need to approve my marriage? ThousandSpire doesn't even *have* a ruler at present. The High King knows that, doesn't he? Is this his roundabout way of saying no?"

"He is responsible for considering the balance of things; it is his nature and his role." Lamorkin looked at Wyn. "You know why the High King has asked this."

Wyn swallowed. "Yes." All his wrongs coming home to roost. He couldn't look at Hetta. "How much time do we have, godparent?"

Lamorkin shrugged. "Not enough."

His lungs were cold, painful stone, making it hard to breathe. "I…is there some other way?" There had to be a way. He'd make there be a way.

Lamorkin pursed their lips. "There is a spell I may be able to do, to give you more time. But it is not an easy spell, little one. There will be a price."

"I will pay it."

"Wyn!" Anger flushed Hetta's face, her eyes stormcloud grey. Like the eyes of the child Lamorkin had 'guessed'.

He shook off Hetta's hand, energy roiling beneath his skin. "No. *I* will pay the price. Not you." This wasn't a debt he was prepared to share, not when he was the cause of this. Not when he'd seen Hetta's misery at the thought of losing the child.

"You could at least ask what the price is first!"

Lamorkin chuckled. "Your lover is right, little one. It's reckless to make such promises in ignorance. But in this case, the price has already been paid, if you are willing." Lamorkin held out slender hands tipped with golden nails.

Oh. His heart squeezed.

"You've been a good godparent to me," he said, taking Lamorkin's hands. Better than his own parents, though that wasn't a high bar.

"What price?" Hetta demanded.

"The one my mother paid for Lamorkin's guardianship," he said softly. "Lamorkin is asking I forfeit the remainder of their term as my godparent in exchange for this."

Lamorkin's beetle-black eyes shone. "You are sure, godson?"

His throat was tight, but the words came without trouble. "I am. Thank you." The price was more than fair, given that if the child lived, Lamorkin wouldn't long remain his godparent anyway. Lamorkin could have reasonably demanded more, and they hadn't, and he was deeply moved by this show of sentiment.

Lamorkin's long ears flicked, their fingers pressing tightly around the bones of his hands, and he was on fire. It burned through him from that point of contact in the space between blinks, incandescent and burrowing down to his core.

His connection with his godparent was older than his oldest memory: a still point around which the world spun. Memories surged of that terrible night he'd left the Court of Ten Thousand Spires. Lamorkin's eyes, wide and frightened, their visage utterly still. *Go*, they had said. *Go now, or I won't be able to protect you. Don't tell me where you hide unless you must.*

Images of that desperate journey flashed through him, and he was helpless to stop them: how it had felt as his broken oath ripped his power apart; the darksink he'd fallen into, where creatures had almost sucked him dry before he'd escaped; the hostile realms of Faerie he'd wandered, lost and alone; the pain of torn flesh and broken bones; and the fear of pursuit a constant drumbeat almost but not quite loud enough to drown the ache of betrayal.

Another memory spun loose. It wasn't his, this time.

They watched from the shadows.

The queen sat at her son's bedside. The eldest prince lay on his side, his back to his mother, his form mostly obscured by his black feathers. What could be seen of his head from this angle was swathed in bandages. It was barely daybreak, pink reflected light limning the gap at the bottom of the drapes, a sharp line of brightness in the otherwise dim room.

"The healers say there was too much damage; the eye will never heal properly." Sorrow in the queen's voice.

"I know. They told me. No more night flying for me."

The queen put a hand on the prince's wings in comfort, but he jerked away from the touch. She pulled her hand back. "What happened, Koi?"

He turned over at that, sitting up. He was lean and limber and bloodied, a young but grown thing compared to their own chick. A patch covered one eye, the other half-obscured by the white-blond hair spilling over his forehead. He pushed his hair away, freeing his undamaged golden eye to search his mother's face.

"You don't know. Why don't you know? It happened here. You *were* here...weren't you?" His voice trailed off uncertainly.

The queen went utterly still, not one of her feathers stirring.

The prince spoke slowly, as if scratching deep to find the words, each one emerging as a small revelation. "But you weren't here, were you? You went away." His eye widened. "And we forgot that you'd gone. Again. I remember now."

The prince began to pull at his bandages, hissing and recoiling from the queen's touch when she reached out to stop him, working frantically until the last of the white strips fell away to reveal a raw, oozing wound. The slash had cut from his temple to his cheek, directly through his eye, which was a swollen, purpled mess. An ugly ruin of promise. He gestured at it, his expression hard.

"This was your fault."

"Is your mind turning on you again? Set did this to you, not me." The queen's voice was gentle.

"She held the knife," the prince agreed. "Father encouraged her. He doesn't like weakness, of course. But I think the real reason he encouraged it is because he thought it would bring you back here. And it did, didn't it? So all you've taught them both is that violence is the solution. Again. It's getting worse. What will they do next time, now they've escalated to bleeding their own kin?"

The queen sighed. "I will talk to Set. But you should remember that I never left." Her tone grew soothing, low and hypnotic. The prince's harsh expression eased, his tensed shoulders suddenly drooping.

The queen picked up the bandages and began re-bandaging the wound. The prince sat passively throughout. "Remember that I have always been here, that everything will be fine. Remember that we are happy."

The lines of the prince's face slackened, his eyelids fluttering, and the queen eased him back down onto the bed. He curled into himself, black wings settling around his limbs like a blanket. The queen stood staring down at him as the dawnlight softened into day.

When she turned away, her gaze went straight to them, piercing through wood and shadow and glamour as if these defences were nothing. They shivered under the piercing green of her gaze.

"I don't like spies, Lamorkin."

"It is my nature—and our bargain," they said, alarmed enough by the queen's expression to need to remind her.

"Mother?" a small boy's voice. Both of them turned. He was so young and shiny-soft, this chick of theirs, a doveling in a nest of hawks despite all their attempts to teach him sharpness. Even his wings hadn't yet lost all their downy baby feathers, soft bits of fluffy white still scattered amidst the silver.

The boy looked from his mother to the bed where his injured brother lay, the same uncertainty that had been in the court's oldest prince's face now echoed in its youngest's.

"What are you doing?" he asked his mother. He hadn't seen Lamorkin, hidden under their glamour.

What would happen, they wondered, if they simply stole him from this nest, spirited him to somewhere safe? But that was foolishness; no such place in this world. They would have to keep him alive long enough to grow his own teeth and claws.

Lamorkin met the queen's eyes. "I have decided my price; I am calling in my favour."

The connection snapped, clean and swift as a knife, and Wyn staggered back, something cold and hard in his curled fingers. His chest felt hollow with absence, and for a moment he didn't know where or when he was. There had been…a room in the palace at ThousandSpire, and, and someone he knew was hurt, but…but it was gone.

His eyes were wet, and he lifted a wondering hand to his face to wipe away tears he didn't remember shedding. Blinking down at his hand, he saw he held a heart-shaped stone, clear as glass. He could feel the magic in it, the characteristic elegance of Lamorkin's magic.

Lamorkin looked at him, and their expression was as soft as he'd ever seen it. They tapped his cheek fondly.

"You have until the stone turns black. Goodbye, Hallowyn. And good luck." With a pop, they disappeared.

Where they had been, an ink-black feather hung in the air, spinning lazily until Wyn reached out and caught it.

14

THE HEARTSTONE

"Honestly, do fae take lessons in making dramatic exits and entrances?" Hetta said, glaring at the spot Lamorkin had recently vacated. "They're not even gone from the estate! I can feel them in their room upstairs." Hetta had offered Lamorkin lodgings on the basis that they were sort of part of Wyn's family. Since he put up with any number of her strange and eccentric relatives, she could house a few of his on occasion—the non-murderous ones, at least. Aroset wasn't invited.

But Hetta's faint knowledge that Lamorkin was still at Stariel meant Wyn's godparent had left them on a cliffhanger *on purpose.* Stariel rumbled a question at her. <No, don't fetch Lamorkin back.> She was pretty sure she could translocate other people about the estate if she wanted, but, firstly, it would be rude. Secondly—it reminded her a little too strongly of how Wyn's father had popped people about on a whim. How could she emulate someone like King Aeros?

Even if Lamorkin deserved it.

"They have a peculiar sense of humour." Wyn stared at the feather in his hand, a black slash of ink. Hetta had a good eye for colour, and she'd only seen a black that rich once before, in the wings of

Wyn's oldest brother when she'd been locked in a cell in the Court of Ten Thousand Spires.

"It's Irokoi's," he confirmed.

But Hetta was far less concerned with the feather than Wyn. Whatever Lamorkin had done had shaken him. His brown skin had taken on a paler hue, and he kept staring unseeing at the feather. She crossed the distance between them and wrapped her arms around him. Normally he ran slightly hotter than she did, but now he was cool to the touch.

"You're not all right." A statement rather than a question.

"I remembered something, when the bond came loose between Lamorkin and me." He shook his head. "My mother."

"A good memory or a bad one?"

He shook his head slowly. "I don't know—the details have fled. A…painful one, perhaps." He took a deep breath and straightened, separating himself from her to bring his open hand up between them. On his palm lay a heart-shaped stone the size of a coin, clear as glass, glittering like a diamond. It couldn't be a diamond, could it? It was far too big.

Stariel perked up, highly interested in whatever it was.

"This is for you," he said. "You should wear it next to your skin."

She gasped at the ice cold stone as he placed it in her palm. "It feels…strange." The stone began to swiftly warm, until it was the same temperature as her hand. Little shivers—like an echo of static—ran across her skin towards the stone. It had been perfectly translucent, but as she watched it grew opaque and turned to white with the faintest hint of blue. "Is it taking in the surplus storm magic?"

"Yes. It will turn black when its capacity is overrun." His eyes were dark, and he answered her next question before she could voice it. "I don't know how long it will last. Long enough for us to complete the High King's task, I hope."

There was a tiny hole in the stone, and she removed the necklace she wore and threaded the chain through it, tucking it securely
under her blouse. It rested against her collarbone, slightly warmer
now than the rest of her.

"So Lamorkin is no longer your godparent?"

"No."

She didn't know what to say; she knew how he felt about
Lamorkin, the sole fae who'd been on his side for all those years.
Paid to be on his side, and Wyn had loved them despite knowing
that, which all felt unbearably sad. Though, given Lamorkin was
currently haunting Stariel's bedrooms, perhaps Wyn's love wasn't
one-sided, when all the prices and oaths were taken away.

"Thank you," she said. "That seems inadequate."

He shook his head. "It was time. They have done their duty by
me and more."

Hetta touched the stone at her throat. "What did you mean
about knowing why the High King wants us to get far too many
approvals?"

He gave a bitter laugh. "It's...justice, of a sort. He asks us to
reforge what my broken oath shattered: common ground between
two warring courts. And to remedy a situation I indirectly caused:
ThousandSpire's curse."

That might make sense by what she knew of fae logic, but:
"ThousandSpire wasn't your fault—Cat did that!" How dare the
High King hold them to ransom for it?

"She wouldn't have had to if I had taken the throne." He took her
hands. "I don't regret my choice, but I'm sorry to be the reason the
High King asks so much of...us." He grimaced at the last word, but
he'd said it anyway, so she threw her arms around him and hugged
him close. "Ah, this isn't the reaction I expected to the news of my
liege's demands."

She pulled back so she could look up into his eyes. "We'll do this.

Free ThousandSpire and bludgeon both them and DuskRose into approving of us."

Honestly, this task was so typically fae, a puzzle box of layers and unnecessary complications. Not that she'd expected anything as simple as a, a request for a dowry or something, but still!

When had her personal life gotten so very political? It made her half-long for the simplicity of her life back in Meridon. If she'd decided to marry in her misspent youth, it would've been a matter between only her and the nearest monk-druid. Why hadn't she appreciated that luxury more at the time? Irrelevant that there hadn't been anybody she'd wanted to marry amid her various love affairs; it was the principle of the thing.

But at least they had a concrete direction now, even if it was an exasperating one. Thinking out loud, she said, "I suppose there's no question of whether we're going to DuskRose's ball or not, then. Though DuskRose's queen isn't going to give us her approval just for the asking, is she?" Fae were never that generous, in her experience. Bar one.

Wyn's fingers tightened around Irokoi's feather. "DuskRose's approval may actually prove simpler to gain than ThousandSpire's. At least DuskRose currently *has* a ruler. ThousandSpire…even if it were free, it refused to choose any of my siblings."

"Well, it can't have you back." Though ought she to consider it, given the circumstances? But Wyn was already shaking his head.

"No, it can't. That is, I don't think it can be undone, even if I wanted it."

"*Good.*" Her emphasis made him chuckle. "Maybe ThousandSpire will reconsider one or other of your siblings now that option's been taken away? Though hopefully not Aroset. In any case, it can't choose anyone while it's under a curse, can it? So we find Irokoi and he can hopefully tell us how to undo it, and then we worry about finding it a suitable ruler who approves of us." There were a few too many 'hopefully's in that. She gestured at the feather. "Is there a reason Lamorkin didn't simply *tell* us where Irokoi is, if they know?"

"I suspect they've said and given all they can."

Of course simple communication would never do when there was a more convoluted option available. "Still, I'm assuming we can use the feather to find Irokoi?"

"I hope so, yes," Wyn said. His expression grew pained. "But I will need Rake's help. Again."

RAKKEN WAS FULLY DRESSED this time when they knocked on his door and seemed entirely unsurprised to see them, though his eyes widened at Hetta's appearance.

"You've stabilised the energy fluxes. How?"

"Never mind that. What matters is: can we find Irokoi using this?" She waved the feather under Rakken's nose.

His eyes brightened, but he shot Wyn a sharp look. "Your mysterious godparent, I assume?"

"Yes and no. Will you help?"

Rakken laughed, a bitter sound. "And *why* do you need my help, brother?"

Wyn closed his eyes, as if summoning patience. "You're a better mage than I."

Rakken looked darkly satisfied. "Yes," he agreed. "I am. If you hadn't wasted so many years playing at being human—"

"So you'll help, then," Hetta said, cutting him off.

He met her gaze, and the rage burning in him was terrible. "*My* priority is Catsmere and the Spires. So yes, I will help you find Irokoi."

She gave him the feather.

He held it up to the light, riffling the filaments before tucking it into a pocket and stepping out into the hallway.

"Where are you going?" Hetta demanded.

"Outside. There's too much interference from the house leylines for this sort of spell."

Wyn took her hand as they followed Rakken through the house. The warmth of him anchored her, even as the fatigue of the day began to creep in. A few people were still awake and moving around the house, she could feel in a vague way, but most of the small people-sparks were abed. It made her think longingly of her own as they reached the entrance hall and she hastily pulled on a coat while Rakken waited impatiently.

Outside, the full moon shone down on the rising fog and made the world strangely claustrophobic. They made their way around to the side of the house, where the raised terrace ran parallel to the lake front. Hetta hadn't had to worry about losing her footing since she'd become lord, but it still didn't make picking her way over the pavement in the dark and damp a pleasant experience.

Rakken sank down onto the lawn without regard for his clothes, with the kind of arrogant uncaring you probably only got from never having to think about your own laundry.

A minor whirlwind whipped about him like a snake, tearing a hair-thin line in the grass. A faint hint of citrus gathered, and Stariel rumbled in protest. <It's fine,> she reassured it. <Or, well, I hope it is.>

She shivered, and Wyn put an arm around her. Burrowing against his warmth, she thought longingly of her own bed and held back a yawn. How could she be tired when there was important fae magic happening? But as the seconds stretched into minutes, the initial rush of relief that had driven her into action was fading, and her limbs grew heavier and heavier, until Wyn was half supporting her.

Rakken's magic swelled within his makeshift circle, but nothing much else happened. After what felt like hours but was probably only ten minutes, he shook his head and rose to his feet in a rustle of feathers.

"The spell needs more power." He narrowed his eyes at Wyn. "I suppose I shall have to make do with the raw material on hand. I will need you, brother, and the Standing Stones."

The Standing Stones. She wrinkled her nose, looking out into the damp night. The location had never sounded less appealing, her bed never more so.

Wyn looked fondly down at her. "You can go to bed, love. I will wake you if we learn anything."

She wanted to protest that she wasn't so weak-spirited, but it came out as a muffled yawn instead. "All right. I admit the thought of tramping about in the cold doesn't appeal much." She groaned. "And I'm supposed to be meeting the linesmen early tomorrow." It had been easy to forget, what with everything else. Guilt rose. *It's fine; I can be a good lord and find the High King at the same time. The two aren't mutually exclusive.* She fixed Rakken with a meaningful look. "No trying to strangle each other."

15

TRACKING

YN WATCHED HETTA disappear into the house with a
complicated mix of relief and anxiety that he managed
not to voice. He could be reasonable. He could. *The*
book said increased tiredness was normal. But what *was* normal, for
a half-fae child giving off very abnormal amounts of stormcharge?
She has Lamorkin's heartstone now, he comforted himself. They
would both be fine.

He began to walk in the direction of the Stones. Rakken fell
in beside him, and they walked in silence through the thickening
fog. The edges of the lake blurred into the darkness beneath the
trees where the Home Wood met the shore. Their footsteps were
nearly silent in the soft earth, the world so quiet the small rustling
of Rakken's feathers was audible.

The approval of ThousandSpire's ruler... Oh, the High King
couldn't have chosen something that would bite deeper. If he'd
taken the throne...but no, the High King would no doubt have
asked for something different then.

A strange image came to him, of King Aeros's hands on his wings in kindness rather than anger… Why would he imagine such a thing? Was it a dream? A memory? But the image slipped away even as he tried to grasp it more firmly.

"Was Father…better, before Mother left?" he asked.

Rakken shifted his wings irritably. "I don't understand why you cling to your fantasy, why it's preferable for you to believe that she abandoned us."

"It's better than believing Father killed her." He knew Rakken's theory.

The dismissive sound Rakken made echoed in the mist. "It wasn't Mother's absence that sent Father spinning towards madness. He was growing harsher, more sadistic even before that. If Mother does live, she merely chose an opportune moment to escape before he could grow even worse." His tone was flat. "An understandable act of self-preservation but not one I can forgive."

The rising fog blanketed the fields, the crown of Stone Hill rising above it like the back of a misshapen turtle. They traipsed up the gentle slope, the night utterly still around them. Wyn didn't need to look at Rakken to know his eyes would be glowing. He knew his own would be the same as he leaned on his leysight for night vision, but there was no one here to see it.

Rakken hissed a directive to stop before they crested the hill, but Wyn hadn't needed the warning. He wasn't foolish enough to wander carelessly into his brother's spellworking, and the scent of Rakken's magic was strong here, soaked into the earth. Moisture beaded on the surface of the stones, painting them a gleaming black.

The Standing Stones marked the location of Stariel Estate's most sacred ceremonies, but Wyn had also used them twice now to forge a portal to the Court of Ten Thousand Spires. That use had not only made the divide between Faerie and Mortal thinner here but also imbued the location with magical residue.

The lines of Rakken's spellwork glowed to Wyn's leysight;

intricate, beautiful work, though Wyn kept that opinion to himself. Rakken didn't need his ego stoked any further, and Wyn had felt like an uneducated fledgling too frequently in the last few days. He tried to decipher the patterns, feeling wholly outclassed. He'd gained many skills in the last ten years, but few of them had been magical, whereas Rakken had become an even more apt sorcerer. *I suppose I could always challenge him to a napkin-folding competition to make myself feel better.*

"Is that Belchior's reverse loop?" Wyn pointed at a sigil near one of the fallen stones, dredging up old memories.

Rakken didn't bother to respond as he strode through the circle, the spell-threads curling back from his feet as he walked, neat as pinions sliding into place. *Is he doing that just to intimidate me?* Probably safe to assume so.

Rakken turned narrowed eyes to Wyn, fixing meaningfully on the parts of him that were most human. With a sigh, Wyn shrugged out of his coat and changed. Changing was always akin to stretching a cramped muscle, but this time the relief was so excruciatingly sharp that it made him dizzy. His senses flared to life, sight and sound, and that deeper awareness of the world that Rakken had spoken of. Wyn fanned his wings in and out. In daylight they were a riot of blue and silver, iridescent as a peacock's. In the dark they looked black, and Wyn had a sharp pang of worry for Irokoi.

Rakken sank to the ground in a cross-legged position and gestured for Wyn to join him. The position woke an old memory of Irokoi teaching Wyn how to cast a circle for the first time. Irokoi was the oldest by a considerable margin; he and Aroset had been born close together. Then there was a gap, followed by the twins, Torquil, and last, Wyn.

Rakken unfolded a pocket of space—a trick he used frequently to store small objects in close reach—and pulled forth a clear, flat piece of crystal.

"To hold the spell, once it's set," he said in answer to Wyn's unvoiced question. "I do not plan to repeat this every time we wish to discover Irokoi's location."

That was impressive. Tracking spells were usually transient things.

Rakken held out the feather in one hand, the crystal in the other, and Wyn met him palm-to-palm, carefully trapping the objects within their two-person circle. Rakken drew in a long, slow breath and let it out, and Wyn let his own breathing fall in with his brother's. Wyn held no pretensions about his spellcasting abilities. He might be powerful, but he lacked *knowledge*. Rakken was a sorcerer, and he took the lead with casual ease, while Wyn struggled to remember how to follow. It had been a long time.

Rakken built the form of the spell, centred on the feather, and extended the invitation, like holding out a hand to a dance partner. Rakken's spellwork was all grace and delicate lines, and Wyn's contribution was clumsy enough to make Rakken raise an eyebrow, but they both felt it when the pattern clicked into place. *Blood calls to blood*, as Rakken had said: his, Wyn's, and Irokoi's.

Wyn's inexperience faded away now that they'd found the point of synchronicity. He could feel what Rakken had meant before, about the spell needing more power. That faint sense of Irokoi-ness petered out before reaching the end of its leash. Rakken built a dam around that line of connection, holding back the building power between him and Wyn with a multi-tasking precision Wyn envied. All Wyn had to do was draw power into that reservoir.

Lightning twined around them and crackled in the air, and every sense grew sharper. Wyn reined in the urge to flare out his wings because it would break Rakken's circle, but he threw back his head and welcomed the fine mist condensing on his skin, the dampness of the soft earth beneath them. He felt so alive, his whole body singing with a wild energy that made him want to launch into the sky and fly to cold and heady heights. Rakken's magic was familiar not only from past experience but because it hummed *kin*. That wasn't something Wyn was used to finding any comfort in, and yet, to his magic, it did not seem to matter.

Tracking spells weren't usually so complex, but this one held more magic than Wyn would have dared alone. Rakken's hold on the patterns never faltered, even as the power became bright as the sun to Wyn's leysight and he closed his eyes against the glare.

How long was Rakken planning to hold the spell? How deep did Wyn's own power *go* now? It was both exhilarating and terrifying not to know where it might end, like jumping off a cliff in the dark.

Rakken's hand spasmed, and that was the only warning Wyn got before the spell released, snapping out with the speed and fury of a shellycoat's attack. It unfurled from Wyn and Rakken, on and on and on until it seemed impossible that it could go further, but the energy they'd built sustained it, that long, long line, past the point where it should have faded.

And then it *caught*.

Wyn jerked as sensations flooded him: sea salt and parchment, and the midnight frost that was Irokoi's magic. Rakken's fingers dug into his in silent demand, and Wyn obediently sent more power into the thread. The line thickened, stabilising, and heat flashed into the feather and stone both. Wyn hissed as it flared white-hot between their palms but held on until Rakken let go, carefully de-powering the spell. The taut fishing line disappeared from Wyn's awareness.

He opened his eyes to examine his hands. The one that had touched Irokoi's feather was now reddened and smeared with ash, the feather disintegrated. Rakken examined the crystal that had been in the other.

"Well?" If it hadn't worked, they'd now lost their ability to cast another tracking spell.

Rakken nodded and held up the crystal. It had changed shape and colour, as if Irokoi's feather had been merged with it to form a single object, an obsidian stone in the shape of a feather. Perhaps that's exactly how Rakken had done it. When Wyn examined it with his leysight, he could see the threads of the tracking spell coiled neatly inside, ready to spring into being with the right trigger: blood, he decided. Rakken had tied it to their bloodline.

"That should last long enough to find our errant brother, unless you plan to waste another month frittering about the estate before taking action."

Wyn didn't rise to the bait. "Where *is* Irokoi? That sense did not match my knowledge of any of the courts."

"Deeper Faerie." Rakken might have been made of the same stone as the tracking spell.

Deeper Faerie. Ice slithered around Wyn's lungs. The fae courts were tame and civilised, in comparison. One did not simply venture into the deeper realms unless one was foolhardy or very, very sure of one's power. They held the oldest and strangest denizens of Faerie, with no faelords to keep them in check. And power came with age, to fae.

"We will need a Gate," Wyn said slowly, thinking aloud. Temporary portals couldn't access the deeper realms, even if he'd been familiar enough with the resonances there to attempt it. The magic there was too strong and changeable; only a Gate was stable enough to bridge the distance. But most Gates were built between allied courts in the surface realms rather than to Deeper Faerie. Where would he find a Gate of the sort he needed? Had ThousandSpire had one? He couldn't recall, but it would be of no use in any case, not with the Spires currently inaccessible.

Rakken made an unfocused sound of agreement, pocketing the tracking spell and getting to his feet.

"Give me the spell, Rake."

Rakken turned, raised one eyebrow, and didn't even bother to voice the response: *And why should I?*

Wyn answered anyway. "Because I don't trust you not to go running off alone, and we stand a better chance of finding Koi and freeing the Spires if we work together."

A slow smile spread on his brother's face, one of dark amusement. But to Wyn's surprise, Rake pulled the stone from his pocket and threw it lazily to him. Wyn caught it, sucking in a breath at the heft of it. It had a weight disproportionate to its size and practically sizzled with magic.

"To be honest, I expected more argument," Wyn confessed.

Rakken shrugged. "I can wrest it from you easily enough if I wish."

"You can *try*," Wyn couldn't help saying, needled, tucking the spell-stone carefully away.

Rakken ignored him, which was probably for the best. Wyn wrestled down his irritation. "Do you know of any Gates to Deeper Faerie, brother?"

Rakken didn't answer, instead putting a hand against the tallest of the Standing Stones. He looked through the gap in the stones as if they showed a view more interesting than Stariel's misty night, and Wyn didn't have to extrapolate hard to know that Rake was seeing the Spires. There was something sharp and leashed in him that made Wyn uneasy, something that made him think of a wild creature, cornered and unpredictable.

"Do you?" Wyn prompted again, when it seemed as if Rakken's plan was to continue ignoring him all night. "I know you're keeping something from me."

"You flatter yourself; I keep many things from many. You are in no way unique in this respect."

"I don't see why you wish to play games about this, Rake. Surely you wish to find Koi as much as I do?"

Rakken gave a sharp laugh, the sound of something breaking, but when he turned there was only weariness in his face. "The Court of Dusken Roses has a Gate to the part of Deeper Faerie where Irokoi is. How neatly coincidental for you. You should have destroyed that fucking plant when I told you to."

16

VISITORS

ETTA WOKE EARLY the next morning, intending to be up with plenty of time to discuss things with Wyn before her meeting with the linesmen today. Her body, however, had other ideas. She re-counted the pattern of lavender bathroom tiles for the tenth time and closed her eyes, *willing* her stomach to return to proper behaviour. This had absolutely no effect, and in desperation she reached out for Stariel.

A glass of cold spring water on a hot day, the relief so immediate and so welcome that she gave an involuntary moan.

<You couldn't have done that sooner?> she asked the land.

Stariel only sent its standard reassurance image of mountain bones.

<In any case, thank you.>

Should she be worried about leaning against Stariel for help with this, given recent issues with entangling herself too deeply? But she didn't release her grip on her land-sense, currently entirely willing to make that bargain if it meant keeping her stomach under control.

She spent a moment examining Lamorkin's heartstone, swinging it back and forth on its chain. It was still a pale bluish white. Was it her imagination that it seemed a little darker than last night? She tucked it away.

She was surprised to find Wyn in her bedroom when she returned, a risk despite the earliness of the hour. Oh, how she wished they didn't have to worry about such things! His dark eyes flickered over her, worried.

"Hetta…"

"I'm all right, actually," she said, checking her timepiece and hurriedly beginning to dress. "No shocks, and Stariel has been surprisingly helpful on the nausea front this morning. But never mind that—tell me about last night."

He told her what Rakken had found with his tracking spell and held out the tangible result. She took the strange stone feather from him, finding it unexpectedly heavy. Stariel nudged around her as she examined it with her magesight, careful not to disturb the dense web of alien magic nestled in its centre.

"How difficult is it to find a Gate to Deeper Faerie, then?" she asked.

Wyn didn't immediately reply, watching her in a way that made her feel…not exactly self-conscious, but oddly flustered as she located her stockings and pulled them over her knees.

"If you can't stop yourself getting distracted, I shall have to ask you to leave," she said primly.

He laughed, giving himself a small shake. "My apologies. Gates to Deeper Faerie aren't exactly common, but Rake says that DuskRose has one that comes out to near where Irokoi is. The Butterfly Gate. Apparently all of DuskRose's Gates are in the same place—so any new one we build will undoubtedly spring forth near it."

Hetta felt for the knot of magic in the greenhouse, but the dusken rose still slumbered. "That seems a rather large coincidence. How does Rakken know the location of DuskRose's Gates, anyway?"

Wyn shook his head. "He wouldn't tell me, but it explains why he gave the tracking spell into my keeping so easily. He can't go to DuskRose."

"Why not?"

Wyn hesitated. "He and Cat killed DuskRose's Crown Prince, Queen Tayarenn's only son. It's what prompted the High King's intervention in the feud between the courts."

"Oh." Right. Hetta stared down at her hands, feeling oddly detached. Well, no wonder DuskRose held such enmity against ThousandSpire. Murder. She couldn't seem to get her head around it, that Rakken had done such a thing—even though he'd proposed to do exactly that before, when he'd planned a coup against his father. It had been too easy to fall into the habit of not taking Rakken seriously, between the flirting and dark humour. Ought she to be giving house room to such a person?

But more immediately, how in Prydein were they supposed to make peace with DuskRose, given that history? Although, the High King hadn't asked for peace, precisely, and she knew from experience how exact fae were. An idea began to form.

"You said that we can't turn down DuskRose's invitation without giving offence—and that accepting it and building the Gate to get there would be seen as endorsing an alliance." She checked the timepiece again.

Wyn gave a tentative nod.

"Does that logic apply in reverse?"

His eyes widened. "That's…"

"Very fae thinking, I know, but do you think it would hold with the High King?"

"Are you truly proposing to invite DuskRose to our wedding?"

She rather liked how flustered he sounded by that. "Yes. I don't love the idea of planting that rose—or of Princess Sunnika at my wedding, if it comes to it—but if it gets us a step closer to Irokoi… Does it commit us to anything more than general peace with

DuskRose? Because I'm all for general peace—and perfectly willing to install a Gate to ThousandSpire as well, as a gesture of equal opportunity allyship in all directions. Peace for everybody. Feel free to come up with stronger arguments for or against it." She glanced at the clock again. "Although, actually, it would be better if you didn't just now as I probably don't have time for it."

He turned back, expression warming as he took in her appearance. "I shall save them then. You look lovely." He smiled, a spark of devilry in his eyes, and she quickly stepped back and out of reach.

"If you muss me up—"

"I can be very careful."

She prodded him in the chest. "You—" but she broke off as he gathered her in his arms and held her crushingly close. She let herself close her eyes and just breathe in the solid comfort of him before pulling herself together.

"I need to go," she told his chest.

"Yes." He didn't release her.

"Wyn…"

He took a deep breath and stepped back, his arms dropping. His eyes were dark with worry. "Good luck."

SHE'D INTENDED TO GO straight down to where the linesmen were working, but she heard the chief linesman arguing with one of the village councillors as soon as she emerged into the stables. She sighed. Did the blasted man have to stick his nose into everything?

She went to rescue the chief linesman; this particular councillor could talk for hours, stalling the lines work for an equal measure of time, and he didn't like that most of the linesmen weren't

Northerners, even if Mr Adeyemi, the chief linesman, originally hailed from Greymark. Greymark was, apparently, not Northern enough despite being the old Northern capital.

Gracious, she reminded herself as she rounded the corner. *I am a gracious overlord.*

"And what if people don't choose to use the elektricity, eh?" the councillor was saying to the linesman. "Won't it build up in the lines and cause fires?"

She managed to extract the chief linesman, though unfortunately not without leaving a disgruntled councillor in her wake. Wyn would have ruffled feathers to smooth over when next the two met; he had more patience with the man than she did. The metaphor made her smile; she supposed he had more practice smoothing feathers than most.

"Elektricity doesn't work like that!" the linesman burst out as they set off down the driveway.

"Yes, I know," she assured him, but the man's indignation was such that he was determined to rebut each and every one of the councillor's points in detail, and she was quite out of patience with both of them by the time they made it to the point along the driveway where the lines had so far reached and where the rest of the crew had gathered.

The greater cities of the South had had elektricity installed for many years now, even in the poorer areas, but in Stariel much of the estate remained without. The phone lines had only recently reached as far as the House, and it still hadn't been wired up for elektricity, though the lines themselves now ran that far. Hetta intended to run lines not only to Stariel House but to all the many cottages and smaller settlements sprinkled over the estate. Her services had significantly improved the cost of the installation, but they still couldn't afford to do it all at once; the later stages to the more far-flung parts of the estate would have to wait until the next harvest season.

The main driveway ran along the lake shore, Starwater a sparkling deep blue in the pale sunlight. She lifted her face towards the warmth when they stopped, determined to enjoy it. The air still held a fierce bite, and the moment the sun went behind a cloud, the temperature would plummet.

A sudden splashing made her turn towards the lake, and the cause of the sound drew her up short.

"Oh." She let out a faint breath of surprise, her heart beating rather loudly.

"My lord?" The linesman looked between her and the lake with a faint frown of puzzlement. Clearly he wasn't seeing the same thing she was, because there was no way he'd be looking at *her* rather than the *enormous lake monster* if that was the case.

Said enormous lake monster craned a neck that went up and up and up, tilting its head like a horse until it could fix Hetta with one gargantuan golden eye. Its hide was dark and sleek as a seal's, gleaming like wet pebbles. A long, fluked tail rose lazily behind it before slamming down and sending up a spray.

She struggled with the hysterical laugh trying to force its way out of her throat. *I suppose all those local legends about the nessan living in Starwater had to be based on something.*

"Is something the matter?"

She and the nessan stared at each other for several eternities. Stariel pulsed at the back of her mind, creating an unsettling duality, as if she were merely the glass through which the faeland was examining the creature. The nessan raised one foreleg with slow deliberation, spreading its webbed foot like a lady unfurling a fan. The gesture was so unexpected that Hetta didn't process what it meant until after the nessan had ducked its long neck and disappeared back beneath the dark waters.

It had been *waving* at her. Goodness. She gave a small hiccup of laughter, all at once delighted.

"My lord?"

Hetta turned back to him with a bright smile. "Right. Sorry. Shall we be getting on?" She began to walk again, the gravel crunching under her boots.

They stopped where a smaller path split off the main driveway towards some of the northern tenant farms. A long line of fresh earth showed the progress of the lines so far.

"It's going to rain tonight," she said. "So I'd better not put in more trenching than you'll get to by then."

When they'd agreed the next bit of trenching should go as far out as Gorse Cottage, she hesitated, uncertain in a way she didn't enjoy. *Oh, for goodness sake! You've already done this many times before!* She let herself sink a little deeper into her awareness of the estate, drawing up a detailed map of Stariel in her mind's eye. Stariel had had a little difficulty with the concept of maps at first, since that wasn't at all how the estate perceived itself, but eventually they'd managed to integrate the two.

When they were ready, she drew a mental line on her map where she wanted the earth to shift and pulled. The sensation was akin to running a finger down one of her own tendons, feeling sinew pull tight.

She opened her eyes, unsure exactly how much time had passed. Had it been only a second, or several minutes? A narrow trench ran away from her feet, disappearing out of sight, and the linesman didn't look concerned that she'd been absent for too long. She let out a long breath of relief.

???

<Yes, well done.> She gave the faeland a mental pat, and it happily brushed against her.

"It's done," she repeated to the linesman, who tipped his hat and said something that she didn't hear because something in the distant sky snagged her attention. A bird? She frowned and squinted, reaching for more information, but whatever it was hung just outside her borders in the direction of the station, maintaining height with a deliberateness that wasn't natural. Oh, how infuriating to see something but not be able to *sense* it.

But even without her land-sense, she knew it wasn't a bird. No bird moved like that. No bird was that big. No bird had wings of shattered red-and-gold so brilliant they shone even at such a distance.

Aroset.

Aroset, who should've been trapped in ThousandSpire, but who was somehow and incredibly here instead. Stariel roared up in alarm and Hetta wobbled, losing her balance as she tried to reassure the land through her own horrified reaction.

"Are you all right, my lord?" the chief linesman asked. He followed the line of Hetta's gaze blankly. Glamour. Aroset was under a glamour. No one else could see her.

Too many things no one else could see today.

"I'm fine, thank you," she lied. Dizziness threatened, and she took a long, slow breath, extending her senses into the land as if she could use Stariel for support like the roots of a tree. *This is no time for dizziness!* she told her body firmly.

How could Aroset be here? Why couldn't she be nice and safely trapped in the Spires? Gods, if Aroset was here, she'd no doubt try to target Wyn again if she could. Where was Wyn? Awareness of his location followed hard on the heels of the thought, and his spark brightened in the web that connected her to all of Stariel's people.

Her attention split, and she was simultaneously here, in a crowd of murmuring linesmen, and in the kitchen at Stariel House. Wyn was talking to Cook, but Hetta couldn't parse his words because the chief linesman was again asking her if she was all right. That had never happened before—usually her awareness homed in on wherever she focused and she lost all sense of herself.

Wyn frowned and broke off mid-sentence, canting his head as if straining to hear something. There was a splash from the lake, a fish jumping. Her head pounded at the sensation—humans weren't meant to be in two places at once—and there was a sudden snap of magic as they pulled together.

Oh no, she thought, dismayed, because she knew exactly what she'd accidentally done as Wyn appeared out of thin air beside her, and knew exactly how much he hated the way his father used to translocate him on a whim about the Spires. He held a mug half-raised to his lips in one hand, and he stayed locked in the position for a single startled moment, eyes widening as he took in his new location.

The chief linesman stepped back with a squawk, surprise spreading to the rest of the crew like a ripple.

"Sorry," Hetta said. "I didn't mean to do that."

"What's wrong?" Wyn scanned Hetta, his gaze resting on her abdomen for a fraction of a second longer than it ought. Really, if he didn't stop his fussing it wouldn't be *her* who gave things away earlier than necessary.

Hetta pointed towards the distant red speck of Aroset, but the sky was empty. "Dash it, she's gone now. I saw Aroset, hovering outside the bounds." Had she been mistaken? It had been so comforting to think of Aroset neutralised; the single good thing to come out of the Spires being stuck in stasis.

If Aroset was truly here in the Mortal Realm, how could Hetta protect everyone from her? Hetta could keep Aroset out of Stariel easily enough, but life didn't stop at the estate boundary. *Gods, Marius*, she thought. He wasn't safely inside Stariel's boundaries—and Aroset had a particular reason to target him. A fierce urgency filled her, to gather up everyone important to her and hold them close, to keep them safe through sheer proximity.

Calm down, she told herself. *Marius is halfway across the country from here, and how would Aroset even know where to find him?* But this wasn't that reassuring, since Aroset had shown an uncanny ability to create portals to wherever she liked.

Wyn didn't change forms as he searched the horizon for his sister, but he sharpened. His fae nature lurked close to the surface, bringing a vibrancy, a sense of otherness not wholly disguised by his neat appearance. "I cannot sense her along the leylines," he said in a low voice after a moment. "But she is very capable of shielding her presence from me, if she wishes."

Hetta's heartrate was slowly returning to normal, helped by the absence of lightning strikes from enraged fae princesses. She scanned the empty sky. Had she *imagined* seeing Aroset? It would certainly be nice to think so—much nicer than the alternative.

"Sir," the chief linesman said, his tone oddly dreamy.

Hetta jerked; she'd forgotten their audience. She turned back to find the entire crew had fallen silent, all weirdly mesmerised by Wyn. He wasn't a stranger to them, and he wasn't in his fae form, but they were looking at him like men dying of thirst who'd just spotted a pint of ale. She gave a choked laugh, even though it wasn't that funny. It was the sort of reaction Rakken usually got. All the royal fae Hetta had met exuded a magnetism that they didn't seem able to entirely eliminate, but Wyn's was normally damped. Had he foregone that now? He always appealed to Hetta, which meant she had to lean heavily on Stariel to double-check whether the glow of him was any different to its usual level. He *did* seem brighter than usual.

Wyn froze, and then a slight shudder of distaste ran through him. The atmosphere shifted, the glow of him dimming to Stariel's perception. He tucked his fae nature away with ruthless efficiency and straightened, smiling pleasantly around at the group.

"Mr Adeyemi." He acknowledged the chief linesman with a nod.

"Forgive my abrupt intrusion." Did he practice the various degrees of nods for all occasions? His Helpful Butler one was similar but somehow implied much less superiority. Did fae get training in this sort of thing? *Though I suppose I did get drilled on degrees of curtseys at school,* Hetta reflected. *So I shouldn't tease.*

The linesmen came back to themselves with a shake.

"Is that all you needed me for today?" Hetta asked the linesman quickly. She felt like there were two Hettas—one of whom was smiling and nodding and pretending that everything was fine, fine, fine; the other simmering with fire just beneath her fingertips, ready to throw at every unexpected shadow.

Mr Adeyemi nodded, gesturing at the trenching. "We've enough to be getting on with."

She and Wyn went straight to Stariel Station. The train line through the valley marked the eastern boundary of the estate. There was no sign of Aroset.

Hetta looked helplessly at the empty skies. "How is Aroset here? Does this mean the Spires aren't in stasis anymore? Or that she was never stuck there in the first place?"

"I fear the latter, though Rake will know for sure." He looked skywards. "I'm going to fly the bounds. I'll be able to see further along the leylines that way, if she is still out there."

She squeezed his arm. "Be careful."

He nodded. "I will." But he didn't move.

"Are you waiting for me to leave before you change?" Hetta eventually asked. She looked around; the stationmaster gave a wave from inside the ticket office. "Or is it Mr Billington's sensibilities you're sparing?"

A sheepish smile curled at the corners of his mouth. "Ah. My vanity surprises even me sometimes." He shrugged out of his coat and handed it to her. A fraction of hesitation, and there was a soft, soundless explosion as his wings unfurled. The dying light gleamed on the tips of his horns, picked up the network of silver filigree in his feathers.

Hetta couldn't help glancing back at the ticket office. The stationmaster's mouth was partly open, his cup of tea frozen halfway to his mouth. Wyn gave him an ironic salute and took off in a whirl of feathers, leaving a faint tang of spice in the air. He rose swifter than a bird, though she suspected his urgency sprang more from a desire to be out of sight than from the need to begin his search.

The stationmaster transferred his attention to her, and she raised a cool eyebrow at him, as if to say, what of it? She was determined that Wyn's nature should be—well, not ordinary, exactly, but not cause for remark from locals.

The stationmaster swallowed and looked away, putting down his cup.

Hetta sighed and began to make her way back. Her family weren't going to be pleased at what she was about to tell them.

17

A DELICATE SITUATION

"NO ONE IS to go outside the estate bounds until I say so, and certainly not until I get back," Hetta told her family later that night. She'd called an impromptu family meeting in Carnelian Hall. "Aroset is dangerous, and she may attack anyone she knows is related to me."

Alexandra shrank into the chesterfield, her face pale. "I thought it was safe now."

"You're safe within Stariel; she can't cross the boundary without permission." Technically greater fae could enter without permission, though it meant they left their power at the border, but Hetta had spent some time giving Stariel strict instructions on Aroset specifically. She was fairly certain the estate would enforce her will even without her being here, but the risk still worried her. *If only I had more practice at this lording business.* Did other faelords grapple with such uncertainty regarding their faelands? *If only I didn't need to leave the estate to go to this DuskRose affair.*

"Thank Simulsen I dried so much rosemary this season!" Grandmamma said brightly, looking around at the assorted cousins. "Who wants to help me make up some more anti-fae charms?"

"This is *not* acceptable!" Aunt Sybil grumbled. "Can you not simply talk to your sister, young man, and explain matters?" she asked Wyn.

"I am sorry, Lady Sybil. I wouldn't hesitate if I thought doing so would do any good," Wyn said softly. He'd spent much of the day flying the borders, trying without success to catch another glimpse of Aroset.

"And just how long are we supposed to stay here for?" her uncle Percival asked. He stood by the mantel, a thin man with spectacles. "I need to be getting back to my classes." Uncle Percival and his wife were both academics at Knoxbridge University. He'd been due to leave tomorrow. "I admire the sentiment, but it's not a practical solution, Hetta. Half the family's already outside the bounds. Your brothers, for one."

As if she didn't already know that! She didn't like to think of her two brothers out there, potentially vulnerable, though Aroset probably wouldn't recognise Gregory. Marius, though. Aroset knew Marius, and probably *would* try to harm him if she could, since last time they'd met the backlash from his telepathy had sent her sprawling.

"She's here, not in Knoxbridge, and she has no reason to go there, since she doesn't know where they are." Hetta hoped that was true, but she had another plan in case it wasn't, involving an entirely different one of Wyn's murderous siblings. If Rakken couldn't come with them to DuskRose, he might as well be useful to them here— and she was fully prepared to wield the supposed debt he owed her against him to make that happen, if need be.

"The same could apply to me, if I take the train down," Uncle Percival pointed out. "You've said fairies don't like iron; why should this woman bother following every train south?"

"Maybe," Hetta agreed reluctantly. "But I'd still much rather you didn't. Wyn and I shouldn't be gone very long, anyway—less than a day, we think, but maybe two." Rakken thought Irokoi's location was quite close to the Gate. "Surely you can put off your return that long, Uncle? Please?"

"You are taking a chaperone with you, of course?" Aunt Sybil said, narrowing her eyes.

Hetta met them. "No, Aunt, I'm *not*. Only the two of us are invited, and the fae don't care about such proprieties in any case."

Aunt Sybil clucked as Aunt Maude fiddled with one of the many charms she wore.

"Perhaps we could convince this fairy woman to leave if we made the right offering?" Aunt Maude asked in her soft voice. She'd been superstitious even before the fae had been revealed as real and had taken the news as permission to further indulge herself.

Hetta rubbed at her head. "I very much doubt it, since she wants both me and Wyn dead." Making offerings to fae? Hetta made a private vow not to tell Aunt Maude about the wing worshippers Marius had mentioned.

There was a slightly affronted pause. "I will light a candle beseeching Mother Eostre to calm angry spirits, then," Aunt Maude said, sounding far less dreamy than usual.

Jack frowned at Hetta. "You sure you should be going to this fairy ball?" *in your condition* he narrowly avoided verbalising.

"It's a ball, not a battlefield. I'll be fine," she said, even though she wasn't at all sure of what they might encounter in Deeper Faerie, assuming they did manage to find and use DuskRose's Gate there. But how much trouble could they really run into in the short time they planned to be there for? Well, probably a lot, but it wasn't as if she and Wyn were defenceless.

"I'll keep my gun by me," Jack said. "In case she comes back."

She swallowed. "Thank you." Her hand sought the lump of the heartstone, but it was tucked safely out of sight under her clothing. *I'll figure out how to deal with Aroset after DuskRose; Stariel can keep everyone safe for a day or two.* After the DuskRose ball, if they found Irokoi, well, that would put them in a better place to deal with the murderous princess.

There was an awkward pause in which it became clear her family's questions had finally run dry. People began to shift, forming small knots of murmured conversation. Uncle Percival picked himself up with a huff. "Well, I am going to pack. I'll take the train down tomorrow," he said testily, waiting for someone to contradict him. Hetta held her tongue but sent a pleading look to his daughter, her cousin Caro. Caro's mouth thinned but she nodded; she'd talk to him.

Lady Phoebe, who hated awkwardness, fluttered nervously next to the coffee table. There was a bridal catalogue resting on it, and she seized upon it as a way to change the subject away from upsetting things, flipping it open to a bookmarked page.

"Have you given any thought to what flowers you want, Hetta, dear?" she said, smoothing out the pages. "Peonies are lovely, but they're only in season until July." She looked hesitantly at Wyn. "Maybe roses would be better."

"I am happy to be guided by your advice on this," Wyn said diplomatically.

"That's a pretty sentiment, but the wedding's bloody well going to be before July, isn't it?" Jack said.

"Language!" his sister Cecily reproached him.

"Begging your pardon," he added, not looking the least apologetic.

"Yes, well…" Lady Phoebe made a helpless gesture. "Perhaps we could settle on some of the arrangements in advance? And then that could help save time once you…set a date." Her voice trailed off uncertainly.

"Of course," Hetta said, trying to accept this peace-making offer for what it was.

The slightly awkward void in the conversation was filled by

Cecily's husband, Mr Frederick Fenwick. He'd accepted the talk of fae without comment, but he seemed eager to contribute to a change in subject.

"I can strongly recommend marrying a Valstar." He looked fondly at his wife. "Cess and the girls are the best things to ever happen to me." His attention roved around the high-ceilinged room. "And this place was meant for families. Be good for this old place to have kiddies running through it more of the time."

"Not till after the wedding, obviously," Cecily said, flushing. Aunt Sybil, Cecily's mother, made a firm sound of agreement.

"Obviously," he agreed. "What do you say, Wyn? Do you see yourself as a family man?"

Hetta stared down at her hands and fought down the fit of giggles she could feel trying to force their way out. She snuck a look at Wyn, who'd lost his usual composure and seemed temporarily unable to speak.

"Ah—I am looking forward to marrying my own Valstar," Wyn said, sidestepping the subject with the care of a man navigating a bog. "We hope the event we are to attend at DuskRose will bring us closer to gaining the permissions I need." They had told her family, in the loosest terms possible, that Wyn still needed an authorisation from the fae High King to marry Hetta.

Aunt Sybil grumbled. "It is all very well to be fastidious about these things, Mr Tempest, but this is taking much too long for my liking—you must realise the impact on my niece's reputation!"

Behind her, the door opened, and a maid brought in a carafe of coffee. Hetta inhaled in anticipation, desperately in need of the comfort, but instead found herself gagging, her stomach giving a worrying roll.

"Ugh—take it away!" she ordered as the horrible smell drew closer. "The beans must've gone off."

The maid blinked at her. "My lord?"

"Take it *away!*" The smell was making her both intensely nause-
ated and also angry. How could coffee let her down at such a time?
The maid jerked into motion and carted the carafe out again.
The smell still lingered, and Hetta dug her hands into her knees
through her skirts, willing her stomach to stop churning. Cool
air curled around her, smelling of rain, and took the scent with it.
Hetta breathed out a long sigh of relief and gave Wyn a look of deep
gratitude for the air magic.

"It didn't smell bad to me," Alexandra said. She looked quizzically
at her mother, who avoided her eyes.

Several of Hetta's family members were giving her strange looks.
Cecily's wide eyes flicked between Hetta and Wyn. Her stepmother
had gone a deep pink and was looking fixedly at the ceiling, and
Aunt Sybil's gaze had gotten even narrower.

Cecily's expression turned knowing, and Hetta had a sudden
urge to throw a cushion at her cousin's head to show what she
thought of her condescending smile.

They know. Her stomach flipped with something other than
nausea. No. She was being paranoid.

"Henrietta, I would like to speak to you privately," Aunt Sybil
said ominously, nostrils flaring.

Hetta was abruptly tired. Tired of hiding, tired of judgement,
tired of worrying. It all seemed so petty in the scheme of things,
compared to the Conclave and Aroset and DuskRose and the fact
that *her baby might die* if she couldn't complete the High King's task
in time. What did it matter if they *did* know?

She tilted her chin. "Whatever for, Aunt?"

A muscle twitched in Aunt Sybil's jaw. "A delicate matter."

"If you are referring to my own 'delicate situation', then I'd as
soon as not talk to you about it. It's none of your business."

Silence expanded out from her, the room slowly falling quiet with little hisses of *what did she say?* But she felt lighter than she had in weeks.

Aunt Sybil stuttered into motion. "Henrietta! How could you shame the family so! This is what comes of you associating with those loose theatre people!"

"I have never been to the theatre, my lady, and you must allow me to be a full and equal participant in this," Wyn said mildly, coming to stand behind Hetta's chair. He put a hand on her shoulder, and she wrapped her fingers with his, hoping to hide the fact that they were trembling.

Aunt Sybil went a deep and furious purple. "You must marry *immediately*!"

Wyn's hand tightened on hers but his voice remained steady. "I fully intend to marry Hetta; I have already explained the reason why that cannot be as soon as I would like."

"You should have thought of that before—" Jack snapped off the end of his sentence.

A hint of rainstorm and spice twined around the room. "I realise there is an…awkwardness surrounding this, in mortal culture, but for me this is a joyful thing." He gave a wry smile. "Although a somewhat daunting one. I hope we can lean on you all for support."

Thank the gods for Wyn; her own voice had stuck in her throat.

"What's a joyful thing?" little Laurel piped up from the doorway.

"Laurel, dear, you should be in bed." Lady Phoebe rose and went to her daughter. There were still spots of colour on her cheeks, but she met Hetta's gaze deliberately. "Hetta, come and have a chat with me later."

Lady Phoebe ushered a protesting Laurel out. The interruption had temporarily derailed her relatives' swelling outrage, and before they could turn their attention back, Hetta stood.

"Good night, everyone." She fled.

18

THE ROSE GATE

I⟨t⟩ T WASN'T COWARDICE that made her avoid mealtimes with her relatives the entire next day before DuskRose's ball; she was simply too busy preparing to have time for them. Her relatives, unfortunately, had plenty of time for *her*.

Jack was, surprisingly, the best of them, because he simply pretended she wasn't pregnant and spared them both the awkwardness of discussing it. He wanted to know just how long exactly she was planning to be gone, and what needed doing in the meantime, and could he shoot Prince Rakken while she was gone? She ended their conversation feeling more in charity with him than she'd been in some months.

Aunt Maude wanted to know whether they'd thought about names, and did Hetta want to know which names had been in the family for more than five generations? Hetta did not at this immediate moment, no.

A red-faced Alexandra shuffled in around noon and said shyly that no matter what anyone else said, *she* would love her new niece or nephew unreservedly, a sentiment that had Hetta hugging her while blinking back unexpected tears.

Her cousin Cecily turned up in her office at afternoon teatime to advise her pointedly on the efficacy of chamomile tea for settling upset stomachs.

"But you mustn't eat anything with spices in it," she warned. "Or strong flavours. They result in a bad-tempered babe." She set out the last word carefully, as if waiting for Hetta to deny it.

"That can't possibly be true." Hetta put her pen down.

"Oh, it is! My friend had *such* a craving for ginger biscuits throughout and then not a wink of sleep for months after little Robert was born! And I made sure to avoid all but the mildest foods, and the girls are so even-tempered—everyone remarks on it!"

Hetta privately held a different opinion regarding Cecily's twin girls.

"I'll keep it in mind," she hedged. She rolled the pen back and forth over the accounts book, wishing one of the female cousins she was closer to could advise her. But Caro and Ivy didn't have children. The age gap between her and Cecily was only five years, but in a large extended family that might as well have been decades, and Hetta was too conscious that anything she said to Cecily might reach Aunt Sybil's ears.

As if on cue, Cecily added, "Of course, it wasn't very wise of you to…anticipate the wedding night."

"You never…?" Hetta didn't want to know, truly, but she couldn't resist asking.

Cecily straightened, the resemblance to her mother strengthening. "Certainly not!"

Hetta looked down at her hands. "Well, thank you for your advice, but I really need to be getting on with this." She gestured importantly at the list in front of her, which was long since complete.

Cecily stood. "Don't hesitate to ask me if you have questions."

"Thank you."

It wasn't rational to be annoyed at Cecily for trying to help when

Hetta had wished for exactly that opportunity so recently. She should've asked about the dizzy spells, and about other things, but it had been kick Cecily out or start throwing pens at her.

Footsteps sounded in the hallway; Hetta knew it was one of the servants in the same way she knew the location of her limbs. There was a tentative knock before a maidservant entered with a tea tray. There were ginger biscuits on the plate.

Hetta eyed them thoughtfully after the maid left, stomach grumbling. Dash it all.

She ate the biscuits.

Ivy let herself in two minutes after Cecily had left, but since she came with a pile of old journals under one arm, Hetta felt much more interested in what she'd come for.

"Well, now I understand a bit more why you and Wyn were feeling so rushed for time," Ivy said as she sat down. She bit her lip. "What's it like?"

"Being pregnant?"

"No, eating biscuits. Yes, being pregnant!"

Hetta considered this. "Mainly extremely surreal so far." She gestured at the journals. "Have you found something more?"

Ivy nodded, pulling the top one from the pile and leafing through to the page she'd marked. "I said old Lord Marius I wasn't much of a diarist, but I've since discovered that his wife Adda was much more reliable. She wrote every day. This is one of her journals, tucked accidentally into one of her husband's." Her nose wrinkled. "I hope the others still exist somewhere else in the clutter and weren't simply discarded for not being the lord's. The number of times—" but she stopped herself from getting off-track at Hetta's pointed gesture at the diary she held. "Oh, yes. Well, Adda clearly wasn't that interested in the wider politics of the time. She writes mostly of the house and her children."

Hetta perked up. "Including Ewan?"

"Including Ewan. Listen to this: 'Ewan is very set on this fairy girl of his, though I must admit to some doubts. The girl herself seems to mean well, but she is still the oddest creature, bringing wild things into the house as if they were pets, turning up in a dress of thistledown! I've told her if she wants to make Ewan a good wife, she'll have to change her ways, and to be fair to her, she seemed willing enough. But Ewan is still so young! I cannot help but wish he would not think of marriage so soon.'"

The hairs on the back of Hetta's neck stood up. Another Valstar had tried to marry a fae, much more recently than her original ancestor. Well, if you could call three centuries 'recent'. Hetta tried not to think too hard about the fact that he'd died before succeeding in it.

"Is there more?"

Ivy made a frustrated sound. "I'm sure there must be another diary of hers covering the time period around his death, but she reached the end of this one just weeks before that." She held it up to show Hetta; all the pages were filled with flowing handwriting. "I'll keep looking."

HETTA CHARGED JACK WITH transporting the dusken rose while she finished her preparations; she didn't trust Rakken not to change his mind and destroy it. Waiting for them in Stariel's rose garden, she turned slowly to examine the small circular space with its geometrically laid out beds and carefully began to unpick the wards against translocation in a defined area. Evening was settling in, making spindly shadows among the greenery. The roses were caught between seasons, new glossy leaves beginning to unfurl. They looked much healthier than the black, leafless stick of the dusken rose.

Wyn landed with a soft thump behind her. "Forgive my lateness," he apologised.

Hetta turned and froze.

Gone was her mild-mannered butler. In front of her stood a prince, breathtaking and unmistakably not human. He wore Spire-garb now, a rich black fabric made of luxurious shadows and dark gleams. The high collar emphasised the strong column of his neck but left a deep V of skin visible. Hetta hadn't previously considered collarbones to be a particularly erotic body part, and yet, there was something in the sight of that narrow strip of skin that sent heat right through her.

Wyn had always been able to assume an air of authority when needed, but it had always been a very *civilised* authority. There was a wildness to him now, despite the undoubtedly expensive finery. Each horn was encased in its own net of filigree, winking with tiny jewels, and his silvery-white hair hung loose around his pointed ears. Even his feathers seemed shinier than usual.

She wanted to touch him, to reassure herself of his solidity. He didn't seem quite real, all glittering darkness and iridescent blue feathers under the sluggish moonlight. And yet she hesitated, trying to reconcile the man she loved with the one in front of her.

And then he smiled mischievously, and familiarity flooded her. *There you are*, she thought.

"Have I stunned you into silence with all my glory?" He turned in a slow circle, spreading his hands. Silver rings glinted on several of his fingers. "Rake didn't wish me to shame the Spires by present-ing with insufficient finery," he explained. "Also, he lent me one of his space-saving spells." He put a hand into the velvet pouch attached to his belt to demonstrate and pulled out a thermos that couldn't possibly have fit without ruining the line of his clothing.

Hetta blinked as he replaced it. "How abnormally helpful of him." She reached out to smooth his shoulder. The fabric was sleek and buttery to the touch, with no obvious fastenings.

"How does it fasten?"

"Behind my wings," he said, holding a wing out in a rustle of dark sapphire to show her.

Hetta frowned at the nearly invisible fastening, unable to figure out how anyone could do it up without the need for impossible contortions. "But how—"

"Magic."

Hetta laughed. "It seems curiously mundane to use magic to do up buttons."

"You thought fae princes would have some more exciting mechanism?"

"Well, *yes*," she admitted.

"I could ask the brownies to fasten it for me, next time, if you'd prefer," he said with a straight face. A note of sobriety entered his eyes. "Though I'd prefer not to repeat this specific outing."

"Me too. Not least because I feel decidedly under-dressed. Can you tell?"

Wyn gave her a thorough inspection. "No. I can taste your magic—and I'm familiar enough with your wardrobe to guess what's real and what's illusion—but I cannot see through it. If anyone can, the display of magic will be more important than mortal fashion in any case—illusion is rare, in the courts. It's not a fae magic."

Hetta had compromised on her outfit. Part of her had wanted to show the fae that she could dress like a queen too. The more sensible part didn't want to go tramping through Deeper Faerie searching for Irokoi in a ballgown.

Hetta wrapped her arms about herself, feeling the sturdy fabric of her coat under the illusion of a flimsier, silken outer garment that was borrowed from a fashion plate in one of Phoebe's bridal catalogues. The heartstone was warm and hidden underneath. The colour had shifted a few shades darker, to summer-sky blue. It seemed to be working, because there hadn't been any more elektric shocks since she'd started wearing it.

His gaze lingered. "You look beautiful," he said, but the words were contemplative, covering some deeper thought process.

"You're not going to convince me not to go or to let you go without me. Especially since the invitation was originally to *me*."

He didn't deny what he'd been thinking. "I know. Just…be careful. They will try to rattle both of us if they can. If you harm a member of Tayarenn's court, it will break guestright."

"What if they attack me first?"

"Then they have already broken guestright, and you are within your rights to defend yourself. But do not let them goad you into striking the first blow."

"I *can* control my temper, you know," Hetta said, more amused than irritated. Her eyes widened. "Oh, you're reminding yourself rather than me." She hadn't realised his control was so frayed. He'd said he was struggling with more aggressive impulses, but it was quite hard to believe it, given his tight self-control. "Are you truly worried about that?"

He made a loose gesture with one hand. "Well, I'm glad to know I give a convincing appearance of restraint, at least." His gaze grew distant, and something dark flickered in the depths. "I am reckless, when it comes to you. I always have been."

She threw her arms around him. "That's a ridiculously melodramatic thing to say."

His wings flared out, silver catching in their depths. "I'm about to wade into a court filled with people who despise me, along with the woman I love, dressed in night and silver. I am feeling… melodramatic."

"You certainly are. '*Night and silver*' indeed!" Their faces were only an inch apart, their breath mingling. His eyes darkened. "The lipstick is real," she warned him, with real regret. She'd clung to that small bit of realness, needing the reassurance when so much of her current appearance was false. It no longer seemed like such a good idea.

He leaned his forehead against hers. "You prefer real lipstick when you're nervous. You always wear it to village council meetings." He gave a heartfelt sigh. "Perhaps I could kiss you very gently?"

She laughed, though his observation startled her. Did she really do that? She hadn't made the connection. "Lips are tricky to illuse well. They move a lot. I don't want to risk the magic slipping at an awkward moment." It came out sounding defensive.

"I am nervous about many aspects of tonight, but not about your illusion. I think you give your own mastery too little credit, love."

He stiffened and pulled away just as footsteps sounded on the paved path into the rose garden. Jack marched with the dusken rose held as far away from his body as possible. Caro and Ivy padded alongside, bright with curiosity. Rakken trailed silently behind the party, expressionless.

"Well?" Jack demanded. "Where do you want the thing?"

"Put it down there." Hetta pointed to a wooden arch between the two flowerbeds where she'd already peeled back the wards.

Jack put the pot down, and Hetta practically felt Rakken's distaste. *Am I really going to do this? Is this really in Stariel's best interest?* The heartstone sat heavily against her skin.

"Can I re-set wards after we plant it?" she asked Rakken. Gate or not, lesser and greater fae still needed her permission to enter if they wanted their powers to come with them, but wards would stop anyone from simply wandering out of the Gate and into Stariel before she noticed; Jack had promised to keep a watch on it until they returned.

Rakken's eyes narrowed on the plant, as if he were reconsidering destroying the dusken rose, but eventually he said, "Yes. Lay a circle out, both physically and magically, if you please, Lord Valstar."

Hetta took a deep breath and concentrated. The earth parted, creating a thin circle of damp loam about them. Unasked, she called for the granite of the Indigoes. She wanted something harder and more permanent than soil for this. The effort made her sway, and Wyn caught her arm. When she opened her eyes, a stone band interrupted the grass surface, the archway in its centre. She blew out a breath of relief that it had worked exactly as she'd wanted it to for once.

"You may plant it now." Rakken sounded resigned.

Hetta instructed Stariel to form an appropriately sized hole in the centre of the circle. *Maybe I should take up gardening as a hobby,* she mused. *Since I get to cheat at digging.* "Is there some special trick to planting it?"

"I think it will work regardless," Wyn offered, so Hetta plonked it ungracefully into the hole.

For a moment, nothing happened.

And then, like a candlewick catching, foreign magic blazed up. Stariel responded instantly, and Hetta had to push the land back. <It's all right. We're just letting it put a connection here. But you may certainly jump on anything that gets outside this circle.> She tapped mentally at the granite circle.

Stariel subsided, and the dusken rose grew. The stunted black stick grew glossier and sent out shoots in all directions, forming thick, thorn-covered vines. They wound around the confines of the circle until they found the arch, speeding over it with startling rapidity. Leaves unfurled, huge and heart-shaped with jagged edges. Pale buds sprung up between the leaves, each the length of a finger but tightly furled. Through Stariel, Hetta could feel the dusken rose's roots burrowing into the earth, and she hastily extended the containment circle downwards, containing the archway within a globe of wards.

When the astonishing growth ceased, the dusken rose covered

the archway and ground around it with a thick mass of vines, leaves, and pale flower buds. It felt *different*. Hetta glanced at the others to see if they felt it too. Jack was glowering at the archway; Caro's nose was wrinkled as if she smelled something unpleasant. Ivy had one hand pressed to her mouth, though it was unclear if this was in delight or alarm. Hetta felt somewhere between the two herself.

"How do we open the Gate?" she asked.

Wyn stepped forward, touched one of the buds, and drew a finger softly around the petals. The petals began to unfurl and grow at impossible speed, until the flower—the dusken rose—bloomed bigger than a person's head. The petals had been a perfect unblemished white, but as they spread, they began to darken to a deep, glowing crimson, pulsing like the embers of a fire. The Gate shimmered to life, showing a view not of Stariel but a foreign garden full of vine-covered archways, where dusken roses glowed in the twilight.

Hetta gripped the invitation firmly in one hand and took hold of Wyn with the other. They stepped through.

The world turned over. She couldn't feel anything, not even the breath in her lungs, and when they emerged, she sucked in air like a swimmer emerging from a dive. She caught a whiff of cherries and beeswax.

"Welcome to the Court of Dusken Roses."

PART II

TO FAERIE

THE COURT OF DUSKEN ROSES

ETTA'S FIRST IMPRESSION was: green. Green *everywhere*. Plants and trees grew in profusion, bursting with life and colour. The air clung to her skin, and she smoothed her hair, feeling how the humidity was already making it fluff. Hastily she wound an illusion into it so it wouldn't lose its sleek appearance.

Was this the rose garden Rakken had spoken of? There were more dusken roses here, pulsating like embers amongst the rampant greenery. The archway they'd emerged from was made of an iridescent blue stone she recognised as star indigo—a substance only found in the Indigo Mountains. *Until now,* she thought uneasily. Had the rock sprung into existence when they activated the Gate, or had this location been pre-prepared? More archways were hidden among the shifting shadows, all different in appearance, but she couldn't examine them more closely with Princess Sunnika right in front of them. Which one was the Butterfly Gate?

"Your highness," Hetta said in greeting.

Princess Sunnika sized her up; Hetta returned the scrutiny.

Sparkling gems hung from the princess's cat ears, not totally dissimilar to Wyn's horn-jewellery, and she wore a long-sleeved, high-necked gown the shimmering colour of starlight. Every small movement made the dress's shining threads glitter. With a shock, Hetta realised the dress was made of a fine mesh of sparkling threads, the fabric flowing lovingly over every curve and making it extremely apparent that there wasn't anything *under* it.

Was being provokingly under-dressed a common fae habit, she wondered, thinking of Rakken's dressing gown? Not that Princess Sunnika could be said to be under-dressed, exactly. The dress was extravagant, if shocking, and with her normally sheet-straight black hair heaped into a waterfall of curls and adorned with twinkling gems a few shades paler than the cherry-pink tips of her hair, Sunnika looked exactly like a fairy-tale princess, if a very *adult* one.

Hetta smoothed her own dress self-consciously. Her own outfit— or at least, the illusion of it—was fashionable, but it certainly wasn't made of magical stars, and *she* knew she was wearing practical everyday garb underneath it, even if no one else could see it. *The next ball we go to, I'm wearing a proper gown, dash it*, she decided.

"Princess," Wyn said evenly, putting a proprietary hand on Hetta's elbow. Princess Sunnika's attention shifted to him, and Hetta didn't appreciate the way her eyes lingered on the exposed skin at Wyn's collarbone.

"You are bringing him as your Consort, Lord Valstar?"

Hetta nodded. She'd requested this, but the title still felt extremely odd. "I am. And no one will harm me or him, if we come to this party?" It was rude to question the invitation, but she found she wanted the reassurance more than she cared about giving offence.

Princess Sunnika's eyes narrowed. "So long as you do not break guestright, I, on behalf of my aunt, Queen Tayarenn, grant you safe passage. DuskRose will not harm you tonight. Follow me."

Despite the twilight hour, it was warm enough that Hetta unbuttoned her coat as they walked out of the rose garden and up a gentle slope. Huge leaves the size of her head swayed to either side of the path. String music played from somewhere out of sight, an instrument and melody she didn't know, but not unpleasant. Tiny lanterns floated in the air above head height, each one glowing a different colour. They weren't illusion.

"The Rose Palace," Princess Sunnika indicated. Emerging from the jungle like a flower was an enormous palace painted in bold colours. It was built as a series of interconnected courtyards and buildings, each one rising higher than the last. The many roofs curved into steep points, and carvings lined their edges. Wound about the whole were vines blooming with enormous flowers in a symphony of colour.

Hetta caught her breath, enchanted despite her apprehension.

Princess Sunnika led them through an archway and into an open-roofed courtyard, which turned out to be a dance floor filled with an astonishing variety of fae. At one end sat a dais with an empty throne, but Princess Sunnika spared it only a single glance, though her tail switched. Giant leopard-like cats in every colour of the rainbow lounged on the piles of cushions lining the room's edges. The nearest lifted its head, baring alarmingly sized canines. Hetta would've frozen except for the gentle pressure of Wyn's hand on her elbow.

"Shadowcats," he murmured, looking meaningfully from the leopards to the catlike fae amongst the dancers.

Oh. He'd told her that greater fae were shape changers, and she'd seen Princess Sunnika's ears and tail, but she hadn't realised... She swallowed. Well. What a good thing they'd come here with the intention of getting on DuskRose's good side.

But even the shadowcats in full cat form were almost normal compared with some of the dancers. A pair of impossibly tall fae with fine blue fur, flat noses, and spindly gazelle-legs spun each other in long-limbed circles, their long necks a head and shoulders above the crowd.

Wings fluttered in wild abundance—bat-leather, dragonfly-glass, feathers of every colour and shape—alongside an equal variety of horns, claws, tails, fur, and pointed ears. Gender was impossible to discern in many instances and seemed to make little difference to who danced with who in any case. The strange shapes and colours were only eclipsed by the costumes—or in many instances, *complete lack thereof.*

Hetta blushed and looked away from a dark-haired man with scales around his eyes, who was dressed in little more than an artfully draped scarf that completely failed to cover any of his key areas. Confirmation—if she'd needed it at this point—that the fae held very different opinions on public nudity.

Wyn certainly managed to keep that under wraps, she thought wryly. *Literally.* More than a decade of starched shirts and waistcoats.

A fae the size of a child hovered in mid-air by the archway, bumblebee wings humming, but it was no child in truth, his features holding an adult's awareness.

"You may announce us," Princess Sunnika told the bumblebee fae. He stared at Wyn with wide, unblinking eyes that lacked whites. His irises were curiously shaped, like flower petals, and the sight was unsettlingly familiar—Gwendelfear's eyes had had that same curious pattern.

"Her Royal Highness Princess Sunnika Meragii of the Court of Dusken Roses. Lord Henrietta Valstar of the Court of Falling Stars." The bumblebee fae paused. "His Royal Highness Hallowyn Tempestren of the Court of Ten Thousand Spires."

A susurration passed through the ballroom. The dancers didn't stumble so much as ripple gracefully, as if each had swiftly adjusted their movements to compensate for their surprise.

Hetta knew what it felt like to hold a crowd's unfriendly focus, but she'd never observed it from the outside—for this crowd's attention wasn't for her. Hundreds of heads turned towards Wyn, and the air grew thick with hostility. His wings pressed tight against his spine as he faced them, but his expression didn't crack. She squeezed his arm.

These people were at war with Wyn's. Why hadn't she fully grasped the weight of that till now? So many eyes, glittering with malice. How many fae had died in the war with ThousandSpire?

And he would've lived in this court if he married Princess Sunnika. He'd told Hetta it would've been easy for his father to frame DuskRose for his murder. *That was an understatement, if anything.* Quite a lot of the fae looked like they wanted to slit Wyn's throat there and then.

They can't attack him without breaking guestright. Princess Sunnika invited him here; we're under her protection. Hetta held the reassurances close, though they felt inadequate against so many people wishing Wyn ill. *We only have to survive this for one evening.* But how were they going to slip away from these predatory gazes to use DuskRose's Gate? And could they really convince DuskRose to support their union, even in so roundabout a way as they planned?

Princess Sunnika held out a firm hand to Wyn without looking at him. "Dance with me, Prince Hallowyn." It wasn't a request.

Hetta appreciated that Princess Sunnika was showing public support and reminding her court that Wyn was an invited guest and not to be harmed. This in no way stopped the jealousy shooting through her, hot and humiliating. She pushed it down irritably. This was no time for such pettiness.

Wyn's feathers shifted, and he raised an eyebrow at her.

"I'll be fine," she told him. *But aren't we supposed to be finding the Gate?* She tried to communicate the latter with her own eyebrow raise.

"Later," he said, which wasn't a very satisfactory answer, but she supposed he couldn't really say more in a ballroom full of eavesdroppers.

Hetta frowned as he and the princess joined the throng. She'd never considered herself particularly prone to jealousy, and it was silly to start now—Wyn didn't want to marry Princess Sunnika, and Princess Sunnika had released him from their engagement. So why did watching them feel like she'd downed a bottle of vinegar?

Because he looks like he belongs with her more than he does with you.

She sucked in a breath at the thought. Despite the court's hostility, Wyn was *fae*; everyone here was fae. Unlike her. Was this what Wyn felt like, at Stariel, this chasm of difference between him and everyone else?

My child will be fae. She stopped herself from resting a hand over him or her just in time. *Would* her and Wyn's child be winged and horned? Would he or she belong here, in this court of strangely shaped people?

Does Wyn ever wish I had wings?

The thought had never occurred to her, and she wished it hadn't now. Now wasn't the time for this kind of introspection or insecurity, not when they needed to show this court a united, confident front. Besides, Wyn loved her and both of them would love this child, regardless of its features; she *knew* that, and even the sight of an irrefutably fae and beautiful Prince Hallowyn Tempestren dancing with an equally beautiful fae princess couldn't shake that certainty.

She watched the pair until a low voice purred behind her, close enough that breath tickled in her ear.

"Lord Valstar, I take it?"

She spun, her pyromancy flaring up in alarm. She had to curl her nails into her palms to stop flames bursting forth, a sign of how on edge she was.

It was the dark-haired not-enough-scarf man, and Hetta's eyes went, inevitably and regrettably, to the place that most lacked scarf. She yanked her gaze away, and scarf-man smirked and rested a hand on his hip. This didn't improve matters. She fixed her attention firmly above chin level, on the pattern of scales that curved along his cheekbones.

He waved a hand towards the floor. "Would you like to dance?"

"Ah—" Would it offend him if she said no? Hetta decided she didn't care. "No, thank you."

Scarf-man—and now she couldn't think of him by any other name—tilted his head. "Something more…intimate, then, perhaps? I have never been with a human." His smile widened. He had unnaturally sharp teeth.

Hetta blinked. Did he mean what she thought he meant? Surely she'd misunderstood. But she hadn't; the state of the scarf made that readily apparent. A laugh of sheer disbelief bubbled up, but she pressed her lips together to stop it from escaping. Fae men probably didn't like being laughed at any better than mortal ones, and angering a random member of DuskRose wouldn't help her find the Gate they needed.

Maybe I should suggest he show me his etchings in the rose garden, the more pragmatic part of her nature suggested. But no, that would probably not be wise. Better to slip off there alone when they reached Wyn's nebulous later.

"Definitely not," she said firmly.

Scarf-man shrugged, not at all offended. "As you like, then," he said and wandered off.

Hetta stared after him, struggling with a sense of spluttering outrage. She'd never considered herself particularly prudish, so it was somewhat lowering to learn a bit of Aunt Sybil lurked in her own soul. There must be a drinks table about, surely? But no, she should keep a clear head even if her stomach didn't rebel at the prospect.

Unfortunately, scarf-man's approach broke the ice, and she found herself fending off increasing amounts of fae interest. Their fascinated gazes unsettled her, as did their remarks. Hetta had dealt with contempt and disapproval before but never…whatever this was. It wasn't hostility, exactly—not like the way they'd looked at Wyn—but it wasn't a warm reaction either.

It came to her in a burning fury that their attitudes were those of people prodding an exotic animal to see how it would react—as if she herself wasn't quite a person to them. She curled her fingers into even tighter fists, and Stariel pulsed through the stone in her ring, a thin and weak connection. *I am not going to set things on fire*, she chanted to herself sternly.

Scarf-man's was not the only proposition she received, nor even the most blatant, little gods save her. Despite the open air above, the ballroom began to feel claustrophobic, with fae pressing in on all sides, eyes glittering, asking impertinent questions about Stariel and the mortal world but mainly about her relationship with Wyn, probing for any weakness. When she answered as best she could, they tittered at off-kilter moments, for reasons she didn't understand, and they made snide remarks to each other in languages she *actually* didn't understand. Why hadn't that occurred to her before now? It did seem unlikely that all fae would speak Prydinian, but she'd never questioned it before. And yet, they all spoke Prydinian to her.

I'll have to ask Wyn about it. She tried to find him in the mess of dancers—how long was this dashed dance going to go on for anyway? Her heart jerked when she failed to spot either him or Princess Sunnika. Sweat broke out on the back of her neck, and she let out a shaky breath, then made herself take a deeper one. Her stomach gave a worrisome roil.

Panicking wouldn't help her, and nor would fainting in a ballroom full of hostile fae. There was no reason to assume the worst. Wyn was probably just temporarily screened from view—it was a large room, and there were a lot of people, even setting aside the luxurious greenery growing over the walls and making it hard to define the room's edges.

Hetta pushed through the crowds, searching. Each glimpse of feathered wings or pale hair lifted her heart, only for it to come crashing down when she saw it wasn't Wyn. The world began to spin in an alarming way. She let the tide of the crowd push her into a side-eddy through an archway, stumbling into a smaller and thankfully less populated courtyard with—thank Almighty Pyrania and all the little gods—*seats*. Seats thankfully not occupied by giant leopards.

Hetta sank down onto one of the benches and spread her fingers across the cool stone, focusing on her breathing and drawing on the thin line of connection to Stariel to steady herself. The nausea began to subside.

The bench she'd chosen was in the shadow of a fountain in the centre of the courtyard, upon which stood a larger-than-life statue of a male shadowcat. His stone face fiercely surveyed the courtyard, and he held a spear in one hand, his tail curled in an S.

Something about him was strangely familiar, and Hetta was staring at his stone features, puzzling at why she thought that when something moved atop the statue. A small paw appeared on the statue's stone shoulder, followed by a muzzle as a leopard cub pulled itself up. It met her eyes and let out a mew of surprise, its grip slipping. It fell into the fountain with a splash.

Hetta found she'd risen by instinct, but before she could move, there was a shimmer and a small naked boy scrambled out of the fountain, dripping wet. Hetta wasn't very good at estimating children's ages, but he looked younger than Cecily's twin girls, maybe four years old or so? He caught her looking and froze, his cat ears flattening against his skull.

"Hello," she said. She'd never seen a fae child before.

"Hello." His tail curled nervously around his waist.

"Are you all right?" she asked him. "I'm sorry I startled you."

He continued to stare, looking her up and down as if sure she must be hiding extra appendages somewhere. "You're a human."

"Yes." The boy's open curiosity was easier to bear than the court's hostile scrutiny, but it still made her feel oddly self-conscious.

He took a few steps closer. "I heard humans can say things that aren't true."

She sank back down onto the bench and patted the seat next to her. Taking this invitation, he scampered over to her and perched beside her. His dark eyes were wide as he studied her, as if he found her features as unusual as she did the fae's. There were streaks of bright purple in his hair.

What lie could she tell a child, in this place where anything and everything might or mightn't be true? She held out a hand. "I have six fingers."

He blinked and then counted slowly. "You don't!"

"I don't have six fingers," she agreed.

His mouth fell open. "Wow." His eyes gleamed. "Say something else!"

"You're much, much taller than I am. Practically a giant," she said promptly, which sent him into a fit of delighted giggles.

"Akiyonn!" Princess Sunnika said sharply, stepping out of the shadows. "You should not be here."

The boy jumped up, and the expression he turned on the princess was one Hetta recognised very well, because it had a lot in keeping with her smaller cousins when they'd been caught doing something they shouldn't.

"I just wanted to see the human."

"Go back to your room or I will take you there myself by the scruff of your neck." Her words were low and furious, but Hetta got the strong impression Princess Sunnika was afraid rather than angry.

The boy huffed, but there was another shimmer and the leopard cub was back. He looked up at the princess plaintively, but she only narrowed her eyes at him until he slunk away.

"Who was that?" Hetta asked.

Princess Sunnika was still frowning in the direction the cub had taken. "Prince Akiyonn. My cousin's child." She nodded at the statue. "That is his father's likeness."

Princess Sunnika contemplated the statue of her dead cousin with more dispassion than Hetta could've mustered in her place. The prince Rakken and Catsmere had killed had had a child? But it had been more than ten years ago; the boy hadn't seemed old enough. Was that because fae children aged differently, or because time in Faerie passed differently? Regardless, it made it worse, to know the boy she'd just met was fatherless because of people she knew personally.

"I'm sorry," she said.

"Are you?" Princess Sunnika turned to face her. "You did not know him."

"I'd be sorry that anyone's relative was dead or that any child was fatherless." Did that really need to be said? Apparently it did, because Hetta caught a hint of surprise crossing the princess's expression. "Where's Wyn?"

"Dancing," Princess Sunnika said. "He holds the court's attention."

He holds the court's attention. "If you wanted to speak to me privately, you could've just asked."

Princess Sunnika's ears flicked this way and that, and she gave the courtyard a thorough examination. Then she stepped closer and said quietly, "You would be within your rights to demand custody of Gwendelfear as recompense for her attack on your consort."

Hetta frowned. "Is she here?"

"It is your right," Princess Sunnika repeated carefully.

Hetta could think of few things she wanted less than a fae prisoner, especially Gwendelfear. Gwendelfear had found Wyn unconscious in Meridon and imprisoned him. Wyn might be willing to let bygones be bygones—his stance was that he and the lesser fae were even now, since he'd imprisoned her at Stariel first—but Hetta remembered the cold dread of thinking Wyn might be dead.

"I don't think that's necessary—" she began, but Princess Sunnika cut her off, her dark eyes blazing.

"I will owe you a favour, Lord Valstar."

Hetta frowned. "You don't want Gwendelfear here? Why?"

"She is being punished." No emotion in her smooth, perfect face.

Hetta tried to work that one out. Princess Sunnika had seemed furious when she'd found out what Gwendelfear had done, so why did she care now that she was being punished for the transgression? Unless that's why she'd been so angry in the first place.

"You care about Gwendelfear's welfare?" Hetta hazarded.

Princess Sunnika's ears flicked restlessly again. "I owe a duty of care to all my handmaidens."

"What does 'punished' mean?" Hetta asked with some trepidation. Princess Sunnika didn't answer, just looked at her steadily, and that was an answer in itself. Horror coiled low and cold in her stomach. "But you're a princess—"

"My aunt," Princess Sunnika said, every word precise as cut glass, "is anxious that DuskRose's relationship with the mortal world is not jeopardised. Gwendelfear is being punished for interfering. My aunt is a wise and powerful ruler." The words were a warning.

Hetta resolved to appreciate her family more in future.

"I will—" She closed her mouth. She'd been about to say she'd take the lesser fae then, fine, but that wasn't how things were done in Faerie, was it? "As it so happens, I could do with a favour."

20

THE THRONE OF THORNS

W YN FOUGHT HIS way through the ballroom, trying to find Hetta's distinctive signature in the riot of foreign magic. The crowds parted before him with hostile resistance, wanting to obstruct his path but unwilling to risk touching a stormdancer. His dance partner had certainly made no attempt to conceal their revulsion. They hadn't been able to refuse their princess' command, but they'd dropped Wyn's hand like a snake when the dance ended.

This is the court I would have been part of if I'd married Sunnika. His feathers tightened against his spine. *This is where I would've died, if Lamorkin hadn't warned me.*

His path took him to the refreshments table, and he helped himself to two glasses of sparkling melon juice. That should ward off any more 'helpful' attempts from Sunnika to pair him up with more members of her court. Storms shivered through his feathers, and he was grateful for the court's wary distance. He hadn't shocked the DuskRose dancer before, but it had been a close thing.

Where was Hetta? None of DuskRose would dare break

guestright, not after Sunnika's show of support. He should be grateful for that, but other more urgent emotions swamped any such feeling, his magic roiling. *Calm.* He *had* to maintain calm, or at least the appearance of it. The fae here wouldn't be forgiving of any sign of weakness, and it would reflect badly on Hetta if her consort couldn't control himself.

There. A faint, tantalising hint of Hetta's magic. Clinging grimly to the hint of coffee and pine, he let everything else fade into the background.

He found Hetta sitting on a stone bench in a smaller courtyard off the main dance floor. She was alone.

"Have you seen the princess?" he asked. Sunnika hadn't directly said that she wanted to speak to Hetta privately, but he'd caught the message well enough. It was the only reason he'd accepted the second dance, assuming that Queen Tayarenn's attention would follow him rather than her niece.

"Yes." She frowned, and he offered her a glass, his instincts screaming with the need to fold his arms around her. But it wouldn't keep her safe, not here. At least the heartstone appeared to be doing its job. The slightly higher elektrical charge around her was mild enough that only a skilled stormdancer sorcerer or someone as familiar with Hetta's aura as Wyn would notice it. *And I am the only stormdancer here.*

"The good news is I've found a way to get to what we want," she said, accepting the drink. He didn't miss the careful way she phrased her words, conscious of eavesdroppers.

Reaching out with his leysight, he found the invisible watchers who'd followed him from the ballroom. Instinctively, he flared out his power in a warning pulse. *I am a Prince Royale and you will not spy on me.* They skittered away.

He came back to himself with a jolt and cursed. Now, more than ever, he needed to keep a tight rein on his instincts, not give in to every passing aggressive impulse! Although at least now no one was listening to them. *Or rather, no one except potentially Tayarenn.* The back of his neck itched with DuskRose's magic. He couldn't tell if the faeland's weight upon them meant anything, but he'd never been able to tell in ThousandSpire when his father was listening in either.

"And the bad news?"

Her lips curved. "We may be getting a houseguest."

Wyn paused, trying to pull the threads into something that made sense, but before he'd assembled them, a much larger distraction drew his attention, the presence ringing through the court like a gong.

Hetta's eyes widened. "What's that?"

"Queen Tayarenn. She's here."

Hetta wrinkled her nose at the archway that led back to the ballroom. "I suppose we have to go back in there."

"We could go to the Gate now." No, they couldn't. They hadn't yet secured anything that would count as DuskRose's approval, even from the most technical of standpoints, and if they went missing now, they were certain to draw the queen's attention. Better to try for the Butterfly Gate later. But he didn't want to return to that ballroom. He felt…tainted, as if the court's distaste had marked him somehow, and the thought of Hetta walking amidst that…

But Sunnika teleported into the courtyard before he could make any unwise decisions.

"Allow me to present you to my aunt."

Wyn exchanged a helpless glance with Hetta. She sighed and got up.

Queen Tayarenn wasn't shielding her presence, and walking into the ballroom felt not unlike nearing a forest fire. Her power woke uncomfortable comparisons to his father. *Heresy,* he thought with amusement, *to compare the Spires to DuskRose.*

Wyn had survived his upbringing in ThousandSpire largely by fading into the background whenever possible, and so the impulse to do the exact opposite here caught him by surprise. Power swelled up without prompting, and his wings twitched, preparing to flare in challenge. He dropped Hetta's hand and winched in his feathers, aborting the motion before it could begin, shocked at his own recklessness. Tayarenn would know what that gesture meant, from a stormdancer.

Hetta shot him a puzzled look that shifted quickly to concern, but he shook his head. DuskRose mustn't know how precarious his control was. He drew in a long breath as they walked through the archway and the crowd parted smoothly, leaving a clear path between them and the dais.

Tayarenn sat straight and regal on her throne, which had a highly distinctive appearance. *The Throne of Thorns*, Wyn had heard it called, the name whispered with an undercurrent of fear. It looked remarkably like a half conker shell. The base of it was green, the shape subtly curved and softly padded on the inside, but long spikes in a multitude of metallic hues protruded from the outer surface. Something about the spikes unsettled him, but he didn't have time to examine the thought before Tayarenn's gaze fell upon them.

Wyn had met the Queen of Dusken Roses once before, on the day of his engagement to Sunnika. Her appearance remained the same now as then: perfect fae beauty; smooth, waist-length black-and-pink-striped hair and fur of the same pattern, like the warning stripes of an exotic wasp. But one thing *had* changed: her power. Oh, it still sank heavily against him, but now it seemed muted, like calm waters instead of storm surge. And now—unlike then—he found he could hold her gaze. He puzzled at it, unsure what effect Tayarenn was trying for by muting her magic so.

His father's power had been muted as well, the last time Wyn had seen him before his death. But that had been because Wyn's broken oath—the oath that also bound ThousandSpire—had weakened King Aeros. Had Tayarenn broken an oath as well?

Or perhaps I've merely grown stronger. The thought startled him enough that he briefly lost his grip on his churning magic. It burst forth from its leash, sizzling over his skin, filling the air with storms and spice. Tayarenn's eyes widened before he wrenched the surge back under control again. If only he dared change back to his mortal shape—it blunted the worst of the magic.

He couldn't apologise for the lapse. DuskRose couldn't know how tenuous his control was, not least because they might seek to provoke him into breaking guestright. So he straightened and pretended nothing had happened when they stopped in front of the throne. Let her think he'd meant to do that. Better ill-mannered than lacking control.

"Prince Hallowyn Tempestren." Tayarenn emphasised his name, putting a little curl of threat into it. Wyn couldn't really blame her, not after his display.

"Your Majesty." His bow was absolutely correct for a royalfae greeting a faelord.

"Lord Valstar. I am pleased you accepted my invitation."

Interesting—she didn't try the same trick on Hetta. That was a good sign. Would Hetta catch that nuance? There were so many pieces of fae protocol, and he hadn't had time to explain them all to her.

Hetta swept a deep curtsey but didn't wait for permission to rise as she'd done when they'd met Queen Matilda in the mortal capital.

"Thank you for inviting us," Hetta said. "Not that I don't appreciate it, but why did you?"

Tayarenn laughed, the spikes glimmering in the light from the floating lanterns. "I'd almost forgotten the bluntness of mortals," she mused. "DuskRose is anxious to re-establish ties to the Mortal Realm, and you are lord of a mortal faeland. There is much we could offer you, if we were allies." Her tone softened and she leaned forward, her manner conciliatory. "It can be an isolating experience, being bonded to a faeland. I could offer advice from my own experiences." She absently stroked one of the spikes near her hands.

Wyn should've been paying close attention to Tayarenn's words, but he realised what was bothering him about the spikes. They weren't spikes. They were horns.

Stormdancer horns.

Hetta said something polite and wary to the queen, but he couldn't hear it over the buzzing in his ears. He was too busy counting. No two horns were identical, which meant each represented a different person. Some were eerily familiar, and an icy knot formed in his chest as he drew up old, old memories of people he'd known in ThousandSpire's court.

Tayarenn's mouth curled slightly at the corner as she caught his reaction. His power thrashed; he wanted to summon lightning, wanted to do anything to wipe that expression from her face. *Think of Hetta, and the Gate!* They'd never survive breaking guestright, not in the centre of Queen Tayarenn's court, and they'd never get to use DuskRose's Gate to Deeper Faerie if Wyn got himself thrown out.

He was a prince who'd grown up in one of the most powerful and deadly courts of Faerie. He could control his reactions and his powers—*would* control them, even if the years in Stariel had left him out of practice. He let expression melt from his face, ice crystallising around his rage.

Would Tayarenn have gotten rid of that throne, if I married Sunnika? He somehow doubted it.

"And what exactly do you mean 'ally with'?" Hetta was asking. She put a hand on his arm. *Stormwinds, let her not realise what Tayarenn is sitting on.*

"The relationship between any two courts is a complicated thing, Lord Valstar, and a formal alliance is worth little if no trust accompanies it." Tayarenn rested one hand delicately on a golden horn, her claws extending to click softly against the metal surface. It took all he had not to flinch at the sound.

"And how do you propose to build trust? I was under the impression that Faerie wasn't a trusting sort of place."

"You are acquainted with only narrow parts of Faerie. Ask your consort how alliances are built. Or perhaps don't, since his experience lies in breaking ties."

"In that case, aren't you glad not to be my in-law?" Wyn said.

Hetta went into a sudden coughing fit.

Tayarenn wasn't amused. "Yes," she said coldly. "I am."

"How fortunate," Wyn said, with the same bland pleasantness that had served him well many times over the years. "For as it happens, so am I."

Hetta's coughing fit subsided as she sobered, reading the currents between him and Tayarenn uncertainly. He was being too aggressive, and it wasn't helpful. He ran back over Tayarenn's words, trying to sift her meaning. *Alliances.* What did she want?

"I could guess what you're suggesting, Your Majesty, but it would be more efficient if you were to simply tell us."

"I see bluntness has rubbed off on you, in the Mortal Realm."

"I appreciate bluntness," Hetta said lightly, squeezing Wyn's arm. She smiled up at him. "Mortal that I am."

He smiled back, coiling his magic in as tightly as he could.

Tayarenn canted her head. "I hope that your choice of consort does not indicate you will be limited to only relationships with courts he prefers." A flash of teeth. "Assuming he still favours the Spires, given their current…weakness."

"I'm not anti-DuskRose," Hetta said. "And I didn't mourn King Aeros."

That was a very fae answer, and Wyn wasn't sure how he felt about it.

"It is common practice for courts who wish to strengthen ties to share blood, in one form or another. I gather you have many relatives, Lord Valstar. Perhaps some of them might wish to spend time here."

Wyn froze, and Hetta's fingernails dug into his arm, as if worried his streak of uncharacteristic recklessness might manifest again.

It was a sadly reasonable worry. Lightning surged in his soul at the suggestion of any more Valstars coming here, and he wanted to fly the present one-and-a-half Valstars as far away from here as possible.

Tayarenn continued, oblivious. "I would be glad to extend an invitation to one of your siblings, even. Perhaps the girl who aided one of my court." Alexandra. She was talking about Alexandra, who had helped Gwendelfear escape her imprisonment in the Tower Room at Stariel Estate. Tayarenn's smile broadened. "Or the telepath."

Wyn hadn't thought he could get any colder, but the word turned his veins glacial. How did DuskRose know about Marius? He'd known Marius's abilities would draw interest, but he'd thought them still safely secret.

"No," Hetta said firmly. "I don't think I can spare them. But thank you for the offer."

Tayarenn didn't seem particularly surprised by the answer. "If you cannot spare a member of your court, then perhaps there is another way you could demonstrate you do not favour the Spires above DuskRose."

Hetta narrowed her eyes. "I don't favour *any* fae court."

"Then why are you providing refuge to Spireborn?"

"Wyn has long since earned his own place at Stariel."

"Stariel has claimed me," Wyn added. "I do not belong to ThousandSpire any longer." Tayarenn would know that already, he was certain.

Tayarenn smiled. "Prince Hallowyn is not the Spireborn I was referring to. Tell me, if you do not wish to alienate DuskRose, then why are you harbouring one of her enemies?"

"I'm not getting involved in the business between you and ThousandSpire," Hetta said. "Besides, I don't think the High King would approve of me ejecting Prince Rakken just so you can hunt him down—didn't he want peace between your courts?"

Tayarenn's eyes flashed at Rakken's name, but her tone remained cool. "It is bold of you to presume to know the High King's mind or to assume he would approve of FallingStar's actions, given his history with your family."

"What history?"

Wyn nearly laughed aloud at the queen's surprise. Fae did not admit ignorance openly. But the queen recovered quickly, speculation in her expression as she answered carefully.

"The Iron Law. I do not think the High King likes Valstars very much after that business."

"Will you tell me what business that was?"

"Mortals," she said wearily. "Information is valuable, Lord Valstar, and you have already refused to accommodate any of my suggestions for showing DuskRose favour."

Interesting. Tayarenn didn't know exactly what had happened between the Valstars and the High King to bring about the Iron Law either, or she would have pressed her advantage harder. *The High King doesn't like Valstars.* His chest constricted. Maybe Tayarenn was mistaken. If she wasn't—well, he'd already known the High King hadn't set them an easy task.

Hetta straightened. "I don't feel that Stariel owes DuskRose any favours; rather, the reverse." She removed her hand from his arm and laced her fingers together neatly in front of her. Wyn suspected it was to keep them from trembling, but she held her head high. "I planted your dusken rose, even though a member of your court attacked my consort."

Attacked was something of an exaggeration, since Gwendelfear had found Wyn whilst he lay unconscious. He wouldn't have been nearly such easy prey otherwise. It probably wasn't the time to remind people of this.

"The lesser fae is being punished for her transgression."

"It's not sufficient," Hetta said coolly. "If DuskRose truly wishes to prove that it values an alliance with Stariel, then I demand custody of Gwendelfear." She looked every bit as regal as Queen Tayarenn, her chin lifting defiantly.

Wyn tried not to look as if Hetta's request surprised him. So this was the houseguest she'd spoken of; what was Sunnika up to?

The queen considered Hetta through slitted eyes. No fae liked to be told they had an obligation, but still less did fae like debts.

"Very well, Lord Valstar," she said after an interminable pause. "The lesser fae is yours to do with as you will."

Hetta shrugged, as if this rather extraordinary development wasn't worthy of any note. "Then, as an extension of goodwill towards DuskRose, I'd like to extend a personal invitation to you to celebrate my and Prince Hallowyn's wedding at Stariel." Hetta smiled at the queen. "Will you accept?"

Wyn recoiled. He didn't want Queen Tayarenn at his wedding, and in that moment, he couldn't hide the fact. His reaction got him exactly the response he'd known it would. Tayarenn smiled, looking directly into his eyes.

"If none of ThousandSpire are invited, DuskRose will attend."

21

THE BUTTERFLY GATE

AFTER THE LONGEST evening Hetta had ever experienced, she and Wyn waited in the rose garden for Princess Sunnika to fetch Gwendelfear. Neither of them spoke. Hetta burned with a thousand questions, none of which she wanted to ask while they stood on DuskRose lands. She knew how easy it was to eavesdrop within a faeland you were bonded to, and she doubted Queen Tayarenn shared her scruples on the subject. She crossed her arms and shivered, though the night wasn't cold.

Wyn put a hand on her shoulder. He was wound tight as a bowstring, his attention skittering from archway to archway, unsettled in a way she rarely saw. Understandable, given the tangible hostility towards him tonight, but he was usually so good at letting that sort of thing roll off him.

"Is something wrong?" she asked quietly, though she knew he wouldn't answer her properly, not while Queen Tayarenn might be listening. Gods, she couldn't think of any person she wanted at her wedding less, but at least the queen *had* accepted the invitation. The High King could quibble that that wasn't what he'd meant when setting his task, and she'd quibble right back about fae technicalities.

Queen Tayarenn thinks the High King doesn't like Valstars. Well, it wasn't as if they hadn't already guessed that might be the case, if Marius I had blackmailed him into the Iron Law somehow. If only she knew exactly how.

Wyn's eyes burned with the same need to communicate, but he shook his head and pressed his lips together.

A soft sound of pressure releasing had them turning. Princess Sunnika had reappeared. A thin figure leaned on her for support.

Horror coursed through Hetta, bile rising in her throat as she recognised Gwendelfear, or rather the shadow of her. Her poisonous blue eyes had always dominated her face, but now they were the only bit of life in the mask of a skeleton. The pale green of her skin had drained to white except where dark bruises mottled her skin, and the multi-hued greens of her hair were now the dry yellow of dead grass. She held her left arm close to her body at an awkward angle, despite the manacles encircling her wrists.

"Say the words," Princess Sunnika instructed. Nothing in her expression showed a hint that her handmaiden's appearance bothered her. Gwendelfear turned those wide blue eyes to her mistress, pleading, but Sunnika didn't soften. "Say it, Gwendelfear."

Gwendelfear didn't meet Hetta's eyes. "I pledge myself to your service, Lord Valstar, to serve and protect you and yours, to uphold the honour of the Court of Falling Stars." The words fell soft as withered leaves, a jarring contrast to her usual biting tone.

Wyn squeezed Hetta's arm. "You must accept," he murmured.

Hetta swallowed. This was a very faelord sort of thing to do, even if she hadn't had mixed feelings about the way oaths bound fae in the first place. But Princess Sunnika's expression flickered, showing a glimpse of desperation, swiftly hidden. *I will owe you a favour*, she'd said. The princess wouldn't have offered that if this hadn't meant something to her, and her help would make accessing the Butterfly Gate much simpler.

"I accept your pledge," Hetta said, and something *shifted* inside her, a lesser echo of how it had felt when Wyn's connection to Stariel had snapped into place.

Gwendelfear sagged.

"Take off her chains," Wyn said grimly, and Princess Sunnika did so without comment.

"Tell Jack that you're there at my invitation and not a prisoner," Hetta told Gwendelfear. The girl's eyes snapped to hers for the first time, confusion in them. "And try not to cause too much trouble in my absence."

Hetta touched the archway that held the Gate to Stariel, and the dusken roses bloomed once again, filling the air with a sweet, heavy scent, underlain with a hint of pine—Stariel's influence, seeping through. Magic shimmered within the archway, and suddenly there was an image of Stariel's rose garden, with Jack anxiously pacing in and out of the frame. Ivy sat on a stone bench, reading in the light of a spell-lamp.

"Go," Wyn said, pulling Gwendelfear to her feet. She gave him a flat look.

"*You* are not my lord."

So she *hadn't* lost all of her fire then. "Go through the portal," Hetta repeated. "And tell Rakken that if he hurts you, I *will* kick him out." She didn't think Rakken would still be within Stariel's bounds, but Princess Sunnika let out a tiny breath of relief at the words.

Gwendelfear looked to Princess Sunnika, and something complicated and bittersweet passed between them. Then Princess Sunnika gestured to the far side of the courtyard, holding out a hand to Wyn and Hetta each. "You will need to be quick," she said to them. Hetta took one of Princess Sunnika's hands and Wyn took the other.

Hetta nodded to Gwendelfear. "Go."

Princess Sunnika's voice was soft. "Goodbye, Gwen."

Gwendelfear took a deep, sucking breath that made her cough, nodded, and stepped through the portal on shaking legs.

The world went dark in the same instant, and then Hetta and Wyn were stumbling next to another archway, this one decorated with stone butterflies; they'd teleported across the courtyard. Princess Sunnika caressed one of the stone butterflies, and it transformed into a living creature, flapping its wings slowly as the portal shimmered to life.

"Go," Princess Sunnika said urgently.

Hetta took Wyn's hand and stepped through.

They stepped out into a brightly lit meadow, the contrast dazzling after the twilight of DuskRose. The Gate snapped shut behind them. Butterflies as large as dinner plates flapped lazily above the grass. Birdsong trilled, and the air smelled of summer. Hetta swallowed, disoriented and a little dizzy. It took several long heartbeats for it to sink in: they were alone, but for the butterflies. Safe.

She turned into Wyn, hugging him tightly, tucking her head against his chest. Clearly he felt the same need, his body curving to hers, pulling her as close as he could. They were both breathing too fast, and Hetta couldn't tell if it was just her heart pounding, or Wyn's, or both of them together.

Gwendelfear's skeletal face and hunched shoulders flashed across Hetta's mind's eye, as did the flat stares of the DuskRose courtiers, eerily like those of the ThousandSpire fae when Hetta had been in King Aeros's throneroom. How had Wyn borne it, growing up in a place like that, never knowing if someone was listening, never able to speak freely for fear of retaliation? She felt the courtiers' hostility clinging to her like grease, and she buried her face against Wyn's neck, welcoming his warm, clean scent, wanting it to banish every memory of both places.

They were safe, here in the warm butterfly-filled sunshine. Safe. Why did she feel on the edge of hysteria, then? She wrapped her arms around Wyn's waist, the sleek, night-dark fabric slippery to the touch, and her fingertips brushed feathers. A fierce and unexpectedly trivial longing for Wyn's usual attire went through her.

As if he'd heard her thought, Wyn changed back to his mortal form, wings and horns sliding away. A knot in Hetta's stomach eased at the tiny bit of normality. Guilt swiftly followed. He hadn't changed for her, had he? She didn't mind his fae form; it was only that she was less accustomed to it. And she'd never *become* accustomed if he kept hiding it from her!

She frowned up at him. "Why—?"

"The magic here," he said tightly. "It's…affecting me."

She tried to feel what he meant, but this place felt not too dissimilar to DuskRose, though less sentient. She picked at the sensation.

"There isn't a faeland here, is there?" There was a strong presence of *something*, but she didn't get the sense of someone looking over her shoulder. That was a relief, after DuskRose.

"No. These are unclaimed lands. But the magic is strong."

"Well, I can handle butterflies. To be frank, I was expecting Deeper Faerie to look much more sinister." Hetta held out a hand to one lazily flapping butterfly, which landed obediently on her palm.

"Hetta—don't—" Wyn jerked her back, but not before she felt the sharp bite as the insect latched itself to her flesh and began to suck.

Elektricity flashed through the meadow, ozone overwhelming the smell of crushed grass and summer flowers. It crackled through the clouds of butterflies between one heartbeat and the next, sizzling on impact. For a single, frozen still-life, the entire meadow lit up, the silhouettes of butterflies dark against the blinding white-blue. Then the lightning snapped out, and the scorched husks of a thousand blood-drinking butterflies dropped to earth.

A hush fell over the meadow.

Hetta looked at her hand. A single drop of blood welled in its centre where the insect had pierced the skin. She looked at Wyn, who was panting, his eyes wide and startled. He hadn't meant to do that, then.

"Well, thank you for defending me, I suppose, though perhaps that was something of an over-reaction. But your control is better than you think." She held up their still-joined hands. "You were touching me the whole time."

Something landed on her foot and she startled before she saw what it was: a blackened butterfly wing. She stared down at it and began to shake. Dash it, it was just an insect! But tears pricked at her eyes, and she couldn't seem to stop shaking now she'd started.

"Oh, my love," Wyn said, putting his arms around her and leaning his cheek against her hair. She could feel his heartbeat racing against her cheek.

She closed her eyes. "They tortured Gwendelfear." It wasn't a question, but it was so horrible that she wanted to make it one, wanted him to tell her she'd somehow misunderstood. "I was so angry with her for imprisoning you. I was *glad* to think she'd be punished. I didn't think—"

"I know, love," he said, holding her more tightly. "I know."

"What were those, those *rings* of bruises from?" She didn't want to know, but she felt compelled to ask.

Wyn spoke softly. "Magic has an infinite variety of uses, some of them terrible. There are…ways to hurt fae without permanently damaging them, physically at least."

"That's horrible." Her stomach roiled with nausea and frustrated rage.

"Yes. But she is at Stariel now, and safe."

"That doesn't change what happened!"

"No. It doesn't. But it is still better that she's safe now rather than not. And we are wasting time when we should be looking for Irokoi."

That startled her—Wyn had never cut her off like that before. She looked up and found him without expression, pupils shrunk to tiny black points in a sea of hard russet.

"Something unsettled you, in DuskRose, when we spoke to the

queen. What was it? And don't be glib." It wasn't fair to push him, not when he couldn't lie, but neither was any of this. "You don't need to pretend to be all right, just for my sake. I think we can cope with us both not being all right with what just happened because it *wasn't* all right, not any of it!"

His expression didn't change, and she thought he was going to fight her on this, but eventually he sagged and said, "Tayarenn's throne is made of stormdancer horns."

"Oh," she said in a small voice. The metallic spikes flashed through her mind. She'd thought they'd seemed familiar. "Oh. Oh, I *hate* this," she said fiercely. "I hate that we invited her to our wedding."

"I also don't relish the prospect, though I suspect that fact is exactly why she agreed so readily." Tired amusement flickered in his eyes. "However, I *did* enjoy telling her I was glad she wasn't my in-law, so that's something."

She gave a weak smile. No wonder he'd been so uncharacteristically belligerent towards the queen. Oh, the memory of her sitting smugly on that throne made Hetta burn. "We'll seat her at the very worst table, I promise. Do you mind terribly that I had to disinvite your family?" It felt extremely peculiar to be deciding on guest lists in the midst of, well, everything else.

Wyn spread his hands. "Her pettiness irritates me more than the thought of doing without Rake's presence for a day, but even if that weren't the case, it's a small price to pay." His eyes softened as he looked down at her. "How are you—" He caught himself. "How many am I up to today?"

"Four." She looked around. "If it's still today. How is it afternoon now when it was evening before?"

"Time moves differently in Faerie, and even more so in the deeper realms. And you didn't answer my question." His mouth curved. "Four times doesn't seem excessive to me."

Hetta put a hand to Lamorkin's heartstone, still hidden under illusion. "I'm fine. We're not going to get back to Stariel and find a hundred years have passed, are we?"

"I doubt it. The realms are becoming more connected now that passage between them has reopened. I suspect the disconnect is greater in Deeper Faerie, but the difference is more likely to be hours or days rather than years." He drew the stone feather out of his pocket and weighed it. "Rake was right about the Butterfly Gate— we're close to where Irokoi is. The tracking spell leads that way."

He pointed at the trees lining the meadow. Their foliage ran through riotous shades of purple, from palest lilac to deepest indigo. Hetta found herself carefully committing the sight to memory; it would make a splendid backdrop. *Yes, for all those plays you find yourself regularly putting on now.*

She gave herself a shake and let the illusionary ballgown and accoutrements drop, finding comfort in the sight of her sturdy walking boots. "Lead the way, then."

She tried not to step on the fried insects as they walked, but it was impossible; there were too many. Wyn didn't look at the ground as the dead bodies crunched underfoot, obscenely loud in the now-silent meadow. She shuddered. Butterflies beautiful as jewels with a thirst for blood. *Once this is done, I never want to come to Faerie ever again.*

22

THE GREENHOUSE

MARIUS PAUSED AND frowned at the seed in his palm as the scent of citrus rolled around the greenhouse. He knew every plant here, and tangerines didn't feature, despite what his nose was currently telling him. The hairs on the back of his neck stood up. Putting the seed carefully aside, he'd just turned to investigate when the opposite side of the greenhouse rippled.

He stepped backwards, his back smacking hard into the workbench. Portal, it was a portal. Aroset's fingers around his throat; the acrid reek of lightning-cracked pavement. Something. He should do something. Was there anything here he could use as a weapon? Iron inhibited fae magic—was there any iron here? There was a spade by the door, but what use would a spade be against a psychopathic fae princess? She had *lightning*! Running would be better. He should run. But he hadn't scrambled free of his paralysis by the time the familiar figure stepped out of the portal.

"Oh, it's you," he said, sagging against the bench. *And a damned good thing too, given my apparently amazing self-preservation instincts!* What exactly had he been planning to do if it *had* been Aroset— faint at her?

Rakken raised an eyebrow. "Not the reaction I anticipated, Marius Valstar." He was in his fae form, and behind him Marius caught a glimpse of a familiar workbench in Stariel's greenhouse before the portal snapped shut.

After a swift scan of his surroundings, Rakken dismissed the rows of unassuming plants as not a threat and returned his attention to Marius. Marius's fingers tightened on the bench behind him, ebbing adrenalin and relief giving way to something much more awkward. He'd forgotten how bloody intense Rakken's presence was, filling the greenhouse like humidity. Or, well, not forgotten, but he'd thought—hoped—perhaps he'd misremembered. Sadly not, because here the aggravating fae prince was, impossibly vibrant even when softened by Marius's lack of spectacles. Rakken's wings—presumably glamoured since they appeared whole—glittered in the bands of sunlight coming through the glass.

"What are you doing here? And how did you build a portal from my greenhouse at Stariel? I thought Hetta and Wyn had set wards against that?" Marius suppressed the urge to fidget, conscious of his inelegant appearance, since he wore a potting apron over rolled-up shirtsleeves. Rakken, of course, looked like he'd just stepped from a tailor's shop—a human tailor, since despite his wings he wore a Prydinian suit.

Rakken raised an eyebrow at him, silently emoting *you do know I'm not required to give you answers for the mere asking of them?*

"Well?" Marius prompted. He peeled off his gloves and reached for his glasses case. He didn't usually wear his spectacles at the workbench, not needing them for close work, but now their absence made him feel curiously vulnerable. But when he put them on, he immediately regretted it. Why had he thought bringing Rakken into sharp focus would be an improvement?

Rakken's eyes were an impossible green, greener than anything in nature, but Marius couldn't stop shuffling through comparisons anyway. The dark gloss of camellia leaves, shaded with the new growth of maidenhair ferns? *Algae*, he told himself firmly. *Pond scum.*

Those impossible eyes gleamed even as Rakken relented. "I came here looking for you, Marius Valstar. I'm interested in meeting this earl of yours."

Marius frowned. "That appointment isn't for ages, and the earl didn't invite you, *Mouse*."

Rakken's eyes flashed at the use of his sister's pet name. "I have not given you leave to call me that. As I have previously explained, the correct address is 'Your Highness'."

"I'll call you by your title if you stop with the 'Marius Valstar' nonsense. Wyn told me that in Faerie, using people's full names is a, a fae posturing thing." Besides which, it felt decidedly odd to be so formally addressed with such frequency.

"You asked him about me, did you?" Rakken shifted closer, sleek and menacing as a panther.

Was there suddenly less air in the greenhouse? Rakken grinned, dagger swift; he was doing it on purpose, this, this *looming*. The bronze horns only magnified the looming effect, catching the light and glittering in his dark hair.

Marius focused firmly on the wall over Rakken's shoulder. "Look, you can stop trying to bait me. It's childish, and I know why you're really here in any case."

That drew Rakken up short. "What am I really here for, then, *Marius Valstar*?" He emphasised the name, the timbre of his voice low and rich as whiskey. It sounded like sex, and Marius hastily shoved *that* comparison into the darkest cupboard of his mind and slammed the door. Dammit, he wasn't a bloody teenager. Why did Rakken have this effect on him?

He took a damn hold of himself. *I'm not letting my desires rule me. Not again.* He'd had quite enough of amoral, manipulative men. Even if Rakken was interested. Which he probably wasn't. Wyn had told him the fae were more open about such things, but Marius was fairly certain all this, this…*innuendo* was merely Rakken amusing himself. Or maybe it wasn't even intentional—maybe Rakken was so imbued with sensuality it dripped off everywhere sort of accidentally, like an invasive slime-mould. *He did manage to seduce the Duchess of Callasham in under half an hour, after all.*

"Wyn told me that Ar—your most murderous sister isn't trapped in the Spires," Marius said, cutting off from saying Aroset's name aloud. Last time that was how she'd latched onto people's locations. "And if you're making portals from Stariel, that means you have Hetta's permission to do it. Which means she strong-armed you into coming here in case your sister decides to target me or Gregory." He sighed. Of course he was worried about Aroset, but it was still lowering to be sent a nursemaid by one's younger sister.

Rakken canted his head. "You seem very certain I'm here at your sister's bidding." He smirked, showing teeth. "What if I came for a different purpose? What if I am merely bored of waiting and seeking…diversion?"

Okay, so the innuendo most definitely isn't accidental, then. Marius swallowed. Everything was too tight and too hot, but anger overrode the sharp and desperately unwanted arousal. How dare Rakken try to wind him up for his own amusement? He wasn't a damn toy!

"Then you can help me prepare anctulus seeds, or you can get out, *Your Highness.* I'm not playing your games," he said flatly. He took a few steps sideways, towards the sink, putting much-needed space between them.

Rakken made no attempt to follow, but his eyes gleamed as he looked him up and down, deliberately. "Are you *sure* you don't wish to play my games, Marius Valstar?"

Marius grabbed for the seedpods of anctulus that were currently soaking in the sink; soft, fleshy things. "Get"—he threw a pod for emphasis—"out!" He threw another.

Rakken dodged the first pod, but water droplets still flicked out across his chest. The second one hit him square in the stomach and burst. A large quantity of reddish juice bloomed, soaking into the white fabric. Rakken peered down at his abdomen with a faintly incredulous expression.

"It does wash out; it won't stain," Marius said after wrestling with his conscience, both appalled and impressed with himself. The seed-throwing had only been half temper; he'd wanted to see if it would actually affect the man. Which he shouldn't have done. The Ethics Committee would never have approved experimenting on unwilling subjects. Although the Ethics Committee had never met Rakken; surely they'd have made an exception?

Rakken threw his head back and laughed. It wasn't fair that anyone had a laugh like that, or that anyone should look so perfectly composed after being spattered with cold water. "How reassuring to know. I must admit this is my first experience of having soggy mortal plant matter thrown at me."

"Keep being an ass and you can help me with my yarrow experiments," Marius said grimly. Yarrow was one of the plants he knew definitely had anti-fae properties. He frowned at the reddish stain on Rakken's shirt, which didn't appear to be causing any discomfort. "I suppose I can cross anctulus off the list of plants with potential anti-fae properties. Unless you want to report otherwise?"

Rakken canted his head to the side. "Are you *experimenting* on me?" He pressed an idle finger to the wet patch on his shirt. The water had made the fabric slightly translucent, and it clung to the planes of his abdomen. Which Marius *did not notice*.

Marius turned hurriedly back to the potting bench. Plants. Nice safe plants. Rakken hadn't even been here five minutes and already Marius felt like setting something on fire—Rakken, himself, the greenhouse. The entire town of Knoxbridge. He hadn't been this fiercely irritated by anyone since he'd come of age, and it would've felt like a childish regression except it really, really didn't make him feel like a child at all and that was the entire problem.

"Maybe the flowers will have anti-fae properties, even if the seeds don't. Do you know if that's the case for other plants? Does any part of yarrow affect you, or only the flower?" he babbled.

A huff behind him. "Do you truly expect me to tell you?"

"Well, I haven't lost anything by asking," he pointed out, pulling the rest of the seed pods out of the water and piling them onto a tray next to the sink. "Although since you don't know the Prydinian names for most plants, I suppose it wouldn't matter even if you did want to be helpful."

Rakken picked up one of the anctulus seeds and inspected it. "Tell me, does your mortal institute support this line of research, or is this a personal project?"

Marius knew he wasn't asking out of idle curiosity. "Don't worry, no one's officially researching weapons of war yet, though I'm sure someone will be if things keep going as they are. You should see what's been in the papers lately."

"I have seen them," Rakken said softly. "I am not here only to discharge a debt to Lord Valstar."

The warning throb of a headache pulsed at the base of his skull. "I'm not sure how you think talking to the earl will help your cause. He hates the fae in general and Wyn specifically, so he's hardly going to embrace Wyn's older brother as some kind of fae ambassador. Also, and as previously stated, you weren't invited."

Rakken shrugged. "I can be very charming."

"If you think I'm going to stand by and let you compel the earl—"

But Rakken was already shaking his head. "Save your threats; I have no intention of compelling your earl." Any virtue in this statement was swiftly undone by his next words: "It's an inefficient long-term solution. Besides, I don't need magic to charm people, Marius Valstar."

"I've yet to see any evidence of that. And you can stop doing that name-thing. I'm not impressed by it."

Rakken smirked. "Ah, but I'm not doing it for *your* benefit."

"I'm amazed neither Hetta nor Wyn has strangled you yet." Marius took the tray over to the other workbench away from Rakken so he didn't give in to the temptation either. "How did you even know I was going to be in here this afternoon, anyway?"

"I did not. Don't let my sister's facility with portals fool you into thinking they can be made wherever one likes. They're a tricky magic that depends greatly on resonance and the portal-maker's familiarity with the destination. I've been in this location before, and this building shares a strong resonance with the similar one at FallingStar."

Marius tried to pretend he wasn't fascinated by the information as he began to sort out pots and soil. "What about when you came through from the Spires into the main library in Knoxbridge?"

Rakken shrugged. "I took a calculated risk. My need was great, and I felt confident we could handle whatever we encountered in the Mortal Realm, regardless of where the portal emerged—and whoever we encountered." He gave Marius a meaningful look, his lips curving. "And I was right."

But the weak attempt at provoking him didn't hide the melancholy in Rakken's eyes at the oblique reference to his twin. Maybe that's why he was being so deliberately abrasive. If one of Marius's siblings had been trapped somewhere… His chest tightened with unwilling sympathy, and he reached out to pat Rakken's shoulder.

"Wyn and Hetta will find your brother, and he'll know how to free ThousandSpire. Won't he?" That was what Marius had gathered from the conversation with Wyn. It all seemed a bit tenuous, but he trusted Wyn.

Rakken looked down at Marius's hand with an inscrutable

expression, and Marius became excruciatingly aware of the heat and muscle under his fingers, of the faint scent of him—not the smell of his magic, but a more mundane one of soap, skin, clothing, and something Marius had come to associate with feathers. He hastily removed his hand. Rakken raised an eyebrow but—thank all the little gods for small mercies—said nothing.

Marius put his gardening gloves back on and began to pot anctulus, his shoulder blades itching with the weight of Rakken's gaze.

Rakken leaned back against the opposite workbench and watched. "Does Hollow know about your experiments?"

"He's not here to hear or see you, so I don't know why you insist on calling him that, or why you've come in your fae form. There's no point in reminding *me* he isn't human—I'm hardly likely to forget." Marius frowned at the tips of Rakken's wings, trying and failing to see through the glamour that hid the sheared-off feathers. Intuition flooded him. "Oh. It's not just to remind Wyn of his heritage, is it? You heal faster in fae form. You're trying to speed up your recovery as much as possible, and you don't like appearing weak while you do so, so you're glamouring to disguise it. Er. Aren't you?"

Marius flushed at the dry look Rakken gave him, filled with a need to dig a hole right here in the greenhouse floor and bury himself in it. Instead, he swallowed and went back to potting seeds.

"Your complete lack of self-preservation instinct continues to astound me. You should be grateful your sister called in her debt on your behalf."

"So that *is* why you're here. To play guard-dog." And Hetta had blackmailed him into it. Splendid. Exactly how one wanted to acquire an unwanted and probably unneeded bodyguard. He sighed. "Do you have any reason to believe your sister will target me or Greg?" After all, why would Aroset come to Knoxbridge, half a country away from Stariel? Oh, he'd no doubt Aroset *would* try to kill him again if she got the chance, but that wasn't the same as actively hunting for him. He wasn't in any real danger, and so he'd told Hetta. Why she'd seen fit to lump him with Prince Difficult—

"I do. I hope I'm wrong."

"What?!"

Rakken's lips curved. "*That* was more the reaction I anticipated upon my arrival."

"But—why? Why would she target me? I was just conveniently *there* last time, and she doesn't know where I am now. I have no particular value to her."

Rakken shrugged. "My sister dislikes being thwarted."

"Don't lie to me." Marius had spent enough time with fae now to tell when they were being deceptive, stating truths designed to mislead. He had no doubt that Aroset *did* hate being thwarted; she'd seemed like that sort of person. Equally, Marius knew that wasn't why Rakken thought him at risk.

Rakken sighed and lost his languid air. "If my sister chooses to target you, it will be partly my fault. I told her something that, in hindsight, would have been better left unsaid." His lips quirked. "Something that I will not tell you, Marius Valstar. In any case, I accept the obligation caused by my own miscalculation."

He met and held Marius's gaze, a challenge Marius didn't understand in their depths. Sometimes, Marius understood subtext and could piece together secrets with piercing certainty. Other times—like now—it was like staring at a high, smooth wall upon which he could get no purchase. The headache that had been slowly building went quiet with a suddenness that made him exhale sharply in relief.

Rakken tilted his head. "And I *do* wish to speak to your earl."

Marius was already dreading the interview, and Rakken's presence seemed unlikely to make it go any better. Though if he took Rakken with him, at least he wouldn't be the sole recipient of the earl's disapproval, and he couldn't imagine Rakken being intimidated.

"I haven't said you can come. And what are you planning to do if Set appears, anyway? You and Cat together weren't powerful enough to confront her last time. And why is she so powerful anyway? I know the Maelstrom is supposed to grant you extra powers, but didn't you go into it as well? Shouldn't you and her be evenly matched now?"

Something dark flickered in Rakken's expression, but the emotion was there and gone in an instant. "Wherever did you come by the conviction that I will answer whatever scatter-shot of questions you throw at me?"

"If I have to put up with you dogging my footsteps, I think it's well within my rights to question whether you'll be of any use."

Rakken chuckled, but to Marius's astonishment, he leaned back against the bench and answered quite reasonably.

"Set is older, and age confers power, generally. If she does make an appearance, I would suggest a hasty and tactical retreat to the nearest resonance location to return to FallingStar."

This was strangely reassuring; much easier to trust Rakken to act to save his own neck rather than believe him to be planning sacrificial heroics.

Rakken raised an eyebrow. "But I'm not precisely useless; I am more powerful now than I have ever been." He opened his palm with a flourish, and a tiny crackle of charge formed in its centre. Marius stared at the contained glittering blue-white ball in fascination. He'd never seen Wyn do that, but then Wyn wasn't exactly showy with his magic.

"Useful if we run out of matches," he said drily.

Rakken laughed, closing his hand. The charge snapped out. He fanned out a wing, and Marius jumped as feathers brushed him, unclear where glamour ended and wings began. Rakken only smiled at his reaction, devilry in his eyes. Gods, Rakken. In Knoxbridge. For who knew how long.

This was a terrible idea.

"You can't come with me to the earl's with your wings out," Marius said, making one last attempt at protest.

Rakken's smile broadened. "Thank you," he said, "for inviting me."

THE TERRIBLE, HORRIBLE, NO GOOD, VERY BAD WEEK

On Monday, the Gate in the rose garden re-opened, only for the creature Gwendelfear to stumble through before it closed. Without Hetta or Wyn, even though half a day had passed and Hetta had said she'd probably be back by now. Thank Simulsen he'd been watching over the Gate, was all Jack could say. What in the hells did Hetta think she was doing, sending them evil fairies for safekeeping without warning or explanation?

And he didn't need Alexandra snapping at him that Gwendelfear *wasn't* an evil fairy—and she should've known he was only joking when he'd said the girl was welcome to the Tower Room again. Well. Only half-joking.

He didn't trust the fairy girl, even if she did look pitiful, as if she'd suffered some terrible wasting illness. And even if Stariel had greeted her as one of its own, sending Jack's land-sense pinging in the same way it did for his relatives—and why and how had Hetta thought attaching yet *another* fairy to Stariel was a good idea? Wyn he could cope with, but Gwendelfear? Wasn't she one of the bad ones, even if she had healed Alex that one time?

Not that anyone had cared for his opinion. The bloody fairy girl was now ensconced in a room down the hall from Alexandra, who'd also taken responsibility for shepherding her to mealtimes with the territorial fierceness of a she-cat. Gwendelfear herself proved a completely useless source of information on Hetta and Wyn's whereabouts.

On Tuesday, the chief linesman complained that he couldn't keep the team hanging around indefinitely, if Lord Valstar wasn't going to keep up the trenching work needed to finish the job; they were due to begin another job soon. Jack told them Hetta was indisposed but would be back to the task soon, and wasted a morning trying and failing to get Stariel to act in her absence. At least the land didn't seem worried, from what he could tell. That had to mean Hetta was fine, whatever the reason for her dragging her feet in returning.

On Wednesday, a royal courier arrived with a message for Lord Valstar and refused to leave without a response.

Jack tried the same tactic as he'd used for the linesman.

"I'm afraid Lord Valstar is indisposed." He couldn't tell the man she was in Fairyland, could he? Or should he? It had now been *three days*, after all.

The ploy didn't work as well as he'd hoped.

"I will wait for her lordship to be sufficiently recovered to respond," the pompously dressed man said.

Jack eyed him with alarm. "There's no knowing how long that may be."

Not even a blink. "Even so. I have my orders."

He and the courier stared at each other. Eventually, the courier allowed, "I suppose a response from you may suffice, if you are acting in her stead."

Jack looked down at the envelope the courier held out as if it might poison him. "Me?" He shook his head. "No. You can leave it here, and she'll answer as soon as she can. But I'm not responding for her." If he opened the queen's message, that would be him involved in whatever this royal nonsense was, wouldn't it, whether he wanted to be or not. This was Hetta's mess, and he refused to get tangled up in it.

Besides, she was going to be back any moment, wasn't she? Wasn't she?

"You can tell her majesty that you delivered her message safely, and that Lord Valstar will respond as soon as she can," he said flatly, folding his arms. "Now I bid you good day."

The courier hesitated, taking in his expression. "Could I have that in writing?"

"I have faith in your recall." And with that, Jack marched out and hoped like hell the courier would be gone when he returned. He'd done the right thing, hadn't he? The faintest fluttering of something like panic stirred in his stomach, like the feeling you got just before a horse bolted.

No, he'd done the right thing, he told himself. Hetta could deal with the queen's message—whatever it was—when she returned. Which would probably be later today anyway, so it was best to leave it for her so as not to confuse matters. He stalked out of the house and round to the rose garden, ignoring the drizzle of the rain.

The Gate was inactive, the unnatural blooms once more colour-less, tightly furled buds. Jack scowled at the plants, feeling Stariel's unease circling them. They shouldn't have let Hetta go in the first place—what the hell had Wyn been about to let her go with him, anyway? Pregnant women weren't supposed to go gallivanting off to Fairyland! Why did Hetta always think she was some sort of special exemption?

On Thursday, the bank manager wanted to know when the Dower House would start bringing in rent.

"The estate agent said there's a fellow coming to look at it next week," Jack told him, pleased to have an answer to this question, if not exactly pleased at the prospect of strangers living on Stariel land.

Jack had lined up an excuse for why Hetta wasn't available to speak with the bank manager, but it proved unnecessary. The man never even asked.

On Friday, Angus Penharrow demanded to know if Hetta was coming to meet the Northern lords he'd invited to his house party. Jack tried his now-standard stalling tactic.

"Indisposed?" Angus said doubtfully. "That's not what the locals are saying."

Jack folded his arms. "What are they saying then?"

"That she's gone to Fairyland."

Bloody hell—could no one keep their mouths shut in this family? Angus took in his expression. "I see that she has, then. When is she coming back?"

"It's none of your business." Jack folded his arms. Angus might've paid in sheep for the wrong he'd done to Stariel, but that didn't mean Jack trusted him further than he could throw him.

Angus raised an eyebrow. "It is if she wants my help with the Conclave."

Why the blazes wasn't Hetta back yet? But Jack wasn't prepared to let Angus Penharrow take the high ground here, even if Jack too privately wished Hetta had given a bit more thought to Stariel before she'd left. "She'll be back when her business there is done."

Angus was unimpressed with this response. "You don't know anything about these wing worshippers the papers have started going on about, do you?"

Jack shook his head.

Angus gave a deep, frustrated sigh. "Well, if she's not back before my fellows arrive next week, are you up to giving a tour of the estate? Lord Arran's planning to arrive early, and it would be no bad thing to reassure him everything's in hand here." He fixed Jack with a meaningful look. "It *is* in hand, isn't it?"

Jack bristled, even though that feeling of riding a runaway horse hadn't left him in days now. "Yes!"

ON SATURDAY, A REPORTER turned up.

24

MISCELLANEOUS FAERIE ENCOUNTERS

W YN CLUNG TO his mortal form under the assault of more magic than he knew what to do with. The afternoon had softened into twilight under the trees, but the weight of, of…*watching* had only grown worse the longer they walked, though they had yet to encounter anyone or anything larger than the blood butterflies.

Uneasy, he drew up his leysight for guidance and immediately stumbled, blinded by the intensity of the leylines.

"Wyn? What is it?" Hetta reached out to touch his shoulder.

He gave her what he hoped was a reassuring smile. "The leylines merely startled me. I'm beginning to understand why Deeper Faerie isn't recommended for young fae."

"What do you mean?"

"You don't feel it? The ambient magic is very powerful. It's…distracting me."

She shook her head.

Perhaps the fact that she was a faelord made her immune to the influence; perhaps it was because she was human. He risked another glance of leysight, more carefully this time. The lines of magic criss-crossing the land glowed with brilliance, a multitude of colours in shades that ran beyond the normal spectrum. Every leaf, every blade of grass, glimmered full of magic, the colours and scents so vibrant they hurt. It sang to him, a seductive song of home-coming that made no sense given he'd never been here before. He wanted to change forms, unfurl his wings and bathe in the intensity of the sensation, but instead he pressed his magic down harder, clinging desperately to his mortal form. Perhaps the ambient magic and the temptation it presented wasn't a sinister trap, but he was suspicious of it on general principles.

"Wyn?"

He started as Hetta touched his shoulder again. She was frowning up at him. Ah. He'd gotten distracted focusing on *not* getting distracted.

"My apologies. This way," he said, choosing a path between two ancient trees of a species he didn't recognise. He'd never seen the like of their towering purple trunks or pale lilac leaves in any of the surface realms.

The forest was full of small noises as he followed the line of the tracking spell. Insects chirped and birds trilled warnings, little flits of feathered things diving for cover as they passed. Ahead of them came the rippling of water and a sound akin to wind chimes, oddly familiar. He carefully examined the leylines again, trying to decipher why the wind chimes seemed so familiar, but everything shone so brilliantly that he couldn't untangle individual threads.

Their path led them to a riverbank, where the water ran slow and clear enough to make out every stone of the bed. Some distance away, a waterfall thundered down a sheer cliff face more than a hundred feet high. Small sprites played in the pool beneath the falls—the source of the windchime sound. In full daylight they would be nearly invisible, burning with a flame so hot it had nearly no colour at all, but dusk showed them as flickering glass figures about the size of dolls, giggling as they chased each other above the water's surface. Steam rose from the surface where their small feet brushed—the equivalent of playing daredevil, for their kind.

"Nightwraiths," he named them quietly, for Hetta's benefit. "A type of flame sprite. They aren't dangerous, generally, unless you touch them."

The sight of their games woke an old memory…

He was a boy and he and his mother sat on a lakeshore, watching the nightwraiths dance.

His mother rose and waded into the water, and gentle ripples lapped against the shoreline, the surface still as glass. The night was warm, full of the dry, earthy scents of summer, and cicadas chirped in the eucalypts. Mother's steps sent distortions through the stars' reflections and the dancing hues of the sprites, who flitted around her excitedly. She extended a graceful hand and coaxed one into her palm.

"Aren't they lovely, Hallowyn?" She turned back to the lakeshore and smiled. "Come and see."

He waded into the cool lake, the water trickling through his feathers to his skin in shivery rivulets. His mother stood only knee-deep, but the water reached his waist when he held out his hands eagerly for the sprite.

She laughed and shook her head. "It will hurt you, little one. They burn brightly."

"Why doesn't it hurt you, then?" The sprite danced in her palm, tiny and delicate, its features flickering shades of flame. Standing this close, he could feel the heat of it, but his mother's skin was smooth and unburnt. "Are you using magic?"

Sadness crept into her expression, a sadness so deep and terrible that it frightened him. She put the nightwraith down carefully, and it ran across the surface of the lake, giggling.

"No," she said.

"Wyn?"

Wyn snapped free of the memory. "I think my mother and I used to watch them," he said slowly, fishing each word up from a great depth. Had they? He frowned. Why had he been so sure of it, just a moment ago? He couldn't recall any particular memory associated with his mother and nightwraiths now.

"They're beautiful."

They *were* beautiful, little figures of living flame with dragonfly wings. His chest grew tight. Why did the sight of them make him feel such sadness, then?

Hetta let out a long, careful breath. "I need to sit for a minute. And eat something."

He found her a suitable rock and tried not to fret. Hetta's smile, half-fond, half-exasperated, told him he hadn't entirely succeeded. He took out a biscuit from his satchel—sending a mental thank-you to Rakken for the spell that enlarged the interior—and offered it to her.

She leaned against him while she ate the biscuit. It always amazed him how small and soft she felt in his arms, the contrast between the iron-willed faelord and the physical woman. He focused on the leylines as they curved around her. She shone as brightly as the magic here. There was a hint of charge spinning lazily around her, draining slowly into Lamorkin's spell-stone, but he stroked the charge off anyway and let it disperse between his fingers. It might not make any difference, but perhaps it would make the heartstone last longer.

"Whatever you're doing makes me feel rather like a cat being brushed."

"What a good kitty." He nuzzled her.

She laughed. "How close are we, do you think?"

He checked the tracking spell. There was still more than half the time left in the spell, which meant they hadn't been here above a few hours. It was hard otherwise to judge.

"A lot closer than before." He grimaced. "I cannot be more precise, I'm afraid."

The forest was oddly peaceful, with Hetta soft against his side, despite the magical assault on his senses. His mind drifted to Stariel, wondering how much time had passed there and how Jack was handling things in their absence. What would the Valstars make of Gwendelfear being thrown back into their midst?

"Will Rakken be able to tell if Marius is…if there's some permanent side effect from Aroset's attack?" Hetta asked abruptly. "I mean, a side effect other than telepathy."

"Perhaps. Mind magic is strange and rare, even in Faerie."

Wyn had met exactly one telepath before, and she had been stark, raving mad, imprisoned deep beneath the palace in ThousandSpire, her powers constrained to within the walls of her cell. The reason King Aeros had kept her alive was as a useful training exercise for those practising mental shields—and as a terrifying way to extract secrets from anyone with any resistance to compulsion. Wyn had gotten the merest glimpse into her mind, once, when his shields had faltered: a hollow shell, filled with chaos not her own. Whatever core of individuality she'd once had had been burned away by the thoughts of others.

She'd died before Wyn had left ThousandSpire. He'd gone to see her body burned, driven by something between pity and guilt. Her head had been wrapped in bandages, but he'd heard her guards muttering about the damage she'd done to herself, how her power had gone rogue, imploding her own skull.

He shivered, not in revulsion but in fear for his friend. *But it cannot have helped her mental state to be imprisoned by my father. Perhaps she wouldn't have lost herself so badly if she'd been treated better. Perhaps she could have gained control of her powers if she'd had someone to teach her.* He'd heard of functional telepaths, though he hadn't met any personally. And Marius's abilities might be much milder than the woman he'd known. Maybe. Marius had sent Aroset hurtling into a wall with the force of his projection—and Aroset was greater fae, should've had iron-hard shields against that.

Were they right to keep the knowledge of his powers from Marius? Rakken thought it too dangerous, but could he truly know the risks? How could Marius learn to control his telepathy if he didn't know he had it? *I will find an expert for him,* Wyn vowed silently. There had to be someone in Faerie who knew more than they did.

Hetta's worry mirrored his. "How much do you trust Rakken's judgement?"

"He likes debts as much as most fae, and he owes you for giving him sanctuary at Stariel. For that alone, I trust him to keep Marius safe from Aroset." Though he had some uneasiness about putting the two of them together for any length of time—an uneasiness he could not share with Hetta, since it was based on a private conversation between himself and Marius.

"What about the telepathy? It was mostly on Rakken's say-so that we didn't tell him, and the more I think about it, the less I like it. Rakken loves having the upper hand, and wouldn't Marius knowing what he can do take that from him? What if Rakken exaggerated the risk for his own benefit?"

The insight startled him. Rakken's shields should be adamantine, telepathy or not, but hadn't Cat said Marius was particularly sensitive to him?

"I confess that didn't occur to me. I hope you're right, and that the risks of his telepathy are primarily to Rake's ego." *Rather than to Marius's life.* "After this, I would like to find someone who knows more about mind magic. Someone who could teach him, maybe."

Hetta made a wordless sound of agreement and burrowed into

his side. The sharp edges of anxiety softened under the physical contact, and he knew Hetta was seeking the same reassurance. After this.

Hetta finished the biscuit, watching the nightwraiths in the distance. "They don't drink blood, do they? I'm rather jaded after the butterflies."

"No, they merely burn to the touch."

She shivered.

"That is Faerie: beautiful, deceptive, dangerous." Hetta had never fully understood the nature of Faerie, not in her bones. Was she coming to understand it now? Did it give her second thoughts?

She swivelled and brushed his cheek. "Kind. Loyal. Insufferably arrogant, on occasion."

His heart swelled. "I prefer *understandably* arrogant, when required." But he couldn't let her deceive herself. "But Faerie is not known for kindness."

"You're fae, Wyn, just as much as those nightwraiths. You can't keep pretending you're not. I don't want you to keep pretending you're not."

"The magic here—" He trailed off under the accusing weight of her gaze. He sighed. It was an excuse, and they both knew it. "I am afraid." He gestured towards the nightwraiths. "What if I am becoming something like my father, something like Queen Tayarenn?"

"Then we shall need to investigate how fae divorces work," Hetta said without hesitation. "Honestly, Wyn, we have quite sufficient trouble to be getting on with without you borrowing more. And how am I ever to grow accustomed to you if *you* refuse to grow accustomed to you? Besides, this is the sort of place where it seems foolish to give up any advantage, and I *know* you can draw more magic in your fae form."

"I also have less control," he pointed out.

"Yes, such as when you electrocuted an entire field of butterflies without affecting me, even though I was *holding your hand at the time*. You've never shocked me, not once. And I have this, besides." She shook the heartstone in front of him.

"Yes, and we don't know how long that will last without my adding to its burden." Was its colour a shade darker even than a few hours ago? He stood, pulling out the tracking spell again. "We should keep moving."

25

THE WILD HUNT

THE FOREST AT dusk transformed into rolling hills at midnight in a way that was patently impossible, and Hetta drew to a halt to glare at the landscape in sheer outrage. She took a step back and found herself standing where they'd been just a few seconds previously, in not only an entirely different landscape but a different time of day. The sun's last dying rays slipped through the dappled canopy of the forest. Trees in strange hues of purple and blue stretched in all directions. There was no sign of Wyn.

She stepped forward into night. Wyn was once more beside her, and they stood together in a sea of rippling grass spread beneath a sky of deep indigo. The enormous full moon cast a coldly silver light across the dips and hollows of the endless plain. Turning on the spot, there was nothing except open sky and grass in all directions, with the exception of the single solitary tree behind them. She couldn't help it; she stepped back under its branches. Even anticipating it, it was still disorienting to find herself alone in the vast, quiet forest, with the sun still edging towards the horizon.

Wonder rose in her, and she felt a bit like a child examining a new toy, stepping backwards and forwards several more times. Still—

"The geography doesn't make sense!" she complained. "Is the tree a portal of some sort?"

"It's a natural border. This is mosaic land," Wyn said absently, as if the landscape's impossibility weren't of that much note.

Instead, he seemed preoccupied with gazing up at the moon, the starlight caressing his skin. Despite being in his human form, he didn't look human. He looked otherworldly, strangely natural in this unnatural place, his hair curling in the gentle breeze, glinting like silver. His fingertips brushed the long grasses, and there was something yearning in his expression as he drank in the moonlight. Her chest twisted uncertainly.

"Wyn?" She touched his shoulder.

His eyes were dreamy when he turned back to her, the russet rich as blood, and he drew her into a kiss that tasted of thunder. It was very—well. Yes. But it also reminded her a little too strongly of a previous time he'd been swept away by strong magic, and when they came up for air, she gave him a shake, rattling the silver clasps on his robes.

"Wyn!"

"Yes, my love?" He cupped her cheek and brushed the pad of his thumb over her bottom lip. It was most unfair, the way he was looking at her, in the silvery light of the moon, and she couldn't really be blamed for leaning in willingly when he bent to kiss her again. Her bones went liquid.

She made another attempt to recover herself. "*Hallowyn.*"

He drew back with a long sigh of regret. "Ah. I did *say* I was finding the magic distracting." He didn't sound very sorry for it, but as she wasn't either, she couldn't really complain. His eyes were still impossibly deep, impossibly richly coloured.

Instead, she pointed at the stone feather he was holding. "How far away are we from Irokoi?"

He touched the stone and lost a bit of his dreaminess. "Close.

This way." He reached for her hand, hesitated, his attention going to the heartstone. It had fallen out of her shirt, and when she went to tuck it back in, she saw that the colour had deepened, the change obvious even by moonlight.

She'd been trying not to think about it, since there wasn't currently anything she could do and so many other distractions going on besides. Not that she could forget that she was pregnant, exactly, but it also wasn't always at the top of her mind, and she still hadn't quite rearranged the pieces of her identity around the concept.

"It's draining faster," Wyn said grimly.

She tugged him back into motion. "Maybe it's because we're in Faerie. If it's affecting you, it's not that much of a stretch to imagine it might have some effect on your baby as well."

Wyn got a peculiar expression that made Hetta squeeze his hand fondly—a sort of awed panic, as if he too had managed to forget about the existence of their baby. For a moment he looked, ironically, entirely human.

Their baby. Their baby that might feel the tides of fae magic like its father. Hetta mused on that as they walked away from the tree, down a gentle slope and then up again. The long grass rippled like the fur of a great beast. How far had they come? How long had they been walking already? She felt bone-tired, but it was hard to know how much that related to the passage of time and how much to the babe.

"Do you think about what they'll be like?" she asked him.

Wyn was still looking up at the sky as they walked, and she thought he hadn't heard her at all. His hair fell away from his ears, which were almost pointed, and his skin glimmered faintly. "Who?"

"I'm having serious second thoughts about broaching the subject now, with you so distracted. I'm talking about our child—do you think about what they might be like?"

That brought him back to her again, some of the otherworldliness draining from him. "I'm trying not to think of it, in case…" He trailed off. The emotion in his eyes knocked the breath out of her. "But yes, I do. I like to think they will have your eyes. And fierceness."

"Let's hope they don't inherit my pyromancy," she said. "Or don't you remember me accidentally setting the drapes on fire?" It had been when her magic was first coming in—and before she'd realised the link between her emotions and pyromancy. Illusion worked differently.

"I do, yes."

She gave him an accusing look. "Now I think about it, that fire extinguished remarkably easily." Almost as if someone with air magic had been present at the time. "You wouldn't happen to know anything about that?"

A teasing light came into his eyes, a relief to see him so present and not distracted by the scenery. "Think how useful I will be if they *have* inherited fire magic."

"Well, if he or she inherits the ability to accidentally start hurricanes, I'm going to blame you."

What would their child be like? On a superficial level, Hetta found she rather hoped they would inherit *Wyn's* deep russet eyes and mild temper, now that the idea had been put into her head. How strange, to think of a person-to-be, a combination of both her and Wyn. Or maybe they'd be entirely different to their parents. She let herself spread a hand over her still-flat stomach, feeling simultaneously a bit soppy and a bit ridiculous. It still didn't quite seem real.

And yet, the thought of losing this undefined child, however abstract… She swallowed, her fingers curling into a fist.

The grassy plains were interrupted by a series of rock formations. The transition wasn't as abrupt as the previous one. Though the rocks had risen out of the grass between one step and the next, she could still see the grassy plains stretching behind them when she looked, and at least they were still under the same starlit sky. They drew up before a great cairn of stones, piled several storeys high. There was no path up its steep, reddish sides; they'd have to go around it.

That was when the horde arrived.

It ought to have been impossible for anyone to sneak up on them in this landscape, but there was scarcely any warning. One moment, the rush of hoofbeats and heavy bodies and the crushing of grass stems thundered; the next, riders were rushing down the hill towards them. Hetta suspected Faerie geography was at work again. Of course.

Wyn reacted faster than she did, changing to his fae form, his wings spreading in a combination of shield and challenge, and the air grew thick with storms and spice. His feathers shouldn't have been so bright in the moonlight, nor his skin so vivid a brown, but it was as if power had lit him up from the inside, painting him with his own personal daylight.

The charge of bodies split and flowed around them, hemming them in against the cairn. Hetta summoned a fireball, which gave the horde pause, their horses pulling up restlessly.

'Horde' had been the first word that had sprung to mind, and it continued to be an apt enough descriptor even on closer inspection. The riders were as many and varied as the fae she'd seen at the DuskRose ball, but there was a wilder, sharper edge to them. Possibly because they were all clearly armed.

They were all mounted, apart from those that were their own mounts. *Centaurs*, she thought in amazement, taking in one huge equine woman, bare-breasted, her hair a long, free-flowing mane down her back. A dark-skinned man—fae—rode what seemed to be an ordinary horse until it snorted, showing sharp fangs. The man bared his own fangs in concert with his mount. Enormous black hounds with glowing red eyes crept forward between the horses.

The temperature—which had been that of a mild summer evening—plummeted, and steam curled visibly in the air as the hounds panted and the horses pawed at the ground. Hetta shivered, and a woman who seemed to be the leader approached. She rode a great stag-like creature with glowing red eyes. The woman had startlingly pale skin, branching horns, and red hair that streamed out around her, the colour of blood. Her eyes burned like coals.

"Trespassers," she said. She smiled. Her teeth gleamed bone white. The wind had picked up at some point in the last thirty seconds, howling like a pack of wolves, and sending the woman's bloody hair whipping dramatically about her. Surely that sort of perfectly timed weather couldn't be natural? Did Faerie weather respond to melodrama? Heavens forfend.

"These are unclaimed lands; we do not trespass," Wyn said, and he blazed bright and tall as his wings spread further. The smell of his magic swirled thickly around them. The horde broke into raucous laughter at that, led by the red-haired woman.

Hetta swallowed and put a bit more power into her hovering fireball.

"We're not looking for trouble," she said, and her voice came out thinner than she'd like. "We're just passing through. Let us go on our way and we won't interfere with you either."

The woman's smile only grew wider, and the hounds crept closer. Their teeth seemed to get even larger and more prominent. The stars dimmed, the night growing darker, the wind fanning her hair out like a crimson halo.

"Look—this is madness. You might be able to hurt us, but not without some of you getting hurt yourselves. Surely we can—" Hetta babbled, but she could feel it was too late, that it had been too late from the moment the horde had found them, that there were no words in the world that would've checked them because that was what they were: wildness and bloodthirst given form.

"Yes," said the woman, and the horde attacked.

Hetta called fire. Wyn acted in concert, taking control of the air currents without hesitation, and her fire fanned out to form a tall, flickering wall between them and the horde. Hetta had expected the horde to leap back, but instead the raucous laughter rose to a crescendo full of metal and cruelty, and their eyes glowed a fiercer red. And then the horde were on fire too—flames not of Hetta's making but a glow of their own red malevolence.

The woman kneed her stag through Hetta's wall of flames. The fires caressed her lovingly, her hair a torrent of burning crimson that kept burning even after she had passed through.

They were fireproof. How was that fair?

"Let's fly," Wyn said, his voice tight as he pulled her against him. But before he could take off, the world was moving—wait, no, not the world, the cairn, up and up and up, with a sound like metal scratching glass.

The thing that wasn't a cairn uncurled, higher than a castle, filling the sky with golden scales. Two slits opened, revealing enormous blue eyes, and the dragon spread vast wings with a roar that shook the earth.

Hetta wasn't really one for hysteria, but she screamed when the dragon's neck snapped down and snatched one of the hounds in its jaws, which had time only for one cut-off squeal before the dragon swallowed it whole.

"Hold on," Wyn said, and then they were airborne in a rush of cardamom and storms. Hetta clung to his neck, her stomach lurching.

The dragon looked up.

Was it going to follow them? But instead it did something only slightly less alarming: it spoke, in a voice like gravel.

"The youngest prince." It made a sound like an avalanche, and she flinched until she realised it was chuckling. "Dragons make excellent godparents, stormchild. Give my regards to your mother."

The dragon turned back to the horde, who were trying to flee, and roared. There was another squeal, and a crunch of bone. Hetta buried her face against Wyn's neck. They flew higher.

26

UNEXPECTED DUKES

Jack was saddling his cob, determined to be out and away from too many people asking too many daft questions when he heard the stableboy call out in surprise: "Mr Gregory!"

Frowning, he put down the saddle and peered out into the stableyard. The hive of activity had temporarily paused in the wake of the stableboy's words, except for the horses, who continued to stamp and whicker as his young cousin came into view, lugging a trunk with both hands. Gregory had a sheepish air about him, which was bloody appropriate since as far as Jack knew he ought to be miles south of here in Knoxbridge.

"Greg!"

Gregory turned towards him and flushed. "Oh. Jack."

"What in blazes are you doing here?"

Gregory rocked back and forth on his heels and then said in a rush, "I've been rusticated. I hitched a lift from the station with Mr Brown." Mr Brown was the local home farmer, who gossiped like a fishwife. Gregory's expression said he was well aware of this and not especially pleased to think every inhabitant of the estate would soon know of his unplanned return.

"Rusticated," Jack repeated. He pushed out of the stall and re-latched it behind him.

"Only till the end of term!" His shoulders came up. "But maybe I won't go back." He looked like he expected Jack to argue with him, or at least disapprove loudly, but Jack wasn't his father or brother, dammit. And Lady Phoebe would fuss fine enough for anyone.

"You see anything at the station?" Jack glanced reflexively at the sky, but there was no sign of a winged figure.

At Gregory's blank look he added, "Didn't Marius tell you Aroset was on the loose?"

Gregory frowned. "Rakken seemed to think she'd show in Knoxbridge rather than here."

Did he now? Why the bloody hell hadn't he said anything? Jack disliked Wyn's secretive nature, but he at least generally had good intentions. Jack had no such faith in Rakken.

"Maybe Marius ought to come back too then."

"He can't; he has classes to teach. Plus he has to go see the earl." Gregory looked at him hopefully, as if Jack had anything at all to add on that subject. Jack hadn't the foggiest why the earl would want to talk to Marius specifically, though Hetta had said something vaguely about an interview.

"Marius all right though?"

Gregory blinked. "Yes?" he said uncertainly, as if it hadn't occurred to him to consider his older brother's mental state. "Same as ever. He doesn't like Rakken much."

"No one likes Rakken much."

Gregory gave him a jaded look that made him wonder exactly what mischief the fae prince had gotten into in the past week and a half. "Yes, they do. They don't know he's fae though. He's passing himself off as visiting royalty from the continent." He looked up at the face of the house. "Hetta's still not back?"

"No." Why did everyone keep asking Jack this, as if he had her hiding under his other coat?

Greg fidgeted with the handle of his trunk, looking up at the face of the house with trepidation. "Is, um, my mother home?"

Jack shrugged. "No idea. I've not been inside since breakfast. But no reason she shouldn't be."

"Right." Gregory paused, as if hoping Jack might offer to accompany him. Jack would rather be dragged by wild horses.

He grinned and made a shooing motion. "Good luck breaking the news, pup."

Gregory glared at him and, to Jack's surprise, made a vulgar gesture before hitching his trunk up again. Jack was half-impressed with his boldness and half-irritated that his young cousin wasn't quite as respectful as he'd been before leaving home.

It was with some satisfaction that he heard a chorus of voices exclaim and demand explanations as Gregory attempted to sneak in the back door at the same time as several of his cousins were heading out. Jack ducked quickly back into the stables, not wishing to get involved. The hubbub disappeared back into the bowels of the house.

It only occurred to him after Gregory had left that he hadn't asked why he'd been sent down from university for the rest of the term. Inevitably, he thought glumly, it was something to do with the fairies. No doubt he'd hear about it sooner rather than later, but hopefully he could avoid being pulled into his aunt's tearful recriminations. He didn't have much patience for Lady Phoebe when she got all teary eyed; Gregory could bloody well deal with that by himself.

The day was overcast, but it didn't feel like rain was coming when he stretched out with his land-sense. The Indigoes got a prickly sort of feeling before storms, and there was none of that now. Something that wasn't quite unease but the echo of it came back to him through the bond. Stariel always had more restlessness to it whenever Hetta was absent from the estate. Maybe he'd hack over to the Thornfield and see how the new flock was faring.

Jack had saddled his horse, and freedom was so close he could taste it when Old Buddle tottered out into the stableyard.

"My apologies, sir, but the Duke of Callasham is here."

For a moment Jack thought he'd misheard. When you lived on one of the most far-flung estates in the North, high-ranking Southern nobles didn't exactly drop in casually for tea.

Buddle coughed. "He asked to speak to Lord Valstar. I've shown him to the Red Drawing Room, sir."

The Duke of Callasham wasn't just a Southern noble, Jack remembered suddenly; he was also Lord Greymark. Which meant it wasn't so strange for him to appear here now, not with the Lords Conclave just around the corner. Probably Penharrow had invited him to his house party.

Jack's heart sank because this all seemed like a lot of politics. Bloody Rakken. What was the point of playing host to fae royalty if they couldn't damn well be there when you needed them? The prince might have been of some use here at last. Typical that he wasn't.

The duke stood by the window considering the view towards the rose garden, but he turned at Jack's entrance. He was a portly man in his mid-fifties, dark-skinned with tightly curled hair, evidence of the strong Noorish blood in the Callasham line. His clothing was fussier than Jack preferred, a reminder of everything he disliked about Southerners.

Through the window behind the duke, Jack spied a glimpse of Ivy on the far side of the garden, sitting knitting on a bench next to where the Gate had opened. There hadn't been any sign of activity since Gwendelfear, but one or other of them frequently found reason to check it anyway.

His relief at seeing the Gate guarded faded as he caught sight

of another and entirely unwanted presence in the rose garden. Ms
Orpington-Davies was striding down the garden path towards Ivy,
notebook in hand. Damn the reporter. He'd told her to get off
Valstar lands. She'd not only paid absolutely no attention to this
directive, but also her byline had appeared beneath a pointed article
headlined LORD VALSTAR IN HIDING?

*I'm going to cart that damn woman to the station myself, and never
mind that she's a female.*

But it would have to wait till he got rid of Callasham.

"I was expecting Lord Valstar," the duke remarked as Jack introduced himself. Callasham looked him up and down, and Jack
became acutely conscious that he'd just come from the stables.

"She's unavoidably detained," Jack hedged, hoping the duke
wouldn't ask further questions.

"It seems a lengthy condition. Has she become an invalid?"

Jack decided it was best to avoid answering this. "What brings
you here, your grace? Are you joining Penharrow's house party?"

"No," Callasham said. "It makes no odds to me if she's accepted
into the Conclave or not, though I cannot fathom Penharrow's decision to gamble on such a flighty wench. I'm here not to represent
my own interests but the Crown's. Lord Valstar failed to respond
to the last message she was sent, and the queen is out of patience
with her."

Jack thought guiltily of the courier's still-unopened message. It'd
slipped his mind, between one thing and another; he'd assumed
Hetta would be back soon enough it wouldn't matter. Yet here
she was, still missing. What in Prydein was she still doing in
Faerie, anyway?

Still, 'flighty wench' was uncalled for. "You're in my cousin's
house; I'll thank you not to refer to her that way." Jack had called
Hetta far worse things, but that was different. That was family.

The door to the sitting room creaked open a fraction. Jack frowned when it didn't open any further—was one of his cousins trying to eavesdrop? But a small black shape slipped confidently into the room and trotted across the carpet, tail erect. Those bloody kittens.

The duke said sharply, "Enough shilly-shallying, boy. Where is—gah!" Callasham broke off as a small black demon darted towards his legs and tapped his shins with a paw before flitting away, hissing.

"My apologies," Jack said reluctantly, though inwardly he had a lot of sympathy for the cat. He scooped up the kitten, which growled in protest, and dumped it out of the room, shutting the door properly this time.

"Her Majesty wishes for assurances from Lord Valstar that the treaty she promised with the fae will in fact eventuate before the Meridon Ball. Which is now less than three weeks away." Every overly rounded vowel chipped from ice. Jack knew his own accent had more of a Northern burr to it than his mother would prefer, but he didn't care. The duke could emphasise his lineage all he liked; the Valstar line was still older than Prydein itself.

Jack was angry enough that the duke's words didn't immediately penetrate. When they did, his thoughts jerked to a grinding halt. What the hell had Hetta promised the queen? She was in no position to be offering treaties with fae courts, not since Wyn had renounced his claim to the throne of ThousandSpire!

Oh. That had happened *after* Hetta and Wyn spoke to the queen in Meridon, and they'd clearly chosen not to keep Her Majesty informed about the current situation in the Spires. Which put Jack in a damned difficult position. Again!

"That's the reason for Hetta's current absence," he said at last and with great reluctance. He couldn't exactly lie directly to his sovereign, could he? "She's in the Faerie Realm. But don't ask me for more details than that, because I don't have them."

The duke's eyes brightened in a way that Jack found unsettling, but his tone remained arctic. "That is an unsatisfactorily vague answer, given Her Majesty's deadline."

"Well, it's all the answer I can give you. Good day, your grace." Jack stood. He was being rude, but if he had to stand here and talk politics for one more second, he risked being much ruder.

Callasham rose with narrowed eyes but didn't object as Jack opened the door for him and escorted him back to the entryway. To his irritation, Ms Orpington-Davies was there, arguing with Buddle. Simultaneously, a chatter of angry voices sounded from the hallway to the billiards room, where someone had evidently left a door open.

"What the hells do you mean, Hetta's breeding?" Gregory's voice, too loud, echoing down the hallway and amplifying in the entryway.

Ms Orpington-Davies looked up. Her eyes gleamed.

Oh, fuck me, Jack thought.

THE TOWER

WYN FLEW THEM into daylight, following the thin line of the tracking spell. The boundary between mosaics was as thin as a wingbeat, and the air smelled of the sea. The salty tang echoed in his soul, awakening an old memory too faint to recall, but the association was pleasant, whatever it was. The world blazed with magic, pricks of it settling at the base of every feather, winding around his body like vines as he flew, as if he'd taken shot after shot of whiskey.

His heart raced and not only with recent fear. He'd flown with Hetta once before, but that only for a few downstrokes, to escape Aroset. This was…something else. He risked a glance downwards; her eyes were sparkling, and it eased the tightness in his chest.

"I'm losing all sense of whether it's morning, noon, or night," she said against his neck.

He set them down on the clifftop. Beyond it stretched a sparkling azure sea, the white crests of waves breaking on the cliff below.

"I think we're far enough away—I cannot sense the Hunt anymore. Or the dragon." The vastness of those golden wings unfurled in his mind's eye, leaving him feeling quite inadequate in comparison. The dragon had been an old, old fae, its power deep enough that Wyn hadn't dared to use his leysight.

Hetta turned a slow circle, examining their surroundings. Below the cliffs, sprites danced in the waves, teasing sea nymphs, who flashed their fins when they saw Wyn watching. Far in the distance, an island rose in a tall, thin needle of stone rising straight from the sea. Between the island and the cliff, the back of something vast breached the surface with a spray of seafoam before disappearing beneath the water. The sight made the hair on the back of his neck stand on end.

"The geography isn't consistent," Hetta grumbled.

"These are the deepest realms of Faerie. Consistency is optional."

"Did a dragon really just offer to be a godparent?"

"I—yes. Yes, I think they did." His legs gave out, and he sagged down to the ground with a choke of laughter. A *dragon*. High King's horns. A true dragon! He'd never thought to see one.

Hetta began to laugh as well. She joined him on the ground, and they clung to each other, shaking with either amusement or hysteria until their limbs grew weak. He pulled her into his lap, holding her close, holding her safe.

Hetta picked at his robes. "And your mother?"

He blinked down at her.

"What the dragon said about her."

He was still entirely at sea. "What did the dragon say about her?"

Hetta looked at him strangely. "To give her its regards."

"Oh." Had it? Surely he would've remembered such a thing? But the import of Hetta's words hit him. "She's alive, then." If he hadn't already been sitting, the dizziness would have grounded him. "She's alive."

He'd always believed that to be the case, or rather *wanted* to believe it. But if she were alive, what had stopped her from return-ing to them? And where was she? If the dragon knew, did that mean she was here, in Deeper Faerie?

His thoughts grew tangled and difficult, and he clamped down hard on his leysight, struggling to focus. What had he been think-ing of? Deeper Faerie. He lifted his head and stared out to sea, to the narrow needle of the island in the distance.

He took out the tracking spell, gripping it tightly until the stone filaments dug into his palms. "That's where Irokoi is."

Hetta's expression was oddly gentle, and she hugged him tightly before sitting back and saying, "I suppose that only makes sense. Having defeated a dragon to win your hand, scaling a tower is clearly the only logical next step. There always seem to be towers in fairy tales, when one is rescuing princesses—I assume the same applies to princes."

He supposed the island did resemble a tower, though a natural one. "Defeated a dragon?" he queried.

"We got past it, didn't we? I'm fairly certain that counts."

"I had not previously considered myself the damsel in distress in this scenario."

Hetta patted his hand. "I shall do my best to heroically sweep you off your feet."

In answer, he swept her off *her* feet, hauling them both up. She squawked in surprise and clutched at his neck. "Hold on," he told her.

"You enjoyed doing that entirely too much," she accused.

"'Pregnant women are known to experience bouts of vertigo'," he quoted, hugging her close. "'A strong masculine supporting hand may be needed at these times'."

He took off amid the sound of Hetta's giggles and her vow that she was going to burn that dashed book when they returned. His muscles strained before he found the right rhythm and balance with Hetta in his arms. The sea air caressed his feathers with each downstroke, warm and buoyant.

He leaned on his air magic for height, thinking of the vast creature he'd seen breaching the waves. Whatever it was, he did not wish to fly too close to it.

The island was farther than he'd estimated, and as they drew closer, its true height became apparent. Wyn bore straight upwards in powerful strokes that made his wings burn. Exhilaration sang through his blood, and a laugh of sheer delight bubbled out of him. Magic came at his call, thick and potent, and he rode the winds he was born to, climbing to dizzying heights before he levelled off above the island, curling the air around Hetta protectively. He could handle a certain amount of oxygen deprivation; she couldn't.

Hetta swivelled to look down on the island, its top a rock-coloured disc at this distance that appeared almost perfectly flat. In its centre, a circular darkness gleamed like a fisheye.

"So where do we think Irokoi is? It looks fairly barren."

"There's an opening in the ground." His eyesight was keener than hers, but he wasn't exactly sure what the opening in the otherwise flat surface of the rock tower led to. A cave, maybe? He stretched out with his leysight and hissed at its brightness. "I think it's a Gate. It's active, wherever it leads." That had to be where Irokoi was; there wasn't anywhere else to *be* on the island; the sharp shape of the rock tower was smooth, hiding no other openings. "Hang on," he said apologetically. "I've given us an excessive amount of height; the dive will be steep."

Lightning hovered on the edge of awareness, and he pushed the temptation away.

It wasn't temptation. Charge abruptly sizzled towards them, and he banked to avoid it. Hetta's grip spasmed, and the terrible scent of copper and old-fashioned roses swamped him.

"Wyn—there!"

Rising like a crimson arrow from behind the tower was Aroset. He was too far away to see her expression, but he swore he could *feel* her triumph. He had the benefit of height on her, but he was losing it rapidly, and she was between them and the island. How was she here, in Deeper Faerie? How could she have followed them? She couldn't have used DuskRose's Gate.

But perhaps, he thought with a deep chill, she didn't need Gates anymore.

"You're going to have to be fast with your dive," Hetta said against his neck. She freed one of her hands, and when Aroset had covered half the distance between them, fog poured fourth in a torrent and surrounded his sister, obscuring her from view. Aroset shrieked in outrage, but Wyn didn't hesitate. He folded his wings and let gravity take hold of them again.

Lightning tore through the air, and the world became white with fog, but Aroset couldn't see him, or the ground, or anything well enough to risk herself in a steep dive from this height.

Of course, he couldn't see anything either. Hetta's illusions weren't glamour, and no amount of effort would allow him to see through them.

But *Hetta* could, and she snuffed the fog out of existence just in time. He flared his wings with a wrench of protest, pulling up cushions of air to halt their momentum just before they hit the Gate. They fell, the world tilting as the Gate transported them, and Wyn flared out his wings again, holding Hetta tightly.

They hit stone, and Wyn winced at the impact. It wasn't his most graceful landing, but, on the brighter side, it wasn't his *least* graceful either. He folded his wings behind him and set Hetta down, looking to see if Aroset had followed.

She hadn't.

Far, far above, like looking up from the bottom of a well,

greenish light shone through a multi-faceted glass dome. A single pane showed blue sky rather than green glass, and a tiny, indistinct face with pale hair peered through.

"Why isn't she following us?"

Wyn couldn't see Aroset's expression at this distance, but he knew, somehow, that she was staring directly at him. Cold crept down his spine.

"She knows something we don't." He put out an arm and stepped them both back and out of Aroset's sight, behind the thick supportive columns and into what appeared to be dimly lit shelves of books. The circular room they were in was at the bottom of many, many floors, connected by winding stone staircases that left the central shaft clear, looking all the way up to that glass dome far above, the only source of light.

He thought of pulling up his leysight to try to figure out where they were, but some instinct said, very strongly, *no*, and one didn't live to a ripe old age in Faerie by ignoring such things.

"This place is old. Very old," he murmured.

"A library," Hetta said, touching a finger to the nearest spines. "Marius would love this. How many floors do you think it goes up for?"

"Too many." Wyn flexed his wings, uneasy.

Footsteps on stone floors. They turned. Irokoi was walking down the stairs from the level above, into the central atrium. Lights flared to life in his wake, pale feylights set into stone sconces along the walls.

Irokoi beamed at them. "Oh, good, you found me. Do you have a plan to get out? That Gate is one-way only."

28

BENEATH THE WAVES

IT HAD BEEN a long time since he'd seen his oldest brother in the flesh. Irokoi looked…entirely himself, and much too relaxed for someone who'd been trapped in Deeper Faerie for who knew how long. Irokoi was as casually unkempt as always, wearing thin gloves but no shoes, and his silver hair hung long and unbound, a sharp contrast against his dark feathers and horns. His expression was open, mismatched eyes wide and guileless, but Wyn wasn't foolish enough to believe it. Irokoi used frankness as camouflage. There was no sense of magic about him, but that too meant nothing; Irokoi had used astral projection to appear in Meridon, a magic so strong and subtle Wyn wouldn't have credited it but for the evidence of his own eyes.

Wyn had half an urge to embrace him, checked by wariness and the adrenalin of Aroset's pursuit still pumping through him.

"Koi, where are we?" he said, instead. The room wasn't circular as he'd first thought, but seven-sided. Seven thick stone supporting columns. Magically significant numbers.

"The floor is a map," Hetta said, sounding odd.

Wyn looked down. She was right. The floor of the atrium was a mosaic of colourful tiles and gems, stretching out in all directions and forming not random shapes but geography.

"It's a map of Faerie," Wyn murmured, awed. It wasn't a static map either, moving so subtly that it was hardly noticeable. Faelands moved relative to each other, faster in some places and hardly at all in others, like a series of sluggish dominoes sliding around each other.

He moved out of the shadows, heedless of what Aroset might or might not see, and found what he was looking for before he even realised he was searching. He knelt, feathers brushing the stone as he placed a hand on a patch of red-and-white tiles. Magical shadows moved across the surface like clouds, obscuring the details: the curse. "ThousandSpire," he murmured. He looked up at his brother. "What do you know about the curse?"

"So you don't know the way out, then?" Irokoi said, his face falling as he looked between them. "Ah, well, I suppose it was too much too hope. Follow me, then." He gestured at the staircase.

"What if Aroset follows us?" Hetta asked uneasily, looking up at the Gate above.

"Then we'll have more of a family reunion than I anticipated just yet. But I don't think she wishes to risk being trapped," Irokoi said.

Wyn couldn't share his brother's calm. "Is Set good enough with portals to penetrate here without a Gate?" he asked.

"It is a very inconvenient gift the Maelstrom has given her, though even she has limits. If she could have made a portal in here, she already would have." Irokoi huffed. "She thinks I know how to free the Spires from stasis."

"And do you?" he asked. His fingers still rested on the shadow rippling over the red-jewelled mosaic. His chest tightened.

Irokoi tilted his head. "Yes. Although knowing and doing are two different things, so it wouldn't help Aroset much even if I told her, which I wasn't planning to."

"Will you tell us?"

"And just what were you planning to do if ThousandSpire *is* freed from the curse, hmmm?" Irokoi asked. "You gave up your claim to it; you cannot take that back, and faelands don't do well without rulers for long. Better to leave it be, brother, guilty conscience or not."

That was an excellent question, and one Wyn had been avoiding thinking too hard about. "We need ThousandSpire's ruler to approve our union, and it cannot choose a new one whilst in stasis," he told Irokoi, rising from his crouch. "Maybe it will reconsider its choices." It had to, didn't it? He'd never heard of a faeland refusing to choose *anyone*, and there wasn't anyone else left of the bloodline but his siblings.

Irokoi smiled in a satisfied way, as if Wyn were a dim student who'd unexpectedly given the exact right answer. "Interesting. Perhaps I will help you then."

He began to walk away, his footsteps echoing loudly in the hushed stillness of this place.

Wyn exchanged a glance with Hetta, and they hastened to follow Irokoi. There was something here…something that unsettled him down to his bones, magic so thick he could taste it, a signature too complex to parse. Too strong, as if each of his senses had been sharpened to the point of painfulness. He couldn't think properly under the weight of the magic. He changed.

Or—tried to.

For the first time in his life, there was nothing there to change *in*to, no other side of himself. He stumbled, catching himself on the balustrade.

"Wyn?" Hetta's voice, concerned.

He closed his eyes, trying and failing once more. "I can't change back to my mortal form."

It was like discovering a limb was missing. He kept reaching and finding nothing to grasp with.

"Koi, can you…?" Wyn couldn't actually remember the last time he'd seen Irokoi in his mortal form.

Irokoi blinked at him. "Oh. You want to know if I can change?" He pursed his lips.

"*Can* you?" Wyn repeated urgently.

Irokoi tilted his head to the side, still looking puzzled at Wyn's reaction. "I am older and more settled than you are, so I imagine I could, yes. But I think it would be a very bad idea to try, here and now. Don't you know where we are? Can't you hear it?"

The terrible thing was that Wyn almost knew what Irokoi meant; there was something like a song here, a hum of magic plucking at every nerve, a tune he almost recognised.

"Or you could just tell us?" Hetta suggested.

"This is a place for deep truths," Irokoi said with an impish grin and kept walking.

Deep truths. Wyn held his wings tight against his back, the rustle of feathers disconcertingly loud. What part of being stuck in his fae form was a deep truth? He wanted to argue with that unsubtle insinuation. Why should this form be any more or less true than the other?

At least Irokoi had suggested the effect was limited to this place, which meant Wyn had only to cope until they found a way out. He could do that. Hetta squeezed his hand, her eyes too knowing.

They followed Irokoi up flights of stairs, around and around the many floors of the library. The presence of so many books had a muffling effect, the resulting quietness oppressive. There were desks set aside for non-existent researchers, and a reading room on one of the floors complete with feylights. There was no dust.

"Are there other people here?" Hetta asked.

Irokoi shook his head. "Only us, now."

Wyn was about to suggest they fly the rest of the way up, since there were still many storeys left to climb, when Irokoi led them away from the stairs towards a wide archway.

"This is the ground floor, sort of," Irokoi said before Wyn could ask. "The library is half above and half below, and we do not want to climb all the way up to Aroset, even if she could see us."

"She can't?"

Irokoi shook his head. "There's an obscuring spell on the Gate. You must have noticed it was rather dark when you looked in?"

"We were in something of a rush," Wyn said drily.

Irokoi led them through to wide stone hallways, the ceilings so high it felt almost as free as open sky above—except for the whispers of the magic, like voices on the edge of hearing. Wyn kept turning his head to catch them, but instead there was only a faint shell-hush, almost like distant waves.

Fae statues three times larger than life stared down at them, the seven-fold architectural patterns of the library tower repeated in the way they were arranged. Each one was unique, as if to showcase the full diversity of forms fae could take. *Which rather clashes with the idea of form as a deeper truth*, he thought, glaring at the statues. Especially since the statues were of *one* individual.

"Who are they?" Hetta asked, briefly touching the chilly stone hand of a woman with antlers and four sets of eyes.

"The High King," Irokoi answered.

"*All* of them?"

"He can take whatever form he wishes. Though probably not all at once."

Depictions of the High King weren't uncommon in Faerie architecture, but this place, speaking right to his bones in a language more primal than words… "Koi, where are we?" Wyn asked again.

"The High King's library."

"Is he here?" Hetta asked.

"No." Irokoi flicked his fingers on the knees of a gigantic androg-ynous figure with the lower half of a goat. "I was looking for answers, but I think I was tricked into coming here so I'd stay put and be safe."

Hetta frowned. "What makes you say that?"

"I wouldn't have locked *myself* in with all these memories; I'm not quite that feather-brained."

Hetta kept asking questions with increasing impatience; Irokoi kept giving his typically circular answers. Wyn knew he ought to be trying to help wring some sense out of his brother, but the song of the magic here hummed through him, increasing in volume the longer they walked, and it was as if he were hearing their conversa-tion through water.

They reached a heavy set of entrance doors that pushed open with smooth ease at only a touch from Irokoi.

"And what does that mean, exactly—" Hetta broke off as she stepped through the doors, jerking to a halt on the paving stones beyond. Wyn was a step behind her, and his wings half-flared in panic as he beheld what lay outside.

It wasn't the fact that the stone building they'd exited, though large, wasn't yet large enough to contain the many storeys and hall-ways they'd wandered through, its largest tower not nearly high enough. Wyn could cope with buildings of impossible internal dimension; he'd taken a tape measure to many of Stariel House's rooms, after all. Nor was the neatly planted terrace overlooking the ornamental lake worthy of much note under the circumstances.

No, it was that the entire thing was underwater.

"Faerie geography," Hetta said in wonder.

Wonder was not Wyn's primary emotion. Transparent walls rose at the edges of a neat garden, curving to encase the building, grounds, and ornamental lake within an immense bubble. Schools of fish swam past beyond the boundary, seemingly oblivious, and further out, shapes moved in the ocean's shadows, ominous and indistinct. There was a strong salty tang to the air.

Wyn looked up and gulped. No sky; nowhere to fly. Only green, directionless light making it impossible to tell how far beneath the surface they stood.

Hetta touched his arm, an anchor point. He closed his eyes and made sure he was looking at his feet when he opened them. The paving stones were a soft golden colour, matching the architecture of the Library's exterior. Right. He moved his attention: a series of bronze urns set along the front of the building, holding geometric topiary. The ornamental lake at the bottom of the steps, its surface preternaturally still. He supposed wind wasn't an issue.

The lakes edges stopped at the bubble, dark lake water held separate from the murkier greenish sea without. *A lake at the bottom of the sea*, he thought and looked up again. A small sound of protest emerged despite himself.

No sky! How had Koi borne it without going utterly mad? Although—maybe he hadn't. Hard to say.

"Yes, I suppose it's a bit surprising," Irokoi said, gazing placidly up at the bubble.

Hetta let go of Wyn's arm and stepped cautiously 'outside' into the strange underwater garden.

"How does it work?" she asked. "How deep are we?"

"Magic, and I don't know."

Wyn stayed where he was and called plaintively after Hetta, "Are you *sure* you don't wish to keep leaning on my arm? It makes me feel useful."

"I'll let you know when I require further coddling." She padded curiously down to the lake's edge.

Sorrow crept into his heart, an emotion so absolute it stilled him. Or it would have if he hadn't already been rooted in place. Where was the emotion emanating from? It tangled with the magic in the air, heavy as the pressure before a storm, and he wanted to spread his wings, take Hetta up and go—but there was nowhere to go. Trapped. The word beat at him, his heart threatening to race. He breathed in, out. *I am not a bird to panic so.*

When he opened his eyes again, Hetta was still peering into the lake, and sorrow still hung on the world like ice. She went to dip the toe of her boot into the water, and Wyn was already moving, a cry of alarm on his lips, but it was too late, she was too close—

"Stop!" Midnight and frost bloomed on the air, and Irokoi's magic wrenched Hetta back from the edge, his hands making a clawing gesture. "Don't touch the lake," he said, releasing his magic, his expression cut from granite.

Hetta stumbled, off-balance with the motion, but Wyn was at her side and wrapped his arms around her. She let out a startled exhale, steadied herself on him.

Wyn narrowed his eyes at his brother. "Why don't you want Hetta to touch the lake?"

"Yes, and if you could explain without going all cryptic and unhelpful, that would be wonderful," Hetta added as she rearranged herself to stand beside him, though she tucked her arm into his.

Irokoi's expression grew sardonic. "Do not touch the lake, Lord Valstar, because there is an enormous lake guardian sleeping beneath the surface who has no love for mortals, and *especially* those of your bloodline, and it would be a very bad idea to wake it."

"Oh." Hetta frowned. "Wait—of my bloodline? You mean Valstars specifically?"

Irokoi's gaze didn't shift, but his blind eye glowed a fractured arctic blue. "Yes."

Wyn exchanged glances with Hetta. "Why?"

Irokoi didn't answer, and Hetta huffed at him. "You seem like you're trying to be difficult. Why won't you just tell us what you know?"

Irokoi cocked his head at Wyn. "I can see why you like the mortals. They're very direct."

Wyn sighed and made an effort to focus, the heavy magic and sorrow here still threatening to pull him into abstraction. He could do this. "Let me add my own directness then. You appeared to me in Meridon via astral projection—and let us set aside exactly when you gained that ability for the moment—and told me to pass a message to Cat. Following which, she flew straight into the heart of the Maelstrom just as the Spires fell under a curse. I recognise manipulation when I see it, Koi. What's going on? You said you knew how to free the Spires. Will you make me bargain with you for the information?"

Irokoi cocked his head to the side. "Lord Valstar has a nice house, or so I hear."

"I'm not giving you my house."

Irokoi burst into delighted laughter. It sounded louder than it should in the still air.

"I am not asking for your house, Lord Valstar. But take me to your house—to your faeland—and I will help you remove the curse from ThousandSpire." Irokoi looked thoughtfully at Wyn. "I will need to gather all the Spireborn who are left in order to do it properly."

A heaviness crept into Wyn. Did Irokoi know? He should, but Wyn hadn't felt Torquil's death from the Mortal Realm, so perhaps Irokoi hadn't either, trapped in Deeper Faerie. Wyn didn't want to tell him; until he did, there still existed a piece of the world where their brother was alive, even if that piece was only in Irokoi's fractured mind.

Wyn hadn't seen Torquil for more than ten years—and they hadn't been close. They'd never grow any closer, now. That knowledge tainted grief with prickling guilt, because he wasn't sure whether he was mourning Torquil so much as the idea of him; mourning for the fact that one of his siblings was capable of murdering another.

He struggled to say the words, but eventually they came out, cold and sharp as mountain flint.

"Torquil is dead."

Hetta squeezed his arm.

Irokoi didn't react as Wyn had expected. His expression grew sheepish. "Ah. No. He isn't, actually. Torquil is alive."

If the bubble had punctured then and sent a thousand tonnes of seawater raining down, it would have been less of a shock. Shock—Wyn stepped away from Hetta as his anger rose hard and fast. Lightning sparked over his feathers as he flared out his wings in challenge.

Irokoi's wings fanned out in response, black as the Void. But there was no sense of power rolling off him, his magic tightly leashed. Wyn couldn't say the same for his own, which was crackling in the air around him so strongly it overrode even the salty tang of the sea. He balled his hands into fists, struggling to find words.

Hetta put her hands on her hips and glared at Irokoi. "What do you mean he's alive?" The temper in her voice matched his own.

Irokoi folded his wings in, looking apologetic. "Ah—I sort of helped him fake his death."

"Aroset." Wyn's voice came out hard. "Rake and Cat believe she killed him. As did I."

"Well, it wouldn't be a very convincing trick if no one believed it, would it?"

"That's not funny," Hetta snapped. "How can you joke about something like that? Don't you care that—"

Irokoi lost all his boyish playfulness. Wyn sometimes forgot that Irokoi was oldest, older even than Aroset. Even now, Wyn couldn't gauge Irokoi's power; it was too tightly coiled.

"No, it isn't funny at all, but it was necessary. I have always done what was necessary, at no little cost to myself, Lord Valstar. Do not accuse me of a lack of compassion; that isn't my flaw."

"No, it's deliberate unhelpfulness," Wyn said, provoked beyond all bearing.

Irokoi whirled on him, words falling as blows. "Cat thought you might refuse the throne, and she wanted to know if there was a way to keep the Spires from going to Aroset if you made that choice. I knew of stasis, but I knew to make it work, a member of the royal blood would need to sleep alongside the faeland. I was looking for some alternative, to stop her making such a sacrifice, but I couldn't find one. And that, Hallowyn, is why Cat flew into the Maelstrom when she did, so which of us, exactly, has been unhelpful to this situation?"

The words hit Wyn as darts, puncturing his fury with painful sharpness. Cat had sacrificed herself for the Spires. *Because I failed her. She expected me to fail her.* The thought bit deep, giving old guilt new life, tiny thorns burrowing into sensitive flesh.

Irokoi ran a hand through his hair, temper fading as quickly as it had come. "I'm sorry. You *have* come to rescue me, after all, and I'm not ungrateful. Besides which, Cat's current situation is…not your fault, ultimately. She made her own choices." His expression was once again all boyish openness, and Wyn believed it even less than usual. "Do you forgive me for yelling at you?"

"There is nothing to forgive." Regardless of what Irokoi said, Cat *was* Wyn's fault. He wanted to wallow in guilt, but it felt too self-indulgent in the circumstances. No amount of wallowing would free Cat from the Spires, but untangling Irokoi's cryptic puzzle pieces might. "Why did you give me that message for Cat—why not tell her directly? And how were you able to perform an astral projection and speak to me from here all the way to the Mortal Realm?"

"Because I have too many of Mother's gifts," Irokoi said easily. "And because you were the only one I could reach. Perhaps it's because I am oldest and you are youngest. I enjoyed having a mirror.

Though I'm sorry you are stuck here too." He looked up at the top of the bubble, following the flickering movements of strange fish.

"Have you tried piercing the barrier?" Wyn didn't like to think of it, the weight of water the magic kept at bay, but if the choice was break it or be trapped, he would choose freedom. And he had air magic, after all.

Irokoi began to walk towards the bubble. Wyn and Hetta exchanged glances but slid into place behind him anyway.

"Can't he just answer questions normally?" Hetta complained, taking Wyn's arm. She looked tired, and she rubbed absently at her ring; he hoped she could draw some power from it, even as far as they were from Stariel.

"Koi?" he prompted, knowing his brother had heard.

"What is normality, when it comes down to it?" Irokoi said without pausing in his stride.

"I'm taking that as a 'no', then," Hetta said drily.

"He's always been like this," Wyn admitted. Why did Irokoi always have to speak in riddles? Others said it was because he was mad, that Aroset blinding him had broken something in him beyond repair, but Wyn didn't believe that. Astral projection was a subtle, complicated magic even Rakken wasn't yet skilled enough to pull off.

Although in fairness, Irokoi's projection had gone to Wyn rather than Catsmere as intended, so perhaps he was giving Koi too much credit.

As they walked along the shore of the terrible undersea lake, Wyn's gaze kept snagging on its smooth surface. Each time, a sharp, piercing sense of sorrow shot once again through his heart, easing each time he looked away.

"Why is the lake sad?" Hetta asked, surprising him. She felt it too? "Or is it the lake monster?"

"The lake guardian is a creature of sorrow," Irokoi said up ahead. "Well, that and anger, I suppose; I wasn't joking when I said you should avoid waking it, Lord Valstar."

Wyn stared at the dark waters, the guardian's sorrow clutching at him. Irokoi reached out a wing and trailed his leading primary along the surface of the water, the movement oddly deliberate.

"You're not worried about waking the lake monster?" Hetta asked.

"It won't speak to me."

Hetta blew out an exasperated breath.

They reached the bubble, and Wyn opened his leysight the merest fraction. The world lit up in incandescent brilliance, rainbows upon rainbows, slicing through him in fractal splendour.

He winced and hastily tamped it down.

Irokoi grinned at him. "If you were any less than you are, little brother, trying to see the wefts of this place would burn your eyes out. As it is, you need to have more patience. Like this, Hallowyn." He held out a hand. Wyn took it warily.

Irokoi extended a mental connection in addition to the physical one. Wyn hesitated. Did he trust Irokoi? Did he have much choice, given they were trapped here with him? Slowly, Wyn lowered his shields. The barest hint of Irokoi's signature: frost and the velvet of a storm gathering at midnight.

"Breathe," Irokoi instructed. "Let yourself feel the world, rather than charging in and demanding it show itself to you."

I wasn't aware leysight counted as a demand, Wyn thought, but tried to obey. What did he feel? He reached out with his senses, following the path Irokoi unfurled before him in his mind. He could hear the eerie stillness of the lake, the absence of the proper sounds a body of water should have made. Starwater always had a sound, even on the stillest of days—the small lapping of its edges on stone, waterbirds paddling, the occasional splash of a fish. This lake held only sorrow so intense it trapped the water itself in frozen paralysis. He could hear his own breaths, and Hetta and Irokoi's, the rhythm of his own heartbeat.

A sense of something whispering on the edge of hearing, a name he could almost catch—

"Who is Nymwen?" he said slowly. "The lake speaks the name," he added, for Hetta's benefit.

A tremor ran over Koi, and when he spoke it was so soft, Wyn had to strain to catch it. "Who knows?" His voice hardened. "But you are supposed to be listening to the barrier, not the lake."

Wyn tried again, concentrating. Between the soft whispering of a wind that didn't exist was wound…something else. Magic. It held the same sadness as the lake, and it surrounded them. He opened his eyes and let it seep into him, his leysight soft and insubstantial as thistledown.

The bubble became a web made of countless tightly interwoven threads that pulsed with magic—a magic that rang with sorrow and power.

"The High King laid this spell," he said, for Hetta's benefit. Not that he'd been in any doubt. Who else could be responsible for the magic here? But it was one thing to know this and another to feel it humming all around him.

Gingerly, he put out a hand and rested it on the bubble-spell. It flared at the touch. He pushed. It didn't budge, but the threads thickened and brightened until he was forced to look away.

"I don't think we can break it. It's absorbing any magic I use on it." He turned back to Hetta, extracting his hand from Irokoi's.

"That's actually somewhat reassuring to hear, given the amount of water above us," Hetta said. She swallowed as a vast shadow moved in the deep, entirely silent.

They watched as it drew closer. So that was what he'd seen the back of before, breaching the surface. A grey-skinned leviathan, walking on two tree-trunk legs, many teeth visible in its blunted snout, tail undulating silently in the murky waters. Wyn felt extremely vindicated in his choice to keep far from the waves.

"Can it see us?" Hetta asked, her voice higher pitched than normal.

"The spell keeps it out as much as it keeps us in," Irokoi said. Wyn knew he was trying to be reassuring, but it was still unnerving to see one great eye roll around and fix on them. The leviathan began to swim closer, vast webbed front feet kicking like an oversized frog's.

"Let's…go back inside," Wyn suggested, fighting the urge to flare his wings out in challenge.

"I completely agree," Hetta said fervently.

LORD ARRAN

J ACK FELT ILL at ease, riding out to meet the lords at the boundary with Penharrow. Of course, he'd imagined himself in the role of lord many times, but in none of those imaginings had he gotten farther than Stariel's border—certainly not as far as membership on the Conclave. Old Lord Henry hadn't bothered much with them. "A bunch of bantam roosters, too concerned with whose crow is loudest," he'd called them dismissively. "Stariel has no need for their approval. We were here before the Conclave was even a notion; they should look to us, not the other way around."

Easy for him to dismiss them, Jack reflected. Lord Henry's right to a place on the Conclave had never been questioned. It seemed both incredible that Hetta's might be up for debate and absolutely typical of his cousin to make things as complicated as possible. To be honest, if not for Angus's concern, he might've thought the whole problem an exaggeration; as it was, he was sure it would all be sorted out easily enough. Probably the other lords just wanted reassuring that Hetta wasn't mad as a hatter.

Though they wouldn't have debated my claim, if things had gone differently. The thought made him irritable, though why should he feel guilty for it? It wasn't like that had actually come to pass, and the

Conclave's attitude towards Hetta now wasn't his fault regardless.

He scanned the skies for Aroset, but there were only high wisps of cloud against the blue. He squinted, just in case it helped, but still nothing. Could be because there truly was nothing, or could just be that his Sight wasn't working today. That was magic for you; unreliable as weather.

Still, it was good to be out of the house. Far too many people had wanted things of him lately; answers he didn't have to questions that were only piling higher as time went on. Hetta damn well should've given more thought to what she was leaving behind before she'd gone skipping off to Fairyland. She'd seemed blithely sure that she wouldn't be gone for long, yet here she was, absent a fortnight and with no indication of when she was planning to return.

What if she didn't come back? What would that mean for him? Jack felt traitorous even thinking it, but it didn't stop the question popping into his mind in quiet moments. Not that there had been many of those; everyone wanted a piece of his time, from the house-keeper to the bloody village council. Land matters he could deal with, but how was he supposed to know about magic?

Jack drew up just short of the boundary and waited for the three riders to approach from the Penharrow side. Probably there wasn't much risk in crossing the boundary briefly, but he'd said he wouldn't, and more than that, that he'd look after Stariel while Hetta was gone. *Someone* had to put the land first. He reached out for Stariel, which twitched restlessly; it had been on high alert ever since Hetta had left. But at least it wasn't—well, it would know, wouldn't it, if there was anything to be worried about, even with Hetta so far away?

He recognised Angus at a distance, riding the roan cob he favoured. Jack scowled reflexively but managed to get his face in order by the time the party reached him. The other two men were strangers.

It was hard not to think of might-have-beens, when Angus introduced the older man as the Conclave's Chair, Lord Arran. He was somewhere in his sixties, short and wiry with thick grey hair, weather-tanned fair skin, and narrow, almost elongated features, as if someone had taken hold of his chin and crown and pulled them subtly apart.

"—and Lord Featherstone," Angus introduced the second man.

Jack took a closer look at Featherstone, darkly amused. He didn't look at all like Rakken, and Jack wondered if he'd heard the tale of the impersonation. Featherstone was younger than Arran, though he still looked as if he had a good couple of decades on Jack, with deep-set dark eyes, olive skin, and an unfashionably full beard.

Lord Featherstone's expression didn't give anything away, and he only nodded slightly in response to the introduction.

"You're old Lord Valstar's nephew," Lord Arran said, pulling Jack's attention back.

Jack felt oddly defensive, and his horse shifted its weight in response; he tightened the reins. "That's right."

"And you're the substitute for the new Lord Valstar, are you? Doesn't she have brothers?"

Jack had to take another moment to control his mount, and it was Angus who answered: "She does, but I believe Marius is away at present, and Jack's always been more involved with the estate. Shall we get on?"

Lord Arran made a disgruntled sound in the back of his throat but didn't object.

They rode. Blackbirds startled at the horses, hopping back under the hedgerows, the blackthorn budding with tiny white flowers. The breeze brought the smell of mud, crushed grass, and horse sweat, and the sun was almost hot on his back.

Stariel hung on Jack's shoulders as they picked their way past muddy fields towards the village. He eyed the rows of young plants with satisfaction; planting season had dragged on longer than it should've, thanks to a wet spell in mid-April, but they'd grown at a staggering rate since. The farmers were all saying it was the best growing season in living memory, typically turbulent April weather notwithstanding. Was that chance, or something else? Jack couldn't stop thinking of that apple tree Hetta had magicked into blossoming at unnatural speed.

"What are you growing, then?" Lord Arran asked.

"This lot is spring barley." Jack told him about the seed trials.

Lord Featherstone seemed interested. "Penharrow says Lord Valstar has been making considerable changes to the estate since she inherited."

"Aye," Jack agreed.

Lord Arran gave him a sidelong look. "I'd heard Stariel followed some odd inheritance laws. Must've been quite an upset for you all."

Jack grunted. "No more than usual. Shall we give the horses their heads? Good day for it." Jack might harbour his own personal feelings about Hetta's inheritance, but he'd be damned if he'd air them to a stranger.

This suggestion was met with tepid agreement, which was all Jack needed; he kneed his horse to a faster pace. The air rushed past, the beat of hooves and the rhythm cooling his blood somewhat by the time they neared the village and had to slow. The streets were busy, it being market day.

They dismounted at the village pub. The grizzled publican's wife looked the lords up and down with every sign of enjoyment, as if she were memorising the details to recount for later entertainment.

A pint of beer and a piece of lamb-and-kidney pie did wonders to improve Jack's mood, as did Angus turning the conversation towards sheep. Lord Arran had strong opinions on this, but he also knew what he was talking about, and Jack found himself in charity with the man.

He should've known things had been going too well to last.

"So what do *you* make of this fae business, Mr Langley-Valstar?" Lord Arran asked when the sheep conversation lulled.

Jack's uneasiness returned in full. "What fae business would that be, exactly?"

"Isn't your steward supposed to be one? A fairy prince, is what I've heard."

Jack shrugged. "He is, but it's hardly relevant most of the time."

Lord Arran scoffed. "That seems hard to believe."

"Believe what you will, my lord." Jack took a steadying gulp of his drink.

"And where is he today? I'd like to speak to him."

Damn Hetta for leaving him to answer awkward questions on her behalf. He cut a look at Angus; Angus was the one who'd talked him into this, after all, but Angus stayed quiet.

"On a leave of absence," Jack said reluctantly. "Not sure when he'll be back."

Lord Arran made a disapproving sound but dropped the subject. Or at least, so Jack hoped.

They went for a walk through the village after lunch. Villagers they passed eyed them interestedly and doffed their hats.

"So I see you've put in elektricity in the village? How did you justify the expense?" Lord Arran asked as they walked.

Jack eyed him with dislike. "You don't have it at Arran, then?"

"Oh yes; years ago."

Why the bloody hell are you asking me to justify it then?

"The inevitable tide of modernity comes for us all," Featherstone remarked, and it was impossible to tell whether he meant it approvingly or not.

The group dispersed amongst the market stalls around the green, and Jack thought it a reprieve until he heard Lord Arran's distinctive tones.

"And what do you make of this fae business, eh? Heard you have one as land steward." Bloody Lord Arran had turned his interrogation upon one of the tenant farmers who'd come to the market day.

"Mr Tempest?" the farmer asked cautiously.

"That's the fellow."

"Don't know anything about the fae business, but he's better than the last steward." Not high praise, since the last steward had actively embezzled from Stariel's accounts. But the farmer followed it up with, "Got our roof thatched soon as I told him it needed doing."

"And your new lord?" Lord Arran apparently saw nothing wrong with interrogating Hetta's people within earshot of Jack! The farmer's expression held an edge of incredulity, as if he too couldn't quite believe the nerve of the man. Jack came up deliberately to stand beside Arran, but the man gave no sign of embarrassment.

"She's ours, born and bred," the farmer said, and Jack made a grunt of agreement. "With all respect, your lordship, I've matters to be seeing to. Got a pig I said I'd take a look at."

Lord Arran drew himself up, clearly affronted at this lack of deference, but the farmer doffed his cap and left—leaving Jack to take the brunt of his ire.

"And your cousin? How long is she planning to avoid us for? Seems mighty convenient timing for her to become an invalid."

"She'll come to meet you as soon as she's able," Jack said stiffly. "And I'll thank you not to speak of her so."

"I suppose we all end up dancing to a woman's whims, one way or another," Lord Arran said, which gave Jack a strong desire to plant him a facer. "Put your back up, have I, young buck? I don't believe in sugar-coating things, and you can tell your Lord Valstar so, since you seem so tied to her apron strings. Tell her to stop cowering and come face me like a man. Though I can see that might be difficult," he added.

Things went further downhill from there.

JACK STUMPED BACK INTO the rose garden, still covered in horse-sweat from the blistering ride after the whole lords-debacle business.

Ivy, who'd been sitting on the nearby bench reading, took one look at his face and excused herself. When he was sure he was alone, he went to stand in front of the Gate. The glossy leaves of the dusken roses seemed to mock him in the afternoon sun.

"Bloody hurry up and come back!" he growled at the Gate. A sliver of guilt prompted him to add, "You can't blame me for putting their backs up; you're the one who left me in this lurch in the first place."

He shut up then, the absurdity of talking to himself catching up with him, and slumped down to sit on the bench Ivy had vacated. He reached out for Stariel; it seemed much as it had been earlier, and once again he tried to find that reassuring. Stariel would know if its lord was in danger, wouldn't it?

FEATHERS

To Hetta's relief, the library also contained bedrooms, presumably for the same non-existent academics who the empty reading room and desks were designed for. It made her extremely curious to know why the High King had built this place and if it had always been so empty.

When she woke, the first thing she did was check the heartstone. Its colour had definitely deepened, now a vivid cornflower blue. The second thing she did was look around for Wyn. She found him draped in a chair on the other side of the room. His wings were relaxed, spread carelessly over the low back, and he was frowning down at the leather-bound book in his hands. A strange, fond feeling curled around her heart. She'd never seen him arranged so artlessly in his fae form; he only went winged when there was some purpose to it.

She studied him, in the moments before he looked up, the man she was trying her hardest to marry. The father of the child she was trying her hardest to keep.

He wasn't human. He was as fae as this strange place of hushed whispers, as the leviathans in the deep and the dragons in the skies. As the blood butterflies had been. And she loved him.

She reached for Stariel through her ring, felt only a faint, thread-thin acknowledgement in return. How long had they been away, now? She'd lost all sense of time, but she thought it couldn't have been more than a day or so. Still, it was longer than she'd hoped to be gone.

Wyn looked up and lost all his artlessness with the motion. His wings rose higher, pressing more tightly against his spine, as if that would somehow make them disappear. "How are you feeling?"

She tested her stomach, found it hungry rather than seasick. "Good. Hungry." At least she'd figured out how to use her thin line of connection with Stariel to settle her nausea. Did that count as making progress with her land-sense?

Wyn produced an apple, putting the book aside to come to her side but retreating again before she could touch him.

"There are kitchens here," he told her. "And a pantry stocked for an army, with preservation spells enough to make me feel a poor housekeeper by comparison."

"So at least we won't be starving to death in our imprisonment." She eyed the apple suspiciously. "Eating it's not going to get me stuck here for a hundred years, is it?" she asked, remembering some of the fairy tales she'd heard as a child.

"We are already stuck." He told her of the exploring he'd done. "Koi has already tried a number of spells to try to break out. Though this is a library, so if the information exists anywhere, it's probably here."

"I take it making a second Gate out isn't as straightforward as I want it to be?"

He shook his head. "The problem is that one needs an anchor, and the anchor for a Gate spell is usually made at the destination and then brought to the origin point. As the dusken rose came to Stariel."

Hetta finished off the apple. "Is that the only method?"

He waved at the book he'd been reading. "Irokoi thinks we might be able to find an alternative, though I admit I have difficulty following his magery. That could be either his madness or my own poor knowledge of such things."

"Hmm." She got off the bed, went to find the facilities and spent a long moment watching running water emerge from a tap. Faerie plumbing. Perhaps it was best not to speculate how that worked when they were underwater.

When she returned to the room, Wyn had withdrawn back to his chaise. She walked over to him and he stilled, feathers flattening down. He wouldn't meet her eyes, but she climbed into his lap anyway, bringing their faces close together.

His eyes went dark and smouldery. Still, there was a hesitation to him as she traced the sharpened lines of his face, not so unfamiliar now as it had been. A guardedness that prompted her to wrap her arms around his neck and haul him into a kiss.

"Hetta…"

Her insides flipped pleasurably, a slow warmth coiling low in her body. She shifted her hands over his shoulders, till they brushed the top of his wings. Wyn tensed at the touch and she pulled her hands away.

"Sorry," she said.

"No, don't be—it's—it's good." All the small feathers at the top of his wings fluffed up. Embarrassment. "You don't—ah—mind?"

"Mind that you're feathery? No. It's new, obviously, but not a bad sort of new." She walked her fingers slowly over his shoulders again, and he went absolutely still. "Should I stop?"

"No." His voice had gone deep. "It's—they're just—ah—sensitive."

"What exactly do you mean, sensitive?" But she cautiously returned to lightly brush the top of his wings where skin met feathers. He made a rumbling sound deep in his throat that she'd never heard from him before, and the gold motes in his irises flared.

To her astonishment and deep delight, he flushed, feathers fluffing up once more. "Ah—exactly what you are thinking, I suspect."

She frowned. "Surely not. That seems impractical, for one, and for another, I've seen you brush against things all the time!"

He drew back one of her hands, bringing her palm to his lips. His warm breath tickled, her skin prickling with anticipation, and when he pressed a kiss there, the point of contact sent heat pulsing through her.

"And you use your hands for all kinds of mundane things," he countered. "Touch is situational." His shrug rustled his feathers. "But the inner wing is more sensitive. Wings are intimate. Wing-touches are reserved for kin, friends, and…lovers." His voice dropped on the last word, and he flared out a wing in invitation.

The heavy currents of desire swam lazily in the room, but Hetta could see the knife-edge of vulnerability in his eyes.

She took the invitation and shifted so she could run her hands over his feathers. The primaries were firm and silken to the touch, and she traced the filaments upwards. *This is you*, she thought. It was admittedly a little strange, yes, but not…unwelcome. There was something deeply satisfying in stripping back a layer of Wyn's carefully built walls. *This is you*, she thought again. *And I love you.*

"Can I?" she asked, tugging at his shirt.

He nodded, shifting so she could reach, both tension and arousal in his posture as she undressed him. The body feathers nearer his back were smaller, bright metallic arrows of silver-tipped blue against his brown skin. They were much softer than his primaries, and when she put a hand between his bare shoulder blades, he shivered.

"Is that—?"

His answer was a wordless sound of encouragement.

She pressed against his back and wrapped her arms around him. "I love you," she whispered in his ear. The tense line of his shoulders relaxed fractionally.

He breathed out in a slow, careful exhalation and let her rest against his back. The room held nothing but the sound of their heartbeats, the heavy warmth of him against her cheek.

She reached up to stroke the planes of his face, subtly sharper in this form. She mentally overlaid his more usual features, trying to reconcile his two halves.

"Oh," she gasped as his hands found their way under her blouse and began to tease their way over her sensitive flesh.

He gave her an innocent look, as if to say 'who, me?', but since his fingers didn't pause in their teasing, it wasn't very convincing.

She squirmed, laughing.

"That wasn't the reaction I was going for," he complained.

"I was just thinking what a good job I did of debauching your innocence."

He began to chuckle and buried his head in her shoulder, his mirth vibrating through her. "Hetta, are you congratulating *yourself* for *my* skills?"

"Yes, I think I am." She grinned at him, unrepentant, and ran her hands through his hair. In his mortal form, the strands were a pale white-blond; now it was as if platinum had somehow been cast into a soft and touchable form. Her fingers moved up, exploring the smooth shape of his horns. He went still again.

"That feels very strange," he admitted. "I am…not as used to this shape as I should be."

He shifted his horns from her grasp and kissed her. How could everything still feel so urgent between them? Hetta had thought familiarity might ease it, except the reverse had happened. Now, desire was intensified by intimacy, by the knowledge of sound and touch and smell.

She wasn't sure which of them the motion came from, but the result was the same. They tumbled back towards the bed in a tangle of limbs and feathers and discarded clothing.

Magic hummed to life around them, hers and Wyn's both, and Wyn paused. She read the hesitation in his eyes, a discordant note amidst the rising heat between them. A tiny flicker of lightning glowed briefly in his irises.

"Trust yourself," Hetta told him impatiently. She caressed the hard planes of his body. A choke of laughter startled from his throat as her wandering hands found their way lower.

"Are you…attempting to distract…me?" he asked, voice strained.

"Yes. Is it working?"

He arched in pleasure, and the sight sent a deep thrill of satisfaction through her. "Yes."

After that there were no more words, only sensation and the heavy haze of magic.

Afterwards, they lay entwined, one of Wyn's wings draped across her body.

"You make a particularly good blanket like this." Hetta stroked the feathers covering her.

Wyn made a sleepy sound of agreement and nuzzled at the back of her neck.

It was wonderful to let the world narrow to this cocoon, her fingers moving with slow meditation, a paler contrast against the deep blue silk. Wyn's feathers were almost the same colour as her ring, she thought idly.

Her hand stilled.

"What?" He'd caught her tension, no trace of drowsiness in his tone.

Hetta stared at her engagement ring, at the piece of stone Stariel had altered in some fundamental way. She held out her hand, the blue stone shimmering with inner fire. "I think I found our Gate anchor."

FURTHER EXPERIMENTS

I T TOOK MARIUS several minutes to realise that one of the undergraduates in his tutorial was not, in fact, one of the undergraduates in his tutorial. With this realisation, the glamour faded. Only for Marius, though; it remained in effect for the other students, who all continued to blithely accept the newcomer in their midst as if he'd been with them all term.

Marius gave said 'newcomer' a ferocious scowl, but Rakken only waved lazily for him to carry on.

Yes, do try to explain my presence to these mortals if you like, Rakken's wicked smile seemed to say, daring Marius to expose him. Rakken was clearly doing something else as well, damping his…Marius hated using the word 'allure' even if it was apparently the correct technical term for the effect, and he was only saying it in his own head besides, but Rakken was clearly damping his *allure* because he was—for Rakken—relatively unobtrusive.

What would happen if Marius exposed him? Rakken's glamour was incredibly powerful, but Marius was coming to know the nuances of it. This slipping-in-unnoticed business would only work so long as no one drew attention to the fact. If Marius did that, well, Rakken could resort to a stronger glamour to disappear, but it wouldn't make people forget the fact that he'd been there in the first place.

Compulsion though…compulsion could make people forget. Not that Marius had seen Rakken intentionally compel anyone since Meridon, but he remembered the power of it then, holding an entire station's worth of people in thrall. Just the memory of it sent a shiver down his spine.

Would Rakken use compulsion on the students if Marius pointed out his presence? *Sadly, he probably won't even need to.* No doubt Rakken would somehow charm them into submission without using any actual magic. Maybe that was simply the mundane magic of confidence, or rather *arrogance*, though Marius wanted to believe there was still some actual magic to it, because the alternative was a sobering reflection on his own life.

"Er…Mr Valstar?" one of the students prompted, and Marius realised he'd been frowning at the space that contained Rakken for a good thirty seconds. He gave himself a shake.

"Right, right. Where was I?"

At least Rakken didn't interfere further, and Marius managed to get through the rest of the hour without giving in to the urge to strangle the man. The students shuffled out of the study, Cholmondeley pausing to ask if there was any possibility of an extension, because really, with the rowing come up, a fellow couldn't be blamed for needing more time, could he?

Marius signed the request off without even a reflexive protest and finally shut the door behind the last of them.

"You know, if you wanted to help with my glamour experiments, you had only to ask," Marius said evenly. He turned.

Rakken had abandoned his human form and was now sprawled on the deep-buttoned chesterfield, one arm flung carelessly along its back, wings draped over the leather. He'd also clearly abandoned the effort to suppress his allure, because his usual metaphorical shininess had returned in full force.

"Does it take effort, suppressing it?" Marius asked without thinking.

Rakken gave him a sardonic look. "Suppressing what, precisely?" He knew exactly what Marius was talking about.

"Oh, never mind," Marius muttered. He turned away and began packing up his things, stacking student papers away with an internal groan at the marking he could already see eating into his evening.

"Yes. Not a huge amount, but some." Rakken grinned, slow and wicked, when Marius looked up. "I am not made to be contained."

Marius made a disgusted sound. "Oh, sod off."

Rakken did not, instead fanning his wings out in a leisurely motion, as if he were sunning them. "What has put you in such a mood today, Marius Valstar?"

"Oh, I don't know; fae princes sneaking into my botany tutorials and distracting me!"

"Do I distract you?"

Marius wasn't touching that. He still hadn't figured out what Rakken meant by all this…flirtation, okay, there wasn't really another word for it. Marius suspected it was for the sole purpose of winding him up, and that Rakken would've done it regardless of Marius's predilections. He turned back to his papers and spoke without looking at the man behind him, though Marius swore he could feel him still, as if melodramatic sensuality interfered with the oxygen content of the room somehow.

"You haven't heard anything from Wyn, have you?" Marius was pretty sure Rakken hadn't, but then again, who knew what methods of communication fae had?

"No."

"They should be back by now, shouldn't they?"

Rakken sighed. "I would know if he were dead, and your faeland would know if Lord Valstar suffered the same."

Marius flinched, and then flinched again at the hand on his shoulder. Rakken was too close, his expression more serious than usual. How had he moved so fast? The faint but familiar smell of citrus and storms, the soft and specific sound that feathers made when their owner twitched his wings subtly.

"Time doesn't move the same way in Deeper Faerie. The delay isn't necessarily a cause for concern."

Mother Eostre help him, Rakken was trying to be *comforting*. Marius moved away, and Rakken dropped his hand. "They're not going to come back in a hundred years, are they?"

Rakken shook his head. "The dilation shouldn't be so great, with the Iron Law revoked."

"Forgive me if I don't find that particularly comforting."

Rakken shrugged. "Hallowyn is a fool, but your sister is tenacious."

"Don't make yourself ill by complimenting a mortal now," Marius couldn't resist saying.

Rakken laughed, warm and genuine, and thank goodness he moved back to the couch, because it was far too easy to forget what he was in these rare moments when he let his guard down. *He's not your friend*, Marius reminded himself. *He will always act for his own interests, which will almost always conflict with yours. Remember what happened last time you let your judgement be compromised by a ruthless man with a pretty face.*

"Not all of you completely lack redeeming features," Rakken allowed, the glint in his eyes daring Marius to ask whether he was included in that category.

Marius didn't take the bait. Instead he took a deep breath and undid his satchel to take out his latest concoction along with another modified quizzing glass. A bit of the rowan-wood had come unstuck, and he hastily tied it back in place.

Rakken rolled his eyes as Marius examined him through it—to

no effect. His wings still looked perfectly whole, not a feather out of place. Damn. Marius lowered the glass, squinted, and for his trouble got only a sensation like itching on the back of his neck. Rakken's feathers still looked perfect.

"I don't suppose you could use a weaker glamour, could you?" He'd seen unaided through the weaker one Rakken had cast on the undergrads before, but he was pretty sure Rakken used the strongest glamour possible on the ragged edges of his wings.

Rakken fanned a wing in and out with deliberate pleasure; the feathers moved seamlessly, impossible to say where the real ones began or ended no matter how Marius stared at them.

"As I have already explained, Marius Valstar, that would be an entirely pointless exercise. You are increasingly able to see through lesser glamours using nothing but your own will. Therefore, if you saw through a lesser glamour of mine, how would you tell whether your 'experiments' were working or not?"

This was a valid point, but, "It's not like I have any other way to test them!"

"—and I do not see that glamour should be your chief concern in any case."

Agreed; the compulsion was a much more concerning magic, but—"Asking you to compel me seems even more pointless." And Marius didn't much fancy bringing on a migraine.

Rakken carefully matched the fingertips on each of his hands. "You are not the only mortal in the world, Marius Valstar. Or even in this town."

Marius glared at him. "No." And thank the little gods that Greg was no longer here and Rakken could no longer suggest experimenting on him. It was the only good thing about his little brother's suspension—well, that and the knowledge that he was likely safer within Stariel's bounds. Keeping Greg safe was the reason he hadn't tried to fight the decision when news of Greg's brawling reached the wrong ears—presumably the earl's. Marius was certainly going to have words with the earl about it.

Rakken spread his hands in easy surrender. "Then don't pretend it is *my* lack of cooperation that is the hindrance in this. You're the one whose logic is flawed, and I'm being generous in pointing it out, since it is not my desire to see you succeed in your stated goal."

"And don't *you* pretend you'd be happy to compel people willy-nilly—because I know you're not. You've been worried ever since the Maelstrom magnified your powers." Marius knew Rakken's compulsive and compulsive-adjacent abilities were now so strong that they disturbed even Rakken. Which was disturbing in and of itself because Rakken wasn't someone who was easily disturbed even when he ought to have been. Oh, not that Rakken had admitted to any unease, but several times recently when someone had been fawning over him, Marius had seen Rakken's eyes widen and the… allure or whatever it was contract, as if it had extended without Rakken quite intending it.

Rakken's eyes narrowed. "I can compel with sufficient precision for your purposes."

Marius crossed his arms. "I'm not letting you compel anyone, even for the purposes of scientific inquiry."

A brief flare in Rakken's irises at the word 'let', and he lost his languor, becoming suddenly very icy indeed. "I think you forget who I am. I am not your tame creature, Marius Valstar; I do not act under your decree."

Marius threw up his hands. "Yes, yes, Your Highness. I know. *Fine.*"

He pulled his satchel over his shoulder and straightened, heading out without stopping to see if Rakken was following. Rakken sometimes dogged his heels and sometimes not, mostly depending on how bored he was, Marius suspected. When Marius had pointed out that this wasn't exactly model bodyguard behaviour, Rakken had said easily, "I will give you leave to use my name to summon me, if my sister appears without warning and I'm not already nearby."

Today, Rakken was apparently bored enough to follow Marius out of the college. Marius ignored him as he headed down to the towpath. It was a mild spring day, and the path had a fair amount of traffic, forcing both him and his shadow to make way whenever they met people coming the other way. None of the people they passed noticed Rakken's feathers, which irritated Marius. Still, it was good to be out in the fresh air.

The foot traffic lessened as he followed the path back to the wilder stretch of the river further from the centre of town, where he'd seen the fae swans. But the river was empty today.

"Damn," he cursed softly, staring at the dark water.

Rakken came to a halt next to him. "You are persistent, little scholar, I'll give you that."

Marius demonstrated heroic strength of character by refusing to rise to the bait. An idea struck him. "What if you, I don't know, calibrate your glamour strength just above what I can see through? Is that possible? How finely can you tune it?"

Rakken sighed and held out a hand. "Give me your latest concoction."

Marius eyed him warily. "I swear, if you're planning to throw it in the river…"

"Oh, please do continue. I'm interested to see what you plan to threaten me with."

"A watery grave," Marius muttered before handing Rakken the modified quizzing glass and the vial containing his latest herb concoction.

Rakken held up the quizzing glass to the light, turning it this way and that. "Tell me your hypothesis. Why this material?"

"Quizzing glasses distort light so as to enable one to detect illusions."

"Mortal illusion is not fae glamour. Glamour has no physical presence."

"Yes, but quizzing glasses have *symbolism*, don't they? A connection to the concept of seeing truly."

Rakken gave him a sharp look. "That isn't how human magic works, as far as I know."

"It's significant for fae magic though, isn't it? Things that are like other things are connected, like resonances for your portals," Marius said, thinking aloud. That was the pattern he kept seeing, in the magic Wyn used, in the stories from fairy tales that might or might not be true.

Rakken's expression went blank, his feathers absolutely still, which Marius knew now was a sign that he was thinking furiously.

"I'm right, aren't I?" Marius pressed.

"And what would you do, if you could allow your people to puncture fae glamour at will? Would you give that knowledge to your mortal queen? To the same people who write lurid reports of wicked fae stealing sheep and seducing mortal women?"

"You *have* seduced mortal women," Marius felt bound to point out. Heat rose in his cheeks.

A dagger-sharp grin. "I don't need magic for that."

No, he supposed that was true, damn him.

Rakken handed back the quizzing glass. "I will not help you build weapons against my people, Marius Valstar. I am greater fae, with many magics to draw on, but many of the lower and lesser fae have little more than glamour to protect themselves."

Marius slid him a sideways look. "Mortals get by without it."

Rakken shrugged, his feathers rustling as they rose and fell. "Mortals get by without a great many things, it seems." He watched the river, the breeze rattling at the reeds. "Tell me…" He hesitated. "Is this where you consider yourself to belong, in this unclaimed land full of dead iron?"

Marius blinked at him. *Dead iron?* "I don't know," he said slowly. "I thought—well, to be honest, I never really thought much beyond my father's lordship. But now he's gone and Hetta's lord and I…I suppose I'm still figuring out where I fit in this new world. What about you?"

Rakken stiffened.

"Oh, come on, it's fair turnabout if you're going to ask *me* personal questions without warning. And I'm not exactly the only one here who's just gotten out from under his father's shadow and also failed to inherit."

A dull ache in his temples as Rakken strongly refuted the assertion that there were any parallels *at all* between them.

"Look, it's not like I wanted to make the comparison, but it was a relatively obvious one," Marius pointed out acidly. "And are you seriously going to argue that while ThousandSpire still stands unclaimed you haven't actually yet failed to inherit? I'm amazed you can even say the words aloud, that's such a technicality. You don't really believe you could still be king there, do you?"

Rakken was looking at him strangely, and the ache at his temples eased abruptly—thank the little gods. He expected Rakken to say something blistering and furious, but instead he simply gave his head a minute shake, his lips curving ruefully.

"You are bad for my ego, Marius Valstar."

THE SEA GATE

WYN LOOKED DOWN at his feet, where the engagement ring nestled in a tangle of spell lines, and tried not to feel melancholy about the fact that the Gate spell would absorb it. Engagement rings weren't even a fae tradition, he reminded himself. His primary motivation in making the ring had been so that Hetta could draw on Stariel's power when she was outside the estate's bounds. But it wasn't the loss of the ring's practical benefits that made him sulk; that was merely an additional blow. Having to destroy the symbol of his intent—was the universe *trying* to emphasise how much it disliked the idea of his and Hetta's union?

They had set up the spell on the ground floor of the atrium, partially because Irokoi thought the tiny mosaic representation of Stariel might help and partially because it was as far away as possible from the lake guardian. It still made him uneasy, looking up to the Gate so many stories above, even with Irokoi's reassurances that Aroset couldn't see them even if she were still waiting there. Wyn hadn't caught a glimpse of her since they'd entered.

"You can make me another one." Hetta patted his arm, careful not to stand on any of the spell lines that criss-crossed the mosaic.

"In fact, I insist."

She could read him so easily. Perhaps it was his fae form, which he'd worn now for the longest span since he'd first left Faerie. The time here had been a strange and dislocated thing, a bubble containing only the three of them. *Well, four, technically*, he thought, sliding a glance at Hetta's abdomen. There was no physical sign, but her personal magical signature burned more brightly than ever, steadily draining into Lamorkin's gem at her throat. The gem's colour glowed a pure iris blue. So dark so soon. He tried to calculate what that meant in terms of the spell's decay rate, but he wasn't sure exactly how long they'd been here for. The greenish light filtering through the dome never changed. Perhaps as long as three days, he thought.

Hetta's sharp prod to his ribs tumbled him out of his thoughts. "I'm *fine*," she told him grumpily.

"I did not ask."

"Yes, but I could hear you thinking it." Her eyes widened at her own turn of phrase. "Gods, I hope Marius is safe. I never meant to be gone so long," she said.

It had taken them a frustrating amount of time to prepare the spell. The dusken rose had come with a Gate spell pre-coiled inside, and it had been made to connect one of the surface realms with Mortal. Constructing a Gate from scratch between Deeper Faerie and Mortal using a resonance point not designed for the task? Even Irokoi's blithe confidence had frayed a little around the edges as the days passed. *Thank the stormwinds we were at least wise enough to become trapped in Faerie's most comprehensive library of magic.*

Wyn wound his hand with Hetta's, pulling her against his side. Disquieting undersea bubble, patrolling leviathan sea creatures, and sleeping lake guardian aside, it was freeing to be able to show affection without a care for who might see or judge.

"I believe Rake will do his best to keep Marius safe, if only because he dislikes being in your debt," he said. "And perhaps Aroset is still perched above the island where we came in, hoping we re-emerge." He imagined Aroset poised like a heron above a fish and hoped he was right and that she hadn't returned to the Mortal Realm yet.

Hetta made an unhappy noise, not disagreeing with his assessment but not liking it either. She shook her head briskly, peering into the gloom among the shelves.

"Irokoi? Have you found the right combination to add to the *arraxis* cross?" She said the word like a child handling a sweet, relishing the syllables on her tongue. She'd always liked magic, and she was rapidly picking up both the theory behind Gate spells and spell terminology. He bent and kissed her, quick and intense, unable to resist the temptation. She let out a startled and then annoyed sound when the kiss ended before it had really begun, turning into him and going up on tip-toes to—

"If you two smudge my spell lines, I shall be most irritated." Irokoi emerged out of the stacks holding a pile of books. He gave Wyn a chiding look, his eyes suddenly old and tired. "Honestly, little brother, is this really the time?"

They separated sheepishly, and some of Irokoi's sobriety ebbed.

"But as it happens, yes, Lord Valstar, I have found the solution. With this, I think we're ready to activate the Gate." He put the bulk of his pile into the satchel slung over his shoulder and opened the remaining volume until he found the page. "This diagram, I think."

Irokoi carefully painted the last spell line in, his magic just a hint of frost and darkness. They all paused to take in the intricate web, which spanned the entire floor, spiralling up to a makeshift arch they'd constructed in the room's centre, which would give the Gate form. As Irokoi unhooked his magic, the spell shivered and… clicked, making the Gate a potential rather than an impossibility. Wyn let out a long sigh of relief.

"You need to remain within the central circle while the spell activates," Irokoi told Hetta. "We aren't building this Gate in a normal way, so the key resonance point is *you*. The ring is merely an anchor for it. Think as strongly as possible of home."

Hetta nodded. Irokoi and Wyn took their respective places. Wyn's role was primarily to feed magic to Irokoi. Irokoi had put him on the edge of the ground floor "so as to interfere as little as possible with the resonance. Your sympathies are too complicated, brother."

Wyn pretended not to know what that meant. He'd almost re-adjusted to the constant weight of wings at his back, to the point that it only occasionally threw him off balance now. His shoulder muscles hadn't gotten such constant exercise in years.

Irokoi triggered the spell, and it drew on Wyn's magic in a sudden rush, like opening the door of a firebox. In the centre of the spell, he saw Hetta swallow, her brow furrowed in concentration.

For a long, hollow moment the call rang out into nothingness, but then something caught, and the magic began to bloom. Stone tendrils grew from Hetta's ring where it nestled amidst the spell lines. They slithered across the floor in tentacles the sparkling colour of star indigo. A faint, foreign hint of pine followed in their wake, and tiny, ghostly starflowers burst from them as the spell hummed to life, stone winding its way up the pillars. Yearning expanded in his chest. Home. It sang of home. Hetta's eyes shone with the same longing.

Beyond the walls of the atrium, something roared.

The sound sent terror thrilling through him, and he spun, searching for the source. No. But his denial didn't prevent something vast and serpentine from crashing into the library on the levels above, where the doors to the underwater garden connected. He caught a glimpse of glittering white scales before the lake guardian's head appeared over the railing. The creature glared down at them, eyes glowing green with rage. It was hard to tell precisely how big it was from this distance, but it was certainly big *enough*.

And it was staring straight at Hetta.

It seemed to happen in slow motion. The lake guardian flung itself over the railing above, its long body spooling out like the coils of a snake. Power flared out of Wyn without conscious thought, lightning pulling all the way up from the soles of his feet and shivering out along his outstretched arms. It arced into the lake guardian, catching it mid-dive, and the force knocked it off course. Instead of landing directly on top of Hetta, it smashed into the far wall.

So that's what happens when I lose control, he thought dizzily. But he hadn't killed it. The lake guardian shook its head, dazed but gathering strength with each second. And now Hetta stood between Wyn and the creature.

Hetta had balled her hands into fists, urging the Gate spell on. Stone crawled up the support structure, nearly as tall as she was now.

Time slowed as the lake guardian got to its webbed feet once again, its focus swinging back to Hetta. Teeth flashed, sharp and jagged as a shark. He could not draw lightning again, not with Hetta between him and the guardian. He was in the air without conscious thought, air magic as much as muscle, soaring over Hetta and the forming archway as the guardian leapt.

He should have met the guardian in mid-air, but instead there was a wrenching shudder of stone, and he landed unobstructed and off-balance between Hetta and the creature. He tracked the distance between himself and the lake guardian, not comprehending why it had aborted its leap and why even now it was holding itself back rather than attacking. There were deep grooves carved into the floor from where it had halted its own momentum so abruptly, and its body bent at an unnatural angle from the effort. It flared out its ruff and hissed at him in displeasure.

"Wyn!" He felt the Gate flare to life behind him.

He didn't question his good fortune, turning and sprinting for the Gate with the others, grabbing Hetta's outstretched hand. The lake guardian cried out, its anger and sorrow thick as ice.

The world spun, and he barely registered that they were in the Sesquipedalian Room in Stariel House before he reached to de-activate the Gate. The view of the High King's library snapped out, and Wyn sank to the floor, shaking with adrenalin. He could still feel the lake guardian's mournful cry, a vast, bitter rage that went deeper than sound. It vibrated in his bones, behind his teeth, jagged and magical and impossible—how could it follow them here?

"Yes, yes, I'm fine, *calm down!*" Hetta told Stariel, which was clamouring at them in alarm.

Wyn stared at the newly formed Gate on the wall between two cabinets stuffed with seashells, heart thundering in his ears. Inactive, the Gate appeared as a pattern of waves and twining serpents on the wood panelling. It was closed. Closed. The lake guardian couldn't reach them here, even if it knew how to activate the gate. Hetta was safe, even if there were now *two* permanent doors to foreign realms within the borders of Stariel. They were safe.

So why could he still hear the guardian's cry, cutting through his skull like a blade?

Wyn scrabbled at the floor as an earthquake rolled along the leylines, as unbalanced as the deck of a ship in a storm.

The world *shifted*, and the guardian's cry cut off. The hairs on the back of his neck stood up, and when he checked the leylines, they were trembling with the impact. The impact of *what*, exactly?

Hetta had got to her feet and was glaring down at him. "Are you staying on the floor or is there some *other* monster you plan to throw yourself in front of?" She didn't seem disoriented—hadn't she felt it? Had he *imagined* the way the guardian's call had rearranged the leylines, like a tray of sand being sharply shaken?

He blinked, so preoccupied with how the world had changed that it took him several long moments to comprehend, firstly, that she was angry at him and, secondly, why that might be the case. He mentally reviewed the last few minutes. Ah.

"You cannot be annoyed that the guardian *didn't* eat me, love."

Hetta gave him a level look. "That is *not* what I'm annoyed about, as you very well know."

He did, and he couldn't blame her for her anger; had their positions been reversed, he would've felt the same way. Of course, Hetta probably wouldn't have been quite so reckless as to leap in front of a charging fae beast with absolutely no plan as to how to stop it. Probably—she did have a temper when provoked and had, in fact, once confronted a drakken with nothing but her bare hands.

He decided not to point this out.

"Can you have your argument later?" Irokoi interjected. He grimaced at Wyn, leaning against a shelf in an awkward sprawl of wings. He rubbed at his temples. "That guardian's call made my head ring. Did you hear it too?"

"Yes—how? What did it do?"

Hetta frowned. "What are you talking about?"

Wyn blinked. She hadn't felt it. Which meant it hadn't been something physical, and it hadn't been something connected to Stariel. Ice began to creep across his chest—the lake guardian had triggered something, something significant enough to dramatically shift the leylines *in the Mortal Realm.*

"The leylines shifted," he explained, inadequately. "And I cannot apologise for throwing myself in front of the guardian as I'm not at all sorry for doing it, since it worked."

Why had it worked? It was as if the guardian hadn't wanted to hurt him, specifically, despite its rage at Hetta for building a Gate. Perhaps it was primarily the forming connection to Mortal it had objected to; perhaps it wouldn't have hurt Hetta either. He was glad they hadn't tested that.

Hetta narrowed her eyes. "You didn't know it was going to work when you did it."

"It was still preferable to letting it reach you. I'm much more resilient than you are. And you needed time to finish the Gate." He levered himself up off the floor.

She put a hand flat on his chest, as if she couldn't decide if she wanted to push him away or throw her arms around him. "Don't do it again. Just...don't." Her voice went wobbly.

He took the opportunity to fold his arms around her. "I will try not to meet any more lake guardians."

She made an angry hiccoughing sound against his chest. "Dash it, I'm *not* going to cry!"

He murmured wordless reassurance and let the warmth of her ease his jagged edges. That guardian had come much, much too close to her. If it had reached her... No, he wasn't sorry at all for putting himself in its path. They rested like that for the space of two heartbeats before Hetta fought her way out of the embrace. Wyn reluctantly released her.

Taking a long, steadying breath, she said in a more even tone, "What do you mean, the leylines shifted? How could the lake guardian do that?"

"I don't know. Koi?"

Irokoi got to his feet, black feathers rustling. "I don't know exactly what it did. I'm not an expert on *everything*. But I don't think it's happy that we left, waving a mortal in front of its nose while we did so. I did *say* it would be better not to wake it." He looked around the room with interest. "This *is* a very nice house."

"Thank you," Hetta said drily.

Running footsteps sounded, and Jack and Alexandra burst in.

Both of them pulled up short at the sight of them. Wyn pulled his wings tightly against his spine and...reached.

His other form came as if it had never been missing, but oh, it felt strange. Everything was oddly muted, his balance off. He clutched at the nearest armchair for balance. Hetta gave him an unreadable look.

Irokoi beamed at Jack and Alexandra while he was still recovering. "Ah, little Valstars! Tell me, where is my brother and also yours? The oldest one," he clarified.

What did Irokoi want with Marius? Irokoi had refused to explain more about how to free ThousandSpire until they'd returned to Stariel, but Wyn didn't like the shape of this game he was playing.

"You're one of Wyn's brothers," Jack accused. He narrowed his eyes at the new Gate before whirling on Hetta. "Where in the hells have you been? And why did you land us with Miss Gwen again?"

Wyn had almost forgotten about the lesser fae, given more pressing recent events, but now he reached out with his leysight and found Gwendelfear approaching the room at a more cautious pace than the Valstars. Her expression held fearfulness—she'd felt the leylines shift too—but she straightened as their eyes met, chin tilting.

She wore a glamour, which surprised him—he hadn't thought she'd have enough magic for it, given how drained she'd been when he'd last seen her. But even allowing for glamour, she moved more easily than she had before, as if her limbs no longer pained her as much. Gwendelfear had healing abilities, but Wyn wasn't sure if she could use them on herself or not.

"How long were we gone for?" Wyn asked slowly. "What day is it?"

Jack frowned and gave the date.

He and Hetta both drew sharp breaths. His estimate of the time dilation effect had been off—considerably off, storms take it. They hadn't been gone three days. They'd been gone nearly three weeks.

"I missed the dinner at Angus's. Not that I was exactly looking forward to it, but..." Hetta trailed off. But it had been an opportunity to persuade more of the lords to support her.

A thousand smaller questions sprung into being, tasks that Wyn worried had gone unchecked. He hadn't prepared for so long an absence. He glanced at Hetta, where the heartstone lay hidden beneath her clothing. Perhaps that was why it had drained faster than they'd anticipated, shifting between realms. How much time did they have left before it turned pure black?

Hetta performed the introductions and gave a succinct and highly edited account of their adventures in Deeper Faerie.

"Yes, yes," Irokoi said impatiently. "But where is your brother, Lord Valstar? And where is mine?"

Wyn calculated what day of the week it was. "In Meridon, in all likelihood." With the earl. Would the addition of Rakken to that mix better or worsen the situation? "I will send him a summons to return." That bit of magic was beyond his skill, but Rakken had left him the requisite charm before they'd left for DuskRose.

Hetta gasped and went rigid. A second later, Wyn felt it too—as did Jack and Alexandra, from the way they stiffened.

"What—what's that?" Alexandra asked, her voice trembling.

When Irokoi spoke, his voice was as grim as Wyn had ever heard it. "The lake guardian sent the leviathans after us."

PART III

AND BACK

COLD VISITORS

ETTA GASPED AS something stung at her in places that had no physicality. She'd had greater fae cross the boundaries of Stariel without permission before, but never quite like this—never actively opposing her. Right at the border, to the north, huge and inhuman creatures pressed against her, sharp and biting.

Distantly, part of her raged at the monstrous unfairness of their arrival. She and Wyn had spent apparently weeks trying to build a Gate out of the underwater library, and the lake guardian had opened a portal here in a matter of minutes. Could they really have been gone for so long? Anxiety over all the things that would mean threatened, but she pushed it aside.

Monsters first; self-doubt later.

<No,> Hetta thought fiercely at her intruders. <No, you may *not* pass.> She clutched at a cabinet for balance and dug her heels in. Stariel roared up in agreement, seeking direction. The faeland's fury was vast and powerful, but only Hetta could give it proper form.

<There,> she told Stariel. In the undersea, she hadn't been able to properly sense the leviathans, but she could now through Stariel,

and their cold, brineish echo sat on the back of her tongue, along with a hostility so strong it made her recoil. <Go away!> she told them. <You don't belong here! This is *my* land!>

They rumbled in response, wordless and full of rage. Hetta had had enough practice interpreting Stariel's sendings to sieve their meaning out: they hated her humanity, hated that she had tainted their realm with it, hated this mortal realm they'd been sent to, and they were here for blood.

<Yes, well, you're jolly well not getting my blood! Go away!> She forced the incursion out, step by step until the leviathans crossed the border and her awareness of them snuffed out.

Warm hands on hers, voices, and she snapped back to herself, senses dimming, contained again in a small, fragile vessel. Was that how Wyn felt, shifting back to his mortal form?

Wyn's eyes were wide and worried, his hands steady on hers.

"I sent them away."

He didn't look reassured. "Where?"

"On the north-eastern boundary. Near…" She trailed off.

"Penharrow," he finished grimly.

HETTA TELEPORTED HERSELF, WYN, and Irokoi to the border, leaving Jack's cut-off protest behind. Fog clung thickly to the ground, here in the lower-lying parts of the estate. There was no sign of the leviathans but for footprints the size of cartwheels. Each dark impression glistened with water that—through her land-sense—tasted slightly salty. How dare the strange dangers of Deeper Faerie follow her home! She glared at the footprints and willed the ground flat again, like smoothing out a rumpled rug.

She pushed the fog away, clearing a wide circle around them, but she had no power to do so beyond Stariel's boundaries, so it piled up along the border, impossible to see through. She could hear nothing.

Irokoi made a gesture akin to swiping a cobweb away, and a path cleared beyond the boundary. Right—air magic. In the distance, large, lumbering shadows strode in the direction of Penharrow Manor. Oh, gods. What would they do if they encountered anyone in their way? What would they do when they got there? Angus had no faeland to back him up, and no magic. *And a bunch of Northern lords are currently staying at his house. So much for making a good impression.*

She curled her hands into fists. "I shouldn't have sent them away; I should've trapped them here." Hetta thought of the trick she'd used once on Rakken, liquefying the soil to bury him up to his waist then re-solidifying it.

"Do you think these ones are under similar instructions not to harm fae as the lake guardian?" Wyn asked.

Irokoi considered the lumbering shadows. "I think they will follow us," he grit out, as if the words cost him. Hetta got the impression that wasn't all he'd intended to say, but he shook his head and closed his mouth, frustration flashing in his expression. His feathers pressed flat against his spine.

Wyn took a breath and changed to his fae form. He gave Hetta a tight grin. "I shall have to give them sufficient encouragement to follow us *back* to Stariel."

Hetta didn't like this plan in the least, but she couldn't think of a better one, and Wyn was much more able to survive the wrath of a giant fae creature than anyone else at Penharrow.

"Be careful."

He nodded. "Koi?"

Irokoi sighed, his shoulders sagging. "I suppose you're right, though it isn't the leviathans' fault they are under a *geas*." He flared out his wings. "I shall leave any close flying to you, brother." His missing eye interfered with his depth perception, he'd told Hetta once.

The two fae took off and Hetta's heart with them. The fog billowed and curled without Irokoi's air magic holding it back, making it hard to tell whether the leviathans had reached the manor or not.

A loud *crunch* echoed through the valley, followed by a sound like a giant's fist hammering on stone.

I suppose that's an accurate description of what's happening. The leviathans had reached the manor. Hetta wrapped her arms around herself and tried not to think about large, gleaming teeth and slab-like hands. What if Wyn and Irokoi couldn't turn the leviathans' attention away from Penharrow? Why had she thought simply standing here and waiting was a good idea? Her pyromancy itched for expression; if she'd made Wyn take her with him, maybe she could've burned those things to ash. *Their powers clearly relate to water*, she reminded herself, thinking of those gleaming footprints. *I don't think fire would be particularly helpful.*

She'd never meant to drag a bit of deepest Faerie back home with her. She wrapped her arms around herself, shivering, and Stariel's presence rubbed against her, unsettled as she was. Hetta searched the horizon, trying to see through the murk, her heart stopping each time a flash of lightning lit up the sky. *Wyn.* He'd be all right, wouldn't he? But she couldn't help think of the tight rein he'd held on his magic, his unease with himself. How he'd changed so quickly to his human form when they'd returned. How could he possibly elude the leviathans' grasp while at war with himself?

Enormous echoing booms grew nearer, and both fear and relief flooded her. She visualised, crisp and determined, sending a false version of herself to stand just inside the border while she blended the real her in the scenery. The power came easily, strong and deep as a river, her own will boosted by Stariel. Oh, how she'd missed that.

The ground vibrated with the leviathans' strides, and Hetta braced herself. <We're letting them in,> she warned Stariel. <Temporarily.>

The estate sent a sensation not unlike a sigh but acceded to the instruction.

A winged figure shot across the border like a dark arrow—Irokoi. Hetta had a sharp, fleeting concern for Wyn—where was he?— before the two leviathans crashed across the border and took up her entire attention. They slammed across her senses like tidal waves, and Hetta felt the impact down to her heels, down further, into the roots that spread beneath her surface. The leviathans roared at the sight of her illusionary self and smashed their fists down, cries of triumph changing to anger as they met no resistance.

Hetta's stomach roiled—there was something deeply disturbing about seeing yourself be crushed under a giant's fist, real or not— and bit her lip to distract herself from the sensation. She needed to concentrate.

She'd spent so much time trying not to lose herself in Stariel's vastness, trying to balance its alien, distant attitude with her humanity, patiently explaining to a force of nature why certain blunt approaches weren't always the most appropriate, but now she…let go, and became a channel for the faeland's primal possessiveness, its absolute black-and-white view of the world, where things either belonged to it or didn't.

And the leviathans didn't belong.

Power surged, and she rose up and struck at the fae creatures who dared cross her boundaries, who *dared* try to harm her people. The leviathans resisted, power spilling out of them as they tried to free themselves from the earth liquefying beneath them. Lightning struck from a clear sky, fire igniting in a sudden contained inferno about them. They grew afraid, and would've fled, but she held them in the white-hot heart of her anger, a place where there was no room for moral greyness, in the absolute righteousness of knowing this was *her* land and her first duty was to protect it.

They buckled, snuffing out, but the magic continued to burn, a conflagration that didn't satisfy her wrath. She swarmed up and down her boundaries, checking and rechecking them, and the sparks of her wyldfae bowed in terrified obeisance at her passing. *Mine, this is mine*, she hissed, restlessly pacing the length of Starwater. She and Stariel brushed against the sparks of the Valstars, those most closely connected to her, reassuring themselves of their safety. They touched the newest member of their court, the little lesser fae, plucking at the bond like a new filling. The lesser fae quivered under the scrutiny, and they sent it an impatient dismissal. <You are ours now; we will protect you.>

There was a key spark missing from the net—their lightning-drenched prince, the one they'd claimed for their own. Where *was* he?

They searched, frantically, the boughs of the pines on the slopes of the Indigoes rustling with anxiety. Clouds raced across their surface, the weather disordered by the lightning they'd summoned.

They stumbled across the foreign spark near their border, its magic nearly unnoticeable, and only the familiar storm-smell of him kept them from squashing him immediately. This foreign spark was of the same blood as their missing prince. They nosed about him, demanding. <WHERE IS HE?>

The foreign fae didn't flinch, but his magic uncurled. They had thought him weak, but they realised now that this was only because he'd kept the full weight of his power so well contained they'd mistaken it for a lack thereof. It flared into being, a beat deep and dark as midnight in the heart of winter's storm, before it snapped back in on itself.

The show of strength made them pause, and then something *hurt* on their skin and suddenly they *had* skin.

Hetta gasped and rocked back on her heels, her cheek stinging. Irokoi stood in front of her, grimacing.

"Henrietta Isadore Valstar," he said.

Hetta rubbed at her cheek, her limbs feeling ill-fitting as a jester's costume. "Did you just slap me?"

He shrugged, feathers rustling softly. "Yes."

"Thank you." Her legs wobbled under her, and she had to jerk away from the urge to extend her sense down beneath the earth to steady herself. "Did your father ever…lose himself in ThousandSpire?"

Irokoi blinked. "Not that I saw, but he was already ancient by the time I was born. You are young and still coming into your powers. The comparison isn't useful."

"Where's Wyn?" Her gaze fell on the scorched earth where the leviathans had been, and her stomach turned. It smelled nauseatingly like fried bacon.

Irokoi's mismatched eyes were old and solemn. "He keeps fighting his own nature, and that's not only foolish but dangerous."

"Yes, but where is he? Is he all right? What happened at Penharrow? Is anyone hurt?"

"No one is dead, that I saw. Wyn will heal."

"That is *not* reassuring." Hetta fought her stomach into compliance and put out a hand commandingly. "Take me there. *Now.*"

BLOOD AND STONE

THERE WAS FAR too much blood. Wyn pressed the wadded scarf firmly against Lord Arran's shoulder. The unconscious man didn't react as Wyn held the wad with one hand and wound the scarf he was using as an impromptu bandage as tight as he could with the other. He had to shift his weight to do it, and he hissed as daggers stabbed his left leg in response. Concentrate! The man bleeding out in front of him was the important thing, not his damned leg, and not the high-pitched ringing in his left ear where the leviathan had crushed him against the side of the house in its attempt to snatch him out of the air.

Irokoi had been right that the creatures would follow them, but he might have mentioned this was because the leviathans were determined to capture the pair of them—presumably to drag them back to the undersea. He put the question of why aside to examine in less blood-soaked circumstances.

"Miss!" He recalled the maid servant who he'd stolen the scarf from. She'd been shaken enough to obey his command, even though his appearance had her eyes wide enough that he could see the whites around the irises.

"Y-yes, sir?" she stuttered, jerking into motion.

"Please fetch the first-aid kit. Has the doctor been summoned?"

She shook her head uncertainly.

"Send for him immediately." She bobbed her assent, the order seeming to steady her, though her attention still snagged on his horns as she left.

"I'll take over; you need your leg seen to," a firm female voice told him. A primly dressed woman knelt beside him and put her hands on Lord Arran's shoulder. There were plaster fragments in her hair. She sketched the winged shape of him briefly but didn't linger, her attention returning swiftly to Lord Arran. "Ms Orpington-Davies," she said. "You're Prince Hallowyn."

The reporter. She'd given up on Marius and Knoxbridge, apparently. "Keep pressure on it," he said grimly.

"I'm not a fool, Your Highness."

He grinned. "Maybe I'll give you an interview after all then."

"I'll hold you to it if you stop trying to martyr yourself. Give over."

He did, standing clumsily as Ms Orpington-Davies took his place. Pain pierced his left leg even though he put no weight on it. Everything on that side hurt, but the leg was the worst. He stumbled, feeling a warm, slick wetness in his left boot that didn't bode well. *Curse my too-slow reflexes. And curse storms-bedamned thick hide!* He wasn't even sure if the leviathans had felt his lightning, and he hadn't wanted to risk drawing more power, not so close to a mortal dwelling. Not when he wasn't iron-certain of his control.

There was dust everywhere—the leviathans had ripped part of the roof off and clawed out a portion of the second floor. The manor swarmed like a kicked anthill, people shouting back and forth. Had anyone else been injured? Wyn tried to find out, but he couldn't seem to find his mild, conciliatory manner through the pain, and servants scattered before him, skittish as sheep. He couldn't really blame them; they had just seen one fae rip half the roof off, and here Wyn was, another fae wandering into their midst. *Though one would think they'd recognise me; Penharrow is not that far removed from Stariel.* Though in fairness, they wouldn't have seen him in *this* form. His left wingbone felt sprained, complaining at every jostle. He shook his head, trying to clear the ringing, or at least recover his hearing; everything sounded muted on that side.

Well, if he couldn't be conciliatory, he needed to at least be mortal, but he couldn't seem to compact himself down into the right form. He rubbed his ear and grimaced; the ringing continued.

Hobbling up the entrance stairs, he came face to face with two people he didn't recognise. Only his reflexes saved him from becoming a pin cushion as one of them brandished a kitchen knife at him.

"Begone, foul creature!" The accent placed the man as one of the lords Hetta was supposed to be meeting this week at Penharrow's house party.

Wyn felt put-upon. "I'm here to help," he complained. "Please put the knife down. I am Lord Valstar's steward."

He *willed* himself back into mortal form and managed it just as Penharrow appeared at the top of the steps. Wyn staggered as the pain became more acute, and Penharrow scowled at him.

"Where's Hetta?"

"At Stariel. Lord Arran is injured." Wyn waved in the direction of the fallen lord. "Are there any other—"

"Some. I've sent for Dr Greystark." Penharrow grimaced as he took in the lord now uncertainly clutching the kitchen knife. "For the gods' sake, put down the knife, Drummond." He met Wyn's eyes. "What were those things?" There was an accusation there, an accusation Wyn had no answer for; the leviathans were, after all, Wyn's fault.

"Leviathans," Wyn said softly. "My brother has drawn them off; Hetta will take care of the rest once they pass the bounds to Stariel."

Penharrow's mouth thinned, but he had higher priorities than

Wyn now. He strode past Wyn and down the steps. Wyn leaned against the stone balustrade for support. The lord lowered the knife, and Wyn heard Penharrow issuing commands, soothing frayed nerves with the ease of someone used to being obeyed. Wyn let people wash around him in eddies, wishing his head would stop ringing. At least in mortal form he didn't have to deal with the pain of his wing, but the pain in his leg had increased tenfold and, more worryingly, the limb *felt* wrong.

He looked down. A rim of ruby was slowly forming around the outline of his boot, the colour bright against the pale stone. During the fight he'd channelled the pain into his magic, but now it had nowhere to go, and it swelled inside him, pressing against his skin in a low, stabbing ache. It would hurt less in his fae form, and, terrifyingly, he found he wanted to change for reasons beside that. Everything felt so muted like this, his body unfamiliar and awkward.

But he felt the unfamiliar lords' eyes on him, watching the way one would a beetle that has wandered into the house, so he forced himself to smile amiably at them, holding onto his form with sheer determination. He would *not* be the reason they voted against Hetta.

The leviathans might be, though, he couldn't help thinking.

They carted Lord Arran into the house; he looked semi- rather than *un*conscious, which Wyn hoped was an improvement. The man was elderly, and the blood loss had been significant before Wyn got to him. *What if it's killed him?* The thought felt like the leviathan grabbing at him again, except this time the dull, ringing ache came from within. Why did other people always end up paying the price of his mistakes?

Kineticar tyres crunched and tore Wyn's attention away from the slow drip of his own blood.

Jack stepped out, but Wyn hadn't had time to process his arrival before Gwendelfear emerged from the kineticar and Wyn nearly lost his grip on his mortal form as his instincts shrieked *enemy!* His

instincts faltered in the face of her cool blue eyes and the hint of
Stariel rather than DuskRose that now clung to her, the same hint
interwoven with his own magic. It was more obvious now than it
had been within Stariel's borders, the contrast between her and the
background magic greater here.

Gwendelfear's lip curled in disgust, and he knew she didn't wish
to feel that flicker of kinship between them either. *But we're of the
same court now.* He spread his hands in a pacifying way; they might
as well grow accustomed to it, since he doubted the lesser fae would
choose to leave the protection of Stariel for unclaimed lands, and
if she'd had another court to flee to, she would not have needed
Sunnika to intervene on her behalf.

Gwendelfear's expression didn't grow any warmer and in fact
took on an edge of satisfaction as she took in his injury. Ah, well.

Penharrow headed back to the door and frowned to see Wyn still
leaning against the balustrade.

"You're bleeding, man."

"Yes," Wyn said, his voice sounding odd in his ears. "I expect it
will stop soon. Who else is injured?"

"A few of the servants have minor scrapes, and my mother's
twisted her ankle. Lord Arran…" Penharrow's expression told Wyn
all he needed to know about the Conclave's Chair.

Irokoi descended in a rush of wings, Hetta in his arms, and Wyn
nearly sagged with relief. They'd dealt with the leviathans successfully, thank the stormwinds. Following hard on the heels of that
thought was fear; they were outside the bounds of Stariel. What
if Aroset made an appearance? He scanned the sky, searching for a
hint of his sister's magic, but there was nothing. *Please let her still be
fanning her wings in Faerie.*

Hetta hopped down. "Wyn!" She made her way towards him,
and he decided on this occasion that he could let her cross the distance rather than meeting her halfway.

His hands clenched on the stone balustrade for support, accidentally jolting his leg and sending a fresh wave of agony through it.
His boot felt too tight, and he suspected it might be the only thing
keeping his foot from swelling to several times its natural size.

He lost time, and Hetta was at his side.

"What's wrong with your leg?"

"Broken, I think. Are you all right?" The heartstone had fallen
from under her shirt where she usually kept it hidden, the colour
darker than earlier today. How much power did Lamorkin's spell
have left?

The next few minutes contained an excessive number of people
telling Wyn he was an idiot for standing there on a broken leg, followed by a painful removal to one of Penharrow's receiving rooms,
where Lord Arran had also been conveyed. Wyn did at least manage
to ask Irokoi to keep watch for Aroset outside. Hopefully they'd
have sufficient warning if she chose the worst possible moment
to appear.

Hetta pressed him down onto a settee, and the other people in
the room gave him unfriendly side-glances.

"Wyn…" She trailed off.

"It does look somewhat worse than I anticipated, I admit." There
was an angle to his leg that wasn't natural, and a distortion in his
trousers that suggested the bone might have come through the skin.

She took a deep breath. "It needs to be set. Has the doctor been
called?" There was an anger simmering beneath her worry, an anger
directed at him that he didn't quite understand. He wanted to ask
its cause, but not here, not in this room filled with people looking
at him like something subhuman. He squeezed her hand.

"Yes," he agreed, to both questions. "But I am not the most urgent
concern; he is." He nodded to where Lord Arran was laid out on the
sofa, still unconscious. The bandage on Lord Arran's shoulder was
soaked through. Mortals should not lose so much blood so quickly,

particularly not elderly ones. For all Wyn's magic, he had no ability to heal people. Healing was a rare gift, in Faerie, and not one possessed by stormdancers.

Wait—there were not only stormdancers here now. He sought out Gwendelfear and she shook her head haughtily, the message clear: *I don't take orders from you.* Her shoulders hunched, waiting for Hetta to command her.

Hetta's hand tightened on his, and he knew she was thinking of the Court of Dusken Roses, of Queen Tayarenn and Wyn's father, and tyranny.

Jack was having no such internal debates. "Well, are you going to help or not?" he asked Gwendelfear.

She examined the dying man on the sofa, and then said, "Get me water that hasn't been changed, that hasn't been subject to iron." When she'd healed Alexandra, they'd carted bucketfuls of lakewater from Starwater to a bathtub in Stariel House.

It took some persuasion, but eventually they managed to get some of the servants to carry down a hip-bath from another room and fill it with water from the ornamental pond at the back of Penharrow Manor. Wyn had no part in the persuasion; Hetta took it in hand. The servants eyed him with suspicion as they followed her orders, and he tried to become smaller even though all he wanted to do was release his wings and lie there panting. Stormwinds knew he couldn't blame them, not after the leviathans. Would those of Stariel, those who knew him better, have reacted differently?

He lay on the settee, time moving in fits and starts as he breathed and began to fold the pain away, building his mental block bit by bit. It was hard in this form, and harder still because his magic writhed, refusing to settle to his command. He was only peripherally aware of Gwendelfear dropping her glamour and summoning her magic, of cool greenish light filling the room and the scent of fresh lakeweed.

He finished his mental block and opened his eyes just as the light snuffed out and Lord Arran opened his eyes. The lord gave a shout of outrage—Gwendelfear was still perched over him, no glamour disguising her true form—and would've knocked her away except that her reflexes were faster than his. She sprang away as he splashed and flailed his way out of the hip bath.

"Get away, you! What is that, that *thing!?* What the blazes am I doing in this?"

Thing. Wyn didn't think; he changed to his fae form between one heartbeat and the next, leaning forward to give his wings space. His magic hummed into the void, and he let it.

"That *thing*," he said, voice crackling with frost, "is the lady Gwendelfear, who you can thank for saving your life, since she has just used her healing magic on your behalf. The water was a necessary part of it."

Gwendelfear's whiteless gaze met Wyn's. Dark circles showed beneath her eyes, her face nearly as gaunt as it had been when she'd left DuskRose. The healing had drained all the power she'd recovered from weeks of rest.

Lord Arran's lip curled. Wyn had to fight down the power that swelled in response, the urge to awe this disrespectful mortal into submission. *You will not look at her like that. You will not look at us like that.* Anger cold and clean as a blade hummed along his nerves, trailing down to his primaries, to the deeper thought beneath.

You will not look at my child like that.

Lord Arran flinched and clutched at the side of the bath for balance, dripping wet. He snarled at Hetta instead:

"I should've known you'd be in the middle of this trouble, girl. Is this what we have to look forward to now? Fairy monsters attacking people now you've gone to bed with one?"

"It's Lord Valstar to you." Hetta's voice was the same temperature as Wyn's.

Lord Arran just shook his head and stalked out without a backwards glance. A heavy silence fell. One of Hetta's hands slipped to her abdomen, the briefest flicker of a touch, and Wyn wanted to chase after Lord Arran—broken leg be damned—and *make* him apologise. Wyn knew exactly what she was thinking, for his thoughts traversed the same path, revolved around the same unhappy question: *Will people call our child a thing?* Wyn curled his hand into a fist. *Not if I have anything to do with it.*

Hetta sighed. "How many lords do you think I've alienated now?"

"I think I must take credit for the two who brandished knives at me earlier. So, between us, three?"

Her lips twitched. "I think you're being optimistic."

What about Penharrow? It had been hard to read the man amidst the chaos earlier, and he'd disappeared into the manor at some point after the hipbath had arrived, presumably to see to the rest of the injured and check the extent of the damage.

"We should get back to Stariel," Wyn said. The longer they were outside its bounds, the more risk of Aroset finding them, and he couldn't face his sister like this, a lame duck.

"*You* are going to stay on that couch and wait for the doctor to set your leg," Hetta told him. "Jack, go and see where Angus has got to and if Dr Greystark has arrived."

Gwendelfear made a hissing sound like a teakettle at boil and stalked over to Wyn.

"I will set it, storm prince." Her expression dared Wyn to comment. She glared at Jack. "Get me a knife. The boot will need to be cut off," she added impatiently when Jack didn't move. A whisper of a smile curled around her mouth. "Though I don't deny the temptation to use it in other ways."

"Thank you."

Gwendelfear pretended not to hear him. When Jack returned, knife in hand, she used it to remove his boot and trouser leg with ruthless efficiency, unmoved by Wyn's sharp breath as agony slammed down to his heel.

Hetta swallowed and sat down beside him, looking away. The way the bone jabbed through skin was very nauseating, Wyn agreed.

Gwendelfear scowled at the injury. "It was wise not to attempt to heal yourself till this was set," she said. "Otherwise it would need re-breaking to straighten it." She looked disappointed this wouldn't be necessary.

Wyn didn't move, but something gave him away, because Gwendelfear's eyebrows went up. "You don't know how to do that, do you?"

"I read the theory, when I was a boy," Wyn admitted. "But…" But he hadn't had the power necessary to attempt it, then. Now… now, maybe he had the power, but he wasn't sure he had the necessary control. In theory, greater fae with sufficient skill and power could redirect their own magic inwards, accelerate their own healing rate. It was an ability that required fine-tuned control as well as raw power.

Gwendelfear just made a sound of disgust. She set his leg, and Wyn lost time again. His awareness narrowed to Hetta's hand on his, to the red throb of pain, and he came back to himself, panting, as Gwendelfear upended a bucket of cold water over him. He winced. Was it truly necessary to splash such an excessive amount every-where? The settee was likely to be unsalvageable after this. Although that wouldn't be a problem for him to deal with. Perhaps not moving immediately to Stariel had been wise.

Gwendelfear thrust out a hand, demanding, and Wyn took it. She…pulled, was the best description he could come up with. He recoiled, an instinctive reaction to someone trying to grab at his magic, and Gwendelfear made an impatient noise.

"I don't have enough magic left for this myself, Oathbreaker. If you'd rather hop out of here…"

"Sorry." Wyn concentrated, but still nearly fumbled the connection—this was much less straightforward than linking to Rakken or Irokoi had been, since they shared blood—but Gwendelfear made up for his ineptness with sheer persistence. And they were, after all, the same court now. An unsettling thought.

The link snapped into place, and magic rushed out of him and into Gwendelfear. She made a sharp, startled noise, but her grip didn't falter. How many times had he been used as a magical battery, of late? He hoped this wasn't an omen of things to come.

His leg flared with heat as her magic washed over him, sunlight on lakewater. The relief from pain was so intense that it made him dizzy. Or perhaps that was merely the drain of his magic.

Gwendelfear released his hand and scrambled away as if burned. Her earlier gauntness had faded; her skin bloomed a healthy shade of green once more, and the colour had returned to her hair, all the shades of summer grass. If she'd looked like this when he and Hetta had tumbled through the Gate, he would've feared months rather than days had passed in their absence.

She panted, staring at him with an expression that unsettled him; it had too much in common with the lords and servants earlier.

"Unnatural," she muttered, a flash of her sharp teeth showing. She'd called him that once before; it didn't hit any more pleasantly now.

Wyn returned his own mirthless smile. "You are welcome." Because unnatural or not, she'd clearly benefited from his magic too. "And thank you."

He suspected the lesser fae had done it only to make it clear she owed him nothing for defending her to Lord Arran, but he didn't care what her reasons were, not when his leg lay smooth and straight and blessedly, blessedly *un*broken.

Although he did look quite ridiculous now, missing a trouser leg and a boot. He pulled the remaining one off, deciding that matching bare feet were slightly more acceptable than being lopsided.

"Yes, thank you, Gwendelfear. Or do you prefer Gwen?" Hetta frowned between the two of them.

Gwendelfear looked to Wyn, a slight movement of her eyebrow conveying her outrage.

"Names do not have the same weight, for mortals," he reminded her. Gwendelfear bristled like an angry cat.

"I know that, *Hallowyn,*" she spat.

He couldn't help it; his power snapped out at the insult, and she sucked in a breath and took a step back before he managed to wrest it under control again.

"Miss Gwen is acceptable, Lord Valstar," Gwendelfear said through clenched teeth.

Irokoi entered the room, and Wyn swung off the settee to full alertness.

"The good news," Irokoi said, "is that Set isn't anywhere nearby. The bad news is that she is indeed in the Mortal Realm once again. Somewhere to the south, I think." His feathers shifted. "Where did you say your older brother was located, Lord Valstar?"

35

MARMALADE

THEY TOOK THE kineticar back to Stariel, except Irokoi, who flew. Jack drove, which Hetta was privately grateful for, since a deep, foggy tiredness had descended over her. Part of her couldn't help thinking longingly of the quiet hush of the High King's library, where she'd only had to deal with herself, Wyn, and Irokoi, and she'd had the luxury of a simple, if fraught, goal: escape. Now that she was back, complications were rushing back in, not least worry for Marius.

At least he's got Rakken with him. Not a statement she'd ever expected to find comfort in, but so it was. At least, from what she'd gathered, Gregory was safely back within the bounds, though she didn't quite understand why yet. From the way Jack had refused to meet her eyes, she suspected it was somehow her fault.

"Rake left me a message-spell to activate to let him know when we'd returned," Wyn said softly. His tall frame was levered awkwardly into the front passenger seat. "It's in my room."

Whether it was Stariel's recent alarm or Jack's precipitous exit from the house that had warned them of something amiss, all of Hetta's relatives currently in residence awaited them at the entryway.

Hetta knew she needed to tell them…something, but her brain felt too exhausted to determine what.

Fortunately, Irokoi chose the moment they arrived to descend from the sky in a whirl of black feathers. His bare feet crunched on the gravel, and Hetta was struck by how out of place he appeared. Rakken hadn't hidden his fae side, but he'd had a veneer of civilisation. But Irokoi—with his long silver hair hanging loose to his waist, whipped into disarray by the wind, and the scar running down one side of his face—well, his appearance was very far from civilised.

"This is Wyn's brother, Prince Irokoi," she told her family.

Irokoi beamed as if he hadn't noticed the way Aunt Sybil was gaping at him.

"Valstars!" he said happily. "How very exciting to meet you all. Will you tell me your names? Or perhaps you should wait for us all to set our appearances to right first. We are all rather messy, aren't we? In our defence, it has been quite a busy day." He looked to Hetta, expression guileless. "May I borrow a bathing chamber, Lord Valstar?"

"Yes, of course." Hetta had no idea of the exact arrangement of bedchambers presently, but Wyn would know.

"Wyn—your foot! Are you well?" Lady Phoebe made a faint motion towards Wyn's bloodied bare feet, the cut-off trouser leg.

"I'm no longer injured, my lady, but I agree with my brother that we are sorely in need of cleaning up." He smiled at the Valstars, and despite their astonishment, several smiled back. Wyn had a singularly charming smile. "Come with me, Koi," Wyn said softly. He met Hetta's gaze, a silent longing there that she shared, but the chances of her being allowed to follow him uninterrupted back to his room were nil. She had to be satisfied with a mere nod as he led Irokoi into the house.

"I need to change as well. I'll see you all momentarily. Jack can answer questions in the meantime." She delegated ruthlessly. Jack shot her a dirty look. Hetta ignored it and fled.

A few minutes later, she sat on her bed, curling her fingers into the mattress, and breathed a deep sigh of relief. It wasn't only that standing on Stariel lands, she could protect the portion of her family already here, nor the magical sense of homecoming settling in her bones. It was the unwinding of a tightness she'd been carrying the entire time they'd spent in Faerie. Nothing had been safe or predictable there, even if parts of it had been astonishingly beautiful. Here she could be certain that butterflies were only butterflies.

Except Wyn is certainly not a butterfly. She brooded over the image of Wyn lying on Angus's sofa, pale and bleeding and still pretending so desperately hard to be human. They were going to have some meaningful words about that. She reached out, just to reassure herself that he was safe, felt the spark of him flare in response from his draughty attic.

Her hand went automatically to the heartstone at her throat. The colour had darkened considerably, now the rich deep blue of lapis. How many shades of blue between lapis and black? She tucked it back under her blouse, just as her stomach rumbled an interruption. For some reason, the tang of marmalade rose to mind, and abruptly it was all she could think of.

Well, there's sure to be marmalade in the kitchen. This is a one-time thing, she told herself as she called up an image of the kitchen door. *Not a habit I plan to get into.*

Translocation was followed by immediate regret; she hadn't taken into account the slightly different space Stariel House occupied compared to the rest of the estate. She swayed and grabbed at the open doorframe for support.

"My lord!" The cook's—Mrs White's—eyes widened. "Are you well?"

The delicious smell of freshly baked bread wafted towards her, and Hetta's stomach gave another grumble. "Just hungry," she admitted, looking around. The kitchen was otherwise empty. "Do you mind terribly if I beg some bread and butter off you now? And maybe marmalade? I've a sudden craving for it."

"Not at all." Mrs White ushered her to the kitchen table, and Hetta found herself in rapid possession of thick slices of still-warm bread set next to the requested condiments.

"Don't let me put you out," Hetta said when Mrs White wavered, as if uncertain whether she should ignore the lord in her kitchen or not. "You shouldn't have to rearrange your morning just because of my sudden marmalade craving."

"Ah, well, they say denying a babe-in-womb begets a petulant babe-in-hand," she said knowledgeably. Then she froze, her eyes wide as a startled deer's.

Hetta paused in the act of spreading butter. She really oughtn't to be surprised, but still! How dare her family get up in arms about her shaming the family name when they couldn't keep their own tongues from wagging!

"So I've heard," Hetta said with a calmness she didn't feel. At least there hadn't been any condemnation in Mrs White's expression.

Mrs White took a sharp breath as Hetta focused intently on the texture of the bread. After a beat, Mrs White returned to her work.

There was a small sound from the entryway. "Good morning, Mrs White. I'm hoping you may know the location of a misplaced lord—ah, my Star." Wyn had managed to change in a remarkably short time, every inch the human butler. His colour was better as well, and he didn't seem to be limping. Hetta was warming more and more to Gwendelfear's presence on the estate, since Wyn seemed to end up bleeding rather more than was reasonable.

Mrs White gave Wyn a look that was a great deal franker than the respectful way she'd treated Hetta. A lot of unspoken things went into the look, and to Hetta's surprise, Wyn flushed. What would the cook say if Hetta wasn't here?

"You should be more careful of her," Mrs White said eventually.

A bit of hauteur sharpened Wyn's features, but he didn't argue with the rebuke.

Hetta reluctantly left the sanctuary of the kitchen. To her surprise, Wyn didn't lead her straight to the hall or one of the sitting rooms. Instead he pulled her through the nearest side door and into a broom closet, hugging her against his chest. Hetta squeaked, though she wasn't exactly displeased. There was something undeniably appealing about him overcome with strong emotion, and she could feel him trembling.

"It's not going to add to my reputation to be seen emerging from broom closets, you know. Not that I apparently have any reputation left to lose. Even the cook apparently knows what's going on now."

"Hetta." His embrace tightened. "I—" He swallowed, piecing his self-control back together. "I'm glad we're home."

She lifted her head to meet his eyes. "Me too."

"I sent the message to Rakken."

36

THE EARL OF WOLVER

MARIUS ITCHED WITH sheer proximity as the train drew into Pickering Station in Meridon. Rakken was unsettling at close quarters and alone—the latter because Rakken had given everyone else who would've joined their carriage a *look* and they'd gone elsewhere. It hadn't exactly been compulsion, but that kind of *nudging* Rakken did with his aura wasn't a whole lot better.

But Marius was almost grateful for Rakken's…Rakken-ness, under the circumstances. It gave him something to focus on other than what they were travelling towards. Gods. The earl. His stomach twisted into knots, remembering the last time they'd met and how the earl had looked at him with such contempt.

Rakken said something.

"Pardon?" Marius said, coming out of his dark musings with a start.

Rakken gave a theatrical sigh. "I asked if there was a reason you were scowling at me—"

"General principle."

Rakken's mouth curved, but he continued without pause.

"—but I gather that you were in fact not thinking of me at all. How lowering."

"It's good for your ego, remember."

Rakken chuckled, low and smooth as sin, and Marius swallowed and looked away.

"I was thinking of what to say to the earl, if you must know. I hope you've come up with some sort of plausible explanation for accompanying me, since I'm planning to disavow all responsibility for you."

"I intend to tell the truth," Rakken said drily. Well, a selection of it.

Marius snorted despite himself. Though he was glad that Rakken was with him, and what had the world become that that was so? But Marius knew that Rakken wouldn't be fazed or self-conscious even if Marius himself dissolved into an inarticulate puddle of nerves— sadly probable—and having Rakken inflicted upon him was the least of what the earl deserved.

The train ground to a halt, and Marius sprang from his seat.

Rakken changed from mortal to fae as he stepped onto the platform, no longer confined by the carriage space. Marius couldn't pinpoint how he was so certain of this, since Rakken still *appeared* completely human and Marius had yet to puncture the glamour Rakken used on his wings with either experimental mixtures or headache-inducing staring. But he knew Rakken generally preferred his fae form whenever possible, and there was something in the way he moved when he was winged that made Marius sure of it.

Rakken raised his eyebrows, and Marius realised he'd been staring. He jerked into motion. "We can walk to Fairway from here."

The suburb was where everyone who was anyone lived, including the Earl of Wolver. The wide, airy Regent's Park separated the palace from the affluent suburb. They could take a hackney, but Marius desperately needed to discharge some of his nerves before the interview.

Rakken didn't object, and they threaded their way through the crowded station. Rakken was doing something again, because the Meridon public were never this respectful of personal space in the crowded train station when it was only Marius. He shot Rakken a narrow look, which Rakken pretended not to notice.

Passing a newspaper stand, Marius couldn't help scanning the headlines, wincing at the number relating to fae. Or Valstars. They weren't too different to the ones in Knoxbridge, which someone always made sure to put in his pigeon-hole just in case he'd missed one. No wonder Greg had been so easy to provoke, if he'd been receiving the same treatment before word of his brawling had reached the wrong ears and seen him sent down. Thinking of that injustice sparked a low anger, and Marius held the feeling close, needing the extra motivation. Anger was better than anxiety.

This meeting with the earl was going to go just fantastically, wasn't it?

As they walked, a headache germinated at the base of his skull, fighting with the knots in his stomach for discomfort. Marius rubbed his head with the heel of his hand, willing it to go away. *Not today, please, of all days!* The only thing that could make confronting a man who hated him worse would be doing it with a splitting migraine. He tried to block out the sounds of the station; sometimes that helped. Sullenly, the headache eased.

They passed a zealous-faced man attempting to thrust pamphlets at passers-by. Marius ignored the proffered document, but surprisingly, Rakken didn't. He came to a complete halt, leaving Marius walking alone for the few strides it took him to notice. He turned, about to remind Rakken that they had an appointment to make, when the pamphlet Rakken was holding up struck him. Printed in large letters was the headline: REJOICE! THE WINGED GODS RETURN TO US!

"Is this supposed to be about *fae?*" Marius burst out, incredulous.

"The winged gods have many names!" the pamphleteer told him happily. He had a Northern accent, and an unsettling light kindled in his eyes. "We are blessed to have them walk among us once more!"

The man believed it utterly. Marius stared at him, head starting to pound again. "How can you believe that? They're not gods! What about all the newspaper headlines?"

"Lies spread by their enemies!" the man said staunchly.

Rakken's voice grew soft and persuasive. "Tell me, have you ever met a greater fae?"

"The Storm Queen is gracious!"

All the hairs on the back of Marius's neck rose. *Storm Queen.* There was only one person that could mean: Aroset.

A faint hint of storms and citrus, but Rakken's tone remained low and smooth as velvet. "And are there more of you? Other 'wing worshippers'?"

"The Storm Queen will reward those who worship her! We are blessed!"

The scent of Rakken's magic strengthened, and the man sagged as if someone had cut his strings. He blinked at them and then down at the pamphlets in his hand.

"I… Who are you?" He bristled. "What's this about? You're one of them! You're one of them!" Panic spiked in his eyes, and he drew back his arm to throw the pamphlets in Rakken's face but froze before he could complete the motion. His eyes glazed over.

"Be calm. Feel unconcerned with the fae and return to your home. Do you remember where that is?"

The man shivered. "I…"

"Remember."

A sharp jerk of breath. "I remember."

"Go there. Now."

Rakken's power released with a snap, and the man dropped his pamphlets, whirled, and made a dash away through the station.

Passengers turned to see the source of the disturbance, wrinkling their noses as they dodged the drift of pamphlets now strewn across the floor.

Rakken stared in the direction the man had taken, expressionless, but Marius could tell he was furious.

"I detest clumsiness in spellwork, and Set hacked through that man's mind with all the subtlety of a mace. I pieced back together what I could, but I don't know if he will ever fully recover."

"She's here?"

Rakken shook his head. "His memories were useless, a single shining point of adoration centred on Set, but the binding was old. He hadn't been in recent contact with her, but clearly she's been in this city at some point." Anger flashed in his expression. "She bound him and set him loose without a care towards his eventual fate."

"And you care?"

Rakken's eyes were hard emeralds. "I don't care for pointless waste, and one owes a duty of care to lesser creatures, particularly those one takes under one's wings."

Lesser creatures. Marius's hands fisted, and he turned and stormed away from Rakken and the crumpled pamphlets. Unfortunately, Rakken's legs were just as long as his were—longer, actually—and he caught up within a few strides.

Marius couldn't speak as they left the station, afraid that if he began, he wouldn't stop until he was shouting. The day was overcast, and the air had a heaviness suggesting imminent thunderstorms.

"I won't pretend to be other than I am, Marius Valstar."

Marius couldn't tell if Rakken was trying to apologise—badly— or justify his actions. Sometimes he knew with unerring certainty what Rakken was thinking, but other times, like now, he had no idea.

"Humans aren't *lesser creatures*," he hissed.

"Ah, I thought that might be it. I will concede then, that not all of them are. But that man was weak and searching for someone to tell him what to believe long before my sister got hold of him. That is *why* she targeted him, of course. It is easiest to sway those inclined to fanaticism. The compulsion sticks better. Setting a long-lasting compulsion in direct opposition to someone's normal personality is nearly impossible." *Though perhaps not for me,* Marius could swear he felt Rakken silently add.

"That's not the— Gah!" Marius shook his head and sped up. *Though I actually didn't think he'd concede even that much. Is that progress?* He gave a bitter laugh but refused to explain it at Rakken's inquiring look.

They met the occasional other pedestrian—the gentlemen doffed their hats politely and the ladies smiled. These greetings were largely focused on Rakken, though they encompassed Marius also. At least that meant Marius looked like he belonged here. Self-consciousness briefly distracted him.

I do belong here—I'm a lord's son. But dredging up his father's authority didn't help his nerves—rather the reverse. What did the earl want from him? Marius knew he ought to be focused on the implications for Stariel and Wyn and Hetta, but the loudest thought was a selfish one: *Is the earl still with John? Will he be there today?*

Why should John be there? Marius tried to reassure himself. This was official business—Chief Inquirer into Fae Misconduct and all that—not about personal matters. Surely the earl wouldn't mix the two together, not when he was reporting to the queen.

"You know, if the earl's worried about all these fae stories, you showing up with me probably won't persuade the earl the Valstars aren't still far too much under fae influence."

"Perhaps you could tell him how very unsuccessful I have been at influencing you in my favour." There was an emphasis to the words that made Marius shoot Rakken a sharp glance. Rakken chuckled. "I wouldn't try to compel you, Marius Valstar. Even if I could."

The words were oddly reassuring. Still, Marius sighed and added,

"Please don't flirt with the earl."

"I *am* capable of other methods of communication."

"I'll believe that when I see it."

They reached the earl's townhouse. Marius eyed the knocker grimly before ascending the front steps. His heart beat so fast he felt dizzy. Angrily, he tried to calm himself. How would it look if he fainted on the earl's doorstep? *Like I'm a coward and a weakling and fifty other things my father has already called me.* What if his father had been right all along? He balled his hands into fists. *Just fake confidence—Rakken does it easily enough. Why can't you?*

He thought of Hetta and Gregory and the dizziness subsided. He could fake confidence for *their* sake, if not his own.

A butler opened the door. Marius summoned his most supercilious expression and presented his card.

"My name is Marius Valstar. I have an appointment."

The butler did not look surprised, but butlers rarely did, in Marius's experience. *Including our own,* he thought, thinking of Wyn's time serving in that capacity.

"May I inquire as to your companion's identity, Mr Valstar?"

"I am Prince Rakken Tempestren of the Court of Ten Thousand Spires."

The butler's eyebrows shot up at that, but he said, steadily enough, "Follow me, sir, Your Highness."

He led them into a drawing room to wait. "I shall inform the earl of your arrival."

They waited. The drawing room was orderly to a fault, which matched Marius's impression of the earl. Maybe that's what had attracted John—John liked things neat. He'd had prettier manners than Marius, for all that Marius was the lord's son and he the commoner. John used to tease him that—

I am not going to think about John.

But how was he supposed to *not* think about John when John was the reason he was here in the first place, if you followed the line of causality back to the start? If Marius hadn't loved John, John would never have come to Stariel. And if John had never come to Stariel, Wyn would never have needed to compel him and John wouldn't have been left with a bitter resentment of Stariel and fae both, wouldn't have used his new lover to try to get revenge. *So really, this entire thing is my fault for showing such bad judgement of character.* Marius did not look at Rakken.

"I find I'm sorry I never had the opportunity to witness my brother serving in such a capacity," Rakken said, gazing in the direction the butler had taken. "It would have been mildly entertaining to have him hold open doors for me."

"You seem confident he wouldn't have shut them in your face."

Rakken grinned. "That would also have been entertaining."

The butler returned.

"The earl would prefer to speak to Mr Valstar alone."

Marius thought Rakken would argue, but instead he said, "I can wait until he concludes his interview."

'*Can*', Marius thought. *Not 'will'.* Hmmm.

The butler led him through the townhouse to the earl's study. It was a large, airy room that reminded him of Hetta's study at Stariel.

"Ah, Mr Valstar." The earl rose to greet him, and Marius braced himself. Last time they'd met, he'd gotten the strong impression that the earl despised him—but there was nothing of that in his expression now. Instead, the earl was coolly evaluative. "May I offer you a brandy?"

Marius didn't feel like drinking at this hour but accepted the offer because it seemed less awkward than refusing. The earl took a decanter atop a small cabinet at the far end of the room and gestured for Marius to seat himself. The silence pressed on Marius as the earl poured two glasses. The man had at least a decade on Marius, but he was one of those men that aged well. He still had to have married rather young to have a son Gregory's age. Did his wife know about his predilections? Did the queen? Was John a rare anomaly for the earl, or did he frequently indulge in affairs?

Don't speculate on the earl's love life, Marius told himself sternly. This interview was already going to be sufficiently awkward without that. They were both adults; they could ignore the great thumping elephant in the room. John wasn't why he was here.

"Thank you for coming. I am aware our last meeting was not… salubrious."

"You mean when you tried to frame my future brother-in-law? Or when you had your newspapers publish various inflammatory columns about my sister?"

The earl had a disturbingly penetrating gaze. "Yes."

"You left John." Knowledge tumbled into him with painful certainty, and his headache flared to life again. "You left John." Of all the possibilities, that one hadn't occurred to him. Sudden, unexpected jealousy rose, not of John but of the fact that the earl had been the one to *end* the relationship. How Marius wished the same had been true for him.

The earl started. "Yes," he repeated, more grimly. His fingers flexed on his glass.

Marius abruptly realised the *other* reason he felt unsettled. There were, after all, such an abundance of reasons to choose from, but this particular one flared into his mind in a burst of crimson embarrassment. How had he overlooked it earlier? And why did he have to be realising it *now* when he would much prefer *never* to realise it?

It wasn't only that the earl liked men and knew that Marius did as well—it was that he and the earl had *shared the same lover*. The weight of that knowledge expanded between them, an awkward intimacy Marius would rather not have experienced. They both knew the shape of the same man, the heat of skin on—*Don't think about it, don't think about it.* But Marius had been cursed with a vivid imagination, and certain memories were hard to forget.

Marius *willed* himself not to flush, but it was a losing battle—he could feel the heat in his cheeks as he met the earl's eyes and knew, he just knew, the earl was having the exact same thought.

"We were both taken in by the same pretty face, it seems." The earl tipped his glass in ironic salute and drank.

Oh, Marius did not want to be here. He wanted to be ten thousand million miles away and not hearing this. Could you actually pass out from sheer mortification? He took a sip of the brandy, the burn in his throat nearly as intense as that in his cheeks.

And yet—and yet, there was a queer comfort, beneath the embarrassment. The earl had spoken with dry resignation, but there was a bitter hurt in him that resonated with Marius's own. The earl *understood* this particular heartache, understood as no one else possibly could.

Marius hunched his shoulders up, unwilling to admit anything. His head throbbed. *You're being ridiculous—he already knows about you and John. You're not keeping anything secret. And he can hardly condemn you without condemning himself.*

"Yes," he said eventually, the word fighting its way through his teeth. What had happened between the earl and John? He couldn't ask but he wanted to. No, he didn't. Why had Marius even raised the subject in the first place? He didn't want to talk about it! "Why did you ask me here today?"

The earl, thank Mighty Pyrania, accepted the rebuff and didn't try to pursue the subject. He twisted his glass so that the amber liquid swirled. "Her Majesty has charged me with investigating the implications of this fae invasion for the Crown." He read Marius's expression correctly and sighed. "I regret that I allowed myself to become…emotionally compromised in my previous dealings with Stariel. I have assured Her Majesty it will not happen again."

"Queen Matilda gave you a second chance."

Again, that cool gaze assessed him. "Yes, she did. Are you always so blunt?"

"If you want a silver-tongued diplomat, you can invite Prince Rakken in, the man currently occupying your drawing room. I'm just a botanist."

The earl put his glass down. "A botanist with a royal bodyguard. A botanist Prince Hallowyn was prepared to both use compulsive magic for and lie to Her Majesty about in order to protect—no, don't correct me. I know perfectly well the fae cannot speak untruths and yet are simultaneously adept at misdirection."

Wyn had managed to slide around admitting his use of compulsion to Queen Matilda with his usual side-stepping, and Marius wasn't about to undo his friend's hard work.

"If you broke things off with John, then you know he's a liar. Whatever he said—"

"Oh, I've no doubt his framing of context was entirely false. But he has a personal and powerful hatred of Prince Hallowyn that rings true."

There was a long silence. Marius knew the earl wanted to know what had really happened at Stariel, not only for personal reasons but political ones. His head throbbed. How far could fae be trusted? Was Wyn truly as committed to peace as he'd said? How should the Crown respond to the potential threat?

Marius let out a long breath. "My sister is going to marry him, my lord. Whatever John told you, Wyn's one of the best men I know. I'd trust him with my life. With my sister's life." Which he was trying very hard to remember with every day that passed with no word from Hetta and Wyn.

"And yet if you are so anxious to protect fae interests, why are you experimenting with plants known for affecting fae?"

Marius flinched. "Are you spying on me?"

The earl's gaze was hard. "Spying is an unpleasant term. The Crown merely…keeps track of interesting individuals."

Marius didn't have an answer to this, or at least, not one he was prepared to give the earl. How could he tell the earl he thought the fae were dangerous without betraying Hetta and Wyn? The fae *were* dangerous, even the ones on their side, and the more than six feet of wing, muscle, and compulsive magic currently waiting in the earl's drawing room was just one example of how.

"Can you tell me you aren't concerned about the fae, Mr Valstar?"

"They're not…simple," Marius said. "You can't just slice them into either bad or good—gods, you can't slice most things into that."

"Then what would you advise me to tell Her Majesty? You must have seen the increasing public anxiety in the papers. The incident between Prince Hallowyn and his sister at the train station was highly visible and deeply concerning for the public. Public meetings have been held, pamphlets distributed, that sort of thing. Protests will be next. And the compulsive ability John spoke of—*that* is concerning indeed, even if it hasn't yet reached the public awareness."

"Yes, and you've done such a good job of keeping anti-fae sentiment out of the papers," Marius said bitterly. "I thought Her Majesty told you to stop that?"

Irritation flickered in the earl's eyes. "I am not actually in control of every media outlet. Nor do I advocate censorship. Though there actually are a number of stories that haven't made the papers, under my watch."

"Yet," Marius bit out. Righteous anger took hold of him. "Don't pretend you have any moral high ground! Gregory's got nothing whatsoever to do with this and he's practically still a child. He's not even nineteen yet!" If the earl threw his weight around to stop the university accepting Gregory back next term… "Oh. You didn't know about that." Marius's anger came to a screeching halt in the face of the earl's blankness.

"What precisely do I not know?"

"Er…your son and his friends got into a fistfight with my brother. My brother was rusticated for the rest of term. Your son wasn't, even though he provoked the confrontation."

"And you naturally assumed I would wage war via hot-headed eighteen-year-olds." There was a tight anger in the earl's voice.

"I've no idea what you would or wouldn't stoop to. You had no problem blackening my sister's reputation."

The earl's fingers spasmed on his glass, and Marius thought he was about to lose his temper. However, when he spoke it was in an even tone. "I would never encourage such behaviour. I will speak to James, and the university. I have left his schooling too much in his mother's care, perhaps. She's very protective of him." Uncertainty coloured his tone. When they'd drawn the careful lines that governed their relationship, his wife had made it clear she considered James' schooling to fall entirely within her sphere. It had seemed the least he could give her.

Marius recoiled, not wanting the insight into the earl's marriage. *Maybe I'm reading too much into things.* The pain in his temples sharpened.

The earl shook himself, leaving the subject behind and drawing the mantle of authority around himself again. "Are you aware Prince Hallowyn promised Her Majesty a treaty between his court and Stariel in exchange for her permission for Lord Valstar to marry?"

Marius remained silent, dreading what was coming next.

"His Highness made this promise on the assumption that he would inherit the throne of his home court. It has come to my attention that this assumption has not been borne out in fact."

What should Marius do? Lie? Lying to the queen's advisor seemed like a bad idea. "He's working on it." That was sort of true, wasn't it? His chest tightened. They should have heard from Wyn and Hetta by now. What if something had happened to them? Rakken had said he'd know if Wyn died, but that wasn't exactly reassuring. There were a lot of things short of death that Rakken *wouldn't* know about, and what about Hetta? Why in the hells had they let her go without more protest? Weren't pregnant woman supposed to sit at home and be cosseted? Could Hetta not be so damn reckless just *once*?

"Working on it," the earl repeated flatly. "Her Majesty has already extended your sister and Prince Hallowyn considerable leeway on this."

"And the deadline she gave them hasn't passed yet." Marius felt on firmer ground.

"Hmmm. And the compulsive magic? How do you propose we are to protect our people from such a thing, with fae apparently appearing behind every bush, if the tabloids are to be believed."

"The ones in the papers—those are lowfae, maybe the odd lesser fae," Marius said. "They have magic, but not compulsion. Only greater fae can compel. And it's not as limitless a power as you think. Compelling people to do something they don't already want to do is hard, even for greater fae. There are protections you can wear, certain herbs made into charms." It felt like betrayal, but Marius pushed the feeling aside. He wouldn't do anything that made it easier for fae to compel people. Besides, the queen already knew about yarrow.

The earl listened with interest, asking several pointed questions. It began to rain, a sudden downpour that filled the awkward pauses in the conversation with white noise.

Something tickled in the back of Marius's mind. The earl had expressed his doubts that Wyn would keep his promise, and he was worried about the wider implications of fae…

"You're thinking about how to stop fae from coming to Prydein at all."

The earl's eyes narrowed. "We already require foreign citizens to declare themselves at the border."

"I'm not sure how you'd enforce that, given the nature of the border we're talking of here—" Marius began, before he followed the thought to its conclusion. "Oh. You'd put the onus of proof onto them to prove they've been permitted in. Make them carry papers? I'm not sure how you'll get them to agree to that." His eyes widened. "Oh. *Oh.* Do you *want* to start a war with fae courts? I'm pretty sure imprisoning or attacking their greater fae would be a good way to do that."

The earl was looking at him with deep suspicion. "That is a dangerous combination, insight paired with an inability to hold your tongue."

"I'm right, though, aren't I? That *is* what you're thinking of doing." Marius rubbed at his head, trying to ease the pounding in his temples.

"I see few alternatives, unless we can reach agreements with all the individual courts, of which I gather there are many who are at war with each other."

Marius hesitated, then decided the risk was worth it. "You need the High King to intervene—whatever he decrees, the courts will have no choice but to fall in with. You know Wyn—Prince Hallowyn—and my sister are searching for him currently."

The earl's mouth thinned into a line. "Prince Hallowyn's promises have so far proved fairly empty. In any case, there is a need for a visible ambassador between Faerie and Prydein—here, in this city, not far in the isolated North."

Wyn would do it—but Wyn should damn well be focusing on Hetta!

The door opened and Rakken strolled in and shut it behind him. The earl started, but Rakken nodded at him.

"Lord Wolver. My apologies for the interruption, but I felt I could add to the conversation at this juncture. You wish all fae to swear guestright within the Mortal Realm?"

"Eavesdropping is considered rude," the earl said in a tone of ice, his hands digging into the arms of his chair.

"Oh, I know," Rakken said, seating himself as though he'd been invited. "But the fate of my people is at stake here, Lord Wolver. Surely you didn't seriously expect me to place more weight on manners than them? Of course I eavesdropped." Rakken had reeled in his lazy sensuality, but he still moved like a predator, confident and deadly.

He and the earl took each other's measure. On the surface they were a study in contrasts, but some kind of shared understanding passed between them, a wolf and a panther meeting in the night. And Marius the foolish rabbit caught out after dark.

The earl broke first. "What is guestright?"

"A promise to abide by the laws of the host and not harm the host's people unless they strike first," Marius said.

Rakken inclined his head. "Guestright works, firstly, because it is an old and respected tradition, and fae like old things. But we are not bound by mere sentiment. Ultimately, guestright works because of the ability of faelords to enforce it. FallingStar—what you call Stariel—is the only mortal faeland in Prydein that I am aware of. But the faelords of Faerie could set rules for their own people, even outside their faelands, if they were given sufficient incentive." A flash of teeth.

The earl considered him. "If you were eavesdropping, you know I was speaking to Mr Valstar about the need for a visible fae ambassador to help alleviate public anxiety."

Rakken smiled. "Yes, I did. And I happen to agree. ThousandSpire is one of the largest courts of Faerie, and I am one of its princes."

Marius felt faintly indignant, even though Rakken had been upfront about his intent. How did he *do* that? And he wasn't even flirting!

"We have received approaches from other fae. The Court of Dusken Roses. They suggested that your brother's court is in some difficulties and that an alliance between Prydein and the Court of Ten Thousand Spires wouldn't be advantageous."

Rakken didn't react. "Did they also name me a murderer?"

Why would he bring that up?!

The earl's eyes widened slightly, but more because of Rakken's frankness than because the information was new to him.

Rakken read him easily. "Ah, I see that they did. It's true: my sister and I are responsible for the death of DuskRose's crown prince." He sat back, utterly relaxed, except that Marius knew intuitively that he was anything but. Sharks swam in the murky depths beneath his unruffled surface.

The earl stared at him. "That's a curious announcement for a supposed ambassador to make. This other fairy court offered very favourable terms."

"And yet you have not embraced them whole-heartedly. Perhaps you dislike the thought of your country being used as a proxy for a fae war?"

"I dislike it deeply."

"I too do not wish ThousandSpire's war with DuskRose to spill onto Mortal soil. That war has cost enough." Rakken laced his fingers together. Marius felt as if he were watching a chess match in the dark.

"What are you proposing?"

"That you not take sides. I see no reason why you may only have a single fae ambassador, unless the High King himself appoints one. Without his direction, we are not a united people. You accept ambassadors from individual mortal nations, so why should the courts of Faerie be treated differently? Let ThousandSpire and DuskRose settle their differences in Faerie and without dragging mortal affairs into it."

"You seem very certain DuskRose will accept that."

Rakken shrugged. "I do not trust Queen Tayarenn, and I trusted her son even less when he lived. But Princess Sunnika is less war-minded than her aunt, and I assume it was she who approached you."

The earl attempted to give nothing away, but even Marius could tell Rakken had guessed correctly. Rakken paused. "It's my understanding that you have not known war here for a generation." He lost his relaxed posture. For a moment, it wasn't beauty or charm that radiated from him but the bone-deep weariness of a soldier that made Marius wonder again exactly how old he was. "I would give a great deal to preserve such a state of affairs, if I were you."

There was a long silence. "I'll consider what you've said."

IT WAS STILL RAINING steadily when the earl dismissed them, and they bundled into a hackney. Marius braced himself for the downpour between the earl's doorstep and the hackney's interior, but it didn't come.

He shot a questioning look at Rakken, who seemed faintly amused by his surprise.

"You used air magic."

"I saw no need to get wet."

"Thank you."

Rakken blinked, as if he didn't trust Marius's words not to hold some hidden barb. *I haven't been very nice to him, after all. Though in fairness he hasn't been very nice to me either.* But Marius supposed being sent on a babysitting mission while others sought the answers to freeing his twin hadn't been Rakken's idea of a good time either.

"And thank you for guarding me. I appreciate it, even if the need for it annoys me. We can use a portal to Stariel once we get back to Knoxbridge. Maybe there's some news. I don't have any classes to teach until after the mid-term break now anyway." If Aroset was still at large then, what was he going to do? *Think about that when it happens.* He'd been terrified when Rakken had first appeared, but the more time that passed without incident, the more he began to think Aroset wouldn't appear.

The way Rakken eyed him made him shift in his seat, uncomfortable with its intensity. After a long, fraught pause, Rakken said, "I don't require reassurance from you, Marius Valstar. But thank you." He said the words as if they were slightly foreign objects, with a weight he wasn't used to. Maybe that was exactly the case. Marius couldn't imagine Rakken thanking people often.

The wall went up between them again.

"Did you…get what you wanted, from the earl?" Marius asked. The entire interaction had left him both flustered and worried. "Did you mean it, about not wanting a war by proxy here? That whole conversation felt like it was purely to combat DuskRose's influence—and how did you even know they'd be talking to the queen as well?"

"Because they'd have to be fools not to." Rakken attention was far away, his face in profile.

Before Marius could stop himself, he found himself asking, "Why did you kill their prince? What happened?"

Rakken didn't turn from the window, his silence so absolute that Marius might as well have been alone.

Marius swallowed. "Er, right. You don't want to talk about it. Sorry. But in fairness, *you* were the one who brought it up with the earl in the first place. And you know, there are other ways to communicate than ignoring me whenever you don't want to answer questions."

Rakken continued to ignore him, but the corner of his mouth twitched, and the silence for the rest of the ride was merely cool as opposed to glacial.

Marius paid the hackney, and they emerged under the shelter of the awnings opposite the station. He inspected his wristwatch. "The train to Knoxbridge leaves on the hour. Which leaves us with half an hour before the next one."

The rain fell in a steady grey drizzle, ageing the day past the actual hour, and Marius grimaced. Should he remove his spectacles? They were nearly useless when covered in raindrops, but walking in public without them made him feel curiously vulnerable, turning everything more than a few feet away into a blurry landscape of indistinct shapes. His gaze drew inexorably to the main entrance, where Aroset had appeared from a portal and tried to kill him. He shivered and took off his glasses and put them carefully in his coat pocket. He could cross a damn street without them.

Rakken tensed and dug a hand into his pocket. He held up a disc the size of a coin made of polished metal. "Hallowyn has returned to Stariel."

"With Hetta?"

"I assume so." He added before Marius could ask, "It works via sympathy—I left its mate at FallingStar to alert me if a portal opened there."

Relief flooded him. "Thank Pyrania." Marius looked at the driving rain. "Unfortunately, I didn't bring an umbrella, so are you up for a bit more air magic?"

Rakken stiffened. Had Marius's presumption offended him? But then Marius caught it—the scent that had haunted his nightmares. The stormy edge was lost in the downpour, but the notes of copper and roses were clear enough.

Aroset. Even blurred, Marius could see the distortion forming around the station entrance, the sign of a portal beginning to form.

"Hang on tightly," Rakken said grimly.

"What?" But the word became a squawk as Rakken unceremoniously hauled Marius into his arms and launched them both skywards.

Outrage fought with utter bewilderment, but both succumbed to the stomach-dropping sensation of *flying*. He latched his arms around Rakken's neck and hung on for dear life.

An analytical part of his mind was saying things like: *he's compensating for his damaged primaries with air magic* and *yes, this probably is a much better idea than confronting Aroset.* The air around them was so dense with citrus and storms that Marius swore he could see reality warp under the weight of glamour, even through the blurry rain.

Marius closed his eyes because everything going invisible was deeply upsetting this far above the ground. *He's trying to prevent Aroset from seeing where we go, trying to hide in the storm. She's older than him, and stronger, but the Maelstrom gave him unnaturally powerful glamour. Did the Maelstrom augment all of Wyn's siblings' powers in unique ways? Why did Rakken get glamour and compulsion and Aroset get portals? And what did Wyn get? The ability to be sane and relatively normal?*

The non-analytical part of him was screaming in panic. How far were they above the ground? How close was Aroset? Could Rakken actually fly for long with his wings still damaged, air magic or not? Marius was flying *in a storm*, and rain quickly drenched all the parts of him that weren't pressed against Rakken. Parts of him were pressed against Rakken. He shouldn't be noticing that. How could he be noticing that while panicking about *literally everything that was happening right now:* the swooping, gut-dropping sensation of each wingbeat, the rush of wind against his ears, the neat slicing sound of Rakken's feathers resisting the air, the freezing cold of the rain lashing his skin, and the hum of magic thick enough to choke on.

But how could he *not* notice Rakken, given how he blazed hot as a furnace in contrast to the ice cold of the storm? Particularly since Marius's eyes were still closed so all he could do was *feel*.

He'd never before appreciated just how strong fae—or at least stormdancers—were. Rakken held Marius's weight with no apparent effort, muscles flexing with every wing beat. Marius might be skinny, but he wasn't exactly a light-weight even though Rakken was manhandling him like one. The thought sparked indignation, which was unreasonable. Rakken was clearly trying to save them both from ending up as two piles of charred ashes outside the train station. Manhandling was the least of his worries.

Marius's heart pounded, though he couldn't separate its rhythm from the beat of Rakken's wings and the dizzying see-sawing motion of the storm buffeting them. He kept remembering the piercing pain in his head from Aroset trying to compel him, the choking feel of her fingers round his throat, lifting him as if he weighed nothing. He shuddered and tightened his grip.

He didn't know how much time had passed when they descended, the shock of landing reverberating through him. He opened his eyes. They were outside the greenhouse in Knoxbridge. On the ground. Oh, thank the gods. He needed to extricate himself, but his muscles were locked in place by a powerful combination of cold, terror, and awkwardness.

Rakken dropped his glamour and came into focus, though everything beyond him remained a rain-drenched blur. Marius suspected he himself was doing a stellar impersonation of a drowned, squinting rat, but Rakken looked like some sort of wildly magnificent barbarian. *Of course he does.* The storm had made wet snaking tendrils of his dark hair, and water droplets clung to him like bits of crystal. His wings were better than the last time Marius had seen them unglamoured but still clipped and missing feathers. How the hell had he managed to fly with those?

"The leylines are quiet," Rakken murmured, folding his ruined wings behind him. "She hasn't followed us." His eyes burned with something more primal than triumph—exhilaration. He'd gloried in the feel of the storm beneath his wings. *Stormdancers.* It wasn't an entirely poetic name, was it? How long since Rakken had last flown? It had clearly cost him to fly on his damaged wings—his chest heaved with exertion and there was a hollowness to his cheeks, shadows under his eyes as if the energy had stolen from his very flesh—but he practically shone with triumph despite his evident exhaustion. His heartbeat pounded against Marius where their bodies touched.

Their bodies were *touching*, and it became abruptly impossible to think of anything except that and the fact that Rakken's chest was extremely warm and firm and—all the little gods help him—covered in a shirt that was now completely wet. Adrenalin, Marius knew, could have strange effects on one's libido, but he could do without this particular stab of it right now.

Marius made an inarticulate noise of protest and released his death-grip on Rakken's neck, sliding gracelessly back into gravity's grasp. His feet hit the soft ground with a shock of weight, and he would've scrambled back except that his shoulder blades immediately hit the wall of the greenhouse.

He couldn't meet Rakken's eyes because it would make the entire thing far too intimate, and his heart was beating so fast he wasn't sure it could take any additional stimulus. Instead he stared fixedly at Rakken's throat.

"We should…the portal. Um. Thank you. Again. Right."

Fingers touched his chin and he started violently. Rakken tsked and tilted his chin up. "By the stormwinds, Marius Valstar, you are bad for my ego."

Rakken's eyes were too green. Marius knew words for at least twenty different shades of green, but he couldn't find the adjective to adequately describe the colour now. Emerald was too cold a word, too bound up in hard stone. Rakken's eyes were a living green. Perhaps some variety of moss growing under the dappled green light of new spring leaves? Why the fuck was he thinking about that with Rakken's fingers still resting under his chin? Actually, maybe green was an excellent subject to focus on, except he couldn't not be aware of those little points of heat against his skin. Rakken was close enough that Marius could see the occasional gold hairs sprinkled amongst the black of his eyelashes. The supple fullness of his lips, which Marius was absolutely not looking at.

Marius swallowed and rasped, "What are you doing?" *Almighty stormwinds, Marius, do you really need to ask?* No one would stand this close and touch like that by *accident.* But what if this was some peculiar bit of fae culture Marius had yet to encounter? Gods, he couldn't imagine anything more awkward than misjudging such a thing from Rakken of all people.

Rakken tilted his head. "I can practically *see* your thoughts chasing in all directions. Apparently, I'm not being sufficiently obvious. What a surprising reflection." He brushed the pad of his thumb along Marius's jawline, heat against rain-cooled skin.

Marius took a deep breath, trying to dispel the surge of lust tightening things low in his body. *Gods, I do not want Rakken to know how he affects me if this is all some bizarre joke to him.* Cold showers. Ice on the lake.

Rakken sighed. "Apparently *still* not sufficiently obvious. Marius Valstar, may I kiss you?"

Marius jerked and whacked the back of his head against the side of the greenhouse. "Ow!" Sweet Mother Eostre. He rubbed at his head, ringing with shock. "You…you *what?*" The words didn't seem to adequately capture the situation. "Why?"

Rakken glanced skywards, as if for patience. "Because I desire it." He met Marius's eyes. "May I," he repeated, "kiss you?"

Lust and confusion ripped through Marius so viciously he could hardly breathe. "You—you can't—why are you *asking?*" He didn't recognise his own voice, it had gone so scratchy.

Rakken looked down at Marius with the predatory gaze of a panther. "To receive an answer, obviously. Which is…?"

Marius's mouth went dry, but he opened it to say of course he didn't want Rakken to kiss him, the arrogant cad, and what kind of question even was that? You couldn't just ask people that sort of thing out of nowhere, and you weren't supposed to actually verbalise it in any case. It was all just supposed to—to *happen*, as it were. In a way that was no one's fault and definitely no one asking for anything.

And weren't they supposed to be portalling to Stariel as quickly as possible? What if Aroset had managed to follow them after all? Was this truly a sensible activity to be proposing right now?

And why in Pyrania's name did Rakken want to kiss *him*, Marius Valstar, skinny botanist with a history of bad judgement? *Yes, like the bad judgement that is happening RIGHT NOW.* He should shove Rakken away.

But the words stuck in his throat and failed to come out, held back by sheer animal *want*. What was he *doing?* He wasn't an animal, to be ruled by instinct, but he was shivering with cold, and Rakken practically radiated heat, and he was *so close*, and Marius thought he might die if he didn't close the gap between them. *Oh yes, try to justify this bout of insanity with some vague need for body warmth!* Marius couldn't argue with his inner voice of cool reason, but he still said nothing, caught in the grip of a much hotter and far less reasonable emotion. The silence wound tighter and tighter.

Rakken canted his head. "As an alternative to your indecisiveness, I'm *going* to kiss you now, Marius Valstar, unless you wish to voice an objection?" He paused, raising an eyebrow.

Marius should say something. Anything. Anything *at all*.

He said nothing.

Rakken kissed him. It was unexpectedly gentle, a slow siege that slid under his guard. He'd never been kissed like this, like he was being seduced. And gods, it was seductive, Rakken's persuasive mouth and the heat of his hand on the back of Marius's neck, firmly directing angles. Marius's fingers curled in the material of Rakken's shirt, unsure if he was holding on for dear life or pulling him closer.

Rakken tasted like rain and citrus, like kissing a storm-tossed lemon orchard or some other, better metaphor Marius's mind was too demented to come up with. It filled the aching loneliness at the centre of him, despair washing away under raw physicality, nothing but heat and the hard, throbbing awareness of his own body, the animal desire to rut. Gods, he hadn't felt this alive in months, not since he and John—and that thought brought him crashing back.

"No," he said, shoving Rakken away. Rakken went easily, but the lines of his face hardened.

"No?" Rakken said, lifting an eyebrow. His tone was dispassionate, but his pupils were blown wide, the black swallowing the green of his irises. His mouth was flushed red. He wasn't as unaffected as he wanted to seem. Good. Why was that good? Marius shouldn't want Rakken to want him. He didn't. *Well done for making sense in your own head.*

"You don't even like me, Rakken. And I don't like you. We aren't even friends." They weren't, were they? When had he somehow forgotten that? He *didn't* like this man—this fae—with his insufferable arrogance and questionable ethics, regardless of how addled he made Marius's hind brain. His hind brain wasn't supposed to be in charge of decision-making. *Remember the trouble it got you into the last time!*

Rakken gave Marius a slow inspection from head to toe, lingering on certain unmistakably aroused aspects of his anatomy. "That need not be an obstacle," he drawled. "You clearly *desire* me."

Marius flushed. *Oh gods, let the earth open up and swallow me now.*

"That's not the point! The point is I'm not a toy for you to play with just so you can get your unwanted attraction to an infuriating mortal out of your system!" He was trembling. He wasn't even sure where the words had come from, but they felt true. Rakken's narrowed eyes certainly suggested he'd struck true.

He doesn't want to want me any more than I want to want him. The realisation stung, and another, more bitter one came on the heels of it: Rakken's magic was drained after summoning such powerful glamour and flying them here with his damaged wings; he needed more magic before he could build a portal to Stariel. But strong emotions could augment fae magic, couldn't they? Strong emotions like *desire?*

"And I'm not bloody fuel for you to recharge your magic with! That's what this was about, wasn't it?"

Rakken didn't deny the accusation as Marius pushed past him. Nor did he make any attempt to stop him, which made Marius irrationally angry. "I'm not some weak mortal you can use just because it's convenient! None of us are!"

Of course Rakken never did things for *simple* reasons; of course everything had to serve some ulterior motive, even something as base as lust. *Gods, I'm a fool.* Shame coiled roots through him, snuffing out the remnants of desire.

Marius shivered as he let himself into his greenhouse, soaked to the bone. He'd been so terrified of being used again, of being overwhelmed by desire and loneliness and falling yet again for the wrong man as a result. But he…hadn't done that, had he? He'd just pushed away the walking definition of The Wrong Man. The comfort was cold but oddly energising. He turned, shoring up that newfound knowledge. He wouldn't let himself be used again.

He turned to close the door, found Rakken watching him hungrily—but there was no apology in his expression.

"Marius—" Rakken lifted a hand and dropped it, as if he hadn't meant to make the gesture.

Marius cut him off. "You can come in when you've recovered enough magic to build a portal. Otherwise, you can damn well stand out there and drown, for all I care." He shut the door.

37

NAMING CONVENTIONS

E WILL RETURN shortly. Our sister temporarily delayed us. Marius is safe.

What did it mean, temporarily delayed? Hetta turned the words Rakken had sent to Wyn over again. Couldn't Rakken have been slightly more explicit? But then, when did fae ever speak plainly if being cryptic was an option? At least he'd said Marius was safe.

Cryptic Exhibit A was chatting unconcernedly with Hetta's stepmother on the chesterfield. Irokoi had changed to mortal form and now wore human clothes and shoes. He hadn't given Hetta any more information when pressed except to express enthusiasm for Rakken and Marius's returning as soon as possible.

I wish I could figure out what he's playing at. Remembering the ancient frost of his power, the deliberateness with which he'd unfurled it, it was hard not to see Irokoi's air of bewildered innocence as pure camouflage. With age came power, Wyn had said more than once, and Irokoi was the oldest, wasn't he?

Camouflage or not, it was working on Hetta's older female

relations. Even Aunt Sybil's rigid disapproval from earlier had softened. But then, Aunt Sybil had a soft spot for all handsome young—or apparently young—men, up to and including Rakken, so her judgement was clearly not to be trusted.

"Alexandra is named for my mother's sister, who died when I was a girl," Phoebe was telling Irokoi. "Gregory for Henry's great-uncle." Her expression faltered at the mention of her son, and Hetta felt a twinge of guilt. She hadn't spoken directly to Gregory yet, but from the way her younger brother refused to meet her eyes, she had a fairly good idea why he'd been sent down from university. Yet another thing to put on her list of problems she'd indirectly caused and now needed to solve.

"You frequently name children after other people, then?" Irokoi asked, fascinated.

"Oh, yes, all the time! And a good thing too because sometimes I think there are so many Valstars that if we didn't reuse names we'd run out! But Laurel is simply because I liked the sound of it. She was going to be Jessica, but it didn't suit once she was born."

Hetta decided to make her exit. The press of things she needed to catch up with weighed on her. Jack had disappeared onto the estate, apparently leaping at the chance to be rid of his delegated authority, and babbling something about a royal message, but she needed to pin him down again and get a proper debrief.

She stood to go, but Irokoi turned to her. "I don't think you should name your children after Aeros, given what Hallowyn did to him. But what was your mother's name?"

"Edith," Hetta said faintly. Her family's attention fixed on her interestedly.

Phoebe took pity on her, asking Irokoi kindly, "And what is your mother's name, Prince Irokoi?"

Irokoi's delight dimmed for a beat. "They called her Ryn."

"But that wouldn't do for a boy," Aunt Sybil pointed out.

"It wouldn't?" Irokoi looked surprised. "Oh, I don't know the rules of these mortal naming conventions. Can you combine them? Edyn? Rydith? Hettyn? Wynetta?" He sounded entirely delighted.

Hetta looked up to see Wyn frozen mid-step on the threshold.

"Brother!" Irokoi said brightly. "Apparently you can name children after other people. Don't you think *my* name is an excellent one?"

"My Star," Wyn said, ignoring Irokoi with a composure Hetta envied. He gestured towards the hallway in an apologetic way. "Forgive the interruption, but would you mind stepping out for a moment…"

Hetta stood hastily. "No, of course not." She tried to keep her pace dignified and radiate an aura of official-business-ness as the two of them made their escape.

"*Thank* you," she said fervently when they'd reached her study. The fragments of Irokoi and Phoebe's conversation skittered around the room, unspoken but as present as the heavy wooden furniture and colourful prints on the wall. "I'd like to strongly veto Wynetta. Actually, I'd like to veto *all* of Irokoi's suggestions."

Wyn swallowed. "Agreed."

The weight of the future reality in which they had a *child* with a *name* pressed down on her. It seemed to be having a similar effect on Wyn; his expression as he stood next to the window was smooth and unreadable, but Hetta was fairly sure of his feelings. Naming their baby—if they failed, did they want to name their loss?

We're not going to fail, Hetta vowed, conscious of the weight of the heartstone at her throat. It had darkened noticeably since last night. But hadn't they already achieved half of what the High King asked? Well, assuming he accepted their extremely technical fae argument.

The day was darkening, Starwater's surface already semi-obscured by wisps of fog, though Hetta could feel the wind starting to rise.

"Did you actually have something to ask me or were you just aiding and abetting my escape?" she asked.

He smiled. "Not specifically, but I could certainly have come up with something if pressed." His expression sobered. "The bank manager is unhappy. Apparently Lord Arran is a shareholder."

The bank couldn't know about the leviathan attack yet, which meant Lord Arran had said something to the bank even before he'd accepted Angus's invitation.

"We've been meeting our repayment obligations. As a shareholder, that should make Lord Arran extremely happy. And those tenants are about to sign the lease on the Dower House. Unless something happened while we were gone? Jack didn't say anything." The experimental seed varietals and new drainage scheme wouldn't bear fruit till the next growing season at the earliest, and they still desperately needed cashflow to undertake maintenance and upgrades that had already waited far too long. Her villagers shouldn't have to go through another winter without insulation.

Wyn shook his head. "All excellent facts that I pointed out, but I fear…" He sighed. "He implied that the extension of any further funds would be contingent on the outcome of the Conclave's next meeting."

Hetta thought of the way Lord Arran had looked at Gwendelfear, and her heart sank to somewhere around her boots. *The Conclave would've accepted Jack without a murmur.* Hetta didn't believe in second-guessing herself, but it was hard not to in this instance. Stariel had chosen her, but Stariel didn't understand politics or finances. What if the faeland had chosen *wrong*?

She shut down that line of thought as unhelpful and picked up the stack of accumulated mail. Wyn didn't say anything as she sorted through it until she found one bearing Queen Matilda's seal and opened it, revealing an invitation addressed to "Lord Henrietta Valstar & His Royal Majesty Hallowyn Tempestren".

She put her thumb over His Royal Majesty, blanking out the incorrect title with a mixture of relief and guilt; she was glad it wasn't true, despite everything, and it was sort of nice to see their names linked together so officially. Gods, what were they going to do about finding a new ruler for ThousandSpire, assuming Irokoi really did know how to free it?

She removed her thumb, and the title glittered accusingly up at her again. Of course the queen had assumed Wyn would be King of ThousandSpire now. Hetta ought to tell her that was not the case and never would be. The invitation was to the Meridon Ball, now less than a fortnight away. There was a veiled threat behind the polite words, *we expect your attendance. Please confirm.*

Hetta gave the invitation to Wyn, who read it grimly as she opened the next missive. It was, ironically, the official summons to the next meeting of the Conclave, in Greymark. A bitter laugh choked its way out of her. Well, at least she'd been invited *before* she'd unleashed bloodthirsty monsters on the Chair.

"I'm developing quite an aversion to letters," she said, handing that one to Wyn as well.

"You're a good lord," Wyn said. "The Conclave should welcome you into its ranks. If it won't… Well, we persuaded the bank in our favour once before."

"*You* persuaded the bank."

"With *our* plan, as *your* steward relying on *your* delegated authority. I will not accept sole credit. Delegation is part of ruling." Wyn paused. "Besides, allow me to be arrogant enough to want to contribute *something* to your life besides trouble."

"Don't you dare make this about you!"

Frustration flashed in the russet of his eyes. "But it *is* about me. If the Conclave rejects you, it will not be because you have failed as a lord. It will be because of your association with me."

Hetta gave an angry laugh. "Allow *me* to be arrogant enough to want to be accepted or rejected on my own merits!"

"I…" He sagged. "I'm sorry. And you are right; it infuriates me as well to think that you may not be. If the Conclave has any sense, the lords will see past their prejudices to what you are."

This, irrationally, only made her angrier. "Stop agreeing with me!"

He blinked. "Ah…do you really want to fight, Hetta?"

"Yes!" She wasn't sure if she wanted to hit him or kiss him. Irritation sparked in her like fireworks. What was *wrong* with her? "Are you calling me irrational?"

A muscle twitched at the corner of his mouth, as if he were trying hard not to smile. "Remember I told you the books strongly advised against doing so."

"Stop trying to make me laugh! I don't want to laugh!" She made an inarticulate sound of annoyance. "You're just so…so…argh!"

His expression was extremely neutral.

"Oh, go away, then! I'm going to talk to Jack." She put out the words as a challenge. Wyn was impossible to provoke, but her cousin would definitely oblige her. And she needed to talk to him anyway about what had gone on in her absence.

"Good idea." His eyes sparkled. "I love you, Hetta."

"I love you too!" she snapped back. "Now go away and do something stewardly." Maybe she'd have a handle on her temper by then. She knew she was being unreasonable, and yet that didn't seem to make a difference to her prickly irritation.

Wyn nodded. "My Star." But his head came up sharply at the same time as something fluttered on the edge of her awareness, Stariel pulling her attention to the greenhouse as the gap she'd left in the wards opened. Relief filled her, re-ordering her priorities in an instant.

"Marius," she said just as Wyn said, "Rake."

"At least they have not strangled each other," Wyn said. He held out a hand. She took it, squeezed.

As they walked out to the greenhouse, she imagined pulling a curtain around her mind, feeling both a little ridiculous and anxious as she did so. Wyn had been trying to teach her how to shield her mind against telepathy, but neither of them had any idea if it would be effective or not, since Hetta was human and they hadn't had a telepath to practice with.

She supposed this would be practice now.

The temperature in the greenhouse was warmer than outside, trapping the weak sunlight. Hetta fiddled with the leaves of a sweet pea as the taut, pulling sensation increased and the portal took shape on the far wall. It slid open, showing a flash of unfamiliar greenery, and then Rakken and Marius were stepping through.

Both of them were dripping wet. They were also studiously ignoring each other. She couldn't read Rakken's expression, but the tight anger in Marius's made her want to set Rakken ablaze on general principles.

Marius went to hug her and hesitated, but Hetta threw her arms around him anyway. He made a startled sound of protest. "Hetta, I'm all wet, you shouldn't—"

"I haven't suddenly become made of glass." She released her brother, admittedly feeling quite a bit damper, and frowned up at him. "What happened with Aroset?"

"Aroset was in Meridon, but we escaped." His gaze tracked over her worriedly. "How are you doing? Did you find Irokoi? Does he know how to help?"

"Fine, and yes, though he's so far being extremely cryptic about it. What about the earl? And how did you escape?"

"What does Irokoi know?" The demand came from Rakken. He was looking towards the house, his focus sharp, as if he could see through stone and greenery all the way to the drawing room containing his brother. Maybe he could; Hetta still wasn't sure exactly how leysight worked.

"He says he knows how to free the Spires, though he's been refusing to tell us details. You encountered Set?"

It was as if someone had switched on a light in Rakken. His mask of indifference slipped, his eyes brightening. He headed immediately for the door, but Wyn put a hand on his shoulder and halted his exit. The mask slid back into place with a beat of citrus and storms.

"Set," Wyn repeated as Rakken glared at him. "What happened?" Hetta found herself reaching out to Stariel, just in case she had to quickly separate the two.

"She portalled into the train station, but we didn't encounter her so much as successfully run away," Marius said quickly.

Wyn frowned. "She continues to grow distressingly good with portals. She opened one to Deeper Faerie while we were there."

Rakken shrugged out of Wyn's hold. "Interesting but not currently relevant. *My* first priority remains the Spires."

Wyn gave him a steady look. "Our interests align in this. I will drag Koi away from Lady Phoebe and meet you in the library. Your storming in dripping wet to demand immediate answers will not speed matters along."

"Still playing the human butler, little Hollow?" Rakken mocked.

Wyn's expression didn't change. "You are a guest here, Rake."

Rakken made an exasperated sound. "Very well. Ten minutes I will grant you." He stalked out.

"Has he been like that for the entire time?" Hetta asked Marius.

Marius was drumming his fingers on the edge of a tray of seedlings, but he heaved a deep sigh at her question. "You have no idea."

WINGS IN THE LIBRARY

YN FOUND IROKOI had already extracted himself from the circle of Valstar women and taken up position in the library. Irokoi sat on the main lower level, perched on one of the windowseats, wings draping over the worn fabric. He was reading one of the old lords' journals with keen-eyed interest.

For some reason, the sight sparked a primitive territorialness, a sudden urge to sprout wings and call up his magic in defense of…what exactly? Hetta didn't need protecting from Irokoi and neither did the library books. *What is wrong with me?* He took a deep breath, filling his lungs with the vanilla-y smell of old books. It didn't dampen the impulse as much as he'd hoped. Hetta frowned at him, half a question in her eyes.

"This feels like home to you," Irokoi observed, setting down the journal. "I am glad you found somewhere to come home to."

"Ah—thank you."

"Which lord are you reading about?" Hetta asked, coming to sit beside Irokoi, who shuffled to make room for her. The stark view of the Indigoes framed them, snow still covering much of their slopes. It would retreat, day by day, until by midsummer, only the highest peaks would be dusted white. The snow still covered his father's unmarked grave.

Irokoi canted his head. "The one your oldest brother is named for, I believe. Speaking of, where is he?"

"Getting changed. They both arrived rather wet from Knoxbridge."

Unease shivered through Wyn. That was the second time Koi had asked after Marius specifically. Hard to believe it mere happenstance. And Koi knew Marius was a telepath. Was it merely caution driving his questions? Any sensible fae would be wary of a telepath. But Wyn could not shake the misgiving filling him.

"Are you going to tell us how to retrieve Cat and lift the curse now, brother?"

Irokoi's mismatched eyes were oddly serious. "Soon, I hope."

Wyn considered his oldest brother, trying to reconcile recent events with the old Irokoi he'd known before he left Faerie. But had he ever truly known Irokoi? Wyn had been a child when Aroset blinded him and changed him in ways that went deeper than his physical scars. Or had it been Aroset at all? Irokoi had always been... different, that uneasy mixture of open and cryptic. At least Irokoi's remarks never carried the hidden barbs most greater fae threw out as easily as breathing—he always seemed *sincere*, if not always *comprehensible*.

Rakken prowled into the library, dry once again, tattered wings folded neatly against his back. Two stormdancers walking winged through Stariel House. What would happen if Wyn followed their lead? Something between terror and excitement gripped him, dizzying as a high-speed dive.

Rakken ignored Wyn, his attention all for Irokoi. *Just once it would be nice not to be dismissed as unimportant by my siblings.*

"Mossfeathers!" Irokoi cried. Beside him, Hetta grinned.

Rakken was sharp with impatience. "If you know how to retrieve Cat—"

Irokoi shook his head. "Oh, I do, but that is only the first piece."

"What pieces, Koi?"

But Irokoi was looking past him, to where Marius had slipped in the door to the library. Marius shut the door behind him with a click and warily approached them.

"Marius Rufus Valstar." Irokoi's voice had lost all hint of playfulness.

Marius drew up short, halfway along the shelves. His eyes widened.

"What's *wrong* with you?" He sounded both horrified and fascinated. "You're Irokoi, aren't you?"

Irokoi's feathers lifted in excitement. "You can see it? I hoped you would. And please call me by the fish-end."

"Koi?"

Irokoi beamed. "I got the *right* one this time," he told Hetta in an aside before returning his attention to Marius.

"Koi, could you at least try to be a little more comprehensible?" What had Marius seen? Wyn wanted to grab hold of Marius and haul him away from this room; he wasn't convinced Irokoi had Marius's best interests at heart.

Irokoi didn't remove his attention from Marius, and his voice was low and serious. "Oh, trust me, I am trying."

Thunder and citrus rolled into the room. "Koi," Rakken began, voice dark with warning. He took a menacing step towards Irokoi "Do not toy with—"

"You're under a compulsion that stops you from speaking freely?" Marius said blankly.

Rakken missed a step, and Wyn felt the same jerk of shock, realisation sharp and stunning as a lightning bolt. There were too many pieces to pull together all at once, and he did not have them all, but the shape, the *shape* those pieces made—he could feel the sense of it coming into focus, and, oh, it terrified him.

"Who?" he and Rakken asked together. They exchanged glances, a shared thought. *Who* had compelled Irokoi? And why—but *who* was so much more urgent.

Irokoi smiled, sad and slow, still locking eyes with Marius. "The storm brings both gifts and curses. Perhaps one can undo the other, for me."

Marius went pale, breaking eye contact and taking a step back. "You want me to tell them you think Rakken can break the compulsion. How do I know that?" He sought out Wyn, grey eyes panicked. "*How do I know that?*"

No one answered. Marius spun, accusing. "What are you keeping from me *this* time?" He winced and rubbed at his head. "What's a telepath?"

"Someone who can hear others' thoughts. We believe you have the ability." Wyn closed the distance between them, trying to will calm into his friend. If Marius lost control now, with Hetta so near...what effect would that have on the babe? Anxiety pushed thorns into his heart, the fierce need to *protect* tearing him apart. But who was he supposed to protect here? How? He drew in a long, brittle breath and tried to find his way back to clinical detachment. He'd been so good at that, once. When had it become such a challenge to find it?

"You're joking." Marius's voice went up, seeking a reassurance Wyn couldn't give him. "I can't—I'm not..."

Wyn put a hand on Marius's shoulder, trying to steady him. Marius jerked away.

A pulse of emotion surged, the panic of a cornered creature. Wyn staggered under the force of it, hastily hardening his mental shields. The sudden relief confirmed the cause; Marius was projecting. Wyn cursed his stray thoughts that Marius had picked up on contact. He'd been unforgivably careless.

"I'm sorry—I am out of practice with my metal shields. Forgive me," he said to Marius, keeping his tone mild.

Marius's breaths came in harsh pants, and Rakken sent Wyn a pointed glare that said he needed to do better, *quickly.*

"You don't want me to panic. You're worried I might go mad or hurt people. I can *hear* you," Marius said.

Knives against Wyn's shields, a building psychic storm.

Stariel rumbled, its presence looming over them in threat. Wyn had no direct line to its emotions, but he could judge them well enough from Hetta's expression, and it felt...it felt like the intake of breath before the land had struck down his father. Hetta's hands were curled into fists, her face gaunt with effort. She was holding it back.

"Marius," he said, then hesitated. Telling people to calm down had never, in his experience, resulted in anyone calming down.

"How long have you known? Gods, don't tell me Jack knows too or I will murder something. Oh gods, how can I be the last to know *even this?*"

Hetta slipped out of the windowseat, her face deathly white. "Since Aroset attacked you. I wasn't sure how to tell you—we thought it might be worse if you knew—and then you left so quickly I didn't have a chance."

"It frightens you," Marius said flatly. "*I* frighten you. Did you tell me you were pregnant because you actually wanted me to know or because you thought I'd figure it out anyway?" He began to laugh, a bitter hysteria that held no mirth, and the pressure on Wyn's shields increased. Hetta gasped, and Wyn's stomach dropped.

Rakken moved fae-fast and shoved Marius against the shelf. A book fell loose and hit the carpet with a thunk. "Marius Rufus Valstar," he snarled, magic rolling off him. "You told me you weren't weak. Prove it and calm down or I will do something you'll regret. Again."

Marius took a deep, shuddering breath. "Damn you." But as he glared at Rakken, the jagged psychic whirlwind began to ease. Thank the stormwinds this once for Rakken's ability to incite anger at the drop of a feather; it was giving Marius something to focus on outside his own fear.

"Yes." Rakken released him.

Marius shook his head like a horse fending off a wasp, pushed away the shelf, and stalked out of the library.

Hetta made an abortive half-motion to follow him. Marius whirled and glared at her from the threshold. "Leave me alone." He met Wyn's eyes. "Tell her it's for her own damn good."

Stormwinds. He really needed to work on his mental shields.

Stariel's violent presence eased with Marius's exit, and Hetta sagged. Wyn looped an arm around her waist, steadying her when she swayed. The guilt in her eyes cut at the heart of him.

"He's still in control of his actions, and he hasn't lost his mind," he told her. "That is much, much better than many of the outcomes I feared." He watched Marius's presence burn along the leylines, through the house and exiting in the direction of the greenhouse. It flickered but didn't intensify, the turbulence churning but stable. That was also a good sign. "Give him a moment to adjust. We have all had time to think about the ramifications. He hasn't. I will talk to him."

"He's *my* brother, Wyn! I shouldn't be afraid of him." Her voice cracked, and she made an infuriated sound and buried her face in his shirt. "I. Hate. Crying."

"It will be all right," he told her, stroking her back. "You're more afraid *for* him than *of* him. The latter will win over the former, given time. Besides, even a telepathic Marius is still Marius, who is many things—but fearsome is not one of them."

"Yes, yes, you're right, but why can't I stop crying?" she wailed.

"Perhaps I should check one of the books for an answer? Only you'll need to remain here while I go and get them, as they're in my office."

She lifted her head and glared at him, then gave a wet laugh and rubbed at her eyes. "I'm afraid you may be trying to marry a watering can."

"A very charming watering can," he said, straight-faced.

She sniffed and smiled, trying to cover her awkwardness with bravado. She hated people seeing her cry. He offered her a handkerchief.

"Next time you plan to take such a risk, warn me, Koi," Rakken hissed, joining Irokoi on the windowseat. He folded himself into an angry cross-legged position and held out his hands for Irokoi's.

Compulsion, Wyn thought with a jolt.

COMPULSION

HETTA TRIED TO pull herself together, despite the fact that her insides still felt wobbly. She was already sick of the way her emotions kept jumping around, like something happening to someone else without any input from her. She'd shed more tears in the last few weeks than in all her life prior. *Is it going to be like this for the duration?* she thought glumly.

Stariel curled around her reassuringly, and she leaned into the land's presence. Where was Marius? The answer came instantaneously as her self expanded: the greenhouse. She blinked and pulled back, not wanting the dizziness of double vision.

<Can you tell if he's well?> Poor Marius—they'd stolen his favourite refuge spot in the library, so he'd been forced to resort to another. At least the land had returned to its usual vague feeling of possessiveness towards Marius now it was no longer concerned with her safety. It patted softly at him, as if it was attempting to apologise for its earlier behaviour.

That had to be a good sign, didn't it? It had shocked her, how violently the land had bristled up in her defence. If it hadn't been for the faeland's own uncertainty when faced with a Valstar, could she have held it back? It worried her that she didn't know for sure.

<Is he all right, though? He's not hurt?> The land returned a deep sense of uncertainty along with something else—a bigger concept that it took Hetta a few moments to unravel. Stariel almost never used words, but if she'd had to translate, it would've said something like: *the world has changed and changed you all with it.* The Iron Law coming down, that's what it meant.

She itched to go find her brother, but Wyn was probably right, and Stariel's reaction before had shaken her. What if she couldn't control the faeland's protectiveness next time? *I will,* she told herself firmly. But it would probably be a good idea to give Marius time to settle a bit first. Stariel curled restlessly around her, twining its way through the web of sparks that made up the Valstars, as if it too needed additional reassurance.

Rakken had completely ignored Hetta's minor breakdown and now sat on the windowseat across from Irokoi. What had Rakken been threatening Marius with? It had apparently worked, but that didn't mean Hetta forgave him for whatever had caused the animosity between the two in the first place. *I'll pluck his dashed feathers out if I find out he hurt Marius.*

Rakken's magic silently built, and Stariel grumbled. It didn't approve of all this magic lately from people that didn't belong to it. Hetta soothed it as the air grew charged, hugging Wyn's waist. He gave her an absent smile, but he was clearly distracted watching his brothers.

The magic built until something shifted with a swell of frost and midnight velvet. She'd been too preoccupied to pay much attention to the complexities of Irokoi's magic, last time. *What, exactly,* she puzzled, *does midnight velvet smell like?* Fae magic didn't actually *smell* as such; that was merely how her senses perceived it. But this was the first time she'd encountered a fae signature that had a texture as well as a scent. How could a smell have texture?

"There are so many layers," Rakken whispered. "How long has this been going on?"

"I am Eldest. I spent the most time with her." Irokoi gave a crooked smile. "That's why I'm the most broken. Well, apart from Father." A deep, bitter sadness washed over him. "You don't remember him before, of course." He looked over Rakken's shoulder at Wyn.

"Are you talking about your mother?" Hetta asked, since nobody else seemed about to clarify. She'd been puzzling at it ever since the dragon's parting remark—a remark that Wyn seemed to have somehow forgotten. *Though how he forgot an enormous dragon telling him to give its regards to his mother, I don't understand.*

Irokoi grit his teeth and his words came out forced, as if each syllable cost him. "She didn't *mean* to break us. She never means to, and she thought she could fix it, but she couldn't, could she? She only wanted to keep us safe, but her very presence broke us all, bit by bit. You can only deny your nature for so long. So she made us forget, and left." He leaned over, panting, his hair hanging over his face.

"Uh…that sounds like 'yes'? Your mother laid the compulsion on you?" She shot Wyn a worried glance; his expression had gone strangely smooth. "But what do you mean her presence broke you?"

Rakken hissed in pain. "I've never seen spellwork this powerful before. This will take some time to undo. How do we free the Spires from stasis, Koi?"

"I found the spell in the High King's library. It will need all of us together, all the Spireborn yet living. But it won't help us to free the Spires, not yet."

Hetta frowned at them both. Why wasn't Rakken reacting to Irokoi's words about their mother? Why wasn't *Wyn* reacting? The tension in his body had eased with a speed Hetta found disconcerting.

Irokoi sighed and met Hetta's eyes. "This would be a lot easier if you hadn't frightened the telepath away." He was trying to tell her something, but whatever compulsion he was under stopped him. Frustration blazed in him.

"Koi, this is much harder when you're not looking at me," Rakken complained.

Irokoi obediently returned his attention to Rakken. "The Spires—*why* won't it help us to free it from stasis?" Rakken's words were urgent, and his power swelled, eyes glowing green.

Irokoi took a sharp breath and pushed the words out in a rush. "Because it cannot choose a new master with us as we are. There's a reason the Spires couldn't choose freely: we're all too bound already to make new bonds. But when they are undone, perhaps the Spires will have its true choice of the bloodline."

Rakken reeled back, and so did Irokoi, sagging back against the cushions like a cut-free puppet. Blood trickled from Rakken's nose, and lightning flickered across his pupils. He flashed his teeth and leaned forward urgently, grabbing again for Irokoi's hands.

Irokoi slid off the windowseat. "Enough, little brother," he said gently. "I've lived many years under constraints; they won't be undone in one night."

"I'm *fine*," Rakken snapped, which made Hetta curious as to what Rakken would consider *not* fine, given the way he was shaking.

"Well, *I'm* not." Irokoi shook out his feathers as if he were airing a damp rug. "And I'd rather you didn't rummage around in my head while yours is ringing with pain." He smiled at Hetta. "I wouldn't mind some more of those ginger biscuits your cook makes. They are delicious." He met Hetta's eyes, and she knew there was something else he was trying to communicate, something his mother's compulsion was keeping him from saying.

Hetta frowned. Rakken and Wyn didn't seem *nearly* upset enough by what Irokoi had told them. Especially Rakken—hadn't he thought his mother was *dead*? Wasn't having another chance at ThousandSpire's throne his deepest desire?

"You're saying the Spires couldn't choose anyone except Wyn because you and the others are under compulsion, and he's not, for some reason? A compulsion cast by your mother? Who is still alive, somewhere?" Hetta repeated slowly. Both Wyn and Rakken looked blank, as if they hadn't just heard exactly the same explanation as her. Her chest tightened.

Oh, she thought. *It wasn't just Irokoi who was compelled.* She stepped away from Wyn and gave him a shake, as if that would dislodge the compulsion affecting him. His brows creased, and she could see something breaking behind his eyes, a slow-dawning horror. *His mother didn't just leave him; she worked magic on him against his will.*

"Oh no; it affects us all," Irokoi said, confirming her suspicion. His eyes burned. "Hallowyn is merely the youngest and so least bound of us. He had less to forget. It's no wonder ThousandSpire made a grab for him; it was desperate to bond to *someone*. Faelands don't do well, untethered for so long." Irokoi made an apologetic gesture towards Wyn. "That's not to suggest that you might not have been its first choice; it's merely that we cannot really *know* what its preferences would've been, since you were its *only* available choice at the time."

"And when you said you needed all the Spireborn to break the curse...?" Rakken asked. He wiped the blood from his nose and looked at his hand in distaste.

"Well, yes, we are going to have to retrieve Cat first. That's actually the easiest bit. The trickiest bit is the timing—without her presence to anchor it, we'll have to act quickly to unravel the curse before it destroys the Spires. The harder part is probably going to be persuading Aroset to help, isn't it?" Irokoi wrinkled his nose. "Though we probably don't actually need her to *do* anything; I think so long as we can get her to be present, it will help the spell catch. I'm fairly certain I can convince Torquil to do his bit. He may actually be quite keen to help once I tell him he has another shot at being chosen king. Do you think the same bribery might work for Aroset?"

Citrus and thunder rolled through the library in a wave that sent Stariel bristling and made Hetta press instinctively against Wyn's side.

"What," Rakken growled, "are you talking about, Irokoi Tempestren? Torquil is *dead*."

Irokoi wasn't at all ruffled, though he did seem tired. "Oh, yes, you don't know that yet. No, he's not actually. I helped him fake it; it seemed like a good idea at the time."

For a moment, Hetta thought Rakken was going to hit Irokoi, but then his magic snuffed out, and he turned on one heel and stalked out without a word. Hetta didn't blame him for being upset, though would the world really end if he just said that instead of pretending he didn't care at all and going off to lick his wounds in private?

She leaned against Wyn; he was so still that she might've thought he wasn't upset either, except she could feel his heart pounding. *He acts the same way as Rakken does, sometimes, pretending things don't bother him.*

"You cannot blame him for his anger, Koi," Wyn murmured. "*I* am still furious with you over it, and I didn't feel Torquil's death, as Rake said he did."

"Yes, that was quite a hard effect to achieve." Irokoi was frowning in the direction Rakken had taken. "You have the luxury of anger, because of me. I did what I thought best; I cannot apologise for it. But perhaps I could have told him more tactfully, yes." He slid off the windowseat with a sigh. "I'll talk to him; I'll need his help with the spell."

Wyn stood in his path. "Koi." His voice was low and full of warning.

Irokoi appeared oblivious to it. "You're quite useful in many ways, Hallowyn, but you're not much use for fine spellwork, I'm afraid."

"I need more explanation."

"I agree," Hetta said.

Irokoi huffed at them. "Which part was unclear? Firstly, we do the spell that will bring Cat to us, and secondly, we need all seven of us for the spell that will undo the curse on ThousandSpire. Our grumpiest brother unpicks the compulsion so that ThousandSpire can choose a new ruler. You get their support and complete the High King's task—and good news, ThousandSpire even has a gate to the High King's realm. Get married, save your child, everyone goes home happy. Simple."

It actually did sound a lot more possible when Irokoi spelled it out like that.

Wyn glared. "There are *six* of us, brother, even assuming we can somehow involve Aroset in this mad plan."

Irokoi looked straight at Hetta. "Not anymore." He folded his wings more neatly. "Now excuse me while I go settle Mossfeathers." He left.

INHERITANCE

WYN STARED HELPLESSLY at Hetta, fear jostling for space amidst his immense confusion. He felt as if he'd been set into free fall with a wing bound. Compulsion… there was a compulsion on him. A compulsion set by, set by… His fists clenched, trying to fight it, but his mind smoothed and he couldn't hold on to the thoughts, the thoughts of, of—

Hetta touched his sleeve, her face worried. "You can't remember what Irokoi said about your mother, can you? I can see it every time you forget. Can you remember that you're under a compulsion, at least?"

It was like breaching the surface, sucking in a painful breath after being long submerged. His mother. His *mother*. He tried to recall her face, and his vision swam. Trying to analyse the extent of the compulsion was like grabbing fistfuls of fog. He could sketch the edges of it now—enough, at least, to be aware that there *was* a compulsion—but the deeper he went, the more unravelled his thoughts became.

"Yes," he bit out. "But it keeps sliding away from me. I can't remember…" What? Hetta hugged him, and he held onto her as the only solid thing in a world that was shattering around him. "We'll get Rakken to de-compel you. I'm so sorry, Wyn."

He wanted to ask what she was sorry for, but Hetta released him and stepped back, digging the heartstone out and weighing it in her hand. It glowed dimly, a deep, pure blue.

"How much time do we have left, do you think?"

Wyn wished that he wasn't quite so good at mental arithmetic, that he hadn't already made his own estimate on that very question.

"We don't know how long we will have after the spell runs out," he temporised.

Hetta gave him a flat look. "How long, Wyn?"

"A week, at most, at the current rate."

Hetta swallowed. "That's what I thought, too. I hoped I was wrong." She glared at the glowing stone and curled her fingers around it.

"So we have a week to free ThousandSpire and get its new ruler to support our union." There was something more to that, he was certain, but whatever it was had slipped his mind. He puzzled at it, trying to recall what Irokoi had said. Perhaps some bit of spell detail he hadn't understood?

"And marry," Hetta pointed out. "That's the bit we actually need to sort out the stormcharge, isn't it, according to Lamorkin? That's what it means. We have a week to get married, and somehow around organising that I have to go to the Conclave as well so they can refuse to ratify my membership." She sank down on the nearest chair, dark circles under her eyes. He resisted the urge to ask if she was all right, and she gave him a look that said she'd noticed anyway. "It's still ten days until Queen Matilda's ball." She gave a weak laugh. "So we need to get married before she actually plans to announce our engagement. Assuming she's still willing to do that after she hears about the leviathans."

"I hadn't actually given much thought to that part," Wyn admitted, somewhat daunted by the coming logistics. "But if we speak to the High King...we could do the fae ceremony first and complete the mortal part later, after your queen has 'engaged' us, with all the mortal trappings Lady Phoebe desires."

Hetta smiled at that. "I think my family are becoming less concerned with the trappings and more concerned that the event actually takes place in any form whatsoever." Her smile faded, and she picked at the curling spine of one of the nearby books, an ancient encyclopaedia. "The Lords Conclave is never going to ratify me now, is it? Maybe I shouldn't even bother going, given everything else."

After the leviathans, Wyn had the same doubt, but to see Hetta consider giving up... He was so used to preferring Mortal over Faerie, but in this, Faerie had the right of it. Faerie might have schemed and manipulated and threatened, but it had never denied Hetta's worth. How dare Mortal reject her?

"You will rule even without their approval, and they will regret that they shunned you." He was sure of it—but it wouldn't make life easy for her or Stariel. Guilt threaded through him. Why did he seem to bring only hardship to the place he now called home, to the woman he loved? He tried to find some better comfort than his own anger. "But perhaps tradition will win out. The Conclave are known to be generally conservative."

Hetta drummed her fingers on the shelf. "Do you think Aroset would come willingly, if we told her she might have another chance at being chosen by ThousandSpire if she helps free it from stasis?"

"To Stariel? No. She will not set foot on a faeland ruled by another. If we could find another resonance point to build a portal from, in unclaimed lands...perhaps."

"And then she'd try to slaughter you all the minute the spell successfully freed ThousandSpire," Hetta finished for him.

"Sadly probable." It still hurt, to know his sister wanted him dead, to know she was capable of it. Aroset believed she'd already killed Torquil. *Broken; Koi said we were all broken, some of us more than others.* What had he meant? It had to do with, with…

Hetta squeezed his hand, startling him out of his reverie. He hadn't been aware of her rising.

"That's very unsettling, watching you go all blank like that. You were thinking about the compulsion laid by your mother, weren't you?"

"Yes." Panic skittered across his skin and he breathed in and out, reining it in, breathing in the warm coffee and pine of Hetta's magic, the soap scent of her skin as she wrapped her arms around him again. "It seems neither of my parents were very good role models." How was he supposed to do this, now he knew the full extent of his inheritance? How could Hetta still want him? His father, a sadistic tyrant; his mother, someone who could ensorcel her own children and walk away without a backwards glance. *It doesn't matter*, he tried to tell himself. *It changes nothing.* Why, then, did he feel as if he'd lost a wing? "Where is Marius?"

"Stariel's been keeping an eye on him. He's…upset but he doesn't seem unstable. I don't think his shields have failed. That's good, isn't it? He's going to be all right, isn't he?"

"I hope so. I'll talk to him."

"*I'm* his sister," Hetta disagreed.

Which was exactly why Marius would not welcome Hetta's presence right now, and not only because—thanks to Wyn's careless thoughts—Marius might be afraid he'd endanger her.

"Yes, his *little sister*," Wyn pointed out. Marius had always had trouble admitting vulnerability to Hetta for that reason. Mortal masculine beliefs around family could get rather complicated.

Hetta's nose wrinkled, and he knew she both understood and didn't like it. "He's an idiot, if he thinks I need protecting from him.

I'm more worried he might need protecting from *me*, given how Stariel reacted before." She sighed. "Fine. You talk to Marius. I'll go and figure out what to tell her majesty; I imagine it'll go worse if she hears about this from Lord Arran first."

He squeezed her hand. "My Star."

He got only halfway down the hallway before he had to sag against the wall for support, his pulse wild as a dust dervish. He pressed his hands flat against the peeling wallpaper. He was a fae prince and an excellent butler. He did *not* panic or lose control in a crisis. He made lists and defused tension with mild humour. Lists. He grabbed the thought like a lifeline. A list would be timely.

Firstly, find Marius and check his mental state. Possibly accompanied by whiskey. Secondly, see if Rakken had recovered and ask him to lift this…this compulsion he could barely hold the edges of. Thirdly, pin down Irokoi again and figure out how to assemble the pieces they needed to free the Spires, including Aroset. Fourthly, go over the estate's most recent figures in case he needed to plead with the bank again. Fifthly, think of anything he might do to aid Hetta with the upcoming Conclave. Despite her words, he knew the thought of failing there bit her deep.

The mental list did not have its usual calming effect. With each item, a physical weight seemed to add to his chest and the spiralling out-of-control sensation grew. His fingertips dug into the wall, and flecks of plaster came free. Stormwinds take it. Stariel had enough maintenance needs without him adding to them.

He was under a compulsion from his *mother*. The list evaporated. It shouldn't matter so much—he'd carried the pain of his mother's loss for years, not knowing whether she was dead or had left them on purpose. There were so many more urgent things requiring attention; this was an old wound he could lick at later.

He pushed off the wall, stumbling in the direction of the nearest stairwell, the servants' staircase to the courtyard. A surprised maidservant met him halfway down, nearly dropping her load of laundry.

"My apologies, Amabel. I didn't mean to startle you—don't mind me." He gave a slight bow. Could she see through his tattered mask of civility? A wild creature clawed at his insides, but he couldn't let it escape here. The heartstone, only a few shades lighter than black. This form, which shouldn't feel so strange but did, senses muted and wings scratching at the compaction.

The maid blinked, dipped a brief curtsey of acknowledgement, and went on her way.

The cool spring air helped, a little, when he pushed open the door to the courtyard. He emerged in deep shadow, the sun's arc not high enough to reach this wall in anything less than the burning height of summer. He knew this in the same way that he knew which of Stariel House's many bedrooms had the best sun and where the central heating system was inadequate in the older East Wing. It wasn't only his years of butlering here that had made him gather every minute detail, holding it close. It had been an unconscious attempt to anchor himself against the pull of Faerie. Even in those ten quiet years before the Iron Law came down, he'd feared his father would one day find him, that he'd be forced to leave to protect the people and estate he loved. But in the end, the danger he posed to Stariel hadn't come from some external force. *I think that is what might be called irony.*

He found Marius seated on a wooden bench outside his greenhouse, staring vacantly towards the lake. The setting sun glinted in the silver threads in his black hair, and Wyn was reminded, oddly, of Lord Henry.

Marius didn't have much in common with his father apart from his colouring and the long Valstar nose—the same nose Hetta shared. Old Lord Henry hadn't understood his oldest son, had tried to shape him into his own mould. Ironically, the old lord had had far more in common with his oldest daughter, even though his views on women had prevented him from seeing it. Lord Henry had had the same drive to protect his people and his land as Hetta did, misdirected though his efforts had been. Trying to force his children to be something other than what they were had only created a deep, irreparable wedge between them. It had made Lord Henry a bitter man, by the end.

Well, that and the alcoholism. Wyn owed the old lord a lot, for taking him in when he'd most needed sanctuary, but he wasn't sure if he could forgive him for the damage he'd done to his children. Especially to Marius.

The thought steadied him. He couldn't fall apart, not when Marius needed him. He shored up his mental shields but made no effort to keep his approach quiet, not wanting to startle Marius.

"Come to make sure I don't explode?" Marius said darkly without turning.

Wyn came to a halt beside him. "I'm sorry you found out like this. I erred, keeping this from you. Can you forgive me?"

"Why aren't you afraid of me?" Marius did look up then, his eyes wild as winter storms.

"Because you aren't particularly fearsome?"

"But…mind reading. It horrifies me, and I'm the one doing it! If I knew someone else could read my mind, I'd be terrified!"

"Well, you are only reading surface thoughts, as far as I can tell, and those only when I forget my mental shields. For which I apologise. If you were any other telepath, perhaps I would be afraid, but I know you, Marius. It seems unlikely you will do anything nefarious with whatever knowledge I accidentally let loose, and I'm used to your sudden intuitions, regardless. If they were going to scare me, they would have done so long since. I fear only hurting you inadvertently with my own careless thoughts."

Marius leaned his elbows onto his knees and put his head in his hands. "Has my intuition—has it always been telepathy, then?"

"I do not know for certain, but I suspect you must always have had some level of psychic ability for Aroset's attack to trigger the way it did."

"At least I know now I'm not crazy."

Wyn sat down on the bench beside him. "I brought whiskey." He put the hipflask down on the bench between them.

Marius's hollow laugh rang out over the countryside. "Very Northern of you."

They watched as a flock of ducks powered their way across the lake. Wyn had always admired the sheer muscle-powered way the birds flew, with persistence rather than grace.

"How do I learn to control it?" Marius said eventually. "Can I turn it off?"

"I can tell you what I know about mental shields *against* telepathy, though I do not know how or if they will be useful to you, since they're similar to what one uses to shield against compulsion, and you're already immune to that." The telepathy explained that small mystery. "But you already do control your ability, subconsciously. I think you've been doing so for years, even before whatever Aroset triggered. It's why we didn't tell you immediately. Rake thought knowing might undo your instinctive control."

Marius's knuckles whitened on the bench. Wyn wanted to ask what his brother had done to earn such a hostile reaction, but Marius said grimly, "Tell me about the shields."

Wyn explained as best he could; neither of them was satisfied by the time his answers ran dry, long before Marius's questions did.

Marius picked up the hipflask and began to tell Wyn about his conversation with the earl. "You *are* going to try to get the High King to agree to some sort of treaty or to rein in the fae when you talk to him, aren't you?"

"Mainly we are going to try to get him to marry us," Wyn

admitted. "But, yes, we plan to appeal to him on that front also." *Though how I am to convince him to help out of the goodness of his heart, I know not.* Especially knowing the High King had a potential history of antagonism with Valstars.

Marius shot him a look. "You really want him to bring back the Iron Law?" He stiffened in alarm. "Did I...? Was that telepathy?"

Wyn shrugged helplessly. "It may be only that I'm more predictable than I'd prefer."

Marius leaned down to pluck a few blades of grass, twisting them restlessly together. "And here I was plotting to throttle you as soon as I saw you again. How do you always manage to derail the topic of conversation from what one most wishes to speak to you about?"

"You're welcome to shout if it makes you feel better."

Marius slid him an irritated look. "Well, I *would* if I thought it might change anything. Bloody hell, Wyn." He looked at his hands, bright stripes of colour appearing on his cheekbones. "I thought you had better judgement."

"Ah...this wasn't exactly something we planned."

"That's exactly what I mean! Hetta I expect recklessness from, but not *you*! You knew you weren't free to marry her when you... Well, you *knew*. But apparently that made no difference whatsoever! And don't give me platitudes about fae culture," he added acerbically. "Because you've damned well been living in Prydein long enough to know what's acceptable here and what's not."

Wyn was relatively certain they were both recalling the same morning, when Marius had inadvertently caught Wyn in Hetta's room in a state of undress. But Marius didn't need to know that was the night the child had been conceived, nor that it had been their first night together. Despite Rakken's teasing, Wyn was a little sentimental about that. It had been an enjoyable night.

Marius winced and blushed a fiery red. "I did *not* want to know that!"

And his shields had slipped. Wyn bolstered them again with an irritated jab at himself. When had he become so careless? Though he wasn't exactly used to spending time with telepaths. Perhaps it was because his subconscious didn't see Marius as a threat, and all his training had been designed to trigger against malicious influence. *Or perhaps it is another sign of my fraying control.*

"Sorry." He took a deep breath. "But I am not sorry for the child."

"I'm too young to be an uncle." A pause. "You're going to be a father. Hells."

Wyn swallowed, the phrasing somehow sliding through all his careful walls of emotional distance. A father. The word shouldn't hold particularly warm connotations, given his own parentage, and yet...

Marius took one look at him and laughed. "Breathe," he instructed. He handed him the hipflask. "And have some whiskey."

Wyn did both. The shock of the liquor didn't settle his emotions; rather, it seemed to knock something loose.

"I'm going to be a father." He thought of small wings beside his own, and his throat closed up on the words.

"And this has only now occurred to you?" Marius said drily. He stared out into the darkening estate. Their conversation had taken them from afternoon to dusk. The sun's dying rays lit the lake in brilliant lines of pink and gold.

Wyn put his head in his hands and made an inarticulate sound.

"How can I possibly be a good parent, given one of mine tried to kill me and the other not only abandoned me but ensorcelled her own children, presumably to make sure we couldn't follow?"

Marius huffed. "You're being ridiculous. Do you think Hetta's going to be a terrible parent, just because our father was?" There was a deep bitterness to the words.

"I am being ridiculous." Wyn swallowed. "I know I am. I just—" He put the hipflask down and looked at his hands with clinical

interest. They were trembling. "I am so afraid of getting this wrong."
He closed his eyes and said the words that had sat like ice in the
back of his mind ever since Rakken had forced him to acknowledge
them. "I killed my own father."

Marius breathed out in a sudden rush, and Wyn felt a need to
explain himself.

"I knew what Stariel would do to him if I brought him here,
given its alarm over Hetta's kidnapping. And I brought him here.
And I don't regret it. And ever since…I thought I could control my
fae side, but I can't." The panic spiked again, sharp.

"I actually know quite a lot about hating your own nature and
the futility of thinking you can change it."

That drew Wyn up short. "That is different. There's nothing
wrong with you, Marius, nothing that should be changed."

"And why should that apply to me and not to you?"

Wyn glared moodily at his hands. "This isn't about desires and
wrong-headed mortal customs. I am…there is something dangerous
in me, something capable of planning and executing murder." Now
that he'd acknowledged it, he could feel the urge to change forms
lurking just beneath the surface, the prick of feathers under his skin.

"You acted to save your and Hetta's lives," Marius said. "I'm not
endorsing murder, but I don't think self-defence counts, Wyn."

"I am more powerful now than I was then. More powerful than
I should be, given my age." *Powerful enough that it affected the babe.*
He gave a bitter laugh. "I thought I could be human, for Hetta, but
everything about this entire situation has driven home the fact that
I am not. Hetta keeps suffering because of my nature."

"Well, she'd suffer less if you'd stop wallowing in self-pity about
it." Marius's bluntness startled a laugh out of him. "Honestly, I
think the only person afraid of what you might be capable of is you."

"I'll try not to be insulted that you don't think I am a fearsome
fae warrior."

"Well, I have no idea about the warrior bit, but fearsome—no." Marius paused. "Are you going to teach your child to hate themselves too?"

41

HOUSEHOLD MANAGEMENT

Hetta set down the phone with unnecessary firmness the next morning. *Well, that went about as well as expected.* She'd finally managed to get through to the palace; unfortunately, not before the queen had already heard about the leviathans from another source. Queen Matilda had also heard there was reason to doubt that Wyn would be in any position to offer any agreements with fae courts. At least the report of the leviathans hadn't yet hit the newspapers, despite Marius's persistent reporter's presence. It was undoubtedly only a matter of time.

The queen had wanted Hetta and Wyn to take the next train to Meridon to give a full explanation, not trusting the secureness of cross-country phone calls.

"Well, at least I managed to put that off without actually refusing a direct royal order," Hetta told the kitten that had crept into her office without her noticing. The half-catshee kittens registered as something like wyldfae against her senses, which Stariel generally considered a sort of background noise, unworthy of its notice.

The kitten eyed her desk, wiggled its tail to build up momentum, and pounced. A second later, a purring black kitten was happily trying to nuzzle her with complete disregard for the stack of papers in front of her. Hetta petted it absently, wondering where exactly to begin the written report she'd promised instead of an in-person debrief—and that only because they were already due at the Meridon Ball and Hetta had made noises about having to attend the Conclave before then and that being summoned would interfere with the self-government agreed between the North and the Crown. The queen had made her general displeasure evident.

"Well, good luck to them trying to ban *you*," Hetta told the kitten, thinking of what Marius had told Wyn about his discussion with the earl. "I can't even keep you out of my office." But surely Queen Matilda wouldn't be that foolish? Queen Matilda couldn't magically eject fae from Prydein like Hetta could with Stariel, but magic wasn't the only threat to the fae.

Iron, she thought uneasily. *Grandmamma's anti-fae charms. Yarrow and whatever other herbs the bank manager's wife used in that potion.* Hetta couldn't imagine Queen Tayarenn—or any other fae—reacting well if the Crown declared open season on fae.

War.

That was what Wyn feared, and she was beginning to think he was right to fear it, surreal as it sounded. Her hand slipped to her stomach. She'd stood for a long time in front of the mirror this morning, wondering if she was only imagining that it was subtly rounder.

She didn't check the colour of the heartstone, though she couldn't stop herself from feeling for it beneath her clothing. Had she focused too much on the immediacy of the High King's task and not enough on the problems of the mortal world? Lord Arran's disgust as he shied from Gwendelfear rose once again in her mind's eye. A hollow, queasy sensation swam around her innards. How could she persuade the Conclave that this was about so much more than whether they thought a woman a fit ruler?

It took her a long time to draft the report for Queen Matilda, and the sun had risen high in the sky by the time she finished. The kitten dozed in slanting rays of sunshine, tail twitching, but woke when she set down the pen and began unenthusiastically sifting through the papers that had accumulated in her absence: bills, invitations, journal subscriptions, letters, a quote for insulation. The only comfort was that Wyn would undoubtedly have an even larger pile, since the minutiae of the estate's paperwork tended to go through him first.

A soft knock on her door.

"Come in." She put down the pen.

Marius teetered on the threshold as they considered each other. He looked tired, dark circles under his eyes, his skin a shade paler than usual. He'd never been good at hiding his emotions when upset, and they skittered across his face in quick succession: concern, hurt, embarrassment.

"I'm not afraid of you," Hetta blurted. "I mean, I don't exactly love the idea that you know what I'm thinking, but I'm not afraid of anything except perhaps embarrassment." She tried to focus on the exercises Wyn had taught her. Stariel lay quiescent, thank all the little gods.

His lips twisted wryly as he closed the door behind him. "I don't exactly love that idea either, sister mine. All I can say is that I promise to try not to. Wyn told me what he knows about telepaths."

"Does it help?"

He held out his hands helplessly. "I don't know yet. Maybe. I'll leave you if what happened yesterday happens again."

Can you read my mind now? Hetta wanted to ask but refrained. Paranoia wasn't going to help either of them. "I'm sorry. We should've told you."

"Yes, you should. Though I understand Rakken is mostly to blame for that." His expression darkened.

"We chose to take his advice though, which I think now was a mistake. That's on me."

All the anger burned out of him, his shoulders drooping. "Well, don't do it again if I develop any other unexpected magical abilities."

She gave a weak laugh. "Stariel seems to think that's a possibility—for the Valstars generally, not you specifically," she hurried to add. "There's more magic running through the estate now, and we're all connected to it."

He ran a hand through his hair and sank down on the settee beneath the window. "Bloody hell. Not just Alex, then?" Alexandra had developed the Sight, with increasing strength over time. A fragment of amusement in his eyes. "Can you imagine the trouble we'll have with Jack's temper if he abruptly develops pyromancy?"

A second kitten appeared—apparently from nowhere—and jumped up onto his lap, making him start. Had it slipped in when Marius opened the door? Hetta considered the one still on her desk. In theory she could track the movements of lowfae, but it required a strong effort on her part to convince Stariel they were worth it.

"I'm beginning to think they can walk through walls," she said wryly.

The one on Marius's lap leapt onto the window ledge, trotted its way along and began to climb up the drapes, complaining when Marius detached it claw by claw.

"Think of them as practice," he said with a smirk. "Kittens aren't half as much trouble as babies."

"Don't you start too." There'd been quite enough slightly gleeful remarks on that subject from too many quarters.

"Aunt Sybil?"

"Grandmamma, actually. But no doubt Aunt Sybil will start on that too once she gets tired of moralising at me. Also, I'm not totally ignorant about what it all entails. I was fifteen when Laurel was born."

"Yes, and at boarding school."

"And you were away at university, so don't pretend you have any more expertise than I do! Why are we even arguing about this?" She sat back with a huff. "It's foolishness."

Marius's grey eyes were penetrating. "This thing with the High King...it's not just about the scandal, is it, or public sentiment about fae?" He grimaced. "Sorry. I don't know if that was telepathy or not." He petted the kitten mechanically. "Gods, I hate that I don't know anymore."

She put her hands on the desk in front of her, examining her nails to avoid meeting her brother's gaze. "No." She explained the situation in a cool, steady tone that didn't shake even when she ended with: "So, in effect, if we can't sort out ThousandSpire and find the High King in the next week, no one will have to worry about me being an unmarried mother because I won't be one."

There was a small, kittenish mew of protest. Hetta looked up. The kitten Marius had been holding spilled onto the floor as Marius crossed the distance between them, leaned down, and hugged her.

Something loosened in her chest all at once, a taut rubber band snapping free. Her eyes prickled. She rubbed at them angrily with the back of her hand; she wasn't going to burst into tears yet again! But the unexpected compassion of her brother's reaction took her off-guard. She'd feared he might think losing the pregnancy would be the best outcome.

"Of course I'm not going to tell you that might be for the best, not if you want it! Credit me with some degree of empathy!" He closed his eyes. "You didn't say that aloud, did you?"

"No." She smiled despite herself. Wyn had been right; he was still Marius.

"Sorry." He took a deep breath, hands spasming at his sides. "So...I'll join Ivy in sorting through the library then, see if I can find anything to give you extra leverage on the High King. Gregory can damn well make himself useful too." He grimaced. "Unless there's anything else I can do to help?"

He looked about as helpless as she felt, but it made her feel strangely better. The kitten meowed up at him, trying to claw up his trousers, and he picked it up distractedly.

"I think more information wouldn't do any harm, if there's any to be found. Though I'm hoping Irokoi might be more helpful on that front as well, if Rakken can get the compulsion out of him properly."

As if her mention had summoned him, the door swung open, and Marius went rigid. Hetta turned, though her land-sense meant it wasn't a surprise to see Rakken standing there. It was a surprise to see how tired he looked, his features carved with exhaustion, bones pricking sharply at his skin. More of his feathers had grown back since the last time she'd seen them, but his wings were still far from complete. Rakken usually gave off a slightly careless energy, but for the first time his appearance conveyed more distracted unkempt-ness than artful dishevelment.

He also seemed extremely angry. The reason for this became clear when he spoke, the emerald inferno of his gaze fixed on Marius.

"I require your assistance, Marius Valstar."

Marius withdrew to the opposite side of the room, holding the kitten like a shield. An ineffective shield, mostly because the kitten took one look at Rakken and slithered out of Marius's grasp with a mew. Marius said nothing. It took a lot to make Marius truly angry as opposed to mildly annoyed, but Rakken seemed to have managed it.

Rakken made an impatient sound. "The compulsion is a living spell that regrows even as I prune it. I need some…mechanism to halt the growth long enough for me to unroot it. Your experiments."

What was Rakken talking about?

"Oh, so you need to use my energies for your own purposes again, is that it?"

Hetta had never heard Marius sound so cold.

Rakken's eyes flashed. "It is your sister who will benefit from this, ultimately. And isn't help with this what you wanted from me? I am not tame, Marius Valstar, and I will not apologise."

Grey eyes clashed with green, the atmosphere sharp enough to cut. Hetta gave a delicate cough.

"What experiments, Marius?"

Marius broke away from his glaring, sagging back against the wall. "I've been experimenting with improving the anti-fae charms Grandmamma made." He told her about his minor successes with glamour and lowfae in Knoxbridge. "I wanted to see if I could make something that would help protect people from compulsion, but I didn't get very far. *Someone* refused to help."

Hetta wasn't sure how to feel about this. On the one hand, Marius was right—given all the trouble they'd had with Aroset, and especially knowing she'd been compelling the general public, if the wing worshippers were any evidence, it only made sense to investigate anything that might give people more protection against her manipulations. But on the other... She thought of Queen Matilda's suspicion, the earl's inquiry, and, oddly, the nessan glittering in the lake without the linesmen being the wiser.

Rakken shifted, looking irritable. "This is wasting time."

Marius ran a hand through his hair, rumpling it into further disarray. "I want your promise you'll support Hetta and Wyn's marriage, if you take ThousandSpire's throne. And Catmere's. And don't tell me you can't make promises on her behalf."

Rakken raised a cool eyebrow. "Very well then, Marius Valstar. You have my word—and my twin's."

Hetta looked between the two of them, feeling as if she'd walked into the middle of something she didn't understand, even though technically both of them had walked into *her* study. But before she could ask for clarification, Rakken had gestured ironically at the door. "Shall we, then?"

By LUNCHTIME, HETTA WAS sick of fae royalty, her entire family, and the fact that coffee continued to smell like something rancid. The last still felt like a personal betrayal. She caught only fleeting glimpses of Wyn, who was weighted down under a pile of queries and complaints from all parties. She knew he'd been up most of the night as well, talking to Irokoi about what they needed for the spell to free first Catsmere and then the Spires.

She stared down at the draft of her report to Queen Matilda, dreading the next task on her list. She didn't want to go back to Penharrow, to face the guilt of the damaged manor and the disgust of the lords. Thoughts of hiding under her desk and pretending to be invisible were far too tempting, but she had to try. This would be her last opportunity to sway any of the lords before the Conclave itself, thanks to the time-bending of Deeper Faerie; she wouldn't get another opportunity to make up for the first impression she'd made on the Chair. Not that she felt particularly gracious towards Lord Arran after seeing how he'd reacted to Wyn and Gwendelfear, but she supposed he *had* just suffered a tremendous shock at the time. She'd give him another chance if he'd give her one.

She was guiltily grateful when Lady Phoebe came in and provided a brief distraction—even if the distraction was the fraught subject of Hetta's wedding. How many people should they cater for? Where should the ceremony be held? What could they use for seating? Did Hetta want Laurel as a flower girl? Who should make her dress?

"I'll wear my mother's wedding dress," Hetta found herself saying to the last, to both her own and Phoebe's surprise. She remembered finding the elegant silk dress in the attic as a child with a mix of excitement and sadness. "I mean, if the fabric is still good. I haven't actually looked at it in years."

Phoebe beamed. "That's a lovely idea. I shall have it brought out so we can check." She got up and then fluttered indecisively in front of Hetta's desk. A faint flush rose on her pale cheeks, paler than the majority of the Valstars. "Hetta, dear. I know I am not your real mother, but I have always considered you another daughter and…well, I know this can be a difficult time. If there is anything you would like to ask…" Her colour deepened, and she twisted her hands together. "Children can be a blessing, but they are not…if one is not ready for such things, one should not feel forced to… I mean, Wyn is a very nice young man, and I'm sure I should be delighted for you if this is what you want, though his heritage makes things a little awkward. But children and marriage are very *permanent*, Hetta, is what I'm saying, and I should not like to think of my own daughters bullied into such things if they were not, not *sure*."

Hetta was deeply touched. She stood and clasped Phoebe's hands, meeting her worried blue gaze. "I *am* sure." Though she wasn't sure she wanted the insight into her father's second marriage.

Lady Phoebe relaxed, smiling again. "Well, I am glad then. I shall go and see if I can find the dress." She left, leaving Hetta staring thoughtfully after her.

She gave herself a shake and went to find Wyn. It took a while to reach the steward's office, as she kept being waylaid by staff and family both. Many of them wanted reassurances about the leviathans. That, at least, she could give.

"They were a one-off occurrence, but they can't get into Stariel in any case. You're safe." If only Penharrow could say the same.

She passed the Green Drawing Room, where Marius and Rakken were still buried, working on the device Rakken said he needed to properly remove the compulsion. She reached out absently for Stariel for reassurance that neither of them had murdered the other.

When Hetta checked in on Ivy in the library, her cousin looked up guiltily from her armchair and admitted to getting completely sidetracked owing to a previously undiscovered set of travel diaries chronicling Hetta's great-great aunt's visit to the continent a century ago.

"Do you know she kept a list of all her lovers? I had no idea Aunt Etheldreda was so outrageous as that! But nothing to do with fairies, I'm afraid. I'll keep looking though," she said, putting the diary away.

Hetta found Wyn in his office, talking softly to the cook, who excused herself as soon as Hetta knocked. He looked up at her entrance, hair falling away from his face, and for a moment his softer human face startled her.

The desk creaked as he pushed up from it. "Hetta?"

She shook her head, holding out the report for the queen and explaining what it was. "I need your diplomatic insight; I wrote it in a bit of a rage, I'm afraid. But first, will you come with me to Penharrow?"

His eyes searched her face. "What about Aroset?"

"That's why I don't want to go alone, though she might still be in Meridon, or Greymark, or wherever she's trying to stir up trouble with these wing worshippers of hers." They weren't sure if the man Rakken and Marius had met at the train station was indicative of larger meddling from Aroset or a one-off.

She made a face. How unfair of Aroset to cause problems in the human world as well as in Faerie. The two worlds were never going to stay properly separate again, were they? She looked into Wyn's warm russet eyes. The good and the bad both.

"I am, sad to say, no match for Aroset."

"You'll make it easier for us to run away back to Stariel, though," Hetta pointed out. "Well, fly." She couldn't read his expression. "Besides, if she does turn up, maybe we can ask her politely if she'll volunteer to take part in this spell of Irokoi's."

She hadn't meant it seriously, but Wyn answered as if she had. "Even if she would agree, I don't want her to have a chance at the Spires, and we'd have to offer her that to have the smallest chance of persuading her."

"Me neither." Without him prompting, she pulled out the heart-stone to show him. They considered its colour in sober silence before she tucked it away again and gave herself a shake. "Are you coming?"

His lips curved. "As my Star commands."

They walked through the house and met Irokoi standing in the entryway, holding out one of his wings for two of her small relatives to examine, looking entirely bemused. His silver hair was once again unbound, spilling brightly over his dark wings.

"Can you take us flying?" Willow was asking him, gingerly reaching out to touch one of his primaries.

Irokoi shook his head. "Small humans are very fragile."

"Please?" Little Laurel's eyes brightened when she saw Hetta. "Prince Irokoi can take us flying, can't he, Hetta?"

"Not now, Laurel." She fixed Irokoi with a look. "Has Rakken removed the rest of the compulsion from you?"

Laurel heaved a great put-upon sigh. "What about later?"

"If your mothers give you permission, I will fly with you later," Wyn said. Laurel and Willow burst into delighted whoops. "Remember, you must get permission first," he repeated sternly, though the corner of his mouth twitched at the reaction.

"Why don't you have wings all the time like Prince Irokoi?" Laurel asked.

"They are a little awkward for human drawing rooms, unless one does not mind the risk of knocking over ornaments whenever one turns," Wyn said.

Laurel accepted this without question, but Hetta couldn't help shooting him a surprised glance. Why had he never mentioned that before? *We can rearrange the drawing rooms, you know.*

The two girls dashed off, presumably to plague their respective parents, leaving the entranceway in sudden stillness. Irokoi inclined his head.

"Mossfeathers over-extended himself yesterday. He's still learning the shape of what he is. The telepath will help, though. I'm about to go to them again."

"The telepath is my brother. You planned that whole thing yesterday, didn't you?" Hetta didn't like feeling manipulated, or people taking risks with Marius's welfare. "You could have warned us."

Irokoi folded his wings back. His expression was bright and open, and she didn't trust it anymore. "No," he said evenly. "I could not have."

They left Wyn's cryptic brother watching them as they left the house and took the kineticar to Penharrow, driving through fields neatly lined with fresh green growth, seeds sprouting towards the sun. Neither of them spoke as they crossed the border, though Hetta couldn't help tensing.

Stariel gave a small, unhappy murmur and then—she sucked in a breath as the land's presence sharply ebbed. Her connection wasn't gone, but it lay muted in the back of her mind now.

"Perhaps we can persuade Stariel to make you another token," Wyn murmured, looking at her hands upon the steering wheel. She'd been absently rubbing at the knuckle of her ring finger.

"I don't seem to be doing very well explaining or persuading it to do much at all, these days."

"You are the newest faelord in all of Faerie by a considerable measure, and Stariel is more awake than it has been in generations. You will learn together."

She loved his unshakeable faith in her, but it didn't quell her own doubts. The wording he'd chosen picked at her as she rounded a curve in the road, hedgerows forming a green tunnel about them. The newest faelord. But that wasn't all Stariel was, was it? It was just as much human estate as faeland.

Her stomach twisted into knots as they neared Penharrow. She didn't know how to make up for her absence from Angus's house party or for the damage to his house and the disastrous impression the leviathans had made when she'd finally returned, but she had to try. *At least the lords can't possibly think any worse of me than they already do.*

She parked the kineticar in front of the house. Gravel crunched under her shoes as she got out, collecting the basket from the back. She scanned the skies, but there was no sign of crimson wings. She let out a long breath.

The house looked…both better and worse than it had. A grey tarpaulin covered the hole in the upper storeys, and the rubble had already been cleared away from the front of the house. She stared at the fluttering material until Wyn squeezed her hand.

"What am I even doing here?" she murmured.

"What you can."

Angus's butler was extremely frosty when they knocked, but he showed them into the same front room where Gwendelfear had healed Lord Arran to wait.

Wyn grimaced at the empty spot where there had previously been an item of furniture. "I expect the water Gwendelfear dumped on me ruined the fabric."

They turned as the door opened and Angus came in. He looked tired, and as grim as she'd ever seen him.

"Hetta," he said heavily. He spotted Wyn standing by the mantel and his mouth thinned. "Prince."

"Is everyone all right? Lord Arran?" she asked.

"Lord Arran is gone, as are the other lords." Her heart sank. Angus frowned at Wyn. "You're considerably more upright than you were when last I saw you. More fairy magic?"

Wyn nodded. "What of the others who were hurt?"

"My mother's recovering well, Dr Greystark says."

"I'm so sorry, Angus, and for the damage to your house—"

"Unless you called those monsters down upon us, it wasn't your fault." His mouth curved. "You didn't set them on me a-purpose, I'm assuming?"

"I didn't…exactly call them down upon you, but they were here for me. They only went for Penharrow because I repelled them from Stariel's borders." Hetta shifted her feet, annoyed at the guilt. It had been much easier when Angus had been firmly in the wrong on all counts.

He gave her a long look, up and down. "I'm not glad of my roofing bill, but what sort of man would I be if I'd rather monsters attacked you than me?"

A sensible one, given that I'm the one who was able to stop them, she didn't say. "Stariel can pay for the repairs—" But Angus was already shaking his head.

"Nay, it would be the height of hypocrisy for me to take from Stariel's coffers, wouldn't it? Penharrow's books are in well enough shape to stand it, besides, and I suspect yours still aren't."

He was right, but she didn't have to like it.

She blew out a breath. "I brought you some of my grandmother's anti-fae charms. I don't think they'll work on anything like the leviathans, but they're better than nothing."

"And will there be more of them?"

Hetta shook her head. "I don't think so." But she couldn't

actually promise, could she? She'd seen the wild, terrifying beauties contained in Deeper Faerie. "We're…working on approaching the High King about fae in the Mortal Realm, to stop this sort of thing happening without consequence—a treaty." A treaty with whom, using what leverage?

Angus looked from her to Wyn, his eyebrows rising. "I see."

"Thank you for all your efforts with the Conclave on my behalf; it's not your fault I've made such a mull of it."

Angus looked out the window towards the drive, where yesterday there had been rubble and dust and screaming people. Today it was quiet, almost serene. You couldn't see the damage to the house. "Well, I can't deny this wasn't the impression I'd hoped you'd make." He looked her straight in the eyes. "You still have a chance to speak your piece before the vote, at the Conclave. They'll take you seriously now, if nothing else."

It seemed like a pretty faint hope, but she thanked him anyway.

42

THE CALL OF BLOOD TO BLOOD

WYN GOT UP from his desk and stretched, ignoring the desire to keep extending until his wings came forth. Marius's words about hating himself kept burrowing deeper, but he didn't know how else to deal with the rising tide of magic in his blood. It was getting worse, and he didn't have any time now to find some other method of control, not with everything else there was already insufficient time for. There would be time later, before the child was born. His child would *not* feel shame for their heritage, regardless of Wyn's own feelings on the subject.

He went and pulled closed the curtains on the deepening dusk. It had been a tiring day, not least because in between mundane matters, he couldn't help prodding at the shadow he now knew lay within his mind. He still couldn't *remember*, but the more he pressed against the shape of it, the easier it was to keep hold of the idea that there was something missing.

Current paperwork dealt with, he stacked the pile neatly and went in search. Irokoi had disappeared into a room with Rakken around mid-afternoon, and he'd heard from neither of them since, for better or worse.

He found Marius snuggled into a windowseat in the library, a book in one hand and a cup of tea in the other. Wyn smiled at the sight of him rugged up like a caterpillar in a blanket. Marius always did feel the cold.

"Any progress?" he asked softly after making sure his mental shields were intact.

Marius jerked out of the book he'd been reading, losing his grip on his cup—fortunately empty—which went bouncing over the carpet.

"Almighty Pyrania, could you not sneak up on me?"

"My apologies." Perhaps Rakken had been right to think Marius had always had some degree of subconscious control over his telepathy. If he didn't, it would be impossible to sneak up on him.

Marius unwound his arms from the blanket and leaned down to retrieve the cup, setting it on the window ledge. "Rakken was being typically obtuse explaining the magic parts, and I can't seem to read his mind when I'd actually like to, but I think progress is being made, yes. Rakken thinks he can get my device to stop the compulsion coming back once he's removed it. It doesn't exactly *prevent* compulsion, as far as I can work out, but it seems to…pause it. He's testing it on Irokoi now." He sounded grumpy, and there were dark circles under his eyes. "Look, I'm not going to explode suddenly if you or Hetta stop checking on me *constantly*."

"I am glad to know it."

Marius narrowed his eyes, but then his gaze shifted behind Wyn, and the darkening of his expression told Wyn who it was without turning. Rakken was masking his presence, the leylines undisturbed by his passing.

Wyn turned. "Good evening, brother."

He wasn't sure he liked the way Rakken considered Marius, the heated meaning in the air between them. He felt a sudden desire to tell Rakken that Marius and, in fact, all of Hetta's family were strictly off-limits.

Then Rakken shook off the connection and met Wyn's eyes. "Our mother," he said grimly and without preamble.

The last person to compel Wyn had been King Aeros, forcing him to his knees in the throne room. He'd managed only a token resistance then. Now, the weight of Rakken's compulsion hit him like gravity, a force so enormous and inevitable that it drove the air from his lungs.

But he'd been weaker, before. Now, aggression woke in him, fierce and unbending. His wings snapped out in a soft explosion of feathers. Marius yelped and ducked out of the way.

Rakken rolled his eyes, but there was a wariness there that said he'd noticed Wyn's flare of power and wasn't sure what to make of it. "Honestly, do you want to be free of Mother's compulsion or not?"

Oh. "You could have explained yourself first, Rake," he said, pulling his wings back in irritably. Ah, stormwinds take it. He couldn't deal with his brother *and* his misbehaving magic in this form.

Rakken made a gesture to halt him when Wyn would have changed back. "Do you wish to lose control of your powers? You're already boiling over with magic; it's no wonder you cannot keep your instincts in check."

"My control is worse in this form. I told you this, Rake, when I asked for your advice!"

Rakken canted his head, a puzzled frown appearing between his brows. "And I told you what to do to resolve the issue."

"No, you did not! You spouted unhelpful metaphor at me about our 'primal natures'."

Rakken's gaze slid sideways to Marius, who'd remained silent, watching the exchange. "Apparently I'm becoming less and less obvious these days, even when I don't intend it." He sighed. "I am not used to parsing my thoughts into blunt mortal shapes."

That was either an apology or a dig. Or, knowing Rakken, a little of both.

"Oh, yes, let's call 'being honest with people' using blunt mortal word shapes. It's clearly not your fault if you deliberately manipulate and deceive people for your own amusement; mortals are just too difficult to understand." Marius gave the last words a bitter emphasis and wrenched himself up. Wyn started; he'd never heard Marius sound so vicious.

"Don't tell me *I* am the one here guilty of pretence, Marius Valstar. I have never tried to hide what I want."

A drawn-out eternity in which Marius and Rakken glared at each other from an uncomfortably close distance and Wyn rather wished he were anywhere else.

For a moment, Marius seemed to waver, his body swaying incrementally towards Rakken, as if he would close that gap. Wyn wondered how to beat a tactical retreat or, alternatively, whether to beat his brother to death. But then Marius jerked his gaze away with a sharp inhalation. "Go to the hells, Rake. And for the gods' sake tell Wyn what he needs to know." He stomped off, his footsteps loud as he left the library.

"What did you do?" Wyn asked. He deeply wanted to avoid his brother's love life, but Marius was his friend, storms take it.

Rakken was staring at Marius's retreating back with an intensity hot enough to crack stones and didn't answer.

"If you hurt him…" Wyn began.

Rakken's head whipped around. "He does not need your defence, Hallowyn. I have shown him what I am; he will keep his distance now." There was a savage undercurrent to the words.

"And you're going to keep *your* distance from him?" Wyn asked meaningfully, shifting his weight. A hint of spice in the air.

Rakken smiled narrowly. "Do you truly think your opinions on this matter hold the smallest interest to me, sparrow?" An evasion if Wyn had ever heard one. "But enough." Rakken's focus shifted in a way Wyn found unsettling, and his next words came with the force of a whip. "You've spent so much time in a mortal form compressing your power that of course it tries to surge loose each time you take your fae form! How else is it to learn the shape of you?

"You've rushed your way to magical maturity before your time with bullish force and no understanding, and now your lack of confidence in your own control is ultimately your undoing; one cannot ride the stormwinds by fighting them. And now you have an unborn child to protect—did you really expect that to have no effect on your own magic? Of course it's trying to manifest properly even as you foolishly try to deny it. Blood calls to blood, as I told you before."

"Is this you trying to explain clearly? Because it's actually quite hard to tell," Wyn complained, though understanding was starting to bloom in his chest. Oh. Oh, he had been so, so foolish.

"Embrace all sides of yourself and your powers should settle. Eventually." Rakken bared his teeth. "If you survive the storm of your own making."

"How reassuring."

Rakken ignored him and gestured curtly for him to sit. Sighing, Wyn obeyed, and tried not to wince as the force of Rakken's will washed over him, inexorable as the tide. It felt like hooks pulling out of his flesh.

After an interminable time, Rakken sat back. He looked even more tired than Marius, and his nose had started to bleed again. Rakken rubbed it away with the back of his hand, irritable.

"Koi was right; there is far less of it in you." He held out an amulet; Wyn recognised it as a repurposed quizzing glass, bound with rowan-wood and shimmering with Rakken's own additional charms. "Put this on. It should stop the compulsion from returning. I've yet to figure out how to keep it back without it; I've never encountered anything like it before. It shouldn't be able to regrow, and yet it *does*." There was unwilling admiration in his voice.

Wyn prodded at his memories, unsure exactly what had changed. It felt...tender. "I cannot tell what has changed."

"It will take your mind a while to heal from the scars. But you should at least be able to hold on to the knowledge of who is responsible for this." His tone had darkened. Their mother.

"Can you remove compulsion from yourself?" Wyn asked.

Rakken gave him a dry look. "Do you think I would un-bind you before myself? I hope I have removed enough. But then, the Spires was still able to connect with you even with the bonds you had tying you in knots." His eyes glowed again; Wyn had never seen him this...dishevelled. "But you were only a boy, Hallowyn, when she left. The compulsion touched you lightly. Removing my own is like unthreading a needle in the dark. And Koi..." Horror surfaced in his eyes. "I do not know how he retained his sanity."

Wyn shivered. "How long until we can undo ThousandSpire's curse, then?"

They both turned as Irokoi's presence came into the library. *He is steadily undoing all my attempts to feign normality here*, Wyn thought with resignation. *Not that Rake was exactly helping either.*

Irokoi had braided his hair neatly, but it wasn't a mortal style, many fine plaits arranged like the fronds of a sea anemone, each decorated with a twist of blue ribbon. He also hadn't quite grasped the finer points of proper mortal attire, the collar of the shirt Wyn had lent him hanging open, no waistcoat in sight.

Irokoi made a pleased sound as he took in Wyn's wings. "You are very strange about showing off your plumage, Hallowyn. I had begun to think you ashamed."

Rakken chuckled, and Wyn gave them both cutting looks.

"This spell, Koi. You said it had two parts," Wyn asked. "Do we need Torquil and Aroset for the first part?"

Irokoi's feathers fanned restlessly. "Well, no, but we will only have so much time after we retrieve Cat to complete the rest of it. We cannot just take the anchor away from ThousandSpire without consequence; the faeland will start to unravel without one. It's not as if Cat initiated the curse for the fun of it! It would be safer not to risk beginning the first part of the spell without all the pieces in place for the second."

It was on Wyn's lips to say they were running out of time, but Rakken spoke before he could.

"How long can ThousandSpire survive without an anchor?" Rakken's voice was hard.

"A quarter moon, perhaps."

"Then that is how long you have to drag Torquil back from wherever he is hiding. We bring Cat back now. That is my price for helping you, brother."

Irokoi looked between them unhappily. "I can bring Torquil back easily enough, but we have no plan to gain Aroset's agreement. It is a risk, Rakken. Would you truly choose to take it with our land, our people?" Mismatched eyes met brilliant green ones, and the hair on the back of Wyn's neck stood on end as a frisson of power moved in the library. Koi was a touch shorter, tilting his chin to look up, holding his black wings motionless.

Rakken didn't back down. "We have more chance of persuading Aroset with Cat on our side, and I will need time to undo the compulsion on her. It is a risk I am prepared to take. We do the spell now." He turned his fierce gaze on Wyn. "Go and get Lord Valstar."

Slightly against his better judgement, Wyn obeyed Rakken's directive—both of them. It felt beyond strange to walk through the house winged, his magic shivering with every step. Was Rakken sure this was a good idea? It felt a lot like inviting a lightning storm upon the Valstars.

But when he found Hetta, his magic surged as if to prove Rakken's point. He grit his teeth, flattening his wings against his spine as he tried to bring it back under control. How had he failed to make the connection?

Hetta tilted her head in silent question at his choice of form, seeing straight through the glamour he'd cast. He told her what Irokoi had said and saw she was as conflicted as he was about it.

"But we don't have time to mess about either." She held up the heartstone; they both watched it sway on its chain for a sombre moment. "And you're worried about Cat too," she added softly.

"Yes," he agreed, to both these points.

They gathered at the Stones for the spell. The day was warm and clear, crickets chirping in the swaying grass. A starling murmuration looped loudly around the stones before continuing.

Koi gave Rakken a serious look before holding out a hand. "I'll need one of Cat's feathers." Wyn had the peculiar realisation that Koi was looking at Rakken with a faint note of *Behave, little brother*, which would've been amusing in other circumstances.

There was a long, frozen moment, but eventually, Rakken clicked his fingers in the clear air and withdrew a feather—a primary, to Wyn's surprise. Such feathers were shed only rarely.

Wyn wouldn't have known by sight alone that it was Cat's and not Rakken's—the twins' colouring was identical. Rakken reluctantly gave it into Irokoi's keeping.

"It will aggravate me if you use that for any malicious purpose, brother."

Irokoi beamed at him before turning back to the rest of them, eyeing their positions critically.

"Four points on a five-pointed star," he said eventually.

"Are you counting me in this?" Hetta asked.

Rakken answered. "What you carry, rather. Their blood is your blood for our present purposes."

Wyn frowned. "Is that wise, using the unborn as an anchor?"

Hetta's eyes narrowed. "Yes, I want to know the answer to that also, because it greatly changes my willingness to participate in this."

"Of course I accounted for that in the spell," Irokoi said, sounding hurt. "Why else did you think I went to such trouble to add an eddy into the design to catch any backlash?" He waved at the lines of spellwork before turning earnestly to Hetta. "Not that there should *be* any backlash."

Wyn frowned at the spell lines, trying to read them. It had been so long, and he'd never had any practice at this sort of advanced magic, but he saw that there were more folds to the spell around one of the anchors, safety mechanisms he faintly recognised. There were also gaps in the spacing—more than four. He frowned at them. "There are pieces missing."

Rakken shot him a dry look, as if he'd announced that the grass was green. "Obviously, Hallowyn."

"Because it's a two-stage spell," Irokoi said.

"Which even if you hadn't already been told such, a fledgling should have the wit to see."

Irokoi ignored Rakken. "The first stage will help us with the second, when we have all the bits for it. Can't do one without the other. That's the trouble with things linking together. We need a lot of power. Otherwise obviously I wouldn't be using unborn people for extra resonance." He nodded at Hetta, who gave a dubious nod in return.

"We are breaking a curse laid by the High King." Rakken's words were sober.

"Well, more like finding a *loophole* in it," Irokoi added. "Honestly, if we didn't have the power of a faeland to draw on, I don't think this would be possible." He grinned at Wyn. "Thank goodness you followed my advice."

Wyn had interpreted that bit of crypticness correctly, then, in the undersea; Irokoi hadn't been surprised by Hetta's pregnancy. He narrowed his eyes at Koi; his brother was keeping far too many things from them still.

When Irokoi had them arranged to his satisfaction, he triggered the spell. Lines of connection sprang forth between them, a space gaping where Cat should have been. Blood to blood.

The spell drew on them all, a heady thing, the magic glittering like a whirlpool, washing around the circle in a storm.

Cinnamon on a sea wind. Catsmere's storm-scent was warm-edged with spice, like his own, and it bloomed into being as the air warped. Power built, and that gap began to beat against the rhythm of the magic, like the wind pulling on a kite string.

The space jerked one last time, and then the spell collapsed.

Cat was on her hands and knees, panting, her wings a mess of broken feathers and dripping blood. The Maelstrom's magic crawled over her, setting Wyn's teeth on edge, and for a heartbeat he was frozen by the memory of the storm snapping his wingbones like toothpicks.

Rakken had already reached Cat by the time Wyn broke free of his paralysis. Rakken helped her fold into a sitting position. One of her wings hung at an unnatural angle, and she held her left arm gingerly and breathed in the careful way that Wyn recognised because he too knew how it felt to breathe through broken ribs. Blood dripped from her hairline—her hair too dark to make the wound obvious—smearing one of her eyes shut. There was so much blood it was difficult to tell the full extent of her injuries.

But she was alive.

Her expression was achingly familiar, the quick, assessing way she scanned her surroundings, giving nothing away of her own emotions as she took in her brothers all arrayed about her. *Oh, Cat.*

"How long have I been gone?" she asked.

"Sixty-seven days, nine hours, and thirty-two minutes, in mortal time," Rakken said, and his voice had cracks in it. His eyes glowed as the words spilled out of him. "How could you, Cat? *How could you?*"

"Someone had to see to the safety of ThousandSpire." Cat fixed on Irokoi. "Is it still in stasis? Did you find some other way?"

"That someone did not have to be you alone!"

"I didn't stop you entering the Maelstrom alone, Mouse, when you judged the risk worth it." There was an old bitterness to the words, a bone that had been picked at many times before.

Wyn had never seen the twins at such intense odds before, and watching them glare daggers at each other felt akin to the sun faltering in its arc.

Rakken's lips drew back from his teeth, but he bit back whatever retort he'd been about to make, remembering his audience. The twins turned, the public facade of unity firmly back in place, though Wyn knew it would disappear the instant the two of them were alone again. Rakken's wings still vibrated with anger.

Cat sought out Irokoi again. "The Spires?"

"The curse holds. But there's no one anchoring the faeland, with you here."

"Why did you pull me out, then?" She tried to get up and failed. "The Spires could've survived without a ruler, in stasis. It cannot survive with no one to anchor it. Would you see the end of our land, our people?"

"It can survive a little while. And we have a plan for the rest."

Cat sagged. "There is no one else left. We have exhausted our bloodline, and the land finds us all wanting."

"There has been a compulsion upon us all that prevented the Spires from choosing freely." Rakken explained the rest in a tight voice. "Look at me, and I will begin to undo it, though it will take some time. Time which we must use as best we can." He looked to Irokoi. "Go."

Irokoi made a face. "Don't order me about, Mossfeathers, as if it were *me* who decided on this order of events. But very well. Don't forget to gather up Set in the meantime. Ask him to explain it to you," he added at Cat's sound of inquiry before sweeping away on wings of midnight.

Cat rubbed her head with her good hand. "Interesting, but first this, I think." She grimly attempted to straighten her trailing wing. The low buzz of the Maelstrom's energy spun in eddies at the movement. "Dislocated rather than broken. Mouse?"

Rakken felt along the bone and nodded. "Yes." He made a sharp, jerking motion and Cat hissed, her face pale as he put the joint back into place. She swallowed and put out an imperious hand. Rakken helped her to her feet. Her wings still hung oddly, feathers torn off or bent akilter in many places and she moved gingerly, as if she didn't trust her body not to betray her. She leaned on Rakken for support despite the tension still singing between the two.

Her gaze locked with Wyn's.

"Hallowyn."

He flinched. "You knew I wouldn't take the throne, even when I did not," he said.

Her eyes glittered. He'd never seen her angry like this before, or at least, not at him. There was more than mere rage in her, and the deeper, colder emotion spiked her words when she spoke: disappointment. "It was obvious where your heart lay. You would not choose Faerie over Mortal. I cannot even blame you for it. You are what you are, Hallowyn."

"Can you forgive me?" He shouldn't ask, and especially not now, when she was so newly emerged from the storm, every movement so evidently paining her.

She weighed him. "If ThousandSpire rises once more, yes. If it falls, then no. I understand, but no."

He swallowed. He didn't think he would forgive himself in that case either.

Cat's gaze flicked to Hetta, and her eyes widened. "You are with child, Lord Valstar."

"Er, yes," said Hetta, and then, with some exasperation, "Can you tell just by looking?"

Cat smiled, genuine. "It's because it's my brother's child, and you used the shared blood to call to me," Cat said. "A *child*, Hallowyn! I will have to teach them to fight," she told him matter-of-factly. "For you will be of no use in such things."

"I wasn't intending that they should live in a world where they need to know such things," Wyn said, though he could not keep from smiling in return.

Her smile faded. "They will be greater fae and half human. The world wasn't made for such, so you must prepare them to face it." Her expression shadowed. "Set will not react well to this news; she will see them as competition."

"If only we could be sure to tell her, it would make for excellent bait," Rakken said idly.

Wyn stiffened. "No."

Cat was frowning between them in confusion, and Hetta looked much too thoughtful.

"Where do we think Aroset is right now?" Hetta asked. "Could she still be in Meridon? Or in Greymark, since that's where all those reports about wing worshippers have come from? It seems very unfair if she's started a cult in the human world, but if she has, presumably she's paying some attention to mortal news." She met Wyn's eyes. "She might come find us, at the Conclave."

"Even if she did, how could we be sure we could persuade or subdue her? She didn't fear all of us together last time and that was before—" He gestured at the twins, Rakken's wings still not fully regrown, Cat covered with blood. As if to make his point for him, Cat made a startled, cut-off sound as one of her legs crumpled.

Rakken caught her weight, and Cat sighed. "I'd like to know why you're talking of baiting Set, but I fear first I may need further medical attention."

43

INFAMOUS

ETTA HADN'T REALLY expected their magical antics and the appearance of yet another greater fae would pass without comment, so she wasn't too surprised to encounter a welcome party on the front doorstep when they arrived back at the house, even if the combination was odd: Jack, Alexandra, and Gwendelfear. However, it quickly became clear it wasn't so much a welcome party as an interrupted confrontation between Jack and the other two. Alexandra was hugging her arms around herself, chin set defiantly, while Jack glowered down at her and Gwendelfear in turn stared silent daggers back at him.

"You can't just go talking to—" Jack broke off at the sight of Catsmere, looking incredulously from her to Rakken. "You're back. Wait, you're bleeding. Why are you bleeding?"

But Hetta's attention wasn't on her cousin. This was the first time she'd seen Gwendelfear in Rakken's presence, let alone both twins simultaneously. Gwendelfear recoiled at the sight, and Alexandra put a soft hand on her arm.

"This is Princess Catsmere," Hetta said into the tension. "And, er, this is Gwendelfear."

Cat's eyes had narrowed. "You are treating with DuskRose, Lord Valstar?"

Treating, honestly? Hetta sighed. "No more than I am ThousandSpire. But Gwendelfear is a guest here. It's all right, Jack, it wasn't an attack," she added for her cousin's benefit, since he was searching the sky as if expecting Aroset to fall from it. *We should be so lucky*. She could deal with Aroset on Stariel's grounds.

Gwendelfear shot her a venomous look, and she knew she'd said the wrong thing.

"Gwendelfear is of FallingStar's court now. She has sworn allegiance," Wyn added. Even Hetta, who liked to think she knew him as well as anyone, couldn't read anything into his tone.

Cat said nothing, and Rakken helped her into the house without looking at Gwendelfear, as if the space she occupied simply didn't exist. Maybe that was for the best. Before Hetta could follow them, Gwendelfear moved, a jerk of agitation.

"I would speak to you, Lord Valstar." Gwendelfear's hands clenched and unclenched restlessly.

A sudden gust of wind made a go for Hetta's hat, but fortunately the pins held it firm. "All right. Come up to my study, then."

Jack dogged her footsteps as she went back inside and removed her coat, demanding to know the reason for Cat's appearance. Hetta heartlessly delegated all explanations to Wyn and left the pair of them standing in the entrance hall, Jack's expression steadily darkening.

Alexandra followed her and Gwendelfear up to her study with a kind of determined awkwardness. Seeing Alexandra so obviously consider herself Gwendelfear's defender made Hetta smile, even if she was still somewhat dubious of her sister's choice of friends.

She closed the door of her study. Gwendelfear had grown even more agitated, her weight shifting as if only the small confines of the room were keeping her from pacing. She looked much healthier after that episode with Wyn's magic, but she was still too thin.

"What do you want of me, Lord Valstar?" she demanded.

Hetta stared at her. "Nothing. Well, I suppose I want you not to harm anyone," she amended hastily. "But you're under no obligation to stay here if you don't want to."

"And what service must I do, to remain? I am bound to your court, unless you mean to abandon me."

"There is no must here, other than not doing harm to me and mine. You're not bound to serve me."

"I told you so, Gwen," Alexandra put in.

Gwendelfear shot her a look. "That is the tie between us now, Lord Valstar. You are responsible for me, and I must do as you ask. That is how it works."

"She's worried about losing Stariel's protection," Alexandra said.

Another venomous look from Gwendelfear, which Alexandra again took absolutely no notice of.

Hetta sighed. "Well, if you want a job here, we can probably find something to suit. Which you'll be paid for. But there's no urgency to it." Of course this must seem a pressing issue to Gwendelfear, but Hetta would quite happily put off thinking about it until all her own pressing issues were resolved. She thought helplessly of Wyn downstairs, knowing she was undoubtedly missing some nuances of fae culture here. When had fae employment relations become Stariel's business? Although, in fairness, the estate had technically been employing fae for years, though that had felt far less like the two worlds becoming entangled. Wyn had always tried so hard to be human, after all.

Not anymore, she vowed silently. *This will be a new world, for all of us. Together.* With that came a decision, settling in her like river stones after a flood. She was going to the Conclave, even if it was hopeless, even if it was dangerous, and not only for Stariel. Bridging the divide between Mortal and Faerie wasn't going to be easy or instant, but it also wasn't going to happen by standing about doing nothing. They could judge her all they liked; she wouldn't be the one who blinked first.

Gwendelfear's narrow shoulders went up like a bristling cat. "Do you mean to punish me?" When Hetta once more looked at her blankly, she added, "For Prince Hallowyn."

"Oh. No, of course not. Even if you hadn't healed him, he already considers the debt between you paid. But even if he didn't, we don't punish people like—like in Faerie," she said, conscious of Alexandra's presence.

Gwendelfear looked from one to the other of them, her expression still full of suspicion. Hetta felt exhausted of both patience and inspiration.

"Look, if you really feel you must have a role here, have a think about the sort of things you might like to do and come and talk to me about it tomorrow. But I truly meant what I said about there being no urgency."

"What I would like to do?" Gwendelfear said as if this were a strange and dangerous concept.

Hetta had never been more grateful for her sister than when Alexandra put a hand on Gwendelfear's arm and said, "I can help you come up with ideas, if you like, Gwen. I'm sure you're good at lots of things. Come on."

Hetta expected Gwendelfear to argue, but she shot Hetta one last wary glance before allowing herself to be shepherded out.

Hetta sagged down in her seat and put her forehead on her desk. Right. After taking several long breaths, she sat back and pulled out the heartstone. It swung in a gentle pendulum motion, picking up reflections from the dying sun.

She looked up as the door opened. Wyn grimaced, managing

to convey both his conversation with Jack and his opinion on her current thoughts in a single expression.

"I deeply dislike the thought of you as bait, Hetta, and even more so when I'm not confident we could overcome Aroset even if she *took* said bait."

"*I* can overcome Aroset, so long as we're on Stariel's lands."

"She will not come here willingly."

"No, but that's not the only way to get someone here, is it?" Hetta hesitated, because she was about to bring up something she knew Wyn didn't like to remember. "What about the way you brought your father here?" she said in a rush. "Lamorkin gave you a translocation spell, and all you had to do was activate it at the right time."

He'd gone still. "Lamorkin won't give me another freely."

"Yes, but what about Rakken? You've said before that he's a skilled sorcerer—could he make such a spell? We made a Gate to Stariel from the deepest part of Faerie, after all, and this would be a much smaller and less permanent version of that. It only need bring me— and whoever I'm touching—to Stariel, from somewhere else within the Mortal Realm. Surely that ought to be possible?"

"Perhaps," Wyn allowed, grudgingly. "But if we are using anyone as bait, which I am not at all convinced is a sensible plan, it had better be me than you. Aroset doesn't know about the child, as far as we know."

She was about to argue with him when Aunt Sybil stormed into the room, brandishing a newspaper.

"Henrietta Valstar, what is the meaning of this!?"

ON ANY OTHER DAY, the headline would have made Wyn flinch: FAE PRINCE SEDUCES LORD VALSTAR, it read. As it was, he stared at the ink of the *Northern Chronicle* with a kind of terrible resignation. His mother was alive and had compelled him. Cat was free. They were so close to freeing ThousandSpire and fulfilling the High King's bargain.

That last made the headline seem particularly unfair. They were so close, or at least, much closer than Wyn had felt for weeks.

"Well, this is just silly," Hetta said, rapidly skim-reading the article. "Apparently you've lured me into 'degenerate ways', which is certainly not true. And I'm a threat to the moral fabric of society—I'd no idea society was so fragile! Honestly, it's not as if I'm the first unwedded pregnant woman to ever exist!"

She threw the paper at her aunt, but Wyn caught it in mid-air and unfolded it.

"You have brought shame on the family name!" Aunt Sybil railed. Crowding behind her were a gaggle of Hetta's relatives. They couldn't all fit in Hetta's study, and they spilled out into the hallway, craning their necks. Even Marius was there, looking pale, though that could've been from the collective racket.

There was a cartoon. Of course there was a cartoon. It showed a woman who was clearly supposed to be Hetta—a poor likeness— with three struggling creatures in her arms. Distantly, Wyn was aware of Lady Sybil berating Hetta and of Hetta's angry response, but mainly his attention was caught by the depictions. The creatures were grotesque imitations of babes, with black eyes, scales and horns and wide, shrieking mouths filled with pointed teeth...and wings. *Fae babes do not look like that.* Or at least—stormdancer ones didn't. Wyn had not seen babes of every type of fae, of course.

Cartoon-Hetta's expression bore into him, desolate and abandoned. A winged man—presumably himself, though they'd forgotten his horns—strolled away from the scene, hands in his pockets and whistling.

The caption read LIKE FATHER LIKE CHILD?

He began to laugh. Lady Sybil and Hetta jerked out of their rapidly escalating argument. He shouldn't laugh; there was nothing truly funny in this, but he found he could not help it. It was so...so *human*.

"Well," he said to Hetta. "Congratulations. According to this we're having triplets."

Hetta gave a burble of laughter. "We're going to need a very tolerant nanny."

Lady Sybil swelled. "This is not a subject for amusement, Mr Tempest! What do you think the queen will say when she sees this?"

"I should hope Queen Matilda will care a great deal more for securing an alliance with the fae than she will about idle gossip," Hetta said firmly, taking the paper off Wyn. "I certainly have better things to do with my time."

"That bloody reporter!" Jack had muscled his way into the room. "I *told* you not to talk to her, Alex!"

"Language!" Aunt Sybil scolded reflexively as all eyes turning to Alexandra.

Alexandra went scarlet and looked at her feet. "I was trying to help! They keep making...well, it's not true, the way they keep making it sound in the papers, and I thought if I just explained that, then— And anyway, she said you'd agreed to an interview"—she looked at Wyn for support—"so I thought it must be all right, then."

"You *what*?" Marius gaped at him.

His misjudgement. Again. "I confess I did say that she might approach me, after Penharrow. But was this earlier today that you spoke to her, Miss Alex?" Alex mumbled an affirmative. "Well, then, this particular article has nothing to do with you; there would not have been time for the paper to reach Stariel. And Marius's reporter does not work for the *Northern Chronicle*."

"She's not *my* reporter!" Marius objected.

"Is Hetta having *three* babies?" Laurel piped up from the hallway, which fortunately put a temporary halt to both the forming mob and further discussion of the topic.

It didn't take long for the wider effects of the article to be felt. The estate agent contacted him to inform them that interest in the Dower House had dried up. *So sorry; people can be so fickle; you know how it is.* The agent didn't mention the article, and Wyn kept his own tone coolly civil right up until the moment when the call ended, at which point he bestowed a number of profanities in both Prydinian and stormtongue on his empty office. Hetta had to fend off yet another demand for explanation from the queen, having only just sent off her previous report, and Wyn suspected a summons would be arriving on the next train.

But he would have dealt with these small blows and more if it would have stopped Hetta from saying, once they were alone again, in the darkness beneath his room's rafters, "Well, Aroset's bound to hear about this now."

Hetta sat on his bed, but he couldn't keep still, agitation sending him pacing back and forth across the wooden floorboards.

"We are not using our unborn child as bait," he said. Lightning hummed under his skin. "It's too dangerous."

"I'm not *thrilled* about it either, as a concept, but it could work, don't you think? Surely we can between us think of sufficient safe-guards to make it as undangerous as possible?" Hetta said. "Besides, I don't want the Conclave to think I'm too ashamed to show my face, and if I don't show in Greymark, that's exactly how it'll be taken. Why not kill two birds with one stone?"

"That doesn't make it a good idea." His feathers vibrated. "Aroset is *my* sister and my responsibility, not yours."

"Even if Aroset was playing by those rules—which she isn't—you do know that marriage means we acquire each other's families, for better or for worse? Which, by this logic, makes her my problem too."

"We are not married."

"Yes, but that's merely a matter of timing, not intent. Or does this change your mind? I am a fallen woman now, after all."

He uttered a mortal profanity, which had the unintended effect of making her laugh. He stopped pacing and groused down at her. "*Hetta.*"

She just raised her eyebrows at him. "Well, does it?"

"Of course not," he grumbled.

She grinned, and then put out a hand and twined her fingers with his. "Not that I mind, but why are you feathery?"

"Rakken says it will help me control myself, though it feels very much the reverse." He flexed his wings slightly, the restless feeling of lightning still a background hum, not having eased in the slightest. "And you are changing the subject."

Her nose wrinkled. "It's not as if I *relish* the idea of danger, but I'm hardly defenceless, and you can't truly have expected me to sit at home safe while you try to solve everything on your own?"

"Last year, when Aroset took you, do you know what I was prepared to do to get you back? Anything, Hetta. Anything." The words were a cry. "And that was before, before—" He gestured helplessly.

"I'm pregnant, not an invalid," she said calmly, but he saw that she understood the magnitude of his admission: *anything*. He would have torn the Spires down to its foundations if he'd had to, regardless of what it cost.

And, in a way, hadn't he done exactly that?

She didn't resist when he dropped onto the bed next to her, hauling her close and wrapping them both in a cocoon of feathers. It didn't ease the fear in him at all, the feeling that both the world and himself were spinning out of control. The wild lightning quivered. Stormcrows, Rakken better know what he was talking about.

"You will not give the same for me. To Aroset, if it comes to it. Promise me, Hetta," he growled against her skin. This was his line in the sand, the cost he couldn't bear. Adding the child she carried into the equation didn't change that fundamental position, only magnified his strength of feeling.

She met and held his gaze, oddly solemn. "All right. In the abstract at least, though I've no intention of either of us needing to sacrifice ourselves."

It eased the fear slightly. "Thank you."

"You're probably the only person I know who finds such a statement of limitations romantic. I'd like to make it clear that I'm willing to give a great deal for you. Just not literally anything." Her cheeks were flushed.

He buried his face in the crook of her neck, breathed in the scent of her. "I know, Hetta. That is a sane approach and deeply reassuring to me. At least one of this child's parents should be sane, don't you think?"

She laughed. "You wish you didn't love me as much as you do. What a deeply unromantic sentiment."

"Not less. Never that. I just—" He made a frustrated noise. "I cannot control it, Hetta."

"Oh, my love," she said, and the endearment warmed him despite everything. "Only you would feel like you should be able to. Think of it as being good practice for our imminent parenthood. I'm fairly sure a lack of control over things is expected."

She kissed him, and it thoroughly distracted him for some moments. When they broke apart, he sighed. "One day, I am going to win one of our arguments."

"One day," she agreed, her lips curving. He kissed her again and had some satisfaction in the dazed look in her eyes when he pulled back.

"If we do this, we are going to be very, very careful." And, storm-crows, they were going to have to ask for Rakken's help yet again.

44

GREYMARK

HETTA HADN'T APPRECIATED how complicated a working a wearable translocation spell would be. Rakken, Catsmere, and Wyn between them worked through the next day and night before the Conclave to make it—a spell that would take her and anyone touching her back to Stariel in an instant. The effort left Wyn's siblings grumpy and as wrung of magic as used dishcloths. Wyn ruefully classed his role as 'unskilled labour', but he too was oddly lethargic when he finally presented the fruits of their crafting to her before dawn on the morning of the Conclave. The spell took the form of a small dark stone, which she hung on her necklace beside the heartstone.

Collecting fae spells as ornaments, she thought wryly. She wished she still had her ring.

They caught the early train from Stariel Station to Greymark. It was a four-hour train journey, but they didn't make it alone. Gwendelfear joined them in prickly silence, the world's least likely chaperone. Hetta hadn't considered a chaperone necessary—after all, wasn't she already as ruined as it was possible for a person to be?

But Gwendelfear had been insistent that she be allowed to do this service, so Hetta had reluctantly agreed. Having someone who could magically heal around wasn't a bad idea if things went sideways.

It made for an awkward journey, though. Wyn and Gwendelfear were excruciatingly polite to each other as they seated themselves on opposite sides of the carriage, which made Hetta feel a bit like she was sitting in the middle of a thistle patch. Eventually, Wyn's tiredness resulted in him half-dozing whilst leaned against the window, the most undignified sleeping position she'd ever seen him adopt.

Hetta spent the train journey continually reaching for the two charms at her throat, her thoughts an anxious knot. The landscape changed—fields, forests, mountains, and finally the sea—and her sense of urgency grew. The heartstone, warm against her skin, had been the colour of the night sky this morning: a deep, deep blue only barely distinguishable from black.

Her thoughts flitted between the Conclave and Aroset, unsure which she was dreading more. The former, she suspected. The Conclave wasn't a risk to life or limb, but at least she could use pyromancy on Aroset.

They arrived at Greymark Central Station without incident. Wyn had regained some energy, whether from restored magic or simply nerves, she wasn't sure. She herself rose with relief when the train pulled into the platform, needing movement to work off her own restlessness. Gwendelfear emerged after them with wary interest for the busy station.

It depressed her to see the pasteboard outside the station: THE WINGED GODS BLESS US. There was no sign of whoever had posted it. Gwendelfear examined it without a change in expression, and Wyn's magic coloured the air around them, the scent of cardamom and fresh rain. Hetta put a hand on his arm.

"After this is over, we can find the ones Set compelled and free them."

"Yes." His fae was close to the surface, deepening the colour of his skin and eyes, turning his hair to burnished platinum. "But she isn't the only greater fae who will treat mortals as her plaything. I cannot stop them all."

There was something savage in him, which Hetta rather agreed with. He opened his mouth then shook his head and closed it.

"Say it," Hetta prompted. "I'm thinking it too."

"Our child will be greater fae." His voice was barely audible, though he needn't have bothered—not with every paper from here to Meridon trumpeting the news of her pregnancy. "What kind of world will they grow up in, if this continues?"

Hetta could see it too, that dark future, and it wasn't only their child's fate that worried her. Wyn was fae too.

"Well, it's a good thing we're already set to speak with the High King soon, isn't it?"

His hand tightened on hers. "I'm worried I may say or do something…unwise if the High King won't be persuaded to act."

"Well, I definitely will," Hetta agreed.

His lips curved. "Hetta, is it sensible for us *both* to be reckless at the same time?"

"Bags I lose my temper first, then, if we must take turns."

He laughed but sobered all too quickly, scanning the train station. No sign of Aroset. Did the presence of the pasteboard mean Aroset had been here recently, compelling people? she wondered.

"Please don't be reckless today," Wyn said softly.

"I have absolutely no intention of recklessness today," Hetta promised. "Not with…her about." She hesitated, deciding not to name Aroset until after the Conclave. Would it be better if she turned up before or after the Conclave? Hetta was dreading the meeting enough that she almost hoped Aroset would turn up beforehand and then she needn't feel guilty for missing the Conclave. Being repudiated by them at a distance would be preferable to in person.

Though I have to at least try to convince them one more time.

Hetta didn't spot any more posters, though her gaze snagged on a man handing out flyers for a public meeting TO DISCUSS THE FAE MENACE. Was that better or worse than the wing worshippers?

They found a hackney cab rather than a carriage to take them to the Conclave, the extra iron a comfort. The traffic drew to a complete halt and then inched along and Hetta, who'd anticipated arriving quite early, began to fear she might be late.

"Sorry, ma'am; there's some kind of protest on today up at the Dome," the driver apologised when she asked him about it. The 'ma'am' struck her strangely. It had been a while since anyone had called her anything except 'my lord' or, before that, 'miss'.

Hetta's stomach twisted itself into knots. "What sort of protest?"

"Something about fairies. The Northern Lords Conclave is meeting today…" The driver trailed off, eyes widening. "You're *him*!" he said to Wyn. "Where are your wings?"

"They are inconvenient for cab-riding," Wyn said, expression smooth as glass. "Tell me, how far away is the Dome?"

"Usually less than ten minutes. In this traffic? The gods know. Begging your pardon, Your Highness."

Wyn and Hetta exchanged glances, weighing risks. "We can walk," Hetta said. "Set us down here, please."

The minute they got out of the hackney, Hetta spun illusion, turning Wyn's hair black, her own blonde and curly, and adding a bulbous nose to Wyn for good measure. Gwendelfear she made into a version of Alexandra. They navigated on foot towards the Dome, Hetta gripping Wyn's hand tightly. Surely Aroset wouldn't attack here, in the narrow, clogged streets, even if she somehow found them? She couldn't smell Wyn's magic, knew he was keeping it as tightly furled as he could. They weren't sure whether his presence would be an additional incentive to Aroset or a reason to steer clear.

The Dome was so named for its main architectural feature, a beautifully ornate roof that rose above the main square in Greymark. A square that was currently filled with protesters, held in check at the bottom of the steps to the Dome by a line of policemen.

Wyn sucked in a breath. Hetta looked straight ahead and tried to ignore the slogans on the hand-painted signs, but she couldn't block out the chants.

They wove their way through the crowd. There weren't that many of them, Hetta tried to tell herself; they'd just done an awfully good job of obstructing traffic. Hetta waited for someone to recognise her or Wyn, her skin crawling, but no one did. Or at least, not until they'd already reached the line of policemen.

"I am here for the Lords Conclave," Hetta told the stern-faced man in her best impression of her father's chilly command. He frowned, but she dropped the illusions and moved past him as if there were not the least possibility of him obstructing her. To her surprise, it worked.

Hetta had never been inside the Dome before. The building was split across two floors, and a smattering of clerks in smart business suits carried papers in an official way, ignoring Hetta and Wyn entirely. Beneath the grand staircase were a set of double doors that stood ajar.

The doorman eyed them both. "Only the lords are allowed entry to the Dome during the Conclave," he warned Wyn and Gwendelfear. "You may wait in the antechamber, if you wish, Your Highness, miss."

"I will wait at the entrance to this place," Gwendelfear murmured, taking up position near the door. Her lips curved. "I will warn you if your sister appears, Oathbreaker, but don't expect me to challenge her."

Wyn's tension increased, but he nodded. The doorman frowned at Gwendelfear but let them into the antechamber.

The antechamber wasn't empty; Angus Penharrow straightened at their entrance.

He had seen the newspapers, that much was clear. Hetta lifted her chin as he traced her shape with his eyes, as if it might've altered in the short time since they'd spoken.

"How is Penharrow?" Hetta asked. Although that might not be the most politic of subjects, it was a much better one than her now-public pregnancy.

Angus grimaced. "The repair of the roof's going to take some time. I've had workmen swarming over it the last three days, with no end in sight."

An awkward silence fell. Hetta could hear the low murmur of voices in the main chamber.

"Is everyone else here?"

"Not quite. Lord Arran hasn't arrived yet." Angus hesitated, then asked in a rush, "Is it true?" He had the grace to look embarrassed about it, at least.

Hetta gave him a flat look but didn't pretend not to understand. "I don't see that it's any of your business, either way."

Angus took her lack of denial for the confession it was. His expression hardened as he turned to Wyn.

"Is this your people's notion of honour, then, or did I miss the wedding?"

Wyn's voice was cold as Starwater in February. "You tried to disinherit the Valstars to further your own ambition. Do not take the moral high ground with me, Angus Penharrow."

Hetta was suddenly tired. "Honestly, Angus, what did I just say about it being none of your business? And you know very well that the queen is planning to announce our engagement at the Meridon Ball this Saturday because I told you so myself." She hoped.

"I'm glad to hear it." Angus still had his gaze locked on Wyn's, putting Hetta strongly in mind of two strange dogs circling each other.

Hetta huffed. "No, you're not, and you're doing a terrible job of pretending. Are you going to vote against my membership now?"

Angus rocked back, a crease forming between his brows. "Do you truly think I'm so petty, Hetta?"

"I hope not. *Are* you?"

He sighed. "No. Your membership on the Conclave should never have been in question; this doesn't change my position on that." His lips quirked in a half-smile. "Besides, if we start excluding people on the basis of what the papers say, where will we stop?" He held out a hand. "Shall we go in?"

Hetta didn't need to look at Wyn to know he'd tensed. It wasn't Penharrow—or mostly not Penharrow. What if Aroset struck during the Conclave? Hetta had pointed out that it didn't change the plan at all and might actually make it easier for her to lay hands on Aroset, since she wouldn't be as wary of Hetta without Wyn by her side. "You'll just have to meet us back at the estate if you miss the translocation," she'd told him firmly.

Still, she couldn't help the shiver that went down her spine when Wyn nodded and stepped away.

"Good luck," he said softly. His expression was fierce. "The Conclave would be fools not to accept you."

THE NORTHERN LORDS CONCLAVE

NGUS'S MANNER CHANGED as they walked into the Dome, folding away all his complicated feelings with a skill that was nearly fae. He made a point of introducing her to the other lords she hadn't yet met with a broad smile.

"Thank you," she said in an undertone as he showed her to her seat at the large oval table in the centre of the room. His lips tightened, but he nodded.

She couldn't help but be grateful for Angus's obvious show of support as the lords examined her critically. She wasn't sure if it was her femaleness or her now-publicly-known pregnancy. If she had to choose one thing she disliked most about her current state—well, aside from the unpredictable nausea—it was the way it made some people look at her as if impending motherhood had become her only relevant personality trait.

She was seated beside the Duke of Callasham—Lord Greymark here. She'd met the duke several times in Meridon, though she wasn't sure he remembered at least one of those occasions, since he'd been rolling drunk. *I certainly hope he doesn't remember Rakken seducing his wife, at least.* He poured her a glass of water from one of the carafes set out on the table, which she thanked him for.

"Blasted traffic's a nuisance, isn't it?" he said, making an attempt to break the ice in the room. "It's held Arran up as well."

"Forgive me, but is it appropriate for Lord Valstar to take her seat among us now? Her membership has not yet been officially ratified by the Conclave." It was Lord Drummond, a thin older man who Wyn had mentioned brandishing a knife at him back at Penharrow.

"Lord Arran is not here; we are not yet in session," Angus said coolly. "And Lord Valstar is a Northern lord. Ratifying her membership on the Conclave should be a mere formality."

Lord Arran strode into the room, barely leaning on his walking stick. Despite his grouchy expression, he seemed no worse for having nearly bled to death less than a week ago.

Lord Drummond shot Angus a smug look and repeated his complaint to Lord Arran.

"Drummond is correct," Arran said. "We have not yet voted on that question." His gaze rested on Hetta; she couldn't read his expression. "But the Conclave accepts petitioners. Lord Valstar, you have the floor. Then I would ask you to remove yourself while we vote on your membership."

Hetta's throat was dry, and she took a sip of water before she got to her feet, trying to look as dignified and lordly as she could. Was Aroset outside, even now, waiting for the Conclave to emerge? But she couldn't think of Aroset now, or of the High King, or even of the child growing within her. Stariel and its people were what mattered most in this moment. She had to try to persuade the lords to accept her, for their sake, even if that now seemed impossible. Sometimes one had to try even when the chances of success seemed so small as to be nil; to do otherwise would be to make the fear of failure into failure itself.

A petitioner, Lord Arran had called her. Is that what she ought to be, begging them to make her one of them? Should she try to soothe their fears that she'd upset their order, defend herself against the allegations she was sure they'd all heard? But the allegations were true, largely; she *was* going to marry a fae man, she *was* carrying his child, and she was planning to eventually upset their order as best she could dashed well manage.

She'd sworn oaths, when she'd been chosen lord; to strive for the good of Stariel and those who lived there. What did that mean, now, with a room full of hostile men focused on her?

She set her shoulders and met their gazes in turn. Her stomach churned, but her voice came out clear and composed, without the quiver she'd feared.

"I am Henrietta Valstar, Lord of Stariel. Lord Arran has called me a petitioner," she said slowly. "But I am not here today to beg permission to join your ranks. Stariel is the oldest estate in the North; the Valstar line predates the Conclave. It is my right to be here. Since when does the Conclave pick and choose its members? Our strength lies in our unity; if we lose it, we will become like the Southern nobles, each separately vying for recognition in the Southern court. Is that what you want?" Queen Matilda wouldn't thank her for invoking Northern parochialism, but Hetta would use whatever she could to make her point.

Including frankness. "This is a time of change," she said. "You'll all have heard now that the fae are coming back to the Mortal Realm. What you may not know is that Stariel stands between the two worlds, Faerie and Mortal both. If you want a part of that united future, then you want me—and Stariel—working with you. If you don't, well, I wish you luck living in the past, but I certainly won't let it hold *me* back."

This provoked a general murmur of consternation. She gave a conciliatory smile. "But if we start regulating membership based on lords' behaviour, where will we stop?" She carefully didn't look at the lord whose notoriety for his very public extramarital affairs had only been recently eclipsed by her own scandal, but she didn't need to.

"You forget my great-grandfather, Lord Valstar—the Conclave has rejected members who weren't fit to rule before," Lord Featherstone interjected.

"Lord Stone-Mad wasn't called that for nothing," Hetta said flatly. "He was both insane and a murderer." In other circumstances, she might've avoided reminding him of his own ancestor's sins, but since he'd brought it up, she felt no such compunction. That had been eighty years ago! How dare he pull out that bit of Conclave history as if it were relevant to her now? She clasped her hands tightly in front of her so no one would see them trembling. "I am merely pregnant. And that is all I have to say on the subject." She sat down.

The intake of breath was audible, coming as it did from everyone in the room simultaneously. The silence went on and on, ringing in her ears, and Hetta thought of the glare of the stage lights at the theatre where she'd used to work. *How the world changes.*

And then sound came back to the world in a rush as the lords found their voices—and their outrage washed over her in a wave. She barely heard it. Her stomach didn't seem to be following her plan to be coolly unaffected; it writhed in a worrying way, and pinpricks of sweat broke out in the small of her back.

"Are you well, Lord Valstar?" the duke asked, leaning towards her.

Hetta swallowed and took another sip of water. "I'm fine," she lied. The world was going slightly fuzzy around the edges. *I am not going to faint*, she told herself firmly, carefully putting the glass down. It took more concentration than it should've.

"Order!" Lord Arran was barking. "Gentlemen! Lord Valstar, you may withdraw while we discuss your petition."

The duke leapt to his feet and offered her his arm. "Let me escort you out, Lord Valstar."

Hetta nearly rolled her eyes, but in truth she could probably use a steady arm. Her dizziness was only increasing, and she wobbled her way to her feet.

"Thank you," she began to say, but the duke was unexpectedly close. She started, clutching the back of her chair for balance. The duke's expression was strangely blank as he reached for her, and there was a sharp, painful tug at her neck.

Her thoughts moved sluggishly, and it took a few long seconds to process what was happening. The duke held her necklace in his hand, staring at the two spell-gems—Lamorkin's heartstone and the more recent one that held the translocation spell. He still had that unsettling expression, as if he were in a dream. *Compulsion! Danger!* She had to get the gems back, but her limbs moved as slowly as her thoughts.

Before she could act, the duke dropped the necklace and smashed his boot down on the gems. They made a crunching sound as they broke, and Hetta stared down at the glittering shards. No. No, they couldn't *both* be broken; that wasn't fair. Aroset would only care about the translocation one; why should the heartstone be caught in the crossfire?

Wyn. She needed Wyn, to warn him, but the air bloomed with storm-scent laced with metal and roses. The centre of the table burst into light as a portal slashed the air.

Aroset's silver-gold hair hung down her back in a long braid, and her wings sparkled like blood rubies as she flared them. The lords flung themselves backwards with shouts of alarm.

Aroset's eyes were the same guinea-gold as King Aeros's had been, glinting with malice, and they were the last thing Hetta saw before the world spun and everything went dark.

46

A MOST INCONVENIENT KIDNAPPING

HETTA WOKE WITH a throbbing head and rebellious stomach. *I haven't been this hungover in years; what in Prydein did I drink last night?* she thought before groggy memories caught up and slammed her awake all at once.

She went to sit up and found she couldn't; her arms and wrists were bound behind her. At least she was alive, but her plan lay in pieces on the floor of the Dome.

She lay on a bed facing towards a window. Neither the bed nor the view of the countryside gave any clues as to her location. The sky was dark with stormclouds, but it was still daylight. The sky above Greymark had been clear. How long had she been here and how far exactly had Aroset taken her?

A cold feeling clutched her chest as she remembered the shattered translocation spell. She was alive, and Wyn would come for her, and Aroset was presumably somewhere nearby, hoping for *exactly that.* Aroset was more powerful than Wyn, or had been, last time they met. And this time they had no backup to convince her to retreat.

Well, the first thing to do was to get out of these ridiculous bonds.

"You're awake."

Hetta twisted awkwardly towards the voice. It came from a woman seated on a stool near the foot of the bed. Her expression had an unsettling spark of zealotry. *Compulsion.*

"I'm going to be sick," Hetta said, her voice dry and scratching. She tried to look as pathetic as possible, which wasn't difficult. "Can I have my hands free, and a bucket—unless you want to clean up a mess?"

The woman's expression lagged behind Hetta's words, shifting into a frown after a long pause. But she rose and drew a chamberpot across the floor and plonked it in front of Hetta.

"Don't think you can escape the Storm Queen," she warned.

Honestly, does Aroset think styling herself as such will magically make the Spires choose her? Though Irokoi had implied any of them might be chosen, if they were freed of compulsion, she doubted Rakken would help Aroset achieve that.

The woman leaned down to untie Hetta's hands and flinched as a spark of static crackled at her touch. After a beat, the woman resumed untying her hands, and Hetta lay still and tried not to think about what it meant that she didn't have the heartstone draining the babe's excess charge away anymore.

The request had been a ploy to get her hands free, but her stomach gave a horrible twist when she sat upright, and she was quite glad of the chamberpot's proximity. The woman watched impassively but did offer her a mug of water when she was done. Hetta stared at the mug suspiciously, fairly certain the duke had put something in her drink at the Conclave. Just how long had Aroset been compelling him? Jack had said he'd turned up at Stariel asking after her too; could it have been that far back?

Her throat ached, and she rinsed out her mouth but didn't swallow any. The woman made as if to re-tie her hands, and Hetta spread her palms and summoned fire.

"I don't want to hurt you," she said, because it wasn't the woman's fault she'd been compelled by Aroset. "But I will if you try to stop me leaving. Go away."

The woman's eyes flashed, but she backed away as Hetta poured more magic into her left hand, increasing the size of the flame there and bending to undo the knot at her ankles with the other.

"You've polluted the sacred bloodline!" she screeched, voice twisting with hatred.

Well, that told Hetta what Aroset thought of her pregnancy. The knots of her ankles took an age to undo, and her fingers were slippery with sweat by the time they came free. So long as the fire sat in her palm, it was under her control and wouldn't burn her, but it still put out a great deal of heat. She eyed the woman warily as she crossed the room and put her hand on the doorknob, but she didn't move, so Hetta let herself out and into the hallway.

"Hallowyn Tempestren," she whispered. Possibly a more self-sacrificing person would avoid summoning her lover, but two of them against Aroset seemed much better than Hetta alone. Her hand slid to her abdomen. Especially because it wasn't only the two of them. She repeated the name as she crept through the house. Its appearance confirmed her first impressions; this was someone's manor house, though it was awfully quiet, absent the sounds and sights of people she was used to in her own.

She was halfway along a hallway when metal and storms washed over her.

"Henrietta Isadore Valstar," Aroset purred from the far end of the hallway. "You are outside your faeland."

"Princess Aroset Tempestren," Hetta said, not sure if saying her name aloud would help Wyn find her or not. It couldn't hurt. She took a slow step backwards towards the door, as if Aroset were a feral dog she was trying not to antagonise. All the fae royalty Hetta had met had that sense of suppressed power about them, that hint of wildness, but in Aroset it held a more vicious edge.

"Queen," the fae woman corrected, her wings arched up in what Hetta now knew was a very stormdancer pose, meant to intimidate. In fairness, it *was* intimidating. Threads of gold glittered in feathers brilliant as crushed rubies.

Aroset appeared to be enjoying the effect. She bared white teeth in an extremely alarming smile. The expression was made more unsettling by the familiarity of her features, the same cut-glass cheekbones as Wyn, the same brown skin and startlingly silver hair. But Wyn had never smiled like that.

"Your new wings are, er, very nice," Hetta mumbled, taking another step backwards. Aroset's smile widened.

"Yes," she agreed, fanning her primaries. "It is the Maelstrom's gift to its future ruler."

"Very nice," Hetta repeated in the hope it would stall Aroset a little longer, repressing a hysterical laugh. She took another step back.

But apparently Aroset's taste for admiration had limits, for she snapped her wings shut and shook her head, chiding. "Now, now, mortal lordling. You're trying to escape from me. Aren't you pleased to see me, a member of your intended *family*?" She bit out the last word with disgust. "How many screams do you think it will take before he comes for you? It is a pity you have no wings to break, but fingerbones are nearly as satisfying."

Oh, to the hells with it. Hetta poured magic into great spouts of flame from her hands, half real and half illusion, down the full length of the hallway.

Aroset snapped out the real flames in a heartbeat, the scent of roses and iron heavy in the air. Fire wasn't an effective magic against someone who could pull the oxygen away from it in an instant. But the illusory flames confused her for long enough that Hetta had time to whirl about and sprint down the length of the corridor.

A whip of air caught her ankle as she fled and she tripped, catching herself on the wall before she fell. Panic scattered her thoughts, so she summoned the simplest illusion she knew: fog. The hallway behind her filled with dense grey mist, and she heard Aroset's frustrated snarl, followed by a gale-force blast of wind. The corridor shook with the air currents, picture frames knocking against the walls, but the fog wasn't real and wouldn't blow away.

"You cannot run forever, little lordling," Aroset taunted, as Hetta fumbled along the wall for balance against the rush of wind, trying not to breathe too loudly, making the illusory fog even thicker. Hetta could see through her own illusions, of course, and she risked a quick glance backwards. Aroset stood tall and narrow-eyed just outside the bedchamber door through the haze of magic, her lips curled back from her perfect white teeth. Her gaze locked onto Hetta's and Hetta jerked away, scrambling faster. Aroset couldn't possibly have seen her through the fog, but Aroset's widening smile had been the opposite of reassuring.

Hetta fumbled for the nearest doorknob and lurched through into a drawing room. Just where *was* she, and, more importantly, how did she get out?

She filled the drawing room with fog for good measure and scrambled across it, escaping through the door opposite and emerging onto a landing. Stairs! Her gaze fixed on the entryway below, and she hurried along the landing and down the staircase, summoning as much fog as she could.

She'd forgotten something essential: Aroset could fly. Suddenly the fae woman was in front of her, folding her wings behind her as she landed.

"Lordling," she crooned. Her golden eyes were bright with pleasure, the kind of look a cat gets when it knows a mouse is already caught. *She's playing with me.* Aroset canted her head to the side, the gesture eerily similar to Wyn's. "I do not think you need to be undamaged."

She moved so fast that Hetta had no time to react before cold and then pain lanced across her arm. She stared down at the spreading wetness in confusion. Aroset hadn't touched her. Had she? But the next strike came while she was watching the fae woman, an icy line just above the curve of her breasts. Air. Aroset was making blades out of air! How was that fair?

Without thinking about whether it was a good idea or not, she launched herself at Aroset in a fiery ball of magical flames. She latched grimly onto the fae woman's arm and poured fire out through her palms. It had to have hurt, but Aroset only laughed, and it was then that Hetta realised that whatever had caused the changes in Aroset's wings and increased her power mightn't have left her entirely sane. Oh dear.

The wind blades picked up speed, the next slash on her abdomen. Hetta gasped, releasing Aroset, her hands going to cover herself protectively.

That was when the lightning struck, cracking open the roof like an eggshell. Hetta covered her eyes, ears ringing with the crack of it.

Aroset spread her wings and looked up. A maniacal grin split her face.

"Ah, Hallowyn. Well met."

Wyn hovered in the space that recently had been occupied by roof. Above, stormclouds churned in angry purple. Thunder rumbled.

Charge poured off his wings, and his eyes burned a flickering blue-silver, not the merest hint of russet visible. He held a sword like he knew how to use it, and Hetta's thoughts snagged on the question of where in Prydein had he gotten a sword from? It looked suspiciously like one of the treasured relics from the walls of the Dome.

Hetta scrambled away from Aroset, partly because being further away seemed like an excellent idea and partly because hailstones the size of fists were smashing into the tiles through the newly formed hole in the roof.

The hailstones, most unfortunately, didn't hit Aroset. She had some kind of thickened air shield, creating a halo of frozen shards around her as the hail shattered on impact.

Aroset smiled mockingly up at Wyn and spread her wings. "Would you like me to kill you or your mortal first?"

Wyn met Hetta's eyes, and there wasn't any hint of mortal butler in them.

"Run," he said. It wasn't Aroset he was asking her to run from.

And then he released the storm.

47

THE MAELSTROM'S GIFT

AROSET COCKED HER head, eyes gleaming the same guinea gold as King Aeros's. Despite the roof, Wyn read only triumph in her expression; she didn't doubt her victory. And why would she? She was older, more skilled in battle, she had beaten him once before, and she stood between him and Hetta now. And Hetta was bleeding.

Aroset took in his proximity, calculating angles. He knew she would try to strike at Hetta first, if she could. A bit of space folded around her hand, and she was abruptly holding a spear. She hefted it thoughtfully.

Wyn had never truly embraced his nature, never let the magic spool out as it willed. He'd always kept a tight leash on his power, but such caution would only hamper him now. He couldn't defeat Aroset by playing mortal.

I am a stormdancer. Hail and wind hammered at him, and he let their songs resonate over his feathers, relishing each wingbeat. *I am a stormdancer, and this is my birthright.*

I am not sorry for the child. And I am not sorry they will be fae. The thought hummed to the rhythm of the storm, glorious and bitter all at once, and he welcomed it, welcomed the knowledge of who and what he was.

"Run," he told Hetta.

The Maelstrom gave gifts to those who survived its grasp. To Rakken had gone compulsion strong enough to hold vast crowds in thrall. To Aroset, the ability to open portals even into Deeper Faerie.

And to Wyn, the Maelstrom had given the storm.

It shook its way out of his soul, white and burning. Lightning struck a javelin into the earth, centred on Aroset.

The world froze, his sister's eyes going wide and startled before it slammed into her. He'd wondered how deep his own power went, if he set it free. Now he stripped it from its fetters, and it was glorious. He let the lightning bear him downwards, embracing the pain and ecstasy of it, and landed with a thump in the smoking crater in the floor.

Charge crawled in white-hot snakes over Aroset's crumpled form, flocking to Wyn's feet like puppies when he touched the ground. He looked down at his sister, lightning writhing through his veins. It would've killed Aroset if she hadn't been a stormdancer, hadn't had significant natural immunity to charge. As it was, only the smallest rise and fall of her chest showed she still lived.

The hail softened into snowflakes, drifting down around them in a chill hush while his thoughts ran cold and crystalline. Aroset had hurt a lot of people, from the bank manager injured in a lug-imp attack she'd orchestrated to the wing worshippers she'd compelled. She'd blinded Irokoi. She'd nearly strangled Marius and pushed his telepathy in unnatural directions. She'd kidnapped Hetta—*twice.*

If they woke ThousandSpire from its curse, it might still choose Aroset as its queen. Oh, Irokoi had been blithely confident they could avoid her stepping foot there, but the risk remained. Aroset was most like their father, after all, and his cruelty hadn't stopped ThousandSpire bonding with him. Faelands weren't concerned with morality.

And if she isn't chosen, it won't stop her from wreaking havoc. She'd already shown herself willing to target those Wyn loved in order to get to him.

She would target the child, his and Hetta's. His grip tightened on the sword, burning white-hot and unforgiving. Blood and magic dripped from his fingers as the wound healed and re-opened with every heartbeat, as the power coursing through him came into contact with the hot iron.

He could end this, now. It would be easy. He'd already killed his own father, hadn't he, already made the terrible calculation once before? And Aroset was as monstrous as King Aeros.

He waited for Hetta to call out as he stared down at his sister's still form, to stop him, to remind him that they might need Aroset alive to undo ThousandSpire's curse, but she said nothing. He heard her footsteps softly approaching the crater, but he didn't turn. Instead, he pulled in the storm's influence, so it reached no further than the circle of his feet, and for the first time it obeyed without question.

Blood pooled beneath his frozen fingers, the same colour as Aroset's wings.

He brought the sword down. It lacked the razor edge of Catsmere's when she'd shorn Rakken, and Wyn was forced to saw at Aroset's feathers, separating primaries from wingbone in rough, ugly motions. Aroset didn't stir, not even when he leaned down and forced open the wing she lay upon in order to reach her feathers.

He met Hetta's eyes. '*I love you*,' hovered on his lips, fighting for primacy with '*I'm sorry*'. Except how could 'sorry' begin to encompass the scope of things? And he wasn't sorry, exactly, or at least not sure what he was sorry for. Sorry for not killing Aroset? Sorry for the way the Conclave had treated Hetta? Sorry for all the various complications he brought with him?

"Where are we?" she asked.

He blew out a breath, the sheer mundanity of the question

pulling him back from the edge. "The Duke of Callasham's estate, near Greymark. Aroset had caught him in her net; the compulsion was apparent even to me when I examined him."

Hetta harrumphed.

"What have you done to your hand?!" She stepped closer as if to take the sword from him, but he flung it across the room before she could. It clattered against the banisters.

"It's hot," he explained. There were lines of red seeping through her blouse on her arms and stomach. "You're bleeding."

She grimaced down at the wounds. "Yes, I know, but they're not deep, and they mostly seem to have stopped bleeding." Her grey eyes were serious, and she put a palm to his chest. "I'm fine."

He wanted to say something, a thousand somethings, but they were all caught in his throat. The cold rage still clawed at him, and he could not remember how to thaw. How to articulate the riot of emotions that had driven him here?

She winced at his blistered palm. "We should put ice on that." She considered the hole in the roof, where hail had been replaced with swirling snowflakes. "Fortunately, we seem to have a lot of ice. In late May." Her lips curved. "Did you steal a relic from the Conclave?"

"Ah. Yes." He shook his head to clear it. "I need to find the nearest resonance point and build a portal. We need to get Aroset back to Stariel before she wakes up."

Hetta ignored him, bending to scoop up a handful of clean hail and offering it to him. He took it without thinking, preoccupied by the leylines curving around her, and the cold burn of it surprised a hiss of displeasure from him.

Living things always cast a shadow on the fabric of magic, and without Lamorkin's heartstone draining the excess charge, he could see the charge building in the centre of her more clearly than before. Carefully, he reached out with his good hand and stroked some of the excess away, letting it disperse harmlessly into the air. It began to build again as soon as he stopped.

She grimaced as she felt what he was doing. "How long do you think we have?"

He didn't know, and he didn't like the answers his mental calculations suggested. "I think…we should find the High King sooner rather than later."

She exhaled a long, slow breath and put a hand against his chest. "Go and find your resonance point. I'll watch Aroset." Snowflakes caught on Aroset's feathers, melting softly as soon as they touched her. "Also, there's a woman upstairs who Aroset compelled."

He nodded. "I will see what can be done."

He found the woman rocking back and forth in a room above. She started at the sight of him and bowed low.

"Mighty stormdancer! I am blessed!"

Aroset wouldn't comprehend the wrong she'd done here, but Wyn felt guilty by association.

"I am sorry," he told the woman, unplucking the strands of compulsion as deftly as he could and wishing Rakken were with him. Though would Rakken think it worth expending energy on an ordinary mortal where there was no political advantage to him doing so? Wyn would like to believe Rakken's finely tuned sense of debts and obligations might win out, if nothing else, but he'd rather not test it. *Perhaps I am being too harsh on him; perhaps he would have compassion.* But that might actually be worse, because Rakken's compassion had to date extended only to creatures he saw as lesser, such as the lowfae.

And this woman wasn't a lesser creature. He found her name among the tangle.

"Bonnie McSymon," he said, pulling the strands away and giving his voice the same bit of snap he'd occasionally used on more junior members of staff with a tendency to daydream. It was a tone that said, with a slight curl of sternness, *you're not being told off—yet—but do pay attention, will you?* It worked; the woman jerked free of the compulsion all at once. The unsettling worship in her eyes crashed into confusion.

"I am sorry for what was done to you. You are not crazy," he told her, as she began to shake. "And I'm sorry I don't have time to help you as I ought." He pulled coins from his pouch and placed them in her unresisting hand. "I am Hallowyn Tempestren; seek me at Stariel Estate if you wish, later, and I will try to set to rights what I can. I am taking the person who did this to you away with me."

She scrambled away from him, a strangled scream starting in her throat, and, hating himself a little, he sent her to sleep. It was much, much too easy. Any natural resistance she'd had to compulsion—and most people had at least a little—had been stripped away by Aroset.

He left the woman on one of the beds, hoping the sleep might do her good. He hoped also that she came from somewhere nearby, that there were others she could turn to for support. Aroset wouldn't have bothered to transport a mortal great distances, would she? It seemed as if she'd simply taken over this place, servants and all, as he met other servants as he stalked the halls, each of them equally enthralled by the sight of him.

Undoing the compulsions took time, as did searching the house for some point of resonance to work with that would get them at least *slightly* in the vicinity of Stariel, and impatience itched at him. What if Aroset woke sooner than he'd estimated? How quickly would the charge around Hetta build, without the heartstone to drain it? What if he missed a compelled servant somewhere in the house?

I will return here and check them all thoroughly, after this is done, he vowed. Perhaps he could think of some leverage to convince Rakken to help him with it. The vow didn't dent the despair winding its way through his blood. *How can the mortals possibly accept the greater fae when we can do such things to them?* He curled his hands into fists. If the High King wouldn't act, Wyn would. There were substances—like vervain—that increased resistance to compulsion, and others—like yarrow—that clouded the ability of fae to see magic. He'd plant them in every garden in Prydein if he had to and throw himself into helping Marius with his experimental devices.

Would I make the world hate my child, though? The question lurked, unsettling, in the back of his mind as he pushed open the door to a broom closet, hoping its similarity to one at Stariel might help him. A broom clattered to the floor, the sound unnaturally loud in the eerily still house now that the servants slept. Wyn replaced it carefully and shut the door. No resonance. But then, it was wildly optimistic to expect a resonance point between this house and Stariel House to neatly fall into his lap just because he wished it. Not only did two places need to share sufficient characteristics with each other in order to resonate, but the portal-maker needed to be familiar with both of them as well. And this house largely did not resonate with the North; it had a very Southern feeling to it, despite its location.

He went back to Hetta, time ticking at him. Her face fell at his expression. Had the charge around Hetta increased? And how much would it increase again before they returned to the estate?

"Nothing?"

"No." If only he were more familiar with the area around Stariel. Perhaps some place outside but near the estate would resonate, if only he knew it better, but he'd only been able to leave the estate recently. Before that, he hadn't wanted to risk flouting the High King's Iron Law by entering the Mortal Realm; he'd been prepared to argue that technically Stariel Estate counted as part of Faerie. *I hope I get the chance to argue that technicality.* The High King still seemed as distant as a star.

Wyn unhappily considered their options; the problem, of course, was Aroset. *Not that her being a problem is exactly new.* But this one was logistical; he couldn't carry both Hetta and Aroset. Air currents stirred tatters of crimson feathers across the floor as he weighed their options, disliking all of them.

"How long do you think until she wakes up?" Hetta asked, clearly following similar lines of thought to him.

As if in answer, Aroset began to wake.

To his astonishment, it wasn't fear that sliced through him first, swift and breath-stealing, but relief. He hadn't killed his sister. *Aroset is right; I am sentimental.* Somehow, he didn't think this would appease her when she woke, de-feathered and defeated.

"Get back," he said, but Hetta had already done so.

Would Aroset survive another lightning strike like the first? Should he and Hetta run and return with Rakken and Irokoi in tow? Aroset would be easier to deal with now, grounded, but what if they couldn't find her again? How much time did Hetta have?

But before he could make up his mind what to do, the heavy scent of cherry and beeswax spiralled out, mixing with the storm. With a slight *pop*, Princess Sunnika appeared. Beside her was Gwendelfear.

48

FAERIE PRINCESSES

ETTA HAD NEVER been happier to see Princess Sunnika. The princess's eyes widened as she took in the scene, but before she could say anything, Aroset woke.

Hetta sort of knew how fast fae could move if they wanted to, but it was still disorienting to see it in combined action. As if there had been some pre-arranged synchronisation, Wyn flared out his wings and grabbed for one of Aroset's tattered wings, Gwendelfear snatched up Hetta's hand, and Princess Sunnika took hold of Wyn's outstretched primaries.

Princess Sunnika's eyes bored into hers fiercely. "Let me through the wards."

The translocation stretched longer than ever before, darkness and a dizzy, disorienting sensation so sickening that Hetta was momentarily glad not to have a physical form. *Home*, Hetta thought, as tightly as she could.

And then the world snapped back into place again, and she knew exactly where she was: the rose garden at Stariel, next to the dormant Gate to DuskRose.

Aroset snarled, and storm magic blasted outwards as air, knocking Hetta off her feet. Charge began to gather, but Stariel swallowed it. The land rose behind her eyes, a hammer about to fall. They could stop this little fae who'd been so warped out of her proper shape, as they'd stopped the leviathans. They would protect their land and their family.

The faeland paused. But their consort would mourn her, because she was family.

Hetta dug her fingernails into her palms, that thought shocking her into her own skin. Stariel considered Aroset family? Hetta wrestled with her own fear and desire for vengeance. <What are you suggesting?>

She was swept back up in the faeland, and they piled layer after layer of magical force upon Aroset. More magic than she'd ever pulled from the land before. Pine forest and new grass and chilli-pricked coffee inexorably overrode iron and rain-drenched roses until there was nothing left of Aroset's magic.

Stariel subsided with grim satisfaction and Hetta collapsed. Strong arms caught her before she hit the ground, and she knew it was Wyn through Stariel rather than her own senses. She was too tired to look up, but she burrowed herself into his chest.

"Hetta, Hetta." He was saying her name over and over, voice hoarse with anxiety.

"Mmmmmf," she managed. Stariel buzzed along her tired nerves, slowly rejuvenating her, but whatever she'd done had impacted the land as well, as if it had been winded and was having to recover its breath.

"Well, that's certainly an interesting solution." Cat's voice. How long had she been here? "Is she alive?"

Hetta reached for Stariel and found something so strange that despite her fatigue she opened her eyes and lifted her head, needing to see it with mundane senses rather than magic.

Aroset was still in the rose garden, but she was frozen, encased completely in blue crystalline. The rock was semi-translucent, so that Aroset's form made a dark, disturbing shadow deep in the stone.

"Yes," Hetta said. "She's still alive." What had she done?

"She's in stasis," Wyn said. "I didn't know it was possible to do that to a person rather than a location. Can she break out of it?"

"Not while she's on Stariel lands, she can't. I'd have to undo it." Hetta was relying on Stariel for the knowledge, but the land felt confident on this point. "I think it may have gotten the idea from ThousandSpire." They both looked at Cat.

Cat extended a tentative hand towards the crystal, her movements stiff but graceful, like an old housecat. Was she thinking of her own time in such a state?

Princess Sunnika got slowly to her feet from where she'd collapsed, aided by Gwendelfear. There were deep circles beneath her eyes, and an air of exhaustion clung to her. It had cost her, translocating their little party across the country and through Stariel's wards, even with Hetta's help. Why had she done it?

Cat went utterly still, and the air between her and Princess Sunnika crackled with an antagonism that owed nothing to magic. Cat snapped her wings tight against her spine.

"Princess Sunnika. So we meet at last." Princess Sunnika's chin tilted. It struck Hetta that this was probably the first time Princess Sunnika had come face-to-face with one of her cousin's killers. Killer. The word unsettled her. It was too easy to forget what Rakken and Cat were, underneath.

"Princess Catsmere Tempestren." Sunnika's tone, in contrast, held enough spikes to puncture kineticar tyres. "Murderer."

Hetta knew enough of fae culture by now to know that the use of Cat's full name meant something. Exactly what, she wasn't sure, but the tension between the two definitely increased.

Cat appeared to be weighing a response, and Hetta tensed,

wondering if she'd need to intervene, wondering if she *should* intervene. Her sympathies lay with Princess Sunnika on this, since even faced with a bristling princess, there was no apology in Cat, no hint of remorse. *At least here I can bury them both to the knees if need be.*

Cat's gaze went from Princess Sunnika to Wyn and back, narrowing. "Thank you for retrieving my siblings." Her lips curved. "And also Lord Valstar."

"I did not do it for your benefit, murderer."

"Well, whoever's benefit you did it for, I am thankful for it," Hetta intervened. She was surprised Cat had offered even that much, though acknowledging obligations was also a very fae thing to do. Hetta was pretty sure they had Gwendelfear to thank for Princess Sunnika's intervention, and that only because Wyn had accidentally sped her recovery by sharing his power with her. Gwendelfear hated being indebted to people, which did make Hetta wonder if Gwendelfear now owed Princess Sunnika a favour, or if there was something else between the two. Her head pounded. Following fae logic through things was exhausting.

"My thanks were sincere. I will take the debt from the lesser fae, assuming it was she who bargained for my brother's rescue just now," Cat said.

That made the hair on Hetta's neck stand on end. What was Catsmere up to?

"Cat—"

Cat shot Wyn a firm look. "This isn't your business, Hallowyn."

Princess Sunnika's eyes narrowed. "Are you attempting to pay the weregild for your crime? It's insulting to compare the debt owed for this"—she waved around at the assembled group—"to the value of a life."

Cat didn't look away, and she spoke with a clipped tightness. "I do not offer weregild for your cousin, Princess; our courts were at war. I am sorry if his death pains you, but I won't apologise for killing him, and I'm not sorry he's dead. Are you, truly, who must've known what he was?"

Gwendelfear hissed and took a step forward, but Princess Sunnika stayed her with an outflung hand. Hetta couldn't tell what she was thinking.

"Do not expect me to come to your aid again, Hallowyn," Princess Sunnika said, without taking her eyes off Cat. "Not even for my former handmaiden."

"I'm not planning to require any further rescuing," Wyn promised. He too was frowning at Cat.

Princess Sunnika didn't answer, disappearing with a pop.

"Thank you, Gwendelfear," Wyn murmured.

"I didn't do it for your thanks." Gwendelfear stalked away on the echo of Princess Sunnika's words.

Wyn whirled on his sister. "What are you playing at, Cat?"

She smiled. "You know, I don't actually have to tell you, little brother."

"And Rake?"

Hetta didn't have to wonder what Rakken would think of this for long, because he crashed down inelegantly moments later in a storm of still-damaged wings and air magic. He had his knives out, but the sight of Aroset frozen into a blue-set statue made him pause.

"The DuskRose princess is gone," Cat told him. She put a hand against the stone. "And Lord Valstar has dealt with Aroset."

Rakken frowned at his twin, and a silent argument passed between them. Hetta could read it as if it were spoken:

What did you do, Cat? You've done something, I can tell from the way Hallowyn is looking at you.

Later.

Rakken didn't like having to wait for an answer, but he grudgingly accepted that. They really did try to keep their unified image intact in company, didn't they?

Rakken clicked a fingernail against Aroset's crystal. "Perhaps a long sleep will improve her," he reflected.

"Well, it could hardly make her worse," said Hetta.

Rakken didn't appear to hear her, studying the crystal. "It would be helpful if you could move her to the Stones. I've begun laying the spell's foundations there in Koi's absence; it is a complicated working."

She still felt like a wrung-out rag, but she closed her eyes and tiredly gathered up enough energy to explain to Stariel what she needed.

Of course, she hadn't banked on fatigue making her so clumsy that she translocated not only Aroset but their entire party to the Stones. Wyn, Cat, and Rakken froze with surprise.

"Sorry," she mumbled, leaning against a Stone for support.

Now that the adrenalin was fading, Stariel was the only thing keeping her upright. She drew on the land to steady herself and then hastily snapped the connection shut when she felt her senses start to spin.

The land pawed at her curiously, wanting to know why she'd stopped.

<I know you're trying to help,> Hetta told it. <But I'm too tired to keep myself from drowning.>

Puzzlement—it didn't understand her fear—but the land subsided anyway. Still, even that brief burst of energy had helped, though she had a feeling she might pay for it later, the way one did after overconsuming coffee.

Wyn looked down at her with concern, then back up at Rakken. "Did Koi give any indication of when he'd return?"

Rakken was still staring at the crystalline stone of Aroset's prison, but he shook his head. "But he knows there isn't much time."

"ThousandSpire hungers," Cat added. Her focus had turned inwards.

Hetta shivered.

"But the spell is nearly ready, if our errant older brother will only fulfil his promises." Rakken glanced at the sky, and Hetta couldn't help following suit even though she knew there was no one there.

They left the twins to it. Hetta briefly considered translocation, but she knew how much Wyn disliked it, and the Stones weren't so far from the house. And, she privately admitted, she was worried about getting lost in Stariel in this state.

"I don't suppose you'd let me carry you?" Wyn said, though his tone was rhetorical.

She shook her head. "I can walk. I'm just tired." The cuts she'd received from Aroset stung, and her wrists ached where they'd been tied, but everything seemed to be working as it should be. She touched her throat and then remembered the heartstone was gone.

When had everything spun out of control so badly? Her plan to get Aroset had worked—more or less—but she hadn't been prepared for the cost.

Wyn reached for her hand, squeezed. They both winced at the spark of static.

"How long do you think we have?" she asked softly. "Without the stone?"

"It will have to be long enough."

Hetta had planned to sneak back into the house when they arrived. Of course she'd have to tell her family about the Conclave, but she didn't see why it had to be right this minute, with her failure as a lord so fresh in her mind. She could still hear the sound of the heartstone crunching into pieces under Aroset's boot.

However, she hadn't counted on the Valstars feeling Stariel's angry response to Aroset's magic and swarming into an anxious mob in Carnelion Hall as a result. The doors were open, and Hetta could hear them all busily discussing what it meant, raised voices echoing.

"Are you sure you felt something, dear?" Caro's mother was

saying. Valstars-by-marriage had some connection to the estate, but it wasn't the same as those who'd been born here.

"What if it means something's happened to Hetta?" Alexandra's voice, high and worried.

"I'm sure there's a perfectly rational explanation." That was Uncle Percival.

"Jack, where are you going?"

An annoyed grunt, the response too low to hear.

She and Wyn exchanged glances.

"I can—" But his offer to deal with the commotion came too late.

Jack froze in the doorway to the entrance hall, his mouth going slack at the sight of her. So much for hiding.

"Hetta." His brows drew together. "How did you get here? Aren't you supposed to be at the Conclave?"

Relatives began to crowd behind him. "What's going on?"

Alexandra's wide eyes, peering over Jack's shoulder. "Hetta's back!"

"How can she be back? She's in Greymark!"

Hetta blew out a long breath. "It's a bit of a story."

By this point, Jack had taken in the full extent of her appearance. Concern sparked in his expression. "Are you well?" Then he blushed, as if just remembering her condition. "Er, I mean…"

Lifting her chin, she gestured for him to move and pushed past him into the hall. Wyn followed her like a sheepdog, as if he would shield her from questions by sheer physical presence. It sort of worked; his wings forced everyone to move and also caused a measure of attention to shift from Hetta to him.

"Yes, yes, as you can see, I'm back." She made her way to the hearth, clasping her hands together. Her throat stuck.

How many times had she stood here now, making one strange announcement or another to her family? The hall was the only room in Stariel House that could hold all her family at once when they were all home without a squash. Perhaps she should have a lectern and a seat from which she could still see everyone installed for next time. Then she thought of Queen Tayarenn's dais and horn-encrusted throne and her stomach twisted. No.

Her family had always treated her lordship with a certain amount of scepticism. All the grumbling about her various decisions from fae to finances she'd been able to bear with the knowledge that she stood by her decisions as being best for the estate. It wasn't as if most of them even really understood the realities of such matters. But the Conclave—they understood that. She didn't regret her actions, exactly, but it did feel like she'd failed them. It was a hard thing to have to confess.

Better to start with less fraught things. She began with the fact that Aroset should no longer be a problem, and how they'd been teleported here from Greymark.

"You ought to be taking better care of her, young man," Grandmamma interjected.

"Ah—I am trying, my lady."

"So the wedding will be soon, then?" Aunt Maude asked, rather pointedly. There was a general, if slightly embarrassed, rumble of agreement.

Hetta lifted a hand halfway to her throat before she remembered there was nothing there to grasp. How long would they have, without the heartstone? "Yes," she said firmly, because she refused to contemplate the alternative. "But in any case, the main point is that you should be safe to leave the estate now." She directed her words at Uncle Percival. Thank the gods Caro had persuaded him to remain while they'd been away. *At least I've managed to keep them safe so far.* It wasn't much comfort, not when they wouldn't have been in danger but for her.

Her uncle, for once in his life, seemed to be having trouble looking at her directly, a faint reddish tinge on his cheeks. Did her now-public condition offend his cerebral sensibilities? *Maybe that explains why Caro is an only child*, Hetta couldn't help thinking. Caro looked both relieved—it couldn't have been easy, persuading her stubborn father not to leave the estate—and alive with curiosity.

"This really isn't acceptable, Henrietta," Aunt Sybil began. "You cannot continue to keep putting off the wedding like this. What must the Conclave have thought—"

Hetta snapped.

"I don't care what's acceptable, or what the dashed Conclave thinks! They're not going to ratify my membership anyway! I care that if I can't find the High King in time, this baby will die! Now, forgive me, but you must excuse me." She didn't wait, striding out of the hall and leaving a susurration behind her.

She ran upstairs two at a time, feeling sick in a way that had nothing to do with her 'condition'. When she reached her bedroom, she slammed the door and immediately burst into tears.

Dash it! She hated being this weepy creature, and she wasn't sorry for snapping at her aunt. At least she hadn't broken down in front of her family; that would've been excruciating. Rubbing angrily at her eyes, she focused on practicalities: removing her slashed-up clothing, warming the pitcher of water set by her dresser so she could wash away the blood from the cuts. A deep, foggy tiredness descended on her.

When Wyn found her, she'd given up all notion of soldiering on and had curled up in bed with the curtains drawn, despite it only being mid-afternoon. He didn't say anything, just came and put his arms around her, stroking her hair.

WHEN SHE WOKE, IT was dusk and she was alone. She reached out and felt the spark of Wyn flare in response from the Stones. She didn't want to speak to any of her family. However, she couldn't keep hiding in her own house.

With reluctance, she dressed and emerged from her bedroom. She was halfway along the hallway to the library when she nearly ran straight into Marius coming the other way. He had a book in one hand and was trying to both read and walk at the same time.

"Hetta! What are you doing here?" He blinked at her, his spectacles slipping down his nose.

She almost laughed. Had Marius been buried in the library all afternoon, oblivious to the various goings-on? He hadn't been in Carnelion Hall earlier.

"Failing at everything," she told him bitterly. "And hiding from everyone."

He took one look at her and said, "The map room, then?"

For lack of a better idea, she let him pull her along the hallway, down the stairs, across the courtyard, and up into the map room in the Northern Tower, where he forced her down into a chair. Hetta watched with some bemusement as he rang the bell for a maid and proceeded to arrange for tea and biscuits to be sent up with uncharacteristic decisiveness. It was only after the maid had bobbed a curtsey and left that he faltered.

"You can still eat biscuits, can't you?"

Hetta just glared.

"Right. Sorry. And before you ask, no, that wasn't some magical telepathic response." He frowned. "I can't honestly tell half the time either way whether I'm, er, mind-reading or not unless I watch people's lips. But you're…quiet, compared to the rest of the family. And I'm not getting a headache, which I'm beginning to think is a side-effect."

It occurred to Hetta that Marius might've been absent from the earlier gathering in the hall for reasons other than being absorbed in a book. But at least the shielding she'd instructed Stariel on was working in some part.

"I'll see if Stariel can shield everyone else too," she promised.

"That's not going to help me outside the estate though, is it?" He sat down opposite her. "So, what happened?"

The map room was a cosy circular room, the bulk of it occupied by the large table in the centre, with low shelves lining the two walls without windows and maps affixed to every bit of otherwise clear space around them. It naturally tended towards clutter, and of late this had only increased, thanks to Alexandra's attempts to map waterways and Jack and Wyn's sketches of planting plans for various fields. Wyn was a surprisingly poor drawer and tended to leave the actual sketching to Jack, but Hetta recognised his handwriting in the calculations in the margins of the nearest bit of paper. Her gaze snagged on it. Notes about barley seemed both so completely irrelevant right now and so completely the reason why she loved the infuriating man.

"Hetta?"

Hetta told him. When she got to the part about Aroset, Marius swore softly, but she ignored him and continued. She was already tired of repeating the story.

"And so we've nearly got everything we need, assuming Irokoi can fetch Torquil as he promised. Assuming we can get to the High King in time." Her hand reached again for her non-existent necklace. "I don't suppose you've found anything more about him?"

Marius tracked the movement with a frown. "Er, actually I think I may have some light to shed on that." He held up the book he'd been carrying. It was a thin, battered volume, bound in pale blue leather. "This is a journal. A *fae* journal."

"*What*? How did it get into our library?"

"I have my suspicions, and they have feathers and one eye,"

Marius said drily. Hetta thought of the books Irokoi had brought with him from the High King's library. "Watch this." He held up the journal to face her. It was stamped with characters Hetta didn't recognise as Prydinian, but as she stared at it, the characters shimmered and changed until they read: *Nymwen.*

The name triggered a memory, and she frowned, trying to recall where she'd heard it before.

"The whole text translates itself into Prydinian, if you stare at it long enough, though it's a bit headache inducing." Marius rubbed absently at his temples.

Memory rolled back; Nymwen was the name Wyn had said the strange undersea lake whispered. A chill went through her, remembering the heavy sorrow of that place.

"Who is Nymwen?" she asked.

"The High King's daughter."

49

NYMWEN

WYN LEFT RAKKEN to his spellwork once he'd done all he could; or rather, once Rakken waved him off, declaring, "I've need for finesse rather than power now. Take yourself away, Hallowyn. Though if you happen to have a map of the leylines on hand, you may bring it to me."

I could do without being dismissed as a superfluous servant, he reflected. But even Rakken couldn't dampen his cautious optimism. He flexed his wings, feeling the stormcharge potential running through them, there but no longer overwhelming. It had been so long since he'd felt in control of *anything*. Perhaps he could take this one small thing as a good omen. For the first time since they'd begun this quest, fulfilling the High King's task seemed truly possible, imminent even.

Except Lamorkin's heartstone is broken. That wasn't a good omen at all. He shook his head and launched himself into the sky. Stariel Estate spread below him, the intense greens of spring growth mixed with the browns of freshly turned soil. Everything always seemed so much tidier from above, perspective and distance smoothing out rough edges.

He landed on his room's tiny balcony, already reaching out with his leysight to find Hetta. The spark of her blazed more brightly than usual, with a very non-Hetta edge to it that smelled of storms rather than the more usual chilli-pricked coffee he associated with her. His optimism fractured, replaced by the ominous tick of a clock. The charge was building so *fast*.

He found Marius and Hetta in the map room. An untouched tea tray sat on the map table, and there was something in their manner that set his instincts buzzing with alarm.

"I came to borrow one of Alexandra's maps. What has happened?" he asked, because something, clearly, had happened.

Marius handed him a book without comment, and Wyn dropped it. Both Marius and Hetta looked at him in surprise.

"It bit me. Magically," Wyn said sheepishly, for he wasn't generally in the habit of dropping things.

It lay accusingly on the floor, shimmering with magic. Hetta bent down to touch it before he could stop her and winced as a bit of static jumped from her to the book. She made a thoughtful noise and looked at her brother. "It doesn't hurt you to touch it?"

Marius picked up the book, tensing and then relaxing as nothing happened. "No."

"Maybe it doesn't like fae magic?" Hetta guessed, frowning at her fingertips.

"That would make sense from what Nymwen said. She wanted to be human."

Wyn frowned at the name rune on the book's cover. It was in stormtongue. "The name from the undersea. Who is Nymwen, and how in the high winds' eddies did you come by that?"

"The High King's daughter, apparently," Hetta said. "I didn't know the High King had children."

Marius's eyes widened. "He doesn't. Sorry." He rubbed at his temples. "You're projecting."

Wyn bolstered his mental walls, trying to rein in the shock roiling through him. He ran a hand through his hair between his horns. "That's…" He couldn't say impossible, since Marius clearly believed it to be true, but even so… "That sounds as believable as saying the Maelstrom itself has a daughter. What makes you think Nymwen is the High King's daughter?"

"Ewan Valstar," Hetta said.

Wyn thought of that dead-end on the Valstar family tree, the young man's life cut short, and of the old lord's grief-stricken words: *The cursed queen gave her word. It won't bring Ewan back, but mayhap it will keep the others safe for a time.* A terrible premonition filled him.

Marius continued leafing through the diary as if the world hadn't just upended. "Er, yes. Nymwen and Ewan were lovers. She wrote about him a lot." The tips of his ears went pink, and Wyn wondered exactly what Nymwen had written. "They met when the High King—well, the High Queen—came to Stariel to witness the signing of the treaty between the Crown and Stariel. The High King left, but Nymwen kept returning to the Mortal Realm to meet Ewan."

"The 'fairy girl' Ewan's mother wrote about in her journal," Hetta added.

"How did he die?" Wyn's voice sounded strange to his own ears.

Marius hesitated. "Nymwen's not…entirely clear. She speaks about struggling with her powers, about trying to stay in human form. It makes for quite depressing reading. '*The power surges in me like the sea in storm. It frightens me. I worry I cannot contain it and keep this mortal form, but Ewan believes in me, and I will be human for him. I must.*' And this is the last entry: '*He's gone, and I cannot bear it. His blood is on my hands. I don't deserve to live.*' Ivy and I have tried to find any more from that period, with no luck."

"That's an ominous last entry," Hetta said softly.

Wyn thought of the deep, piercing sorrow of the undersea, the lake guardian's mournful cry, and ice crystals formed in his blood. He didn't want to follow his thoughts to their logical conclusion.

He didn't have to; Hetta spoke it for him. She'd felt that sorrow too. "What if the High King hates Valstars because his daughter killed herself after Ewan's death?"

She took his hand, and a spark of static snapped between them. Wyn brushed it away.

"Then he has known all along, but he will still be bound by his word if we complete the task he set us."

Hetta eyed him warily. "You're not being as melodramatic about this as I expected."

"I'm not...thrilled at the parallels to be found with a fae falling in love with a Valstar in a tragic love affair, but then, it isn't as if I expected a warm welcome from my liege no matter who I was proposing to marry. I suppose my expectations didn't have far to fall." He half-furled his wings, trying to disperse his unease. Hetta's hand was warm in his, and he knew she felt the skitter of charge pass between them. Her scent wrapped around him, subtly wrong, a storm edge where none should be.

"It sounds as if Nymwen blamed herself for Ewan's death. I wonder why?" Marius mused.

Nymwen's words reverberated in him. *The power surges. I cannot contain it and keep to this mortal form.* What had Rakken said, warning him that if he didn't find the shape of himself, he'd have to survive a storm of his own making?

Oh, Nymwen. He felt a powerful swell of horrified empathy across the years for this fae who'd met such a tragic fate so long ago, if what he suspected was true.

"You think she might've been responsible, trying to be human for too long? Sorry." Marius nervously ran a hand through his hair.

Wyn shored up his mental shields. "Call it a...working theory."

Hetta's eyes met his, her face drawn. "Well, it's not exactly the helpful blackmail material I'd hoped for, but the High King seems committed to peace, if nothing else. I'm going to tell the High King that our marriage will be a symbol of renewed unity on a number of fronts; maybe that will persuade him to agree to a treaty with the rest of the Mortal Realm as well. You never know—maybe this once thing will go abnormally well rather than the opposite."

Wyn laughed, because it was better than despair, and there was no time for despair, not now, with the clock ticking ever louder.

Are you all right? He wanted to ask Hetta. There was a worrying brittleness to her, as if she were navigating a path made of stitched-together eggshells, but the question served no purpose: she wasn't all right. Neither of them was. So he did the only thing he could, bundling her tightly into his arms, leaning his cheek against hers.

"Could you *not?*" Marius spluttered.

There was a knock at the door, and they disentangled reluctantly as it opened.

Lady Sybil stood there, side by side with Jack. She gave Wyn a withering look that he found oddly heartening, since it didn't splinter even in the face of his wings and horns. It was precisely the same look she'd been giving him for several months, ever since he'd made the mistake of kissing Hetta in front of an assortment of Valstars.

"Have the two of you learnt noth— Oh." She broke off as she spotted Marius and realised she couldn't censure them for being unchaperoned. Marius gave her a small, ironic wave.

Lady Sybil ignored him, folded her arms, and glared down her nose at Hetta. "I wished to tell you that I am going to write to Lady Arran immediately. The Conclave wouldn't even exist without the Valstars, and so I shall tell them! And you, Mr Tempest."

"Yes, my lady?" Wyn asked politely

"You had better not disappoint me or my niece." She gave a firm nod, turned on her heel, and stalked out like an angry crow.

Hetta turned wordlessly to Jack, who hunched his shoulders and said without meeting her eyes, "I saw that damned reporter off while you were gone. She tried to claim it wasn't her article." He gave a snort.

Hetta began to giggle, and that brought Jack's head up sharply.

"I assume that was some sort of peace offering?" Wyn said to Jack, since Hetta couldn't speak with one hand pressed against her mouth, trying to muffle the sound, dancing on the edge of a hysteria Wyn had a lot of sympathy with. He put a hand on her arm.

Jack huffed. "Yes, all right. It was. Can you stop laughing?"

"Sorry," Hetta mumbled, wiping at her eyes. "It's just—Aunt Sybil!"

Jack folded his arms. "She does care about you, Hetta, and us all."

Before anyone could challenge this statement, more footsteps sounded on the stairwell.

"This is a terrible hiding spot," Hetta said accusingly to Marius, who shrugged.

"Oh, are we hiding?" Wyn asked. He frowned at the tea tray. "Forgive me, but, in what sense?"

Grandmamma, Alexandra, Ivy, and Caro jostled at the doorway.

"What's gone wrong now?" Hetta asked tiredly.

"Nothing!" Alexandra said.

"We came to help," Grandmamma said placidly. They spilled into the room, which immediately became overcrowded. "Really, Henrietta, you cannot just make announcements like that and expect us not to act." She surveyed the untouched tea tray and fixed Wyn with a narrow-eyed look. "What sort of husband do you think you'll make if you can't even get her to drink the tea? It grows strong bones," she said in an aside to Hetta. "And I imagine your babe will need quite a lot of that, if they're growing wingbones as well? *Do* fae babes have wings?"

Wyn found himself the focus of multiple pairs of interested eyes. Ivy was pulling out her notebook.

"Ah…not fully formed ones, I don't think." Heat rose in his cheeks, and it was with a deep relief that he felt something ping at the edges of his awareness, the spark of a greater fae, unmasked and blazing along the leylines. The spark was familiar but one he hadn't felt in more than a decade. "But forgive me; my brother is at the border awaiting us. Brothers," he amended.

THE LAST STORMDANCER

THE SIGHT OF Torquil, alive and well and standing on the other side of the train line, eased a tension Wyn hadn't known he'd still been holding, muscles relaxing around his lungs. A soft, sentimental emotion swelled. *This is probably the fondest I've ever felt of him*, he reflected wryly. He and Torquil hadn't been close; Torquil was prone to flares of cruel temper, and he'd seen their proximity of age as a reason to compete rather than collaborate. But Wyn couldn't forget how it had felt to think his brother dead, the sharp, surreal sorrow of it, and he didn't try to stop the smile that came to his lips.

Irokoi bounced across the raised tracks that marked the border here, beaming. "I found him! I must say, it's so nice when people stay where you put them."

Torquil's expression was guarded, and he stayed where he was, arms crossed, assessing the party gathered before him: Hetta, Wyn, Rakken. The day was still and warm, and blackbirds chirped from the hedgerow, which needed clipping back.

Torquil's eyes lingered on Wyn's new plumage, but he didn't

comment. *He's shorter than I am,* Wyn realised with mingled shock and satisfaction. Torquil obviously couldn't fail to notice this either, and his expression soured. Wyn fought a childish impulse to flare out his wings so the light caught the colours better. It would not be politic to emphasise that Torquil hadn't yet grown his own bloodfeathers, regardless of how temporarily satisfying it might feel. Torquil's wings remained the same silvery-white as ever.

"Brothers," Torquil said at last. The word was neutral, neither affectionate nor threatening.

"I'm glad to see you, and especially glad to know your death was greatly exaggerated," Wyn said. Was it foolish to admit it? But Wyn didn't see how it could be used against him, and they did, after all, need Torquil's help.

"You always were sentimental, Hallowyn." Torquil's attention moved to Rakken, his feet shifting subtly into a more defensive stance. "Tell me, did you give up your claim on the throne to stop this one slitting your throat?"

"No," said Wyn.

Rakken's posture was carelessly relaxed, and he smiled, razor sharp. "Are you afraid of me, little brother?"

Torquil's hand strayed towards the pommel of one of the twin blades strapped to his back. He'd never been much good at hiding his temper. "Perhaps you should fear me, Rake. I haven't renounced my claim to the throne, and I won't, no matter how many veiled threats you make." The scent of his magic rose in warning. "And I see there's no Cat here to back you up." Cat still couldn't fly.

"Oh, that wasn't a veiled threat, dear, ever-dramatic Quil," Rakken drawled. "If I threaten you, you will know it. Perhaps you should consider that Cat is not here to hold me back, should I decide to remove my competition."

Wyn met Hetta's eyes and saw that she was both appalled and trying not to laugh. He made a helpless gesture with one hand.

Probably Rakken was merely provoking Torquil for his own entertainment. Probably—but his words cut too close to the truth. Wyn
knew how badly Rakken wanted ThousandSpire's throne.

"Rake mourned you," Wyn said. "When we thought you were
dead. We both did."

Rakken gave Wyn a disgusted look, like a cat that has had its
prey taken off it.

Torquil gave a sharp bark of laughter. "How unexpectedly sentimental of you! Did you mourn Father too?"

Rakken dusted a bit of lint from his shoulder. "Death is final;
one mourns the potential it takes from the world. And dead people
are so very rarely of use." He straightened. "Are you intending to be
of use here, Torquil, or shall we dally on FallingStar's border all day?"

"I haven't invited you in," Hetta said, looking between them all
with a dry expression.

Torquil blinked down at Hetta. "I apologise for my manners
in not introducing myself immediately, Lord Valstar. I am Prince
Torquil Tempestren. I understand you wish to marry my younger
brother." He sounded doubtful, as if he couldn't understand why
anyone would wish to do such a thing.

Wyn fought the temptation to flare out his wings and re-draw
Torquil's attention to Wyn's bloodfeathers and Torquil's lack of them.

"Yes," Hetta said. "If I let you in, will you abide by guestright?
And agree to support Wyn's and my marriage?"

"I will."

"Welcome to Stariel, then."

Torquil stepped across the border with an edge of defiance, his
wings tightening as Stariel sniffed around him. He weighed up
Wyn, eyes narrowing as he worked out that Wyn was connected
to the faeland he stood on. It was jarring, Wyn had to admit,
for his brothers to ping against his senses as other rather than

kin; particularly so when the reverse was true for Gwendelfear, a DuskRose fae. Would he ever get used to that?

"Has Irokoi told you our terms?" Wyn asked.

Torquil nodded. "He said ThousandSpire should have its choice again, and I believed him, though…" His brows creased and he trailed off. A chill went down Wyn's spine.

"You can't remember being told there's a compulsion on you because there's a compulsion on you," Hetta told him.

He stared at her. "Yes…" he said uncertainly.

"You'll de-compel him?" Hetta asked Rakken.

Rakken heaved a sigh, and Wyn thought he was going to make some remark about mortal bluntness, but he simply said, "Yes."

They went back to the house. Cat greeted Torquil with more enthusiasm than her twin but less patience.

"Rakken will remove the compulsion from you in exchange for your willing participation in breaking the Spires' curse. Do you agree? We are running out of time."

"I don't trust Rake."

Rakken gave a sharp-toothed smile. "Whyever not?"

Torquil just gave him a flat look.

Rakken sighed. "Very well. I promise to do nothing to your mind beyond what is needed to remove the spell."

He bore Torquil away, leaving Wyn and Hetta alone. Hetta wrinkled her nose, looking after them. "He's not what I expected. He's not…glossy like Rakken."

Wyn shrugged. "Torquil was never very good at diplomacy. Fortunately, he's a skilled warrior, or I don't think he'd have survived in the Spires as long as he did. But it's perhaps not surprising he left when he could. He did not belong there either."

He pulled at that thought, that commonality between them, not sure whether he was reassured or disturbed by it.

"I don't think any of you belonged in the Spires when it turned on itself," Hetta pointed out. "Some of you just took longer to realise than others."

"And yet one of them may soon be ruling the Spires, regardless."

It took nearly twenty-four hours to set up the spell at the Stones, and Wyn felt every minute of them ticking past. Irokoi and Rakken wrangled over spell parameters and ignored the others except for issuing irritable demands periodically. It didn't seem to occur to them that they might be disobeyed.

Wyn exchanged a glance with Torquil after Irokoi had absently sent him to fetch 'a simple pitcher filled directly from a spring'. Torquil had just arrived with another stack of books from the library at Rakken's request.

Torquil raised a wry eyebrow. "They do know we're no longer children, don't they?"

"In fairness, I am not much more skilled at spellcasting now than I was then," Wyn admitted.

Torquil canted his head. "I've never understood how you can be so free with your weaknesses."

"I am not exactly weak." He flexed his wings, the vivid colours sparkling—in contrast to Torquil's own white. Torquil scowled.

Wyn looked up to find Cat watching them with the suggestion of a smile. She was perched on one of the stones, sharpening a blade. Her colour was a lot better than it had been, the cuts on her face scabbed over, her movement freer. Her wings were still a mess.

"Are you sure you aren't still children, children?" she said.

Wyn went to fetch the pitcher without comment.

Hetta dragged him to bed when it grew dark, and even Irokoi

snatched a brief few hours of sleep. Rakken did not follow. More importantly, Cat made no attempt to make her twin rest, even when Rakken was dark-eyed and shaky with exhaustion late the next morning, which told Wyn exactly how urgent she felt.

"Belchior's loop was never intended for such a purpose!" Rakken was arguing with Irokoi, jabbing at a section in the sketch he'd drawn.

"How do you know? Have you even met Belchior?" Irokoi said.

"Can you even explain why it should go in such a pattern, or is this one of your"—Rakken made a dismissive waggling motion—"feelings?"

Irokoi was unruffled. "You're just sore you didn't figure it out without me. It's obvious why it goes there. Don't you trust my judgement?"

"No," Rakken said flatly. "I require an explanation before I will commit magic to this madness. You are of questionable sanity, unlike me."

"Debatable," Torquil muttered.

Wyn laughed, though it didn't ease the tension winding through him. Hetta had suffered too many shocks today. They were running out of time.

"How long is this going to take?" Jack asked impatiently, beyond the bounds of the circle. He, Hetta, and a small knot of other interested Valstars sat on a picnic blanket at what Wyn hoped was a safe distance. Hetta was eating a muffin. Wyn weighed the charge surrounding her, trying to judge the rate of increase. It hummed in the air around her, and her relatives were being careful not to accidentally brush against her. How much time did they have left? He balled his hands into fists. It had to be enough; he would wring agreement from the High King with his bare hands, if he had to.

Rakken and Irokoi pretended not to hear Jack, though Wyn knew Rakken at least was irritated at the reminder of his audience. There'd been a few travelling fairs passing through Stariel-upon-Starwater in his years here, and Wyn was strongly reminded of people gathered around the Fantastical Beasts.

Though we are at least real fantastical beasts. There had been a wretched 'unicorn' one year, consisting of a long-suffering white horse and a spiralling horn whose origin Wyn hadn't known except that it certainly had not come from any unicorn.

And yet, Wyn was strangely glad that the Valstars had come to watch. It wasn't exactly a show of support, but it wasn't exactly *not* a show of support either, and it injected a welcome note of normality into the proceedings. He smiled. What would they do if the villagers decided to show up too? *Perhaps we should charge for tickets.*

"No one is making you stay," Hetta said lightly, setting the muffin down. "And no one promised you it would be exciting."

"It *is* exciting!" Alexandra watched Rakken and Irokoi's movements, entranced, sketching rapidly on the pad she'd brought with her. Could she see the magic they were weaving? *I will have to teach her how to shield herself,* he made a note. The Sight was a rare ability, but like most gifts, it came with a dark side. If Alexandra was powerful enough to see leylines, that meant she might catch glimpses of other, less benign things, and Wyn didn't want to find out how they might affect her. He thought of the blazing leylines in the undersea, how they'd felt burnt into his eyelids.

"I think the spell is nearly done," Wyn offered, assessing the wefts of it. Rakken shot him an acid glare, but Wyn was becoming immune to them.

Jack subsided with a wordless grumble, measuring the sun's position in the sky. "The morning will be gone by the time you're finished."

Marius too was making notes, and at this he looked up and frowned at the horizon. "Is the time of day important for the spell?"

"A bit," Irokoi offered absently as he dragged his outstretched primaries over the Standing Stones that had last held a portal between the two faelands. The touch left a faint, delicate imprint that was somehow connected to the wider coil of spellwork Rakken was constructing between the other stones and the plinth in the centre of the circle.

"Is it the time of day here, or the time in the Spires?" Ivy asked, looking up.

It was a surprisingly astute question, and one Wyn didn't know the answer to. He said as much, hazarding a guess. "I think it's probably about the resonance."

"Tell me, brother, do you have any additional commentary you would like to make before we continue? Any further audience you'd care to invite to observe?" Rakken's eyes glittered, almost feverish. "Don't let my spellcasting keep you from your conversations. We are only about to try to pull off an insanely complicated spell to free a land you are directly responsible for cursing in the first place."

"You're losing your touch, Rake, if you can't block out idle chatter," Irokoi said placidly. "But Mossfeathers is right—we are ready. Now give me a feather." He marched over to where Torquil stood and held out a commanding hand.

Torquil considered him through slitted eyes. There were a number of unpleasant magics that called for part of a person's essence. He reached slowly behind his shoulder and plucked out a small covert.

"If you try to use this for anything nefarious…" he began, but Irokoi simply tsked, grabbed the feather and marched over to Rakken expectantly.

"With the same caveats as last time, Koi." Rakken handed one of his own feathers to Irokoi. Cat gave hers over without comment. "How are you planning to acquire dear Aroset's?"

"Oh, I already retrieved one," Irokoi said cheerfully. "But thank you for reminding me." He reached into his pocket and added two feathers to the ones already in his palm: one of his own black, and one of bright crimson.

The sight of the different feathers in Irokoi's palm stirred something in Wyn. When was the last time they had all worked together on anything? *For a given value of working together,* he thought, glancing at Aroset's frozen form.

Wyn had never felt particularly close to his family, but a warm, sentimental emotion swelled in him now. Perhaps it was merely the proximity of the Valstars, who for all their faults, valued family. But he didn't think he was alone in it, from the others' expressions. Would it survive the competition for ThousandSpire's throne, if they succeeded in bringing it out of stasis, if what Irokoi had said about the faeland having its true choice now stood? *Though at least I am out of that specific competition, now.*

One of his siblings ruling in his father's place, ruling the faeland he had abandoned. How would that change things here, in the Mortal Realm? For Stariel and Hetta?

For his child?

"And you, Lord Valstar."

"I don't have any feathers," Hetta pointed out, getting up from the picnic blanket.

Irokoi waved a hand. "Hair will do. This is just to set the initial pattern up—the real connection will be in blood."

"How reassuring." Hetta dutifully pulled out a few strands of hair with a wince.

"And now we arrange ourselves ever so nicely," Irokoi said, skipping back to the Stones and depositing his treasure in the centre of the seven-pointed star. "Is everybody enclosed in their own circle? Good. Seal it with a drop of blood."

Hetta's expression spoke volumes, but Wyn had warned her, so she didn't comment, just sighed and took a small peeling knife out of her pocket. Wyn carefully cut his thumb and let a drop of his own blood fall.

He hissed when the blood hit the spell, the leylines shimmering with potential. Hetta, too, took a sharp breath, her wide eyes meeting his.

Irokoi spoke, soft and intent. "Seven and seven; the price and the cost."

The spell began as a small thing, lines of connection springing forth between them, magnifying as the currents hit each point of the star, doubling over and reverberating back towards the centre. Building, building, the pull of power towards an insatiable void. He could taste ThousandSpire, a faint, metallic edge on the back of his tongue. Cat had been right; the faeland was *hungry*.

The spell drew on them all, but for the first time Wyn didn't fear the depth of his own power. He'd embraced the lightning to defeat Aroset, and that loss of self had somehow given him back control, even in the midst of the most powerful spell he'd ever seen short of the High King's. Awe filled him as the storm of magic grew.

The storm held many signatures: dust after rain, drenched forests, the sharp hiss of ozone, sea wind, cardamom, citrus, cinnamon, frost. Pine and coffee pricked with chilli. The combination of stormdancer and Stariel magic made him feel...he didn't know. A warmth in his chest.

Would this mingled storm-and-Stariel be his child's signature, one day?

Hetta's eyes were closed, her jaw set, and he knew she was wholly focused on keeping Stariel at bay. He could feel the faeland, scratching madly at the edges of their spell like a dog at a door, trying to find a way in. Hetta's brow furrowed as she tried to reassure it.

The magic pulled and pulled, drawing deep, deeper than any spell had ever required of him. A new fear sparked in him—that the spell would burn him out, leaving only a husk behind. Had he been too trusting of Irokoi and Rakken?

But the smaller circles around each of them flared to life, the drain on his magic snapping off so abruptly that he staggered, only keeping himself on his feet by sheer willpower. That's what the additional loops were for; a safeguard against the desperation of a faeland sucking them all dry.

The spell blazed along the unprotected lines with the ferocity of a wildfire, sucking them dry and leaving black, singed lines criss-crossing the hilltop. Only each small circle where they stood remained green.

The spell died.

But something had woken.

Wyn's knees were weak and trembling. He hurried over to Hetta, who was bracing herself on one of the stones, her cheeks pale. Colour came rushing back, and he knew she was drawing on Stariel's energy to recover more quickly.

"Did it work?" she asked him.

As if in answer, a portal flared to life between the Stones. It came out on top of one of the prison spires. In normal weather, it would look out towards the city. Now it showed only the storm, driving rain and wind reducing the visibility to nil. The magic ran wildly enough that Wyn felt Stariel bristle.

Irokoi stood to one side of the portal and gave a mocking bow. "Well, do we want to agree to let ThousandSpire settle this, or shall the backstabbing commence?" This remark was particularly addressed to Torquil.

Torquil scowled. "It is pointless to try to force a faeland's hand." He marched through the portal without a backward glance, Rakken and Catsmere on his heels. Irokoi followed, disappearing into the driving storm.

Wyn hesitated. They could wait until ThousandSpire made its choice, but—

Hetta took his hand. "Let's go," she said softly. "You need to see it done."

Ah, she understood him even now. He had caused this, in some part; he owed it to his past self to witness this. They stepped through the portal together.

The magic slammed against him as he stepped into what was now a foreign faeland. It was disorienting to stand in the Spires and not feel a connection to it, but even without that bond, Wyn could feel the faeland's turbulence. Cat had been right; this couldn't have waited any longer.

The others stood in a loose circle where they had stepped through, already soaked to the skin though it couldn't have been more than a few seconds. Wyn felt the moment the faeland realised they were there, some residual part of him still attuned to its attention. The wind died in an instant, and the storm simply stopped, fell away like glamour to reveal sullen sunshine and the city below.

Dark, feathered wings rustled from a thousand drakken atop a thousand towers, all of the creatures looking towards the prison spire.

"Oh." Cat let out a breath and went boneless. Only Rakken's grip saved her from falling as he bore her gently to the ground. She began to glow, and Rakken hissed and released her.

For a moment, his brother's soul lay raw and vulnerable in his eyes, and Wyn saw straight to the heart of him. Rakken knew what was happening—they all knew—and he was both triumphant and utterly bereft. He and Cat had operated as two halves of one whole since they were born, different but equal, and now they were irrevocably cleaved apart. There would be no more the-twins, no more Prince-and-Princess, no more Cat-and-Mouse. From now on it would be Prince Rakken.

And Queen Catsmere.

THE GATE BEHIND THE THRONE

S O THIS WAS what being Chosen looked like from the outside. Hetta put a hand self-consciously up to her hair, which as far as she knew hadn't started glowing post-lordship. Perhaps that was only a fae thing. Or perhaps Marius and Jack had been too polite to mention it.

The Spires felt different, though Hetta couldn't put her finger on exactly how. There was still that unsettling sense of being watched. She hoped people unconnected to the estate didn't feel that at Stariel. Perhaps it was only her own connection to Stariel that made her so aware of ThousandSpire.

Catsmere had never been a particularly expressive person, but she was curiously laid bare now. Hetta had never considered what she had in common with other faelords—Queen Tayarenn and King Aeros had been so alien and remote—but here was someone who knew even less about being Chosen than she did.

"It's a lot, isn't it?" Hetta murmured.

Catsmere turned to her, eyes wide and full of wonder, the shared knowledge passing between them. They both knew, in a way no one else quite did, how it was to be so intimately connected to a faeland. How it changed you—well, perhaps not that quite yet, but Cat would find out soon enough.

Catsmere nodded. "Welcome to the Court of Ten Thousand Spires, Lord Valstar." She spoke with weighty ceremonialism.

Oh. They were rulers of two different lands, technically meeting for the first time. "Thank you, Your Majesty, and congratulations," Hetta said, attempting the same. "Er, do you want to be addressed formally all the time now? Because I'm quite okay with just Hetta."

Catsmere blinked but appeared to give Hetta's words serious consideration. "You may call me Cat." A pause. "…Hetta."

Hetta smiled at her. "Welcome to faelord-ship." Though she had mixed emotions about Cat's ascension. Given the alternatives, Cat was probably the best they could've hoped for. She wasn't malicious, but she would always come down on the side of Faerie rather than mortals—and no doubt Rakken would be there advising how they might best take advantage of the Mortal Realm. Which was probably best for a faeland, but not necessarily for the human world.

Well, at least Cat was fond of Wyn. Maybe that would be enough.

"I owe you the weight of an obligation," Cat said formally. "If you still wish it paid."

"Yes," Hetta said, taking Wyn's hand and wincing at the shock. Hers, not his. "Where is the Gate?" Irokoi had said that ThousandSpire had one to the High King's Realm, but what if he'd been wrong?

Cat's eyes went distant, as if she were listening to something only she could hear. Did Hetta look like that, when she was talking to Stariel? "It is behind the throne, as Koi said. It feels…strange. I cannot interpret what ThousandSpire says of it. I don't know how it came to be there, and ThousandSpire cannot tell me. Or perhaps I don't know the right question to ask." Cat's expression grew troubled. She bared her teeth in a sharp, fierce expression. "You are no longer the newest faelord, Lord Valstar."

"Perhaps we can share tips," Hetta said lightly, her heart racing. There was a Gate! "Er, later, preferably."

Cat nodded. "I will take you there."

The taking consisted of flying and walking rather than translocation—which gave Hetta some satisfaction, since she hadn't learnt how to do that straightaway either. Maybe she wasn't as terrible a faelord as she'd thought.

They flew through a city gripped with the same hushed wonder as Cat. Rakken kept snatching glances at his twin, triumph mixed with anguish.

"This is our city now," Cat murmured, as the light struck the jewels set into its many towers. Hetta had only seen the city at a distance before, but now they flew through the maze made of its many aerial bridges. Hetta just wished her stomach would cooperate with the rather spectacular view, which she would've enjoyed under other circumstances. *Not now*, she told her churning stomach, wishing she hadn't lost her engagement ring. She'd gotten too used to relying on Stariel's anti-nausea properties. She tried reaching to her faeland, but the link was hair-thin without the amplifier of her lost ring. It helped a little, but not nearly enough.

The skies began to fill with winged fae, in as vast a variety of forms as she'd seen at DuskRose's ball, though there were more feathers here. The fae had no attention for anyone but Cat, watching her with something between fear and hope.

Hetta couldn't read Wyn's expression as he carried her through the skies, the beat of his wings a steady rush. This had been his home, where he must've flown as a child.

"Maybe we can bring our child here to visit, someday?" she murmured against his shoulder.

It took him a long time to answer, so long that she thought her words had been lost to the wind, but eventually he said in a low voice, "Perhaps."

The throne room was a mess. Last time Hetta had been here, it had been lined with members of ThousandSpire's court, full of mocking, watching eyes as King Aeros staged their confrontation. Now it was empty, a monument to ruined ostentation, filled with dust and broken ceramic tiles. All the jewels in the tree-trunk-thick columns and walls had shattered. The wind swept dried leaves across the cracked stone floor.

Hetta hadn't given much thought to the immediate aftermath of King Aeros's death, when Aroset had briefly held the Spires. It looked like no one had had time to clean up.

Cat rested a hand on a pillar where all the jewels were dead, looking up to the vast open space where there was no roof over the room. There was something intense and complicated in her expression, and Hetta knew instinctively what it was. Home. Hetta looked away, feeling like she was intruding on something private.

Rakken was staring at the raised dais where the throne stood. The throne had cracked in two, and the sockets that had held diamonds and rubies were empty. A strange, glittering red sand covered its seat. *That's where the rubies went*, Hetta realised with a shock. Something had turned them to powder.

It felt wrong to break the silence, but there wasn't exactly time to dally. "Where is the Gate?" Hetta asked, the vast space swallowing her words.

Cat shook herself out of her abstraction. "This way," she said softly, leading them towards the throne. She touched her hand to the broken mosaic on the wall, and it sprang open to reveal a concealed passageway.

"Did you know this was here?" Hetta asked Wyn, who was frowning at the opening.

"I…yes," he said after a beat. "Yes, though I think I had forgotten it. We used it as children?" His voice went up slightly, making it a question.

Cat canted her head. "Yes," she said, thoughtfully. "Yes, we did."
Irokoi only smiled.

The passageway led to a pool surrounded by stone walls. The pool
was set in stone steps, leading down to crystal clear waters. Lilypad-
like flowers with huge pale leaves dotted the surface. The jewels here
weren't dead, and unusually they weren't the red-and-gold colour
scheme that predominated elsewhere in the throne room. They
were blue and green, the pattern of tiles like the ripple of water.

"This is the Gate," Cat said, waving at the pool. She still had an
abstracted look, as if she were listening to something far away.

"How do we open it?" Hetta asked, walking carefully down the
steps to peer into the water. It only appeared knee deep at this end,
but the bottom of the pool looked as if it were slanted, growing
deeper towards the middle. Her experience of fae magic so far made
her cautious. "Is it safe to touch?"

"I remember swimming in here as a child." Wyn pulled off his
boots and rolled up his trousers before wading in. Nothing happened. He looked expectantly at his sister.

But Cat was frowning at the waters and shook her head. "I don't
have the key."

"Blood," Irokoi whispered, helpfully holding out a small knife.
Rakken's eyes flicked from the knife to the pool, narrowing, but he
said nothing. He hadn't spoken a word since Cat had been chosen,
Hetta realised.

"Thank you," said Wyn drily.

"Both of us?" Hetta asked, eying the knife with trepidation.

"His," said Irokoi. "But you should be in the water too. Speak the
High King's name."

Hetta pulled off her shoes and carefully stepped into the pool.
The water was tepid, not the cold shock she'd been expecting. She
and Wyn looked at each other.

"Remember our persuasive speech about unity," she murmured.

He swallowed, gave a nod of acknowledgement, then carefully pricked a finger. The drop of blood welled, hitting the water with a small cloud of colour, quickly dissipated.

"We have done as you asked; you owe us a boon, Oberyn. I call you, Oberyn, High King of Faerie. Oberyn!" Wyn called, his voice low and solemn.

The water began to churn. The world went dark.

THE HIGH KING OF FAERIE

THE WORLD'S DISORIENTATION righted itself and left Hetta standing next to a wall in a vast plaza filled with silent fountains. Alone.

Where was Wyn? Hetta whirled, but there was no sign of either him or the Gate they'd stepped through, only fountains of every shape and size, filling the enormous plaza as far as she could see. She searched the sky in hope of wings and gasped. There were two suns, making the light extremely odd and the time of day difficult to determine. Of course the High King's realm would have the most faerie geography of all.

Giving herself a shake, she peered into the fountain nearest her and gasped again because the water showed not her own reflection but a familiar mountain range: the Indigoes. The pool was a Gate, a Gate to Stariel. How was it possible there was a Gate to her estate that she didn't know about? So much for having secure boundaries.

Hetta turned away from the image and walked over to the next fountain. A little bit of static jumped when she touched it and she pulled back, her heart in her throat. Where was the High King?

She peered into the fountain, careful not to touch anything. It showed a similar disconcerting non-reflection, though this time of an unfamiliar landscape. She inspected several more fountains without touching them and found the same thing. All Gates, all to different faelands. Did every fountain contain a Gate? Did this plaza hold a Gate to every faeland there was? She swallowed. The plaza stretched into the distance in three directions; she couldn't begin to estimate how many Gates that would mean.

The stone wall that bounded the fourth compass point was too high to see beyond, and the long, smooth line of it stretched unbroken along the horizon with no discernible exits. Exactly how big was this place? The quiet of it was unnatural, giving Hetta an urge to keep constantly turning to check there was no one behind her.

Hetta went back to Stariel's fountain and leaned over it, thinking. The snow on the highest peaks of the Indigoes contrasted sharply with the dark slopes and the clear blue of the sky. If she clambered into the fountain, she'd be home in moments. She took a firm step back.

There was a *Gate* to *her faeland* in the High King's own realm. It made her feel oddly bristly, that the fae High King apparently saw Stariel as part of his kingdom. And just why had Hetta emerged here, coincidentally next to an oh-so-helpful exit point, and without Wyn? It was hard not to interpret her location as a hint: the High King wanted her to leave. Or perhaps the hostile, prickling atmosphere was merely her imagination.

"I'm not going to leave without talking to you!" Hetta said loudly, just in case the High King was listening. The words echoed into nothing without a response. "And certainly not without Wyn," she added for good measure, scanning the sky for blue wings without success. Where was he?

The High King values fae lives, Hetta comforted herself, thinking of the lake guardian and how it had avoided harming Wyn. Which meant Wyn must be all right, wherever he was, though it couldn't be a good sign that the High King had separated them.

She walked towards the wall. The black stone glistened in a strange pattern of overlapping diamonds. She laid her palm against it, planning to ignore the expected bit of static, but snatched it back immediately at the unexpected warmth. Cautiously, she tried again. The stone held a low, warm heat, as if it had absorbed a full day's sun. Maybe it had; Hetta wasn't sure what time it was, but it could've been dusk. One of the suns was near the horizon.

She cupped her hand and summoned a flicker of flame. It hovered above her palm obediently, and her magic swarmed up, eager to feed more power into it. The strength of it surprised her, since she didn't stand on Stariel's land; this was her own magic, unboosted by her faeland.

How thick, exactly, was this stone wall, and—more important-ly—how hot did fire have to be to melt it? She looked up. Perhaps she could melt footholds and climb over it? The thought made her a little dizzy—the wall towered over her—but she had to get out of this place and find Wyn and the High King, wherever he was hiding. They'd completed his dashed task, hadn't they? She let the knot of anger manifest, turning her flame from cheerful orange to a pale, almost translucent blue.

The fire hit the stone with a scorching smell, but the stone didn't melt. Instead, it rippled and made a noise like the shriek of tor-tured glass.

And then it moved.

The wall peeled away from the ground, and Hetta could only stand and watch, horrified, as she realised it wasn't a wall at all. It was the coiled body of a gargantuan serpent, the diamond pattern its scales. Beyond it grew a riotous forest in impossible colours.

Hetta darted underneath the rapidly rising 'wall' towards the forest, blind panic thundering her heartbeat in her ears. She was within a stone's throw of the forest edge when black scales filled her vision, and she pulled to a screeching halt.

The serpent had curled its enormous head between her and her destination, its eyes glowing a bright, vivid green. It hissed from a mouth the size of a shepherd's hut, showing alarmingly long fangs.

She took a step back, pouring energy into her hands until she held two towers of flame.

The serpent recoiled but not nearly far enough.

"I'm here to see the High King!" she told it desperately.

It spoke, although unfortunately what it said, in a voice like gravel, was: "Go away, Valsssstar."

"No! He owes me a boon! I demand to see him!" She made the fire in her palms flare up even higher. Her heart pounded.

A sound came from behind her, or rather, a vast absence of sound that shaped the world around it. It formed syllables out of thunder: *Henrietta Isadore Valstar.*

A chill ran down her neck. She took a couple of steps backwards without turning, putting more distance between her and the serpent before she risked a glance behind her.

A tall figure stood amidst the fountains. Like Lamorkin, the figure wasn't static, but unlike the maulkfae, the shifting wasn't a fluid transition between forms but an aura of power that blurred whatever lay at its centre, making it difficult to see clearly what the High King looked like. She had no doubt this was the High King; the power of him burned, like standing too close to an open furnace.

She looked back to the serpent, feeling dizzy even from that single glance.

"Are you going to stop trying to eat me and let me talk to him?" she asked it. It didn't reply, but it closed its jaws and began to settle its coils back against the ground. She took another step backwards towards the High King, then another. The serpent didn't move, its eyes slitting as it watched her. She kept backing up through the maze of fountains, until she could see the High King out of the corner of her eye and the serpent was a good distance in front of her.

She let the fire snuff out. The serpent still hadn't moved. All right then. Swallowing, she turned to face the High King, nervously keeping an eye on the serpent.

The second glance wasn't any easier than the first. The High King's hair—was it hair?—fluttered lazily all around him, as if he stood in the centre of his own personal updraft. A thousand colours caught and shifted in the strands as it wafted, from midnight blue to silver, crimson and gold, rose-petal pink and emerald. His horns, if he had them, were many-branched, like the antlers of a great deer. He had wings, or perhaps he didn't. They flickered, one second great feathery expanses, the next dragonfly gossamer, the next batwing leather, the next insubstantial as fog. Similarly, he might've had a tail, at turns furry and scaled, though it too slipped in and out of focus the more Hetta tried to tell for sure.

His impossible beauty was only a minor footnote against the power radiating out of him like boiling thunderclouds. It made a part of her want to curl into a ball and gibber with fear, and that made a bigger part of her even more furious.

She closed her eyes to stop them from watering. How was she going to approach him when she couldn't even look at him for any length of time? Wyn had said that if the High King favoured you, he'd tamp down his power and assume a single, static form of whatever took his fancy.

Clearly he doesn't favour me. Well, if she had to do this with her eyes closed, she would.

"Good evening, Your Majesty," she said, taking a stab at the time of day. It probably didn't matter. "Where is Wyn? My fiancé." Maybe she shouldn't use that word, when the High King hadn't yet given them his blessing, but she was damp, angry, somewhat nauseous, and couldn't summon up any diplomacy.

There was a subtle feeling of something changing, and Hetta risked a quick look. The High King had chosen a shape, and she let out a breath of relief.

He was now a stormdancer, dark-skinned, dark-haired, green-eyed. His sharp-cut features held an uncomfortable echo of Wyn and his siblings', and his wings were almost a perfect match for Wyn's—was that some kind of threat?

"Why are you here, Henrietta Isadore Valstar?"

She didn't like how he said her name; it gave her a sort of chill. Was this how Wyn felt about true names?

"You said you'd grant us a boon if we met your conditions. That you'd give Wyn your permission to marry."

"And have you met my conditions?"

"Yes. DuskRose is coming to our wedding, and the new ruler of ThousandSpire has given us her approval too."

The High King laughed, and the world shone brighter. "A very fae answer. Very well then, he may marry you, if he wishes."

Hetta narrowed her eyes. This felt too easy, not that she was objecting to easy, but… "Where is he?"

"He is safe." Voice and face expressionless; it was like having a staring contest with a statue.

"He's not yours to keep safe," she said. "He belongs to Stariel."

"FallingStar is within my domain."

"The human half isn't. And I don't see that the fae half gives you the right to kidnap its people, if that's what you've done. I'm pretty sure none of my ancestors would've agreed to that, and I definitely haven't."

"And what would you give for his return?"

Had he kidnapped Wyn, then? "I don't see why I should have to give anything to resolve a problem you've just now caused."

Honestly, Hetta couldn't even be surprised at this treachery, but it did make her anger burn hotter. "Why are you playing games? We completed your tasks! What more do you want?"

"For you to choose: Mortal or Faerie."

Well, that certainly sounded ominous. Hetta stared at the High King. "I don't understand what you mean by choosing. Is this about the Iron Law?"

"It is about the child."

He knew, then. Hetta put a hand to her abdomen and winced at another stray bit of static. Had the shock felt stronger this time? "Can you fix whatever is wrong?"

"I can. It's a matter of balance."

"And what, exactly, does that mean?" Honestly, he was worse than Irokoi.

He echoed her phrasing back at her. "And what price, exactly, would you pay, for this? Would you give up your rule of Stariel?"

She inhaled sharply. "To save the child? Or for you to give Wyn back?" It seemed best to be clear on this point, even if nothing else was making sense.

"Both."

"I don't see why any such sacrifice is necessary; if I marry Wyn, won't that fix whatever is wrong?"

"Do you think you can find him in time, in *my* realm? How much time do you think you have?"

Hetta glared at him. "Do you *want* this child to die?"

His expression didn't change. "What price, Henrietta Valstar?"

"I thought breaking my lordship wasn't possible, that the bond was for life."

The High King didn't speak, but meaning bloomed in her mind. Bonds could be unmade, with sufficient intent and magic. Her land bond could go to another Valstar. Would that really be such a sacrifice, giving up her life there? One life for another; it was traditional.

Hetta crossed her arms. This was ridiculous! He couldn't truly think he could railroad her into this, could he?

And yet, she couldn't stop herself from thinking about it. Sometimes it felt like she'd always been the lord of Stariel, but actually it wasn't even a whole year since she'd left Bradfield and the company in Meridon. She'd liked her old life; she'd been good at it. Was she good at lordship? Images flickered through her mind: the shocked faces of the Conclave, the newspaper articles, the sharp letter from the bank, the damaged roof at Penharrow. Jack had managed perfectly fine in her absence.

What would it mean to give it up? She'd be an individual again, without fear of losing that under the weight of either duty or land-sense. She and Wyn would be, well, not ordinary, but a couple of far less interest to the world at large. Maybe they could go to Meridon. She could return to working at the theatre.

"But Wyn would still be fae," she murmured, almost to herself. "So would our child."

"Do you wish that they were not?"

Again, possibilities bloomed in her mind without words being spoken. What if Faerie and Mortal were separated again? What if the High King could take the child's fae nature and bring back the Iron Law?

She shook her head. "No, don't." That was an easy rejection. As for the other… Could she give up Stariel? She'd never gotten a choice in her lordship; Stariel had chosen her against all her wishes and plans for her own future.

Did she want Stariel, if the choice was hers?

Yes.

There it was, deep down, a truth she'd been ashamed to admit to herself. She liked being Stariel's lord. She liked the magic, and the challenge, and the purpose of it. If she'd had the choice—well, maybe she wouldn't have chosen it at the time, but now, with all that had passed? She didn't want to give it up.

She also didn't see why she should have to. Her fingernails curled into fists. "I don't understand why you're doing this. Is it something about my ancestors? Are you holding a grudge from what happened with Nymwen?"

The world went cold, and something large and reptilian and that she really shouldn't have forgotten about whacked into her. She reached for fire, but she was already stumbling backwards, hitting the water in the fountain with a cold splash—

—She was back, impossibly, at Stariel, standing ankle-deep in Starwater. In the evening's stillness, the waters lapped gently at the shore. Gravel shifted under her boots, and under that, Stariel. It was evening, and stars glimmered down and reflected in the lake as she stood there with soaking feet and a mess of furious emotions.

How dare the High King simply kick her out when she'd refused to take his false bargain? How dare he separate her from Wyn! Had his questions been a test? Had she failed it?

A shock ran through her—a literal one—and she scrabbled for balance, because this one hurt a lot more than any of the previous ones had. She panted, harsh breaths loud in the still evening, and knew, in a deep, visceral way, that her ticking clock was about to run out.

No! The High King had said it could be fixed. A matter of balance, he'd said. What did that mean? She hadn't reached for Stariel, but the land was nonetheless there, a storm of agitation circling around her. What was wrong?

She didn't answer, staring out across the lake, feeling the depth of the waters like the weight of an anchor.

A shining streak blazed across the sky, its path mirrored in the black waters below. The Court of Falling Stars—Valstar. This was the hub of Stariel's magic, the heart of her faeland, groundwater and tributaries all draining into the lake. This was the lake she was named after. As a child, she'd swum in its shallows in summer and skated its surface in winter. Fish from its depths had fed her. She'd drunk from the rivers that fed into it. She thought she'd left it behind six years ago, sick of her father, her family, her roots. But the lake was in her bones, and she'd carried a part of it with her always.

She waded further into the lake, her boots heavy and water-logged. Her skirts were next, soaking in an ever-increasing strip and plastering around her legs, her stockings sodden. In the back of her mind, a small, practical voice suggested that it might've been sensible to remove some clothing beforehand. She ignored it, focused on a deeper, more primal part of her psyche.

Hip-deep, she stopped, swishing her fingers roughly through the cool water. Ripples expanded outwards. She stretched, out, out from the tips of her fingers, a metaphysical ripple in the still waters. The lake's surface had been warmed by the sun, but as she plunged down to its heart, the waters grew cold and dark, until she brushed the bottom of the lake. She turned and arrowed across the bed, unfurling until she encompassed the entirety of Starwater, above and below, reaching up the streams that led to it, down the river that ran from it. Water was magic, in its way, tracing leylines as it moved beneath the earth, channelling power in its streams.

She'd only gone this deep into Stariel once before, when it had

first claimed her. The fear of being lost in its vastness had kept her
to shallower merges since—a fear confirmed by all the times she'd
nearly lost herself.

But there was no fear in her now, even as Stariel wound itself
around her and under her skin, even as she and it became less and
less separate, one creature rather than two.

How did you hold your identity against the weight of something
so old and vast? How did you stop it from swallowing everything you
were, remaking you into something better suited to its own needs?

Lord Valstar or Hetta—which one was more important? She
knew the answer now:

Both.

Neither.

A false dichotomy, because how could she be a good lord if
she wasn't herself? Stariel couldn't remake her into what it needed,
because what it needed was her. That was *why* it had chosen her.

She'd never understood that before, the essential ingredient of a
faelord—not only an anchor, but a bridge. How else could something so vast and alien comprehend the lives within its borders? *All*
of the lives, which for Stariel meant something it meant nowhere
else in Faerie.

This was their home, their land, their family. They were human
and fae. They were a thousand years old and twenty-five years young.
Stariel had chosen her, but now, now she chose it *back*.

Before, it had always been Stariel supplying information at her
request. Now it was Hetta's turn; to say this, here, is what's important, turning the might of a faeland to something even more fleeting
than the lives of mortals; a life barely begun. To take Rakken and
Lamorkin's and the High King's words and forge them into action.
If they could all see the extra energy gathering within her, then
logically, so ought she.

Where they'd been vast, they became now small, enclosed within a single body's physicality. Smaller still. Distantly, cold shook their physical form, and they brushed it aside.

Stariel quivered—dangerous, to go so deep into their own body. <I don't plan to make a habit of it,> she told it. <But this is necessary.>

Deeper. They were blood, and the beat of hearts, and magic, knotting where it should flow, pooling where it should not.

Deeper still. They were leylines and streams and threads of life across this land, connected to them all. They moved hands that weren't hands, delicate as thistledown.

Like aligning two magnets, slippery and fighting against natural forces. They'd thought only fae would be able to stabilise this, but Hetta was a little bit fae too. And Stariel was a *lot* fae. Abruptly, the energy fluxes snapped into place, as if they'd always been whole and perfectly aligned.

She opened her eyes with a gasp. It was done, and she was entirely herself.

And drowning. Her legs had gone out from under her, and water filled her mouth. Darkness above and below. Were those the stars or the bright sparks of leylines? Which way was up? But a powerful body pushed against hers and bore her upwards. She surfaced, the air a cold shock, and she coughed, water coming up in painful sputters. The same force that had hauled her upwards nudged her towards the beach.

"Thank you," she said before the nessan's glowing eyes disappeared back into the depths.

She dragged herself onto the gravel and collapsed, shivering. She put a hand over her baby. It was okay. *They* were okay. Triumph and delayed terror warmed her as she attempted to wring water out of her skirts. Her hands were shaking, and part of her couldn't believe what she'd just done.

What *had* she done? Stariel hummed, but there was something different about the feel of the faeland, something that made her close her eyes and reach out again, more carefully this time.

Her eyes snapped open. She'd always been peripherally aware that there were two Stariels—fae and mortal, lying close but not quite together, one atop the other. There was only one now, and it was neither and both, entirely itself. The sparks of all her people—fae and human—flickered through her land-sense.

She blew out a long breath. Well, almost all her people. One was still missing. She curled her hands into fists. Now to get him back.

53

OBERYN

WYN STOOD ON the edge of a familiar lake. Cicadas chirped, but no other sound disturbed the placid heat of the evening, and the smooth surface of the water lay untroubled by wind.

The single note of discomfort in the tranquil scene came from within, a scratch of thought he couldn't quite catch. He stood beneath the gentle drapery of the willows and tried to draw it forth, but the longer he stood, the less it seemed to matter. Tension drained away, unknotting his muscles and settling his wings into a lower position so that they almost traced the ground when he abandoned his ruminations and walked slowly down to the shore. Dry grass brushed against his primaries, as reassuring and grounding as the smell of warm earth and water.

The sun was setting—wait, were there two suns?—but, no, he was mistaken. In any case, the sun was setting, its golden light spilling out across the water and limning in fire the figure standing a little way into the lake.

The figure. Everything tilted, became unsettling and sinister. It hurt to look directly at them, their shape blurring with a primal, untamed power that warped reality around them.

They were fae—the most purely fae being he'd ever seen—but he couldn't tell which court they hailed from, not when their form flickered so swiftly. A recollection sparked, so deep below conscious thought he could only feel it rising towards him, a connection as yet without comprehension.

Statues…an undersea library…many forms… He nearly had it—

"Hallowyn."

He opened his eyes, and the world shifted again, his train of thought evaporating into so much steam.

He'd been… There had been…

He stood on the bank of a lake, looking out across the water lit by the dying sun, the light too bright to stare at directly. The sun slipped behind the distant cliffs between one heartbeat and the next, revealing a blue-winged male stormdancer standing thigh deep in the still waters. He was facing away, but he had deep brown skin, ebon hair, and gold horns. His wings were a match for Wyn's, deep blue, edged with silver, iridescent with flecks of purple and emerald at the feathers closest to his body.

Wyn blinked, the sight somehow not what he'd expected. He didn't recognise the fae, and yet…something in his chest twanged in anticipation. The stormdancer turned and met Wyn's gaze with eyes of brilliant, impossible emerald, and the twang became a shock, a jerk of recognition and powerful emotion.

Wyn couldn't breathe, drinking in the sight like parched earth as the stormdancer tilted his head, green eyes glinting with interest. He was changed, of course, his face and form hardened from the more feminine version Wyn remembered, but his signature remained the same. It held the sea in storm and smoke from a driftwood fire, a hint of strange spices and apple blossom on the wind, and Wyn knew it as well as he knew his own.

And those eyes… There were only three people in the world with eyes that impossible shade. Two of them were Rakken and Catsmere. The third…

Wyn was moving before he knew it, striding into the lake, heedless of his clothes, heedless of everything. Water splashed up his wings, and he drew to a panting halt a bare two feet away from the—no, not a stranger. Never a stranger. Wyn still had to look up to meet his eyes. That hadn't changed.

"Mother?" he asked, his voice catching.

"Well met, little Hallowyn," the fae man said softly, and the voice was almost but not quite the same as Wyn remembered, the timbre lower. But still so familiar, falling into place as if it hadn't been more than two decades since Wyn had heard it.

"Mother."

He wasn't sure which of them stepped into the embrace first. For a heartbeat there was only the cutting joy of the boy he'd been, reunited with a parent long-lost. The signature winding around him twisted in his chest, so true and right it hurt.

And then he was no longer a boy. The moment passed, leaving a terrible, clawing anger in its wake, and he stumbled back as if bitten. He'd believed, with iron certainty, that his mother wouldn't have abandoned them willingly. But to find his mother here and well, not dead, or imprisoned, or trapped… A bigger question beat against his consciousness for a second, pounding against his skull, but he looked into his mother's green eyes and the pounding faded away, leaving only a faint bruise in its wake.

"You're—you're alive. Why did you leave? Did father— How long—" Wyn didn't know what he wanted to ask. "You left us." That's what it came back to. "You left us."

Ryn's expression turned grim, the light of h—his—eyes, Wyn mentally stumbled over the unfamiliar pronoun, a trivial thing but still clumsy in its newness.

"I did," Ryn said. "I left you."

The betrayal hurt, worse than breaking his wings, worse than having his Spire-sense torn out of him. Accusations and questions tumbled together, fighting their way up his throat, but in the end all that came out was a hoarse cry.

"Why?"

Ryn trailed a hand in the waters, his fingers creating ripples that spread out and out. "I did not belong there." He sounded impossibly sad. "I let myself forget that, for a time. I *made* myself forget that, for a time."

Wyn felt as if he were falling, despite the firm lake gravel beneath his feet—they weren't even hip deep in the water. "Because…you changed forms?" He didn't understand why that should be the case, but, then, nothing currently made sense to him.

Ryn absently lifted a hand to touch Wyn's jaw. "You've been too long in Mortal, little one, to ask such a question. No. This form isn't what made me leave. It's hardly the first time I've changed in such a way." Ryn examined Wyn slowly from head to toe. "You look well, my son." Ryn flexed his own wings with a swish of water, blue glinting with silver. "I confess I hoped at least one of you would bear my colours when you came of age."

"Father was planning to kill me." Wyn hadn't meant to say that, not with so many other questions jostling for space on his tongue, but somehow that was the one that came tumbling out. "He encouraged Aroset to maim Irokoi, and he was going to kill me to continue his war with DuskRose. Did you know that, when you left?" There was no way Ryn could have known, since the latter event had happened years after he'd left, but Wyn couldn't contain his bitterness.

"Aeros." The way Ryn said the name held too many complicated layers of emotion to decipher. A half-smile, fond and bittersweet. "You didn't know him when he was young, little one. He would not have done such a thing, when I first knew him." The smile faded. "My being with him changed him. I thought I could change myself into what I was not, but it only hurt us both. I had hoped, with time, he would stop trying to draw me back…" He shook his head, and for a moment his dark braids looked as if they'd unravelled, as if strands had taken on an energy of their own and were dancing like snakes around him. Wyn squeezed his eyes shut and when he re-opened them, the odd double image had dissipated.

"I don't understand," Wyn said plaintively. It was like scrabbling through shards of glass, trying to piece together his senses, cutting himself to ribbons in the process. He tried to find his centre, to ground himself as he'd been taught since his earliest days of magic, starting with the heart and moving out, but it hammered too hard, as though he were mid-battle rather than standing in perfect tranquillity. There was a bright green thread within him, worming upwards against the tide of confusion. He didn't know what it was.

Ryn looked tired. "Love can make you forget duty, but I remembered mine eventually. But I made sure you would be kept safe, after I had gone, at DuskRose. Princess Sunnika would have grown to love you."

Wyn frowned. "You knew about the engagement? How? Where have you been all this time?" That green thread thrashed within him. He glanced around at the lake, confusion filling him once again. "Where are we?"

There was something he desperately needed to remember… The bright green threads were still relentlessly worming through him, bringing clarity in their wake, enough that he finally recognised what they were.

Rakken. This was Rakken's anti-compulsion at work. He touched the amulet Rakken had given him; it burned to the touch. He needed it to remember because his mother…his mother…

"You compelled us. You're compelling me now." It was like

crashing into ice-cold water. He stared at his mother, horrified. "Why? What don't you want me to know?"

Ryn looked at him. His eyes were the same green as the twins', but somehow more penetrating, as if they could see clear to the heart of the world. "Oh, my Hallowyn." He reached out to cup Wyn's face again, and Wyn jerked back from the touch. Sorrow etched Ryn's expression—and then a sudden dark amusement, turning inwards.

"Children," Ryn grumbled, his wings swishing irritably in the water. "Never doing as one wishes them to do. I suppose I have only myself to blame. None of you have ever shown much inclination to do as told or stay safe where put."

"You're avoiding my question—why did you compel us to forget? Why are you still compelling me now?" Even to ask was a great effort, a fog only kept at bay by the sharp burr of Rakken's spell.

Ryn sighed, and his gaze bore into Wyn's, burning, painfully bright. "Oh, Hallowyn, it will only hurt you to know."

Wyn was sitting on a flat rock on the shore, the tips of his bare feet just touching the water. Next to him sat his mother, their wings overlapping. The cicadas sang in the dusk as the shadows deepened. His chest ached.

"Mother." How had he come to be here? There was something… something he had to say…

Wyn bent his wing around, touching one of his primaries as if that would help centre him. Feathers…he had given another feather to Hetta—

He sat bolt upright, glancing around wildly. "Hetta!"

"The mortal," Ryn said flatly.

"Where is she? How did we—" His memories were disjointed; he couldn't seem to pull them into shape.

Ryn brushed his wing against Wyn's, the reassurance steadying. "She is safe. Tell me, what future do you envisage for the two of you?"

"There is a child. Mine and Hetta's." He held the knowledge tight; how could it have slipped his mind, even for a moment? "We need help."

"I know," Ryn said. "What if the child weren't fae? Perhaps the High King could do such a thing, separate Mortal from Faerie once more. Would you bring back the Iron Law, if you could?"

Wyn frowned. "Is that the only way?"

Ryn picked up a pebble, weighed it in his hand, and Wyn had an eerie recollection of Hetta performing the same motion. Ryn threw. The pebble skimmed across the water in a series of declining arcs and sank out of sight. "It is *a* way."

The High King. That's who they were looking for, weren't they? Only Wyn couldn't remember how he'd come to be here, exactly, or why his mother was here, asking such things.

Ryn held his gaze, waiting for an answer.

Wyn didn't need to dwell on it for long. "If—if that were the only way to save them, then perhaps. But it wouldn't be my preferred option."

Ryn laughed, the sound bright. "That's a very fae answer, Hallowyn."

"I am fae."

Ryn smiled. "You are. Would you be mortal, if you could? Would you give up your fae nature?"

"I—"

Hallowyn Tempestren.

His name rang through him, a summons. It came again, and again, and there was magic in it; magic he knew intimately, connecting him to his faeland. It was furious and fire-tinged, and he burned bright in response. He might not understand what was happening, but that connection—that, he was certain of.

He pulled his wing sharply away from Ryn's. "I have to go," he said.

He backed away from his mother, who watched him unblinking. The world began to change. The forest surrounding the lake was melting away. The lake itself shrunk, becoming a mere pond, and around them stretched more ponds in a wild variety of styles and edgings. Not ponds. Fountains.

Had it all been glamour? He looked at the fountains in confusion.

One of them was humming his name. As if in a dream, he walked towards the fountain edged in the shimmering blue of star indigo. He was missing something, something important. If he could just think!

"Hallowyn," his mother said from behind him, a warning.

Hallowyn, said the summons. It tasted like coffee on the back of his tongue, and he knew its name: Hetta.

He didn't need to think to know there was one place in the world where everything would make more sense; it was the only place that had ever really made sense, in his soul.

He stepped into the fountain.

HE WAS STANDING IN Starwater, but he barely had time to process this before a wet, furious Hetta threw her arms around him.

He blinked down at her, his arms coming up automatically to return the embrace. Home, he was home, although Stariel felt a little bit different, and Hetta was shining with triumph and fury both, her power blazing more brightly than he'd ever seen it—and that odd sense of wrongness had gone from her signature.

"What is—there's no charge building in you anymore." He'd never been more terrified.

She stepped back. "It's all right—I fixed it. No thanks to the High King." She gave an angry laugh. "What did he say to you?"

The High King… His thoughts moved strangely as they made their way to the shore. He whirled back towards the lake, his hand once again going to Rakken's amulet.

The lake of his childhood, or at least the glamoured appearance of it, had been in the High King's realm. Why had his mother been there? He'd seen the High King in the lake when he'd arrived, but then his mother had come, and he'd somehow forgotten what he was doing there…

An older memory rose: his mother, playing with nightwraiths on that same lake, unhurt by their flames despite using no magic. Powers a stormdancer shouldn't have. Compulsion so strong and long-lasting even Rakken had trouble breaking it. Changing forms. *Everyone knows the stormdancer children are unnatural.*

He gripped the amulet so tightly it hurt.

"Wyn?"

Something terrible rose up in him, bringing clarity with it. His heart thrashed like a bird caught in a net.

"Oberyn!" he shouted. "Oberyn!"

The summons had gone unanswered the last time he'd made it. This time, he drew in his power, his unnatural power, calling blood to blood. He was the Maelstrom given form, lightning churning through him, spooling down his arms and into his clenched fists. He didn't ask; he demanded. *You owe me this. Stormcrows, if I am right, you owe me this.*

"Oberyn!"

And the High King came. Sorrow hung on the air around him, his traitorously green eyes dark with it.

Wyn had never been so angry. "Mother."

Hetta's hand spasmed on his.

A long pause, time for the world to fall apart and be remade. "Oh, my Hallowyn."

Accusations and questions tumbled together, fighting their way up his throat, but in the end all that came out was a hoarse cry.

"How could you? How could you!?" His voice emerged distorted. He could feel his wingbones snapping under the force of the Maelstrom. Images flashed like lightning: Irokoi's eyes as they'd been before one of them was blinded; Father's expression as he'd piled compulsion onto his own children. "Don't tell me it was all part of some grand plan; that you had no choice!"

"Not all of it was part of some grand plan."

"You left us! You lied to us! You compelled us! Why?"

The High King's feathers rustled, the sound barely audible above the soft lapping of the waves.

"You owe me that, at least. Stormwinds, no wonder the Spires couldn't bond properly with any of us." Wyn had only been a boy, the burden of compulsion lightest on him; he'd had less to forget, he supposed. How many signs were missing from his memories, small discrepancies, seeing his mother with powers an ordinary stormdancer shouldn't have had? How much more must his older siblings have seen and forgotten? They'd been grown when their mother had left. How could a faeland possibly penetrate that many layers of compulsion, laid down over so many years? Compulsion performed by the High King?

Rakken is stronger than he knows, to undo that, Wyn thought with sudden horror.

"I lied to *myself.* I compelled *myself.*" The High King smiled, a bitter thing. "Do you know what happens when one such as I forgets their duty in such a way?"

"You're Wyn's mother?" Hetta burst out. "How? I don't understand."

There was a long, tired silence from the High King. "It will hurt you to know," he repeated, meeting Wyn's eyes.

Wyn didn't blink.

"Very well, then."

The story came in a flash of memory not his own.

Centuries ago, as the Mortal Realm gained in power and the humans grew more numerous, the High King decided to intervene: an injection of powerful fae blood into the oldest bloodline in Faerie, twins intended to bridge the divide between realms. It had been a long time since he'd allowed himself children; he'd forgotten the joy and terror of it. He had brought Nymwen, the oldest, with him to the Court of Falling Stars. Where better to start than the one faeland already poised halfway between two worlds?

Except it had all gone wrong, and both Nymwen and her mortal lover had ended up dead at her own hand. In grief, the mortal lord had demanded the fae be kept away from humans, to prevent what had happened to his son happening to others. The High King had agreed to the bloodprice: for seven generations of mortal faelords, he would keep the ways closed, a heavy recompense for a heavy loss.

In his own grief, the High King had wanted to retreat further than ever from the Mortal Realm, retreat and forget the pain of the loss, the burdens of duty. Become something other than Faerie's ruler, just another greater fae. He would have more children. He could not bear to remember Nymwen.

He carved the memories and sorrow out of not just himself but all of Faerie—anyone who knew of his link to Aeros, everything anyone ever knew of Nymwen—and put them into a living creature. That creature he bound to the great library, for what better place to keep memories? And then he cast the last and greatest compulsion upon himself.

But his own power had worked against him. Sometimes it leaked out, despite all attempts to suppress it. And sometimes he had had to leave, at times when the High King was needed badly enough that he was forced to remember who he was for a short while. He had charged the maulkfae Lamorkin with the ability to remind him of his duty if the need was great enough, in exchange for Lamorkin being the sole creature in Faerie to keep their true memories—even though they were bound not to speak of them.

To forget so much, and to keep forgetting whenever memory threatened, to lay down so much compulsion over such long periods—there had been side effects, greatest in those who'd been closest to Nymwen. Aeros. Irokoi. Aroset. It had warped his children in ways he'd never intended, warped his lover into something Aeros should never have become, caused a serious imbalance of power between fae courts.

He hadn't wanted to know, hadn't wanted to see the damage his own presence was causing, hadn't wanted to give up his family nor return to his duties. But he had promised Lamorkin a powerful favour, in exchange for their service as his youngest's godparent, and eventually Lamorkin had demanded the payment: that he remember both himself and his duty.

He'd thought it would be better if his family didn't dwell on his absence, if their thoughts slid from him like water. That way they would not come seeking him.

"Except here you are, seeking me anyway," the High King finished, speaking aloud after that flash of shared memories.

"That is…you cannot…" Wyn went silent, unable to express either his outrage or disbelief. The High King had been right; it hurt. He clung tightly to Hetta's hand, unable to look at her. He couldn't imagine what she must think of this. An urge to laugh took hold of him; *even I didn't realise quite what a complicated family I was inflicting on her.*

"So you just meddled with your family's minds until some of them turned into sadistic monsters and then left them to it?" Hetta said angrily. "You made me and Wyn run around Faerie trying to complete your tasks for no reason at all?"

"Not for no reason. You were righting imbalances, ripples of cause and effect. Besides, you wished me to grant a boon, and such things come with a price. I cannot show favour."

"You're his mother! You're supposed to show favour!"

"That is only a small piece of me now I have reclaimed my proper self. In time, perhaps I will forget that piece too."

Oberyn met Wyn's eyes. "You did not answer my question, earlier. Would you be human, if you could?"

Hetta stepped forward, already sounding an objection, but Wyn stopped her with a hand on her arm. The answer came to him easily, a bit of knowledge slipping into place with strange peace.

"I already *am* a little bit human, just as Hetta is a little bit fae. I am both; I will not choose either." He found Hetta's hand again and squeezed it. "I am Hallowyn Tempestren of the Court of Falling Stars, and I do not seek your permission to marry my queen. If that breaks me, then so be it."

Wyn didn't look away as Oberyn's wings fanned out with slow grace, each feather ticking into place as the world held its breath, as Wyn's soul lay exposed beneath the hammer of that gaze.

"Both and neither," Oberyn murmured, and the world began to breathe again. "Even if you do not seek my permission, I still owe a boon. Give me your hand, child."

Wyn could no more have disobeyed than stopped his own heart, but he tried. The High King gave him a wry look as he took his hand. "I am giving you what you ask, Hallowyn, if you would truly be the waypoint between two realms. Though I don't envy you the task you would take upon yourself."

Power pulsed through Wyn in an arc, the smell of the sea flooding all his senses, his vision whiting out. The pulse went through him and...on, as if a deep gong had sounded not just here but everywhere, a thousand threads connecting him to a thousand different locations. When he came back to himself, he was kneeling in the sand, panting.

"What did you do?" Hetta demanded. She was holding fireballs in both her hands and looked ready to hurl them at the High King. "If you've hurt him…"

The High King canted his head. "Perhaps you *are* worthy, little Valstar. Ewan Valstar gave different answers. You have my blessing, even if you no longer wish it." He gave Wyn a dry look.

Gratitude and anger twined together on Wyn's lips. *Thank you*, he wanted to say, and *I missed you, but I do not forgive you.* The words fought with each other as he rose, his limbs trembling, a trembling that went out and out and out beyond the edges of his physical self.

"What have you done to me?" he settled for, in the end.

His mother smiled. Oh, Wyn knew that singularly charming smile, and he couldn't fight the ache of familiarity it brought to his chest. The atmosphere softened, like the calm after the storm, like sunshine warming wet ground, like the gentle unfurling of wildflowers. It took him back to the steps of the summer palace, to a time and place when his mother was the person he loved most in the world.

"Both and neither, Hallowyn. I have made you my emissary. You have the power to negotiate treaties between Faerie and Mortal on my behalf. Binding ones. Be careful what you wish for." He hesitated before reaching out. Wyn froze as his hand cupped his cheek, fleetingly. Oberyn's smile widened, but his eyes remained deep and sad. "Let the others find me in their own time. Good luck tonight."

The High King launched himself into the sky, losing his hold on his form as he did so, becoming a blurry storm of power.

Wyn stared up at the sky after the High King—after his mother.

"Wyn," Hetta said.

His mother. He sat down, hard, on the gravel beach.

"Wyn." Hetta was kneeling beside him.

"I..." He began to shake, a seizure that he couldn't stop. It felt like bits of glass in his chest.

Hetta kissed him. He wrapped his arms tightly around her, encasing them both in the cocoon of his wings, holding onto the one true thing in the world.

"You're soaking wet," he realised slowly. It had taken abnormally long for mundane sensation to penetrate, but this was something he could focus on, a small thing he knew how to remedy. He hauled her into his arms, got slowly to his feet. "Let's get back to the house."

To his surprise, she didn't object to being manhandled. He raised an eyebrow at her.

"I'm providing moral support," she said in answer to his silent question. "You looked like you needed it. Also I hate walking in wet shoes."

He chuckled and held her close, and they squelched their way up from the lake. Stariel hummed in quiet satisfaction around them. It felt different. He felt different. He plucked at the 'gift' his mother had given him and got a complicated jangle of magic in return.

"I can feel whatever you're doing," Hetta said thoughtfully in his arms.

"You are my Star," he agreed. "We're connected." He considered the strange new dimension to Stariel, and the blazing brightness of her along the leylines. "Now more than ever, I think."

"You called me your queen, before."

"Would you prefer that address?"

She shook her head. "No. But...is that how you think of me?"

He looked down at her, surprised. "Of course. I thought you knew. I am yours; I always have been. And you are mine." Usually he would have softened that a little, the possessiveness that sprang from the more primal side of his nature, but he'd been cut back to his bones tonight.

She made a half-fond, half-exasperated sound. "Oh, all right then, I suppose." She went quiet for a bit then began tentatively, "Wyn, your mother…"

He shook his head. "I am glad he's alive. But I cannot forgive him, even with this." Wyn considered his hand, where the power had passed from the High King into him. It wasn't dissimilar to his bond to Stariel, except this thread hummed in many voices rather than just one. He spread and unspread his wings, as if he could stretch his way into the shape of it. Awe dawned as he explored it. It didn't undo the betrayal, but…

"Well, we don't have to invite him to the wedding. Or if you're feeling magnanimous, we can seat him next to Aunt Sybil."

He stopped. "Are you sure?" He wasn't asking about seating arrangements.

"Yes, I'm still sure I want to marry you, ridiculous man."

"You didn't know just how complicated my family connections were before," he pointed out.

"Well, I can't say I appreciated the tests my future mother-in-law saw fit to put me through, but it hasn't changed my mind."

He laughed, because there was nothing else to do.

She put a hand over his heart. "It's all right," she told him. "We're all right. Our child is all right. Stariel is all right. Everything else is secondary." There was a fierceness in her expression. "But I agree with what you said about not choosing."

"The waypoint between two realms," he murmured. *That* was the difference he'd felt in Stariel; neither one thing nor the other.

She grinned. "Good thing I can make my own treaties with Faerie, isn't it? If only I knew someone who could make treaties with *me*."

He plucked at that strange connection and smiled. "If only."

"Brother!"

They turned. Irokoi was perched on the edge of the balcony that ran along the terrace. He swung his legs back and forth, but his expression was uncharacteristically serious.

Irokoi canted his head. "You're going to be late if you don't hurry. You're supposed to go to that ball tonight."

Another three days lost, Wyn mused. It had only felt like a few hours, in the High King's Realm.

"That ball is in Meridon," Hetta pointed out. She let out a long breath. "We're already too late."

"I know that," Irokoi said. "So I've been extremely helpful and found you a resonance point. You're probably going to need to put in a permanent Gate to the city, sooner or later, given what Mother has given you." The amulet Rakken had made him glowed in the hollow of his throat.

Wyn stiffened. "You knew," he accused, the terrible anger rising up once more.

Hetta wriggled, and he reluctantly put her down. "How old are you, Irokoi?" she asked.

Irokoi smiled. "That's not a polite question. But old enough."

Ah, stormcrows. The anger in him went cold, cold and sick. "You knew Nymwen. Our...sister."

Irokoi flexed a dark wing, in and out. "What I know...it's all tangled up. Sometimes I remember and sometimes I don't, though I think I always remembered more than the others. But even when I remembered, I could not speak it." He looked to the night sky where Oberyn had disappeared. "He always found me hardest, I think. I am oldest now, after all, and I've always seen more than I ought. Such is my gift and curse. Tonight, I remember enough, and my tongue is less chained than it has ever been."

The others... "Set knew her too. Nymwen." Aroset was still at the Stones, frozen in time and crystal.

Irokoi nodded. "She was very young, but she loved her as I think perhaps she has no one else since. I've always wondered if that was why she focused on me so viciously, if she subconsciously sensed the mirror of what she'd lost but couldn't recall." He gave a crooked smile and spread his feathers in an echo of a shrug. "Or perhaps she was always destined to become a terrible person. *I* never resorted to violence to bring our mother back, subconscious reaction or not. That does give me some moral high ground, don't you think? Though I think I always remembered more than Set and Father; perhaps that's why I turned to madness rather than murder," he added thoughtfully, touching his scars.

"Nymwen was your twin," said Hetta, horrified.

Oh. *Oh.* The night was still, so still that the only sound was the faint chatter of the house's occupants. There was a light on in the upper storeys where the sitting room was located. The amulet at Irokoi's throat burned even brighter, and when he finally spoke it was with a slow clarity Wyn had never heard from him before.

"Yes," Irokoi said. "Nymwen was my twin. Nymwen," he repeated, lingering on the word. How long since he'd been prevented from speaking it?

"Koi—" Wyn began.

Irokoi shook his head and slid off the balcony. "It was a long time ago. You never lose the grief, but it gets…easier." He looked between the two of them. "This is a second chance. Make it worth it. Bring us the world she would've wanted."

54

THE MERIDON BALL

THE RESONANCE POINT Irokoi had found turned out to be between the Dower House and Malvern Place, the dilapidated townhouse the estate owned in Meridon. Wyn gave Irokoi a long look when he handed them conveniently already-prepared outfits suitable for tonight's ball. Wyn's own outfit, Spires fashion, could almost be explained as borrowed finery, but not Hetta's.

Hetta's dress was made of blue sea silk embroidered with tiny silver feathers and had long sleeves that attached via an intricate network of silver bands that ran up her arms to the knot at the back of her neck. The familiar line of the Indigoes was picked out on the bottom of each sleeve in star-shaped gems.

"Think of it as an engagement gift," Irokoi said cheerfully when Hetta queried both the convenience and lavishness of the garment.

"He's never quite as innocent as he appears, is he?" she said to Wyn in an undertone as she went to change.

"No." *We are going to have a long talk about exactly how his precognition works when we return,* Wyn vowed.

It did odd things to him, the sight of Hetta in Spires fashion, the bare nape of her neck, and her lips painted with illusion rather than cosmetics. He took advantage of that last fact before they made their way to the Dower House. Something fierce and uncompromising burned in her expression when they pulled apart, something that resonated in his own chest.

The resonance point was on the ground floor, and the portal to Malvern Place emerged into a dingy room filled with battered furniture covered in dust cloths. He and Hetta's entrance startled a flock of piskies, who streamed out a broken window and into the yellow-grey night of the city. Malvern Place was in a quieter part of the city, but there was still a background of noise not present at Stariel.

"A project for another day," Hetta mused, taking in the state of the house. "At least we have some practice now, although still no money for it."

Wyn made a vague sound of agreement, distracted by the ley-lines. They leapt towards his touch with disconcerting enthusiasm, despite the fact that the ambient magic of Meridon wasn't high, warped as it was by all the iron.

Hetta shuffled her feet. "I can feel rather more Stariel than usual here."

"The townhouse does belong to the estate. In theory at least, that means the faeland could claim it too, with enough power and resonance," Wyn said, thinking aloud.

They picked their way carefully through the house, skirting rotting floorboards and jumbles of broken furniture. There was a small garden at the back of the townhouse, overgrown with weeds.

Hetta smoothed the sleeves of her ballgown. She looked up at the grey-washed sky, the stars hidden by the reflected lights of the city. Then she turned back and took him in, not just his finery but the fullness of his wings, unglamoured.

"Are you sure?" she asked.

He nodded and fanned out his wings. "Are you?"

She stepped into his arms. "Of course."

He took off.

They flew to the palace, and he set them down outside, where the grand driveway curved around a statue of Pyrania and fancy carriages were still pulling up. Hetta's eyes glowed, her cheeks flushed even though he'd carefully curved the air around them to save her appearance from the wind.

"I hope our child has wings," she said softly, and he couldn't do anything else but kiss her.

She was breathless when they pulled apart. "Well, we're making an excellent start of scandalising everybody. Let's go make the Conclave even gladder to be rid of me," she said with a grin.

Despite her words, he knew the rejection still hurt her. "They're fools," he said. "Let's go make them realise it."

The latecomers and palace staff stationed outside gaped at the pair of them as he fanned his wings in and out a few times deliberately. Well, it was either that or they'd seen the indiscreet kissing. He smiled at them.

Given their entrance and his form, he had to smile again when they were asked to produce their invitation. Hetta managed to turn her giggle into a cough as she handed it over, and they made their way to the ballroom entrance through a tunnel of hushed whispers. The herald gave them a wild look when they gave their names. Had Queen Matilda completely given up on them, then, to not have prepared her staff?

Perhaps she just hadn't expected him to come winged.

They moved through the doors as the herald announced them, the pronunciation as correct as if he'd put sugar tongs around each syllable and carefully dropped them into place. The ballroom was enormous by mortal standards, large even by fae ones, hung with fabric so it resembled the inside of a vast jewellery case. The dance floor swirled with couples, its edges crowded with chattering aristocrats.

The herald's announcement took a few moments to take effect, whispers beginning as those nearest the entry staircase looked up. A hush spooled outwards as hundreds of eyes turned towards them. The music died a slow, awkward death as the orchestra lost its focus, and all the dancers came to spinning halts. *We are starting to make a bad habit of such entrances.* Though at least none of these courtiers looked like they wished to murder him.

Wyn spread his wings to their full extent, holding the pose for several heartbeats before settling them back against his spine. There was something powerful in this, in laying the truth of himself bare for all to see. *This is me*, he thought. *Melodramatic and winged fae prince. Consort to a mortal. I don't apologise for any of it. Do what you will.*

He could tell Hetta was in a similar mood; she tucked her arm in his and smiled ferociously around at their audience.

"The Duke of Callasham is here," Hetta murmured, pointing out the man in the crowd. "Do you think he knows it was you who broke his roof?"

"Hopefully not. Though I will need to check him for remnant compulsion." Wyn's gaze swept over the room, and he made an unpleasant discovery. "Sunnika is here as well."

Sunnika was in mortal form and dressed in mortal fashion, surrounded by a knot of admirers. Her eyes widened when they met his across the ballroom. Did she see the change in him? Or had she merely not expected him to come?

"The earl, too," Hetta observed. The Earl of Wolver watched them with cool interest.

Queen Matilda cut a graceful path through the room, the crowd parting like a flock of starlings in flight. She was a tall woman with piercing blue eyes. Her pregnancy was only obvious because Wyn knew to look for it, the cut of her ballgown designed to hide the subtle swell of her stomach.

"Prince Hallowyn, Lord Valstar," she greeted them.

He dipped his head. "Your Majesty. Apologies for our lateness."

"I apologise for the inability of my orchestra to ignore distraction," she said with a meaningful glance in their direction. The orchestra hastily began the opening chords of another song.

Queen Matilda considered Hetta. "Congratulations on your recent elevation to the Northern Lords Conclave, Lord Valstar."

Hetta's fingers spasmed on his arm. "I beg your pardon?"

The queen smiled. "I know the vote was passed only narrowly, but a victory is still a victory. Take them where you can. I heard your speech to them was very…forthright."

Something unwound inside him. The Conclave *had* voted her one of its own after all, despite everything.

"Good," he said fiercely. Hetta looked dazed by the news.

Queen Matilda turned to him, uncertainly lingering on his wings. "Do you dance, Prince Hallowyn?"

"I do."

The queen seemed to steel herself and held out a commanding hand, which he took.

"I would be honoured," he said drily. Though he was also beginning to feel cursed to spend all his balls dancing with people who weren't Hetta. He gave Hetta an apologetic glance as he and the queen went out onto the floor; Hetta just shrugged, her expression caught between amusement and exasperation. Probably she was thinking the same thing.

"We surprised you," he said to the queen, grateful that the dance was a formal, traditional one, the rhythm slow. Hopefully that would reduce the risk of him accidentally flaring out a wing for balance. He'd never practised mortal dancing in this form.

The queen didn't deny it. "I did not expect you to come winged."

She pursed her lips. "You could have arrived in a somewhat more timely fashion. Your counterparts from other courts did." Her gaze flicked briefly to Princess Sunnika. "It has been suggested that your court is…unreliable."

He didn't have time to respond before the dance separated them. At least any clumsiness on his part would go unnoticed, since his presence had all the other couples so distracted they kept losing place.

"I have seen the High King as I said I would, and I am going to marry Hetta," he said when they met again. "Are you still willing to give us your blessing?"

This time it seemed to take an age before the dance reunited them. Her mouth was pressed into a thin line.

"I do not like scandal, Prince Hallowyn."

"Neither do I."

She did not speak again until the dance ended. "I wish to speak to you both before I make any announcement. Come and see me tomorrow morning in less…crowded conditions." They both spoke in low tones, aware of the many interested parties trying to eavesdrop.

Politics, Wyn thought. "You said you would announce our engagement at this ball."

"That was before…certain complications arose."

Wyn didn't know if she referred to Hetta's pregnancy, the wing worshippers, DuskRose, or something else, but it didn't matter: he still refused to accept it.

"I can negotiate a treaty between Faerie and Mortal, Your Majesty." He smiled, the truth sharp in his mouth. He still didn't know what to make of that truth, except a determination to stand exactly where he'd told his mother, between both realms. His child would not be ashamed, and they would know what they were and where they belonged in the world from the beginning.

"And yet your title has not changed; can you truly speak for your court? It has also been suggested to us that your court's influence is limited."

He didn't have to look far to know who'd suggested that, Sunnika's presence a low burn in the leylines. "I was not speaking of ThousandSpire. I can negotiate on behalf of Faerie. All of it."

The queen looked doubtful, so he pressed his advantage.

"I would rather us be allies, Your Majesty. My child will have a foot in both worlds. But if you send us away, I will make the agreements between Stariel and Faerie alone, and we won't look kindly on such measures as your earl has been considering."

The queen didn't look surprised at the reference to Hetta's pregnancy, though she didn't look pleased either. "Could you not have waited?" she asked with some asperity.

He only smiled. She studied his face, her mouth thinning as the seconds ticked by.

"Very well. Bring Lord Valstar to the dais on the hour. I will make the announcement."

Triumph thrilled through him, heady as sloe gin, but he merely inclined his head in thanks and left to find Hetta.

He found Hetta valiantly making conversation with a group of women. None of them were any good at masking their fascination as Hetta introduced him, but at least none of them regarded him with hostility. Instead, they stared at Wyn's wings and horns with emotions that varied from mild curiosity to lewd interest. Stormwinds. He hadn't anticipated the latter, though he should have. Some mortals were more susceptible to the magnetism of greater fae than others. He tamped down on his allure.

"My apologies, ladies, but I need to steal my Star from you for a moment." He smiled, and one tittered; another blushed.

"Is it true you fought off giants at Penharrow?" the blushing lady asked breathlessly. The others all perked up. If they'd been fae, their ears would have twitched. "I read all about it in *Lady Peregrine's*! It sounded so terrifying!" she gave a delicate shudder. "But you were so valiant!"

Wyn blinked. Of course some version of the leviathan attack would make its way south, but Wyn hadn't expected to feature as a hero in the tale.

"Yes," Hetta said firmly, taking hold of his arm. "He was extremely valiant, but please excuse us." He could hear the hint of laughter bubbling under her words. She drew him away. "I think Ms Orpington-Davies was telling Jack the truth about not writing that article in the *Chronicle*."

Wyn wanted to know exactly what their intrepid reporter had said about him, but Hetta looked surprisingly relaxed about the possibilities when he said so.

"I'm going to get a copy framed. 'Prince Hallowyn combines a kind heart with a singularly charming smile.' *And* she quoted some nice things the villagers said about me too. I take back every harsh word I ever said about reporters."

Wyn frowned at Hetta. "How—"

"One of the ladies had a copy," she explained. "I had to occupy myself somehow while you were dancing."

"I will dance all the rest of the dances with you," he promised.

He made good on this for a bit before a gong rang at ten o'clock precisely. The room hushed.

"I am pleased to make a public announcement tonight, of an historic union between our realm and another." The queen paused. "The engagement of Lord Henrietta Valstar and Prince Hallowyn Tempestren."

Wyn felt the weight of the room's attention fall on him and Hetta. Hetta squeezed his hand, and he unfurled his wings with a snap. You couldn't change the world overnight, but you had to start somewhere.

A ROYAL WEDDING

HAVING FOUGHT THROUGH everything up to and including dragons to get here (for a loose definition of 'fought'), Hetta had been prepared to take matters into her own hands to ensure the weather was perfect for her wedding, but the day dawned bright and clear without her help. Perhaps Stariel had intuited her desire and manipulated things even without instruction; perhaps it was an entirely natural phenomenon. She decided to take it as a good omen regardless.

Her stepmother, a cluster of her female cousins, and her aunts fussed and fretted around her as she made the final adjustments to her gown.

"Are you nervous about being married?" her cousin Ivy asked.

"No," she said. She watched dust motes sparkle in a shaft of sunlight above the dresser where she sat. "But I'll be glad when the ceremony is done. It's taken us such a lot of work to get to this point that I can't quite shake the fear that we'll be interrupted on the brink."

Aunt Sybil descended, narrowing her eyes in an expression Hetta couldn't quite pinpoint. She scanned her critically from head to toe and eventually allowed grudgingly, "You look well, Henrietta."

"You look *beautiful*," Alexandra added with flattering enthusiasm.

"I jolly well ought to, after all that effort," Hetta said, smiling. She hadn't spent the better part of the morning taking pains over her appearance for nothing.

"All brides are beautiful," Ivy agreed. "Radiant is also traditional."

"Beautifully radiant or not, everything's ready," Caro said from the doorway. She came into the room with eyes sparkling. A star-flower was woven into her red hair, matching the flowers in Hetta's bouquet. "But you do look nice. It's time."

Hetta stood, smoothing her dress, which didn't entirely disguise the swell of her belly. She had started to show several weeks ago, and the changes still felt odd. *And only going to get odder*, she reflected, *given there's still months to go.*

For a moment she thought she felt something. Had that been the baby moving? The midwife had said last week that she might feel it any time from now on. Hetta waited, to see if it would come again, but it didn't.

<Everything is all right in there, though, isn't it?> she asked Stariel. This was, in a funny way, Stariel's first pregnancy too.

Stariel not only thought that all was well but offered up an additional piece of information that took Hetta aback. *Well, that's certainly going to make our lives interesting.*

They held the ceremony on the village green, since the crowds wouldn't fit in the temple. At least they'd managed to avoid holding the ceremony in Meridon, despite pressure from the queen. In Meridon, with the queen herself in attendance, they would've been gawked at by every member of the aristocracy who could beg, borrow, or steal an invitation, all of them trying to use the situation to better their positions in Prydein's social hierarchy.

At Stariel, there were still more strangers present than Hetta would've preferred alongside her family, but they were at least mostly Northern strangers, and not all of them were noble. The people of Stariel were well-represented too, with seats set aside for the village councillors and the staff at the house.

There were also fae, and that was the other reason Hetta was glad to be home and also outdoors, since this had the advantage of making the guests much more relaxed than they would've been in an enclosed space. Hetta wasn't sure if this benefited the humans or the fae more.

Fae and humans, she thought, looking at the wings and tails and horns of the greater fae present, at the even more varied shapes and appearances of the wyldfae who'd made a rare exception and dropped their glamours. Urisks peeked from behind bushes, large goat-eyes blinking curiously; tiny flower fae buzzed in the hedge-rows; around the architecture of the temple twined strange and wonderful lowfae. The great nessan had coiled itself between the oaks bounding the green, though in its case Hetta was glad it had kept its glamour up as it would otherwise have frightened the villagers. In the crowds along the riverbank she saw naiads and shellycoats, some glamoured, some not. She waved at them as she passed, and they nodded solemnly.

Princess Sunnika had come in place of her aunt and didn't appear thrilled to be attending the wedding of her former fiancé, but Hetta was still glad she'd come. Hetta spotted Gwendelfear looking almost happy sitting next to Alexandra, though every now and then she shot a melancholy glance at her former princess.

The humans weren't entirely comfortable with the fae presence, of course, but everyone was doing their best to behave, though there was a lot of furtive staring going on. Hetta had to give credit where it was due: Princess Sunnika didn't seem even slightly self-conscious under the intense scrutiny she was getting. Hetta saw the princess stare down her nose at one onlooker with icy intensity, and the onlooker gulped and quickly dropped his gaze from her furry ears.

I suppose one has to start somewhere, Hetta thought, resting a hand on her abdomen. *Though hopefully we're somewhat further along by the time you arrive.*

They were still adjusting to a faeland that was neither fully Mortal nor Faerie but a mix of both, working out the details of what it meant to have the power to negotiate between the two worlds. The Dower House was turning out to be a useful waypoint and accommodation for fae emissaries from other courts, especially with the Gate they'd since constructed between there and Meridon. Jack had suggested they start charging either the courts or Queen Matilda for the use of it, which wasn't actually that terrible an idea; perhaps it would please the bank, Hetta thought idly before pushing it away. They had time to work it out. Today was for her and Wyn.

The ceremony itself was to be under a great oak tree on a rise at the far end of the green. As Hetta made her way towards it, news of her arrival spread, so that by the time she found herself at the start of the long, flower-carpeted aisle, those that wished to be seated were seated, and everyone was staring expectantly at her.

She'd lied to Ivy, she realised as she paused to take a deep breath: she *was* nervous. She could hardly ignore that her marriage marked in a very official way the start of a new era for not just her and Stariel but for the whole Mortal Realm. She and Wyn should've just eloped and got the business over with, but Wyn had stood surprisingly firm on that point. She rubbed at the new ring he'd given her.

Wyn was facing away from her, exchanging words with Lamorkin. She saw the moment he realised she was here, for his wings suddenly pulled upwards. She could nearly see the effort of will it took him to turn in a measured movement.

He looked very handsome and very self-conscious, though he

was hiding the latter well. He was dressed in silver and indigo, the style for the Spires but the colours for Stariel. It matched her dress, the full skirts spreading in a vast pool around her, hiding the delicate sandals she wore.

What a pretty and colour-coordinated couple we make, she thought absently. Wyn canted his head to the side as she drew near, silently asking what her source of amusement was, and she said in an undertone as she reached his side and the music faded, "Thank goodness your feathers don't clash with the colour scheme!"

Wyn choked, but the monk-druid performing the ceremony scowled, overhearing and not approving of this levity. They'd already put his nose out of joint with the extensive modifications they'd requested, plus the fact that the ceremony needed to be conducted jointly by a fae. Lamorkin was performing this aspect of the service, and they beamed at the pair of them, making up for the monk-druid's censure.

Marius, who was standing as best man, was blinking rather a lot, and Hetta's heart swelled with warm affection. Oh, Marius. He'd always been an incurable romantic under it all.

The vows had been a point of contention, with Hetta trying to minimise them and Wyn recklessly—in her opinion—wanting to promise everything and anything, but they'd come to a compromise eventually.

"With this ring I pledge myself to our union, Henrietta Isadore Valstar," he said, voice clear and carrying. Her hand trembled when he took it gently. His hands were trembling too.

"With this ring I pledge myself to our union, Hallowyn Tempestren," she said, her own voice far less steady.

He gripped her hand so that their forearms aligned. Lamorkin was ready with the ribbon for the fae part of the ceremony. They wound the strip of white silk around their joined hands in a lattice pattern.

Wyn's eyes were deep and solemn, the colour of horse chestnuts lit with flecks of brandy.

"I take you as my mate, Henrietta Isadore Valstar, and I entwine my path with yours," he said, squeezing her hand. "Your honour is my honour; your troubles are my troubles; your pleasure is my pleasure." Amusement flickered in his eyes at his words. "Your children are my children."

Hetta repeated the words, her pulse fluttering strangely.

"By the power of the High King, I entwine the fates of these two here joined," Lamorkin said. Some bittersweet emotion sparked in their dark eyes briefly.

Hetta gasped as magic surged up where she and Wyn clasped hands: unfamiliar magic, like strange spices tossed over an unruly sea. Her hand grew hot, and she instinctively jerked away, but both Wyn's grip and the ribbon prevented it. The heat eased just at the point of pain and the ribbon dropped away, charred with magic. Wyn released her hand to examine his own palm, looking terribly smug. She followed his lead and gasped again. Inked on her skin was a strange and beautiful tattoo, centred on her palm and running down the length of her forearm. She traced the lines of it. It made her think of feathers, somehow, and frost. Wyn held his up next to hers.

"We match," he observed. "Looks like you *are* fae enough for the *sengra* to work." He grinned, bright and delighted.

It was a lucky thing that the monk-druid pronounced them married and instructed them to kiss at that moment, because Hetta wasn't sure she could've refrained from doing so.

She hadn't actually expected anything to feel different once they were married, but to her surprise, it did. There was something extra there, a resonance that hadn't previously existed. She felt that thread of connection thrum tight with emotion between her and Wyn as they kissed.

"Yes," he gasped as they broke apart and before she could ask. "I feel it too. It's the bond. More…official, as I said."

"I have some very interesting ideas about how we might make use of that," Hetta murmured, and desire flared in his eyes, but that would have to wait. People were cheering, and they cheered louder as Hetta and Wyn turned towards the crowd and raised their joined hands in acknowledgement. Wyn flared out his wings to their fullest extent, as if to challenge those assembled to accept him exactly as he was.

Music swelled suddenly, a soaring aria, even as her land-sense pinged. The song was piercingly beautiful, the two singers' voices pure and perfect complements to each other. Hetta couldn't make out the words, and it took her a moment to realise this was because they weren't in a language she understood.

She searched for the source of the music and found it in the sky: four sets of wings hovering in mid-air, and Rakken and Catsmere were singing as if they'd practised such a duet a thousand times before. Maybe they had. The sound was amplified by air magic. Rakken raised an eyebrow when he caught Hetta's glance, as if to say, "and what of it?"

She'd told them they weren't invited, explaining DuskRose's agreement, but here they were anyway—a fae technicality if ever she'd seen one. The song finished, and they flew down and settled amongst the back of the crowd.

"I can throw them out if you want," Hetta said, craning to find Princess Sunnika. The princess was determinedly pretending she hadn't seen the stormdancers, but her expression was resigned rather than angry. *Fae technicality accepted,* Hetta supposed.

Wyn shook his head, eyes bright with emotion. "Don't throw them out."

Good enough for her.

She'd expected a mixed reaction to her marriage from her people, but there was more joy here than anger. There was the cook, smiling broadly, and she was far from the only one. Wyn had lived as one of the staff for a long time, and she knew his recent elevation in the eyes of the world had shaken them, but almost all of them looked genuinely happy. The villagers were less enthusiastic but, she judged, still cautiously in favour. Wyn might be a fae, the sentiment seemed to go, but he was *their* fae.

A good few of Hetta's old company had come, to her delight. They seemed generally bemused by the entire business, but Bradfield beamed and waved when he caught her eye across the crowd, lifting his drink in silent toast.

Hetta's family showed a surprising degree of sentimentality. Lady Phoebe was sniffing and wiping tears away, and Alexandra was smiling so hard her whole face glowed. Grandmamma looked as self-satisfied as if she'd been responsible for the whole business.

Irokoi beamed and waved at them from where they had landed past the seated audience, and Cat's lips curved subtly, but the other stormdancers were harder to read. Torquil gave a rough nod of acknowledgement, and Hetta wondered if he'd been bullied into attending, probably by Irokoi. Rakken looked entirely neutral about the whole affair—but he'd sung at her wedding, after all; she decided to take that as endorsement.

Wyn stilled beside her, a wolf catching a scent. She followed his gaze somewhere to the back of the crowd.

"Hetta," he said quietly, "is there another greater fae here?"

Even distracted as she'd been, she would hardly have missed such an arrival, but she reached obediently for Stariel. To her surprise, Stariel's answer was affirmative though strange. The faeland didn't seem at all worried about an unannounced visitor; rather the opposite. Stariel was practically purring with happiness about it.

The High King, Hetta thought, not sure how to feel about that. "He was here," she confirmed.

Wyn took a deep breath, and she watched him decide not to let his complicated feelings about that overshadow this day. He smiled down at her. "So, my dear wife," he said, pausing to relish the taste of the new word. "Shall we go let your people congratulate us?"

"Very well, dearest husband." She couldn't help a laugh; the word sounded so strange, too staid for the man beside her, and yet the most perfect word in the world. She saw her own emotions reflected in Wyn's expression.

"Undoubtedly the label will grow more familiar with time," he murmured.

They went to celebrate. Of course, Wyn wouldn't be Wyn if he didn't keep trying to manage the ongoing wedding celebrations, but Hetta took it as her wifely duty to distract him whenever he appeared in danger of doing so. Other people could be in charge of making things run smoothly for one day.

He didn't seem to mind.

The wariness between the fae and humans eased a bit as the merrymaking reached full swing. The addition of liberal amounts of food and alcohol probably also helped. Hetta spied two village children petting a starcorn, having escaped adult supervision. Jack was even brave enough to ask Princess Sunnika to dance, to his mother's horror.

Even Rakken and Marius appeared to have reached a truce for the day—or maybe more than that, Simulsen help her, Hetta thought after taking in how close they stood together under the trees. Did she want to know what was going on there? She decided that right now she didn't; she could always bury Rakken up to his knees again if it became necessary later.

She looked away and found Cat had been watching her watch their respective brothers. Cat gave a sharp smile before pulling a slightly terrified Gregory into a dance.

They feasted, and danced, and laughed, and suddenly it was

dusk and finally they were farewelling the crowds, who catcalled good-naturedly as Wyn swept Hetta off her feet in a move of sheer theatricality.

"What are you doing?" she said, clinging to his shirt, feeling his heart thudding under her palms.

"It's mortal tradition, isn't it, for a husband to carry his new wife across the threshold of their house?" he said mildly.

"Wyn, we're miles from the house!" she laughed and then let out a breath of surprise as he took off in a swirl of storm magic. Exhilaration shot through her as the wind whipped against her cheeks, and she stared down at the land below as he bore them upwards and towards the house. She could feel Stariel around them just as strongly as if she stood on solid ground; the air above belonged to the faeland too.

They landed on the balcony of their new joint quarters with a thud, and Wyn wobbled before he righted himself. "I could still use more practice," he admitted, making her laugh. He set Hetta on her feet and raised an eyebrow at her. She kissed him, and the world narrowed to the two of them, to the hot thrill of flesh on flesh, and the primal stir of desire.

Later they lay facing each other on the old-fashioned four-poster. The sun's dying rays painted the room in shades of gold, lighting up all the colours of Wyn's wings and glinting off his horns.

Wyn drew small circles on her shoulder, almost absent-mindedly. "I wonder what he thinks of Aroset, frozen down in the basement?" They'd put her there after it became clear the stasis wasn't going to lift any time soon. Hetta didn't have to ask who 'he' was.

"I think he should be very grateful that I've managed to find a way to de-fang your most psychopathic sibling without resorting to murder," she said baldly. "In my opinion, Aroset can only be improved by having time to think about her life choices for as long as possible." Maybe they'd convince Rakken to try de-compelling

Aroset eventually and see if that changed her at all. So far Rakken had been flat in his refusal.

Wyn chuckled, and his touch grew more purposeful. "Perhaps you're right." He traced his knuckles down over the curve of her waist. "But I find I'd prefer to think of something other than my family right now."

Later still, Hetta rested her head on Wyn's chest and gave a deep sigh of contentment. Outside, the sky was ink, stars twinkling through the open balcony doors. Inside, the smallest of flutterings. So she hadn't imagined that earlier. It felt peculiar and also wonderful, making things real rather than abstract.

Wyn looked at her curiously but didn't resist as she took his hand in hers and drew it to the curve of her belly.

The fluttering came again, so subtle she wondered if he'd feel it, but his face went slack with wonder.

"Oh," he said. "Hello, little one."

"Little *ones*. Stariel told me earlier today that there are two of them. I think it was too early to tell, before, or maybe I just didn't know what to look for." She sighed. "That probably explains why Lamorkin's charm didn't last as long as we thought it would."

Through that new connection between them came a jumble of competing emotions: pride, joy, excitement, fear. Love. A degree of panic Hetta shared, thinking that there was *twice* as much to deal with as expected. Wyn stared at his hand against her stomach as if too overwhelmed to do anything else.

She grinned at him. "Maybe I should've asked your mother for tips on dealing with twins."

He gave a strangled choke, wrapped his arms around her and pulled her close. "Hetta," he said, his voice vibrating on an edge between alarm and joy. "I love you. And we are not asking my mother any such thing!"

"I love you too. And you'll be fine," she reassured his throat where she was tucked under his chin.

"It's not me I'm fretting about," he said wryly, but she could hear the softness in his voice. "It's—stormcrows—all *three* of you. My hair will be white."

She had to laugh at that, but, "*We'll* be fine then, all *four* of our little family. After all, this is our home."

"Ours," he echoed, his voice thick. She felt him pluck at his land-sense, and Stariel swirled idly around them in response.

She reached out too, feeling equally sentimental in the moment. *Ours*, Stariel agreed. *Home.* The word had mountain bones in it.

<Yes,> she said, to it and Wyn both.

They lay entangled for long moments before she eventually wriggled back a bit of space. "Now, tell me about dragons," she said. "Do they actually make good godparents?"

THE END

AUTHOR'S NOTE

So, here we are at the end of the Stariel Quartet!

Well…only mostly, as it turns out. I found while writing *The King of Faerie* that there was one character whose story needed a bit more telling than I could fit between its pages. Which is to say, yes, Marius will be getting his own book.

The King of Faerie wraps up Hetta and Wyn's storyline, but *Of Plants & Princes* will be a one-book spinoff that begins shortly after the events of *The King of Faerie*, featuring a certain telepathic botanist, an arrogant fae prince, magic—and murder. Look out for it in early 2022.

It feels ironically appropriate to end the Stariel Quartet by announcing the impending existence of, very technically, Book 5, because everything about this series snuck up on me. When I began the first draft of *The Lord of Stariel*, it was supposed to be a single standalone 'practice' novel to help me figure out this whole writing gig. I never planned to let it see the light of day, let alone kick off a series, but it wouldn't let me go once I began, and the story grew and grew.

It's been a wild journey. I started this series in my 20s whilst living on the other side of the world; I finished it in my 30s back in New Zealand, with our international borders closed for the first time in history.

It's a lovely, bittersweet thing to put *The King of Faerie* out into the world, the end* of my very first series. Thank you so much for coming on this journey with me!

If you want to follow along with my next projects (including *Of Plants & Princes* news), you can sign up to my newsletter on my website ajlancaster.com. I include writing updates, snippets of what I'm working on, discounted book sales, and pictures of my cats. I tend to send out a newsletter every month or so, and you can unsubscribe at any time.

If you enjoyed *The King of Faerie*, please consider leaving a review. Reviews help get the word out to new readers, and as an indie author without the support of a publishing house, I rely hugely on word of mouth.

*Let us not quibble over the very technical existence of Book 5 here.

ACKNOWLEDGEMENTS

This final book was a particular struggle. I loved it. I hated it. The world had a pandemic. I rewrote multiple scenes countless times and the entire manuscript twice. There were lengthy times when I despaired of ever finishing. I owe a debt to all the people who kept me sane and helped me drag *The King of Faerie* over the finish line.

Thank you to all my beta readers who read this book at various stages of drafting. The book is better for your feedback, and your enthusiasm kept me going when I had exhausted my own. Priscilla, you've read more versions of my books than any human should have to. Erin, thank you for talking to me about my characters as if they were real (and for suggesting there could always be more kidnapping). Kirsten, you are endlessly enthusiastic even when my action scene choreography makes absolutely no sense. Rem, your live commentary and commitment to cracktastic ship pairings gives me life. Toni, I can't believe you managed to somehow both read and give insightful feedback on the draft of this with a newborn draped over you, but I'm incredibly grateful that you did. Mel, kudos for finding those pesky typos that made it through all the previous rounds.

I have never been pregnant, but I come from the sort of large extended family where *someone* is always pregnant. Thank you to all my relatives and friends who generously shared your own experiences. Any faults in portrayal are my own (or, I'll admit, creative liberties for the sake of the narrative). Particularly thank you to my cousin Toni and my friend Marie, for answering my questions whilst being pregnant with your respective firsts.

Thanks to my writing group, the Wellington Speculative Collective (with special shout-out to Mel for herding all the cats). You are my people. I'm sorry I keep posting so many pictures of pretty wings in the Slack (or rather, not sorry at all, but thank you for tolerating my quirks).

Carla, thank you for the book cakes and patience for my rambles. You are the best sister anyone could ask for.

Steph, E, and Marie, thank you for all our crafter-zoom / crafter-noon teas during and after lockdown and for listening to my anxieties and moments of triumph both.

And last but by no means least, thank you, readers. Thank you for your reviews, your recommendations, your fan art, your enthusiasm. I never anticipated how much other people would love this series. I thought it might just be me, and I'm so, so glad it's not.

ABOUT THE AUTHOR

Growing up on a farm in rural Aotearoa New Zealand, AJ Lancaster avoided chores by hiding up trees with a book. She wrote in the same way she breathed—constantly and without thinking much of it—so it took many years and accumulating a pile of manuscripts for her to realise that she might want to be a writer and, in fact, already was. On the way to this realisation she collected a degree in science, worked in environmental planning, and became an editor.

Now she lives in the windy coastal city of Wellington and writes romantic, whimsical fantasy books about fae, magic, and complicated families.

You can find her on the interwebs at:
- instagram.com/a.j.lancaster
- facebook.com/lancasterwrites
- twitter.com/lancasterwrites

Printed in Great Britain
by Amazon

13712958R00315